OUT OF NOWHERE

What struck me was that it happened so quickly. They were playing along in an easy, mellow shuffle and then came the crash of the shot and the shattering of the glass. I didn't actually hear the "bang"; the sound of the breaking glass erased anything that may have come before it, like a low-grade retrograde amnesia. Everyone dove to the floor. Me, I was already on the floor, so I froze. I know, I know, it's not very heroic, but that's what I did. I looked around; no one seemed to be shot. It's funny, but I immediately interpreted it as a gunshot, without question. People were bleeding a little—cuts from the glass—but everyone was up and moving around. My pulse slowed, my breathing deepened. I was almost feeling—what, relief?—when I saw the guy slumped over the piano keys. I was squatting at the left side of the bandstand as you look at it, looking at him from about ninety degrees, toward what had been his left profile, eighteen inches away, and as soon as I saw him I knew he was dead....

NINE FINGERS

Thom August

LEISURE BOOKS NEW YORK CITY

A LEISURE BOOK®

January 2008

Published by

Dorchester Publishing Co., Inc.
200 Madison Avenue
New York, NY 10016

Copyright © 2008 by Thom August

ISBN 10: 0-8439-6025-6
ISBN 13: 978-0-8439-6025-9

The name "Leisure Books" and the stylized "L" with design are
trademarks of Dorchester Publishing Co., Inc.

Printed in the United States of America.

10 9 8 7 6 5 4 3 2 1

Visit us on the web at www.dorchesterpub.com.

NINE FINGERS

PROLOGUE

Twenty years ago . . .

Even with the blindfold on, I could see the light, tiny shards stabbing where the fabric bridged my nose. As they walked me down two flights of stairs—fourteen steps each—the light dimmed.

Even with my nose broken, I could tell it was humid. A basement? A warehouse? A faintly metallic taste touched my tongue, like old meat, like cold blood.

We were waiting. They had lifted me onto a cold steel table, maybe an examining table, maybe a butcher's table, maybe a desk. It was heavy; when I rolled it didn't budge. The temperature was cold, not much more than forty degrees. I was still sweating from the brief resistance I had put up, and the sweat was drying, making me shiver.

Don't shiver, I told myself. Don't let them see you shiver.

We were waiting.

I tried to count how many people were there. Not people: men; when they had grabbed me from behind they had that smell: sour, tangy, with an edge. Sweat, coffee, cigarettes.

The man on my left had a noticeable wheeze. His breath came in short rapid gasps, at a tempo of forty breaths a minute. There was another man directly behind me who kept tapping his foot on the cement floor in a unique beat, accenting the first beat of each measure, then the first two beats, then the first three, then all four, like TAP-two-three-four, TAP-TAP-three-four, TAP-TAP-TAP-four, TAP-TAP-TAP-TAP. He was consistent, kept good time. A third man, at an oblique angle to my right, was humming, no particular tune, roughly in the key of F. He had no rhythm, and his pitch kept wandering off-key, flat. I heard other noises—footsteps, creaking boards, a sneeze, an occasional low grumble—but all of this was farther away. There were more men here than the three, and I couldn't make them out. But in the inner ring, within a yard or two of where I was sitting, I could hear three.

No, four men. Someone to my left suddenly cleared his throat, very rhythmically—mm-HMM, mm-HMM. It was Wheezer, TAP-TAP, Hummer, mm-HMM, and me. Waiting.

I heard a door slam in the distance. There were footsteps, quite a few of them, coming closer. Leather-soled shoes. From the sound of them, the floor was cement. One out front, others following behind. They came closer, then stopped. Deep breaths, I told myself, deep breaths.

"Want me to take the blindfold off?" one asked.

"Not yet."

It was him, the husband. He was close to me, right up against my face. I had seen him in the papers, had glimpsed him from a distance once or twice. He was older than the two of us, by close to twenty years. I was forming an image of him in my mind when I could suddenly feel his breath hot against my cheek. Something happened—a signal, the reading of a well-known look—because I could hear everyone else in the room back up two paces.

"So, tell me," he said in a whisper, "did you?"

It was vague, maybe on purpose. I was trying to form the words to respond, when, from behind, TAP-TAP took two steps forward and punched me in the back of the neck. Not a slap, a punch. I started to roll forward. Hands reached out and propped me up.

Again: "Did you?" The voice was breathy, a ragged baritone, sandblasted to sibilance.

"Did I—" I started to ask. I heard the scrape of the floor behind me and felt another punch to the back of the neck, more toward the right side. I rocked forward. TAP-TAP stepped back. I was reeling, close to passing out.

"Listen to this," he said to the others. "The man is seeking clarification." The others chuckled. An inside joke.

He came up to me even closer. TAP-TAP had stopped tapping, getting ready for another blow. It occurred to me that there is an etiquette to these things, a protocol.

"I'll be more specific: Did you sleep with her? Yes or No. Did you sleep with her?"

I slowly but firmly shook my head back and forth.

"I need to hear you say it," he whispered. "You need to say it."

I cringed, waiting for the punch. It didn't come. I paused, for just a few beats. It's not just the sound, but the silence that counts. "No, I didn't sleep with her. Never, not once."

Out of nowhere, another punch on the back of the neck.

"Easy, my friend. I want him conscious."

Two steps, backing up behind me.

"Maybe that was too ambiguous. Maybe that was too quaint. We're all grown-ups here. Let me be more precise: Did you ever have intercourse with her? Did you put your dick inside her pussy? Did? You? Fuck? Her?" More insistent now.

"No. Not once. Not ever." I paused. "I swear."

"You swear," he echoed. "You swear."

"I swear. I never had intercourse with her." Then bluntly: "I never fucked her. Never."

"He's fucking lying," a different voice chided. It was his brother.

There was a pause. Maybe ten long seconds passed.

"But tell me," he whispered, "you loved her, right? You still love her, right?"

I sighed, "Yes."

"Then why not?" he asked. "Why didn't you?"

I dropped my head, shook it back and forth. "I don't know. It's complicated."

"Complicated?" he said. "You fuck her or you don't fuck her. What's complicated?"

"I don't know. I wasn't sure she loved me. I wasn't sure she *should* love me. And then, there was you . . ."

The other voice again, high-pitched, whiny, insistent: the brother. "Come on, Zep. Let's do this. Why are we fucking wasting time with this fucking piece of shit?"

All the little miscellaneous noises stopped.

Then the hoarse voice again, the husband speaking, not to me but to his nephew, a little louder; speaking to the room, to all of them.

"Here's the thing: she says they didn't."

He let it sink in.

"She says they didn't. She swore to me three times. He's wrong: she *does* love him, she's crazy for him. If it was up to her, she would have done anything. But she swears she didn't. If I kill him, that makes her out to be a liar. I don't really care if the fuck is lying, but I will *not* make my bride out to be a liar."

This was a sermon. It spoke the syntax of justice. "On the one hand . . ." Now it was time for "on the other hand."

"But he's got to pay. He can't just walk, can he? It's our fucking *honor.*" The brother played his part in the call-and-response, desperate, a tenor to the older man's baritone. Wagnerian overtones.

It's got to be uncomfortable for them, I thought.

"Yeah, he's gotta pay. They always gotta pay. That's how it works. That's how we get respect. But it has to fit what she said happened. You have to consider the larger picture. I will not confirm others' perceptions of her. I will not give a reason to the rumors."

"So he walks away, just like that? He walks away clean?" The brother was enraged, a petulant teenager, angry that someone else seemed to be about to get away with something.

There was another pause. He was making this a lesson, to me, obviously, but to them as well. When you give the lesson, the one to whom it is administered needs time to understand it, to sort it out, to know that it is not capricious or random. But this wasn't just for me; he was preaching to the choir. He was giving them all time to understand, so that when he pronounced judgment they would already have thought it through that far.

Then, softly, "He'll pay, but he'll pay what he owes. You mentioned *'honor.'* That's what honor is—he pays what he owes, not more, not less. Beyond that isn't honor, it's anarchy."

I was stunned by his words—wise, articulate. Or was I elevating the style because they hinted that I might live? Stop thinking about him. Stop getting ahead of yourself. The sounds—the wheezing, the tapping—had faded from my awareness. All I could hear was a crescendo of white noise rushing through my head.

The brother scuffed his feet on the floor, turned away.

"No, stay," the Don said. "You're so ready to exact revenge, you can help. Hold him down."

The sound of feet on concrete, shuffling closer. Rough hands grabbed me, sat me up, held me by my arms and shoulders.

Slowly they quieted. And he spoke.

"Piano player, huh? Hotshot piano player. The great Franco Giamelli. Mr. Symphony. Could have had any woman in town, any *two* of them, if he wanted. But he had to go after mine."

His voice had changed, lost its patina of grace.

"Maybe that's your problem, going after what you can't have. You knew who she was, you knew who I am."

He turned away, said, "Right side pocket, my jacket." Then, "His right hand, stretch it out."

Then I felt cold steel wrapping around my right pinky finger, slowly tightening until it was touching all around. Some kind of curved knife? A pair of shears? A cigar-cutter?

"Next time you don't even try. You see, if you *had* fucked her, I'd be cutting off something else and stuffing it down your dying throat. But even though you didn't, you had the thought. In your mind you considered yourself worthy of her. And that has to have consequences."

A short pause. This speech wasn't for me, but for them. His voice had modulated back toward its loftier plane.

"Here's the deal," he said. "First, you never see her again. I don't mean you don't go out with her—I mean your eyes never land on her again. You see her on the street? You turn around and walk the other way. You see her at a restaurant? You walk out and you never go back. You never see her again—you don't even look at her picture in the newspaper."

I nodded.

"Second, you never see this town again. This is *my* town. And because it's my town, it's her town. This town is closed to you. So you go find yourself another symphony. You go play your piano somewhere else. You never come back to Chicago, you got it?"

"Yes," I muttered, "I don't see her again, and I never come back to Chicago."

"Good. Very good. And one more thing. You don't go reaching for that high note, ever again."

A sudden, searing pain, hot blood on my hand. I screamed, despite myself. Pain in my little finger. I tried to wiggle it but nothing happened except more pain. Then the flick, unmistakable, of a Zippo, and hot flame against the base of my finger—he was cauterizing it! I screamed again, and passed out, and came to, and screamed again, alone, in the dark, in the cold.

CHAPTER 1
The Cleaner

The Near North Side
Thursday, January 9, This Year

8:00 P.M.: Drive over to the place we keep, up the Near North Side. Close to everything. Get anywhere in thirty minutes. Down the Loop in ten. What's the word? Convenient.

Park it down in the alley. Lock it up nice and tight. Slip on the latex gloves.

No excuse for carelessness.

Pull down the fire stairs. Quietly. Climb up the fire stairs. Quietly.

When we rent the place? This safe house? One of our guys puts a key-lock in the rear window. Easy in, easy out. Across the alley from a warehouse. Nobody sees nothing.

At the landing. Third floor. Find the key. In the lock. Slide open the window. Step over the transom. Close the window. Lock it up. Pull the shades. Flip the switch.

8:11 P.M.: Have a look around. Have a *good* look around.

Traps are in place. All clear.

Another job. A simple one. Got a location. Got a target. Got a description. Got a time frame, couple hours away.

Plan is, get there and back in the van, the one parked two blocks away. There is a set of panels inside, with magnets—Cook County General Hospital, Little Sisters of the Poor, Leukemia Hospice Service, Joe the Cleaner. Little joke, that one. Pick one out. Slap it up. No one is gonna give it a ticket. Park near the place. Walk on over. Do the job. Drive away. Easy.

Got a plan. No reason to be careless. No excuse.

Review the objectives:

Do not get caught
Do not get seen
Leave nothing behind
Hit the target
Do it at the right time
Avoid civilians

Walk to the trunk in the closet. Who to be? North Loop, late at night, from the outside, in the snow. Narrows it down some.

Here is one. Workingman? Watch cap, plaid coat, lunch bag. But what's he doing up on Lincoln? At night? In the snow? No.

Next? Officer, some kind? Police, Fire, Parks, you name it. Got them all.

Always the same pluses, the same minuses, this one. And besides. Been saving these.

Here is one. Could be the bag lady. Not too conspicuous, common enough. Dirty, messy. People do not want to look at her. Invisible.

Have not used this one in a while. Could work.

Open the wall safe. Pick a weapon. Close range, line of sight, one shot. Has to go through a pane of glass. And glass, not that other stuff, what is it? Plexiglas. No rifle, no shotgun, no scope, no silencer. Just a simple pistol. Revolver or automatic? Automatic ejects the shells. Do not want to be trying to find empty cartridges in the snow.

That pane of glass. Need something with a little oomph. One shot only.

Here is a big-ass Colt forty-five. Long barrel, big loads. Could stop a horse. Glass? What glass? Maybe too much. Go right through the target. Go right through three people, the other side of the target. Also got three nine-millimeters, a three-fifty-seven. Too much. All too much.

Here we go. A thirty-two-caliber Police Special. Mr. Smith & Mr. Wesson. Good stopping power. But with the four-inch barrel, not the two. Makes it accurate enough, this range. It is a revolver. Shells stay inside. OK. This is the one.

9:10 P.M.: Pull back a small flap in the curtains. Look outside.

Check all perimeters. No reason not to. Snow starting to pile up. Be less people on the street. Less cars. Bad visibility. Van has snow tires. Long as there is no rush? An advantage.

Strip down to shorts, T-shirt, socks. Reach inside the trunk. First is the bodysuit. Latex. Fastens in back with Velcro. Next the long underwear—dark enough to cover the hair, my arms and legs. Next the panty hose—the warmth feels good.

Next the dress. Extra touch, really. No one would see it under the coat. But if spotted, extra security. Fits OK. Looser than it used to be.

9:15 P.M.: Early yet. Sit and wait. Do not want to leave too early, drive around. Get in. Get out. Instructions are very particular: 10:05, no earlier, no later.

Call comes in yesterday, usual channels. Not my friend, not the Guy Himself. Someone lower down. A messenger. Know the voice, from before. Big-ass guy. Tiny little voice. Says: Here it is, here is the details. Terminate. 10:05. A little picky, you ask me. But no one asks me.

Do not know why. Do not ask why. Not the one who decides. Just the one who acts.

Take the time to fieldstrip the thirty-two, oil it, test-fire it. Good action, no problems. Load the rounds—five shells. One is enough. But. You never know.

9:20 P.M.: Put on the wig, flatten it out. Tape it on. Tie the scarf on top of it. Just to be sure.

Choose a purse, midsize. Plenty big enough for the thirty-two. Get a pair of gloves, black wool with no fingers. Put them on, over the latex gloves. Fit is OK.

If the gloves do not fit, it can all go to shit. Ha-ha.

Boots, for the snow. Tie the laces behind the tongue-flap to make them look untied. Laces tucked in. To avoid tripping. Check them. Look loose, but they are on good.

9:25 P.M.: Time to leave. Into the bathroom. Pull all this stuff aside. Take a piss. Flush. Flush again. Straighten up. Then the coat. Then the topcoat, for camouflage. This will stay in the van. No one will see the outfit underneath on the way out of here.

Sounds like nothing. Some meaningless detail. Wrong. Part of a method. A plan. This is how you keep doing this. One job and another and another. You want to kill lots and lots of people? Not get caught? Use the method. Follow the plan.

One last check. Pain. Scale of one to ten? Four. Dull ache, not too bad. About average. Same place, one inch below the ribs, a shade to the right. Some back pain, too. Try to stretch it out. Like it's got anything to do with being stretched out. Right. Grab the bottle of water in the coat pocket. Take a long pull.

Slide the water bottle back into the coat. Bump into the pill bottle. Pull it out. Hold it up. Four pills. Two blue. Two white with the dark red stripe. Just in case. Tuck it away.

Grab the front door keys, the van keys off the hook. Open the door, step out. Stand, wait, listen. No one is around. Lock up, walk down the stairs.

Out the door. Walk two blocks to the lot. Snow is piling up. Couple a inches now. Open up the van, turn the engine on. Get the brush. Clean the windows. Pull two panels out of the back: Little Sisters of the Poor. Pop the panels into place. Get behind the wheel.

9:30 P.M.: Put the van in gear. Head out on the street. Over to Halsted, left and south. Not much traffic. Not in the snow.

9:35 P.M.: Taking my time. Going slow in the snow.

9:50 P.M.: The place is a nightclub. Up on Lincoln. The 1812 Club. Nothing to do with what's-his-name, Beethoven, or that war. Address is 1812 North Lincoln. Old days, used to be just Murphy's Pub. Added music, couple years ago. Changed the name. Big window in the front, three paces from the entrance. Bandstand in the window, band facing inside. Coming up on it now. There it is on the left. Check it once on foot.

Turn left. Find a space. No Parking? No problem. What Chicago cop is going to ticket the Little Sisters of the Poor? Turn the flashers on, leave the engine running. Check the extra key. On a rubber band. Around the left wrist. Step outside. Lock the door. Put the purse with the gun on that arm.

No one around. No workmen, no cops, no streetwalkers, no homeless.

9:57 P.M.: Directions are very clear. Five people in the band. Trumpet and sax up front. Bass, drums, piano in back. Shoot the black one in the back line, not the black one up front. Black, white? Just a way to mark them. They are not going to be wearing name tags.

10:00 P.M.: Coming up on the window. Move to get a good line of sight. Shit. Three blacks, not two. One in front, the trumpet player. Not the target. Drums and piano in the back, both black. Something is not right. Stop. Kneel down, tying the boots. Tying the boots with no laces.

Instructions say the black in the back. They are finishing a song. Hear the sound of clapping. They point to the drummer, little guy, turns right and bows, turns left and bows.

Drummer is not a guy. It is a girl. And she is not black, exactly. More like Japanese, Chinese. Got the short hair, got some muscular arms. But tits, definitely, smooth face, no stubble. The eyes, those folds, what do you call that? Fooled me there.

Standing up again, slowly. No sudden moves. Face turned out toward the street, walking ahead. Then around the corner. Pause. Lean up against the building.

10:04 P.M.: Stick with the piano player. They told me, the only black in the back. He is sitting there, hunched over. Not moving. Piece of cake. Grab the gun. Check the safety. Flick it off. Gun behind the purse. Purse against the chest. Walk around the corner.

Close to the building now. Dark and snowing. Wind is blowing.

Hear the music now. Something slow and sweet. Jazz. Nice.

Stop. Look around. No cars. No people. Just the snow and the wind.

And me and the gun.

Stop. Two deep breaths. Discipline.

10:05 P.M.: Take two steps into the light, a quarter turn to the left. Aim at the head.

Fire.

Glass explodes, people scream. He is done.

Keep moving. Just a bag lady stumbling along. A gun by her side.

Around the corner, to the left. Open the van. Toss the purse on the seat. Slide inside. Flip the safety on. Tuck the gun between the thighs. The van is still running. Left foot on the brake. Put it into drive. Flip the flashers off. Turn the directional on. Check the traffic.

Drive due west. Nice and easy. North, then west again. Away from Lincoln. West over to Halsted, north up to Belmont, then one block past. Look around. No cars.

Pull over by a Dumpster. Open the window. Hear the howling of the wind. The sound of sirens far away.

Take the gun out. Make sure the safety is on. Empty the bullets into a hand. Empty the hand into a pocket. Hold onto the one empty cartridge. Close the cylinder. Wipe it all down with a rag. Wrap the gun in the rag. Wrap the rag in a McDonald's bag. Toss it all in the Dumpster. Drive.

Drive three blocks away. Stop at the light. Roll down the window. Flick the empty cartridge down a storm grate. Gone. Clean. Easy.

10:20 P.M.: Head to the lot. Park the van. Get out. Put the panels in the back. Lock up.

Clean up. Get dressed. Lock up. And down the fire escape and into the car and through the snow to home.

One more done.

CHAPTER 2
Vinnie Amatucci

Inside the 1812 Club
Thursday, January 9

What struck me was that it happened so quickly. They were playing along in an easy, mellow shuffle and then came the crash of the shot and the shattering of the glass. I didn't actually hear a "bang"; the sound of the breaking glass erased anything that may have come before it, like a low-grade retrograde amnesia. Everyone dove to the floor. Me, I was already on the floor, so I froze. I know, I know, it's not very heroic, but that's what I did. I looked around; no one seemed to be shot. It's funny, but I immediately interpreted it as a gunshot, without question. People were bleeding a little—cuts from the glass—but everyone was up and moving around. My pulse slowed, my breathing deepened. I was almost feeling—what, relief?—when I saw the guy slumped over the piano keys. I was squatting at the left side of the bandstand as you look at it, looking at him from about ninety degrees, toward what had been his left profile, eighteen fucking inches away, and as soon as I saw him I knew he was dead.

Half his head was splattered all over the piano, an exit wound right out of Zapruder, but backward, his mahogany forehead puckered out in red and gray, a great big brain-kiss pointing straight at me as he leaned to his right, dead eyes looking but not seeing.

The dude was dead. No doubt.

I guess you'd have to say that I was in shock. All the adrenaline left me too alert to function, able only to sense. And sense I did: my eyes saw every speck of stubble on his chin; my ears could hear conversations from every corner of the room; my nose could smell past my own sudden sweat to the metallic tang of his blood, pooling on the floor near my feet.

I had been kneeling not three feet to his right, adjusting the soundboard, when it happened. I watched the reel of the tape recorder spin slowly around, one turn after another, clockwise to the right. I had an impulse to turn it off, but I couldn't seem to act on it.

Time jerks you around when something like this happens, because I looked at the couples moseying toward the door, and I looked at the door, and the cops were right there. I mean, right fucking *there*. I didn't even hear the sirens—so much for my suddenly acute sensory focus. There were blue flashing lights behind me and a dozen of Chicago's Finest wedging into the room, half in uniforms and half in plain clothes.

A tall, gaunt cop in a rumpled gray suit, an old black topcoat, and bristly steel-gray hair stepped forward. His face was all loose; it looked as if someone else had been wearing it. His eyes were deep and active. He spoke up, in a deep and raspy voice.

"All right, no one leaves until your statement is taken. Everybody take a seat right where you were when it happened. We'll need names and addresses, so get your licenses out. Everybody stay calm. It looks like it's all over but the paperwork."

A hush fell over the room. All that adrenaline flushed out of my system, and I felt a sudden sleepiness. I wasn't sad or anything. I didn't know the guy at all. I mean, he wasn't part of the band; he just sat in those last two tunes. I didn't even know his name—"Roger Something," I think Paul said before he sat down on the bench. Played pretty well, too, with a nice little solo on a medium-tempo version of "I Got Rhythm." It was quite lyrical, actually; unassuming, melodic, not too showy, except he didn't have much of a left hand.

I don't mean to speak ill of the dead, but he had been sitting in for *me*, so it was hard not to judge.

I looked around; people were having trouble breathing or their eyes were wet or they were looking pale or flushed. Most folks just looked stunned, with vacant looks in their eyes, thousand-yard stares. Even the professionally impatient hadn't had time to get restless.

The band was scattered all around, except for Paul, who was standing right in the front of where the window had been, holding his horn to his chest like he does when he's playing but not actually playing at that moment. It looked like he was still listening to the song's changes in his head, getting himself ready to solo when his turn came up. One of the cops tried to get everyone to sit where they were when it happened, but no one but Paul was going to go in front of that open window anytime soon. Everything was covered in fragments of glass. The wind was blowing and the snow was starting to frost the backs of the chairs. The cops finally herded the rest of the band toward the stage and sat them in front of it, on the floor, sitting with their backs up against the risers with their elbows on their knees. Paul kept standing until a cop tugged on his sleeve. I turned off the Uher, then flopped down where I was.

Jeff was holding his tenor sax, his fingers unconsciously playing some riff. Sidney, legs lotused like an enormous

Buddha, his string bass standing next to him, was staring at something very close to him and very far from the rest of us. Paul, once he settled, seemed to be taking a nap, or at least resting his eyes. Akiko, her drumsticks clutched in her left hand, her head down, was showing nothing but short dark hair for anyone to see, but her eyes were darting everywhere.

Then there was me. When Roger Something started his first song, I had moved to the bar and had been hitting on the blonde sitting next to me. As the second song started, I had Groucho-walked to the soundboard to turn up the volume on the piano. Maybe he was shy, and maybe the system had been tuned to me and I just play too goddamn loud. But I could hardly hear the guy. I had knelt down and had my hand on dial number three when it happened. Now, I kept turning my head to stare at the piano, a good one, a Baldwin, then seeing the blood dripping from the keyboard to the floor, a splat at a time, and quickly looking somewhere else, anywhere else.

The ambulance took longer than the cops, and it seemed as if you could hear it coming from miles away, the siren wailing through the storm, its pitch getting higher as it neared, a classic acoustical Doppler effect. Three EMTs—two women and a man—came out of the van with their green scrubs on, no coats or hats in the snow, with those silly booties on their feet, pulling on their latex gloves, hauling a stretcher, rushing like mad, shouting. They took one look at the piano player and everything slowed right the fuck down. One of the women reached in to find a pulse. Just a formality; it didn't take long. You could see her shake her head: No. Gone.

"Has anyone else been shot?" she asked, looking around the room. About ten people had blood trickling down their faces, and about half of them tentatively raised their hands maybe halfway, the way you used to do when you were in third grade. They were cut up a little from the flying glass, and some of them were wearing what had previously been parts of Roger Something's prefrontal cortex, but they hadn't really been shot, and most of them knew it.

But blood is blood, so the medics set about going around checking each one, picking slivers of glass out of them, wiping them down, patching them up.

I sat back, and tried to breathe.

Who knows? I mean, who the fuck knows, you know?

CHAPTER 3
Ken Ridlin

Inside the 1812 Club
Thursday, January 9

It is the last night of my last shift on the last rung up the ladder back to Homicide when the call comes in.

"Attention: All Units."

I am thinking about Narcotics, about how I hate it, about how I am trying to claw my way out of it. I am thinking how I am almost there, just at the lip, about to shimmy over the edge, and my first thought is—oh, no, not another idiotic drug bust.

The thing is, most dopers are too stoned to stay out of trouble. You might say, it's a victimless crime, they're only hurting themselves, what's the point of locking them up? Won't get any argument from me, in principle. But in reality, they throw themselves in front of the cops. Guy goes to score some blow, he's in a hurry, so he leaves his car parked in front of a hydrant, and the badge on the beat has no choice but to ticket him and toss him, and oh, is that a crack pipe in your pocket or are you just happy to see me?

Or that pothead basketball player who was in the papers a while back. Going on a road trip, has to bring his half-ounce of weed with him, because you just know there's no dope anywhere in New York or Atlanta or L.A. And he has to wrap it up for safekeeping. In aluminum foil. Which even the assholes at the airport can't help but notice, first when he tries to walk it through the metal detector—duh—and then when he puts it into one of those little bins and sends it through the X-ray.

What are you gonna do? It goes with the territory.

So my first thought when the call comes in is, these junkies are going to get me killed on the last night I have to deal with them. After all I am going through to get back, it's all going to stop in some nasty alley with some filthy mook who can't stop sniffling, can't aim a weapon well enough to shoot the wall behind me, but who is wasted enough to drop it on the ground and have it go off and kill me by accident.

But it isn't that. It's:

"Shots Fired, Possible Homicide, 1812 North Lincoln."

And then I have to listen to it again. Because I remember this address—this is a club I used to know, from back in the day. And because it is only six blocks away. And because I am not a homicide detective yet, not until midnight. And so I am thinking—will I piss somebody off for poaching on his turf before I even get on the job? Thinking—will I somehow manage to screw up a simple crime scene and give them second thoughts before they have time to think their first ones? Thinking—how can this go wrong on me, just when I need something to go right? Maybe I can drive around, let a couple hours pass. Maybe the radio is not working in the storm we are having here. Maybe I am out getting a cup of coffee and I'm not hearing it.

And I am thinking all this when the car suddenly glides up in front of 1812 North Lincoln and I am applying the brakes and opening the door and clipping the badge to my lapel. And by then it is too late to think of anything because here I am. My blue lights are on and I do not know when I turned them on, and a squad room full of uniforms is standing right behind me, looking at me the way the linemen look at the quarterback in the huddle—ready, hopeful, expectant.

It is chaos inside, people buzzing all around, throwing on their coats, trying to get out. All except for the band; most of them are standing in front of what used to be the window.

I flash the tin, summon up the big voice, say, "All right, everybody take a seat where you are and we'll get to you as soon as we can. No one leaves until your statement is taken by an officer. We'll need names and addresses, so get your ID's out. Might as well stay calm. Looks like it's all over but the paperwork."

I get the patrons settled, set the troops in motion. It's a routine, a process, a dance we all know how to do. We settle into the rhythm of it.

I check the vic. He is dead. Whoever did this is either one good shot or one lucky bastard—one in the middle of the back of the head, from ten feet away, in the middle of a driving snowstorm, through a thick plateglass window—that is some good shooting. This is someone who put in some effort. There is no collateral damage—everyone else is fine. This is no crime of passion, no sudden impulse. This looks professional.

One of the plainclothes guys is going through the vic's clothes and fishes out a wallet. He holds it up like a twenty-pound fish he caught with five-pound line. "Driver's license for . . ." he holds it up . . . "one Roger Tremblay—Los Angeles address. Baggage stub from O'Hare, Flight 631 arriving from L.A. at five P.M. Lucky he was able to land before the storm hit."

Irony. Black humor. It's a cop thing. We're supposed to be jaded.

"Business card," he says. holding up an ivory-colored rectangle, "Firm of Shields, Manfreddi, and Goldfarb, the

Practice of Law" he adds. "He doesn't look like the Goldfarb."

"Or the Manfreddi, either," another chimes in.

"One less of them—it's tragic," he says.

"One less what?"

"One less lawyer."

Another detective is going through the coat, draped on the back of the bar stool where the vic had sat: "Card key for the Marriott, downtown. Taxi receipt—Checker number four-nine-three-nine, from the Marriott to here, eight bucks, plus a good tip. Cash—maybe a hundred. Pack of Tic Tacs—peppermint. Picture of what looks like the wife and kids. Ad cut out from the *Reader* for this place. Drinking . . ." He picks up a half-empty glass and sniffs it, rolling it around in his gloved hands . . . "Scotch, rocks. J&B? Cutty?"

I remember precisely how each smells—the distinctive medicinal aroma of the J&B, the oily tones of the Cutty Sark. I taste them in my mind as he says their names.

I turn and walk over to the band. There are three of them sitting on the front edge of the bandstand, a big furry bear of a guy, a tiny Asian female, and a sweaty Irish American male. The trumpet player, a tall African American male about thirty-two, is standing right in front of the window, his horn at the ready, snowflakes beginning to coat his short Afro. There is another guy off to the side of the bandstand, by some equipment over there, a wiry guy with dark hair and a beard. We take down names and addresses first. Then it is all the same questions, questions so standard I can recite them by heart.

Their answers come across all snotty. Maybe they all watch too many cop shows on the TV. Maybe it's what they call a distancing mechanism, a defensive thing. Then one of them chuckles. I can go with the black humor, trust me, but we are standing here and there is blood on the floor, and that deserves some respect. I give him a look. He shuts up.

We go around and around and finally, the trumpet player jumps in, bypassing the other detectives and talking straight to me. Is it this obvious, that I am the one?

"Officer, we're all going to tell you the same thing. The man walked in here a few minutes before nine o'clock, as we were about to start the first set. He seemed to be a professional man of some sort, conservatively dressed. He had one drink at the bar, and sipped it very slowly. He listened to the first set very attentively. At nine forty-five, during the break, he came up and asked if he could sit in on piano, just one or two tunes. He said he used to play when he was in school in New York. He mentioned a couple of people in the business, not top rank but recognizable, and said that if we didn't like his playing he'd sit his ass right back down. He looked like a very sober sort of guy. I checked with Vinnie," he cocks his long neck toward the guy by the equipment, "and he agreed. He played fine on the first tune, so we let him play another. We had just started in on that, and were in the middle of the second chorus when there was this noise. Then there was glass and blood everywhere and he was dead. None of us knew him at all. I don't think he had ever been here before. At least, not when we were here."

There are people who will tell you that this detecting thing is like filling in a puzzle. Don't believe them. It's not like that at all. With a puzzle, you already know what the picture is—it's right on the box. So you work from the outside in, from the background to the foreground. With this, you have no idea what the picture is supposed to look like. And you start with the central figure, because he is dead, and you work your way outward, toward the context.

Somebody tells you, "Hey, I saw the dead guy alive around eight forty-five, on the street out front, having a fight with another guy," and you ask what the other guy looks like. Someone else says, "Hey, Roger Tremblay? I met him at the convention and he said some guy was threatening him," and you ask about that. It's not like you have a pattern and you have to find the pieces that bring it to life. It's like you only have this one piece, and you try to find another piece that connects to it, then other pieces that connect to them. So you see if there's another piece that leads you somewhere, and another one that fits that one, and it may cover one little corner of the picture and it may wander all across the frame, and it may go straight to the piece with a picture of the killer standing in the snow with a gun. (It happens, sometimes.) And you can't just look at all the pieces and see what fits where, because the pieces aren't there, you have to find them, one by one. All you can see is what you already know, and when you really look at it it's not much, a few pieces here and there. And outside of that is everything you don't know, and that's most of it. Most of that you'll never know—what the vic was like with his wife, whether he was good at his job, what he did on the weekends, what he did to get to sleep at night. Most of that is part of a larger puzzle anyway. So it's like you're crawling around in the dark, feeling for one or two pieces that can maybe connect you to one or two more, until all of a sudden one piece locks into place and a pattern emerges, and there you are.

Or it never does, and you never know, and you file it away with the cold cases and you move on.

And as I am thinking about this, another cop is *doing* it, and chimes in: "Detective, this lady says she thinks she saw someone outside walking past, staring in the window a few minutes before the shooting, headed . . ."

I traffic-cop my hand to him, turn to her, lean in.

"What did you see, ma'am? What did he look like?"

The woman volunteering this information is tall but shy about it, like a lot of tall women are, hunching her shoulders forward, slumping down. I squat down to get to her level. They teach you to do this, to make it a peer thing, not an authority thing.

Her eyes flick across mine. "It wasn't a he, it was a she," she says. "She looked like, like a . . . a bag lady."

And just like that, a piece clicks into place, maybe a big piece, maybe half a puzzle all by itself. I feel a sudden heat on the back of my neck, instant sweat in the hollows of my armpits, a tightening around the edge of my scalp. A bag lady?

"Heading which way, ma'am?"

She points.

I turn, single out three uniforms who are busy taking up space. "Heading south," I tell them. "Use caution—he's armed. And don't mess up the footprints." They reach for their weapons and step gingerly outside, looking left and right.

I turn back to the woman, squat down to her level. "A bag lady? Stocky build? Scarf on her head? Rolled-down stockings?"

The woman nods to each of these, surprised, except the last one, saying "I couldn't see her legs," but can't add anything else. "Does it mean anything?"

"Did you get a look at . . . the face?"

She lowers her head. Her hair is longish and a little matted, and it cascades in hanks over her eyes. I read that as a "No."

Two of the other detectives give each other a look, ask the room in general, "Did anyone else see this bag lady?" No one says anything.

I look around the room, and the skinny guy is still squatting over in the corner. He has headphones on his head, and is staring at the floor. At all the electronic equipment.

Equipment like a tape recorder.

CHAPTER 4
Vinnie Amatucci

Inside the 1812 Club
Thursday, January 9

The cops herded us together and kept asking the same questions, over and over and over. We muttered and mumbled and said what we could. Paul ended up doing most of the talking; he's good at that.

A pack of cops broke off from the herd and tiptoed out. They left in a rush and came back at a crawl.

I started to feel cold, the wind whipping in harder off the lake and whistling in the broken window. When the cop with the used face got around to me, I told him the basics: Vince Amatucci, I live in Hyde Park, I have a taxi license, I play piano with the band. I'm also sort of the manager; I book all the gigs and tape all the sets. I had my headphones on and was trying to get the balance right and had my head down. Didn't see a thing. Did I tape the shot? I don't know, I must have . . .

I crab-walked over to the Uher, rewound, pressed PLAY, focused in. I heard it, a burst like a loud cough, then stopped, rewound the tape a few turns, held out the headphones. The guy with the long face, the detective in charge, slipped them on, looked at me, nodded. I hit PLAY. I could see him following it. With what must have been the gunshot he blinked.

I touched REWIND, let it run a bit. I hit PLAY. After he blinked again, he said, "Rewind it one more time. No, don't play it. Just stop there, right before the shot."

He leaned back and turned to one of the uniforms. "Bag this tape and give this man a receipt. Maybe the lab can turn something up. And maybe all we'll find out is how good a piano player the vic really was."

I started to protest, but realized he was going to let me keep the Uher, when he could have taken the whole system. Besides, there was something in his eyes that I couldn't identify, something lurking at the edges. I popped the tape out and held it in my hand. A cop in a uniform came over with a plastic bag and opened it. I dropped the tape inside. He sealed it, took out a Sharpie, wrote something on it, then asked me for my name and address or a card so they could get it back to me. The detective with the sagging face said, "Already got it. It's noted."

Then he took me by the elbow and wheeled me around to a small table. He motioned for me to sit. I did. He flipped open a notepad, steno size. "Mr. Amatucci, we've run your name on the computer—you're clean, aside from some . . . 'vehicular incidents.'" He paused, his left eyebrow arched. "Can you think of anyone who would have a reason to shoot you?"

"I hear you," I said, "I've seen the movie—Truffaut, wasn't it?" He stared at me. The guy wasn't playing along at all; he was making me do all the work.

"I can't think of anybody. I've had some angry customers, sure, but murder? Assassination?"

He looked at me. "Your choice of words . . . What makes you say 'assassination'?"

I turned around, stared at Roger Something. I turned back to the cop. "Look at him."

He did, and soon turned back toward me. He was wearing an expression I couldn't read, either that he was impatient to get on with it, or that he had all the time in the world. It was like he was excited, and also bored. And it wasn't like two opposite expressions flickering back and forth, but more like wearing both on his face at once.

"We'll be in touch," he said. The other cops were wrapping it up as well. He stood up and slowly pushed his chair back in.

Louie, who manages the club, didn't seem to know what to do, and kept looking at the cops, trying to make eye contact with one of them. The tall cop saw him and stepped over.

"Looks like you'd better call it a night. You got insurance, right? I was you, I'd get some plywood and some nails and at least close it up temporarily until you can get a glazier in in the morning. Doubt you can reach one this time of night."

"A . . . a . . . glacier?" Louie knows how to pour a decent drink and how to count the house, but he's not exactly Mensa material.

"A *glazier,* a glass guy. There's a place down off Sixteenth Street if you need a reference."

"No, I got the number of the guy who installed it last time. I can call them."

"Don't leave anything in the register or behind the bar. This is a safe neighborhood, but . . ." The guy wasn't looking at Louie; his eyes seemed to be scanning the long rows of bottles behind the bar, almost as if he were cataloging them.

"I'll stay here myself tonight," Louie said. "I got protection." He nodded toward the bar.

"That's nice for you," the cop said. "You have a permit to go along with it?"

Louie raised his eyebrows, reached into his back pocket, and pulled out a wallet the size of a campaign chest, brimming with layers of mysterious papers and cards of many colors. He located a particular piece of detritus, pulled it out, smoothed it flat against his considerable stomach, handed it over.

The cop looked at it. Louie reached out his hand, but the cop pulled it back a bit. "This expires next week. You'll want to get that taken care of while you're getting the window fixed."

"Sure, officer. Right away."

The cop handed him the permit. Louie stuffed it back into the wallet, and somehow managed to wedge it back into his hip pocket. When he looked up, the cop was holding out his card, so Louie went through the whole routine again to feed it back into the jaws of all that chaos.

And then, just like that, it was over. People were starting to straggle out, hanging on to each other. Some were quiet, others had gotten all excited and were jabbering away.

I looked at my watch. Shit. Almost 10:30. I was supposed to take an eleven-to-seven shift in the Fat Man's cab and I was going to have to hustle to get there in time to pick it up, especially in this weather. The Fat Man hated anybody being late, and some guy getting shot wasn't going to get me a hall pass, especially since it wasn't me who got shot. I closed up the sound system, packed it under my arm, nodded at the guys, told Paul "Duty calls," and booked out to my car. The snow was starting to get serious, coming down sideways in big fat flakes.

Not your average night.

After fishtailing down Lincoln and sliding down Michigan I got to the cabstand at 10:58. I gathered up all my stuff, locked up my car, walked over to the cab, found the clicker for the cab, flicked the doors open, started her up, got behind the wheel, wipered off the snow, and eased into traffic, heading back downtown. I didn't get two blocks when some guy flagged me over, hopped in, said "Airport," and we were off.

Great, I thought. O'Hare Airport, land of the fifty-dollar fare.

"Midway Airport," he said.

Shit, I thought, Midway Airport, land of the long and pointless wait.

First it's one thing, and then it's another.

CHAPTER 5
Vinnie Amatucci

Waiting at Midway
Thursday, January 9 / Friday, January 10

I was drifting through the vastness of space, slowly spinning in a weightless void. I could tell it was a dream—there was a languor in my limbs and a rattle to my breathing—but I just stayed quiet, watching it flow through me. There was no joy, no sadness, no feeling at all, just a smooth alpha state, bathing me in warmth, as I slowly sidestroked through the emptiness of deepest darkest space, my head back, my neck loose, letting it all flow in. But in my dream, space was reversed: the black vastness was a dull white, the stars, random dots of burnished black. My breath came deep and slow. The cold silence embraced me.

Then there was a honk. A honk? In the middle of the vastness of space? I jerked awake.

I tried to focus my eyes—the white space and black stars came clear to me: I was sitting in cab number 691, staring at the ceiling—little black holes in white leatherette.

The honking seemed to be coming from behind me. I

looked around; the windows were an opaque white. I leaned forward and tapped the wipers. The cab was covered with snow, but as the windshield cleared, I saw I was in the cab lot at Midway Airport, and the cabdriver behind me was trying to get me to move up. I had fallen half asleep, zoned out.

And I was cold. Freezing fucking cold.

I cranked up the engine and set the heat to Dante's Seventh Circle of Hell. I reached down below the right-hand seat on the front, pushed aside the detritus that had collected there and found the scraper—gotcha! I popped open the door and got hit with a gust in my face.

I hauled out and started scraping the windows. There were about six empty spaces ahead of me, and the line in front of that was only four or five rows from the front.

The way the cabstands work in Chicago—both Midway and O'Hare—is that you drop off your incoming passenger at departures, circle around, and enter the cab lot. Each lot is eight to ten columns wide, ten to thirty rows deep (O'Hare's is bigger by far, for obvious reasons). You pick a column (I've always been a Bernoulli's theorem kind of guy; I head for the edges), pull up, and wait. A row at a time gets called up to the terminal, in single file, and as you pull out you get a ticket from the cabstand master, which he or she time-stamps. This is so cabbies don't "poach," drive in off the street and cut in line, which—I'm shocked, *shocked!*—has been known to happen. At the airports, in a rare exhibition of egalitarianism, you have to wait your turn. Once you get to whatever terminal has called you up, you pull up at the curb and wait in line again. Eventually, the starter whistles up a handful of cabs at a time, until it's your turn. You get no choice in passengers, they get no choice in drivers. Finally, the fare gets in, tells you the address, the starter takes your ticket, and you're on your way.

The cab business in this town *lives* on trips to the airport. Ninety percent of the time it's O'Hare, and that can run thirty-five to sixty-five bucks, not counting the ever-important tip, depending on the traffic and the weather and the time of day. Any gratuity less than a ten is egregious penury. It can also take from thirty minutes to an hour and a half to get out there, depending again on traffic and weather and the time of day, so when you *do* get out there, it usually makes sense to get a fare back. Double your money, double your fun. One of my optimal flow patterns for the day starts with a fare to O'Hare, and then a quick fare back downtown, starting the day by tucking a C-note's worth of confidence into my pocket before breakfast.

The catch is that there are times when you can wait for an hour or three to get a fare back to town. This is true of O'Hare, which is huge, and also of Midway, which is slow. In the summer you'll bake, in the winter you'll freeze. So it's a gamble—you get there, appraise the situation, and make your bet. Should I stay? Should I deadhead back to town? The weather, the flight schedules, the other cabs in front of you all get factored in.

They do have a great feature here they don't have everywhere, which changes the equation significantly: a short-trip ticket. Say you're at O'Hare and you wait for two hours and get some joker going to DesPlaines, five minutes away. Shit! That's a five-dollar fare, instead of the real money you'd be getting to go downtown. Get two or three of those in a row and you're losing your ass. So they have an irregular radius drawn on a map. Any address inside that radius and you get a short-trip ticket. It's time-stamped, and if you can get to where you're going and zip back to the lot in thirty minutes, you get to go to the head of the line. Before they had this, cabbies would refuse fares and would get into fights: "*You* go to fucking Downer's Grove. *I've* been waiting here all goddamn day."

To me, a short trip is actually a good deal. I look forward to them. Plus, at the edges of the radius, it can be a challenge. Keeps it interesting.

I had finished giving the windows a wipe, and jumped back inside to recalibrate myself.

My first fare after the shooting, at eleven, the guy got in and said, "Midway Airport." At night. In the snow. Great.

With him snoozing in the back and me fighting the snow in the front, we slid down the Eisenhower past the pluming smokestacks out to Cermak Road, then waddled south about fifteen blocks, from the high Fifties to the low Forties. It's desolate out here, semi-industrial all the way out, and near the airport it's strip malls with check cashing on every other block, which ought to give you a hint. This airport used to be close to dead, but then they revived it, because O'Hare was growing to roughly the size of Mesopotamia, and nowhere else wanted to give up their tacky suburban homes for a new runway. But bringing Midway back did *not* bring the neighborhood back. The middle-class folks getting ready to move out of the heart of the city hopped right over the West Side and out to the new suburbs around I-294. And Midway was left just about as it had always been, except for more traffic and more noise.

It was almost midnight when I got there, so I figured that since there were not going to be any fares to be found on the streets, I'd try the lot and see what developed. I had heat, I had music. I wouldn't even mind some rest, I remember thinking at the time.

Which is what I guess I got.

Now that I was awake, I kept the wipers on intermittent and tried to clear the cobwebs from my head. I was still in the fourth row, but we had all bunched up in anticipation.

The Fat Man's cabs are something special. He has three of them. One of them he drives, when he's in the mood, and no one else touches it, ever. The second he leases to two guys, twelve-hour shifts each. The third, the one I'm in, is eight-hour shifts, three of us plus a floater. I'm the usual day guy, but I do some graveyard shifts, like tonight. All three taxis are old Marathon International Cabs, the old Yellow/Checker type, the big, bulbous beasts they stopped making almost twenty-five years ago. They've got to have a million miles on each of them, easy. They get about twelve miles to the gallon, but they go through anything, and they never quit. And when other drivers see these old beasts bearing down on them, riding way up high, let me tell you: they get the fuck out of the way.

They're huge inside, even with the bulletproof partition, which he's had motorized so you can actually roll it down and out of the way. Great heat, great visibility, new paint. The Fat Man keeps them in mint condition and people get a kick out of riding in them—like a blast from the past. They're a lot more distinctive than what the big cab companies mostly use today, which is those stupid Chevvies or the rear-wheel-drive Ford Crown Vic's, the same ones they use as cop cars, except without the big police engine and without the decent suspension.

The Fat Man has juiced these up a bit, too. Double overhead cam multi-port V-8s, tuned suspensions, a little extra turbo boost, fat new Pirellis, glove-leather interiors, bitching CD / cassette eight-speaker stereo with a subwoofer under the seat; not at all the way they were delivered. And outside, not a nick or a dent or a scratch anywhere. "You be putting a fucking dent in my fucking cab, I be putting a fucking dent in your fucking head!" is what he tells his drivers when they come aboard. And he means it.

I looked around. There was a stirring around up front. I flipped on the parking lights, flicked the wipers again, moved up a row. Now three rows to go. Time for a systems check.

Cash money? Check.

Trip ticket? Check.

Cigarettes? Let me see . . . Check.

Weed? Where did I put the weed? . . . Fumbling around here . . . Ah-Ha. In my kit bag, tucked between the front seats, where it's supposed to be. Take the pipe out, tuck it back in the kit bag. The canister's in there already. OK. Check.

No wonder I was floating through the deep vastness of outer space.

It would be nice, I think, to get a fare back to town, then

work the hotels and the clubs and the hospitals the rest of the night, downtown, where the roads will be plowed and the people will be awake, doing something, going someplace. Well, some of the people. There are no radios in the Fat Man's cabs, no dispatcher sitting someplace warm, pouring money into your ear.

I asked the Fat Man about this once, early on. He gave me his standard-issue Marine Corps stare, and asked, "How much you have to pay the dispatcher at Yellow, when you was there, get you some calls?"

"The bribe? The kickback? The *baksheesh? La mordita?*" He nodded. "Yeah, that."

"Ten, fifteen a week," I said.

"That get you all the best calls? All them long, good rides?"

"Well, no, not really . . ."

"How much you 'spect you gotta pay to get them *sweet* rides?"

"I don't know," I said. "Maybe twenty-five? Thirty?"

"That all?" he said.

"I don't know. Forty? Fifty? You tell me."

He looked away, coughed. "Sixty?" he asked. "Seventy, eighty?"

"I don't know," I said. "What's the point?"

" 'What's the point?' " he asked, mimicking me. "Point is, you don't know. I could be keeping my hand out, and you could keep filling it up, until you be giving me more to get you the good rides than you be making on them good rides. You need somebody telling you where to go, what to do? Go back to Yellow. You be working for me? You on your own."

The lights ahead of me flicked on. Up to the second row, I jammed my hat on my head, grabbed the brush and scraper, and hopped outside to scrape off the snow again so at least it *looked* like I could see where I was going. Some of your customers will appreciate gestures like this, and tip accordingly. Some won't care in the least; you never know. I even cleaned off the roof and the hood and the trunk. I was Mr. Thorough.

I was giving the rear window a final swipe when I heard a loud bang, and the sound of breaking glass. I dove for the ground. I heard it again, on my left, and flinched again, edging under the rear bumper. I looked up, combing the snow out of my beard. Drivers were throwing bottles at a Dumpster twenty feet behind me. I saw another one, a pint of Smirnoff, sail through the snow and miss the edge of the Dumpster, splintering against its side.

I was panting; my eyes were wide. The whole scene of the guy getting killed at the club flooded back in precise detail: the shattering of the glass, the bullet hole in his head, the cold wind on the back of my neck, the EMTs, the cops, the chaos. My pulse was pounding loudly in my ears.

Deep breaths, Vince, I told myself. Get a grip.

There was another set of honks, and the cabs around me revved up. I brushed myself off and jumped back in the cab. I closed the door, clicked on the belt, and my row pulled up to the front. We started revving our engines in time with our heartbeats. I had a long pull of water and popped two Certs. Then the starter waved us on to Terminal B, handing each of us a ticket to a fresh encounter, a new mystery.

I could only hope that my own encounter would be uniquely interested in the deep and profound mysteries of life . . . especially of life back in the direction of downtown.

CHAPTER 6
Vinnie Amatucci

In the Fat Man's Cab
Friday, January 10

The fare who got in wasn't sure he wanted to get in and wasn't sure he wanted to be a fare. He was a good-looking guy, maybe mid-forties, around six feet, a thinner-than-medium build, trimmed salt-and-pepper hair. He got in the cab carrying one bag, a funny-shaped kind of carry-on, with a zippered bottom to it.

"Chicago . . ." he kept muttering, "Chicago . . ."

I didn't drop the flag right away—I was thinking that this guy was going to bug out and I'd have to eat the fare. Whenever that happens there's paperwork. Lots of paperwork.

"Where to, sir?" I asked.

He still didn't look up, his two hands tented over his mouth and nose, his index fingers massaging his nose. The guy seemed to be way down deep. His eyes were fixed on some middle distance, staring.

I've had people before who didn't want to go where they have to be going—wives heading to the county lockup to visit, older folks heading to the hospital for just one more test—and this one had all the signs.

The starter came up—we were holding up the line by now—and waved me forward a little. I rolled up, hit the switches and brought both left-side windows down. He came over to the left side and leaned down. Skinny tall black guy, skinny little company jacket—freezing his ass off, his shoulders hunched against the wind.

"What's the problem, man?" he asked.

"The problem," the fare says, pulling his hands away from his face but not changing his posture, "is that I'm in Chicago, stuck in a snowstorm, and I don't want to be in Chicago, stuck in a snowstorm, and I'm being somewhat petulant about it."

Surprise, surprise; he was actually lucid. No tone, no edge to it, just self-observant. Maybe a level or two removed from current sensory reality.

Not that there's anything wrong with that.

"You don't got no choice," the starter said back. "Airports 're shut down, both a them, shut down all day tomorrow, too. Talking ice storm. Same with the trains, not going nowhere, accident down in Indiana. If there's someplace else you need to get to, hunh-unh, not gonna happen. You stuck here. Let's make it painless, aw'ight?"

The fare didn't budge. The starter leaned down and inside a little, breathing our warm stale air. "You got the cash for this here transaction?" he asked. This was a courtesy he was doing for *me*, and I appreciated it, because I never ask. It's one of my more noble failings.

The fare looked up, reached into his front left pocket, pulled out a gold money clip, showing a couple of hundreds and some smaller bills. His eyes tracked the roll and then rotated up to look at the starter.

The starter leaned back, took a step forward and leaned into my window. "Let's expedite this here shit, aw'ight?" and slapped the side of the cab as he walked back, blowing his whistle.

"Sorry to put you through this," the fare said, "is there a hotel near here?"

"Well, not one you'd want to stay in unless you want to pay by the hour . . . if you know what I'm saying. You'd probably do better downtown. Where are you trying to get to?"

He jumped right in, but took it in another direction. "What about O'Hare? What hotels are out there?"

"That's good thinking. You can get to almost anywhere from O'Hare. Midway here is mostly short hops to second-tier cities . . ." Good move, Vince, you just implied he just flew in from some shithole. "Of course, all the good hotels up there have Midway vans, every hour or so, if you need to get back here."

Go ahead, make it worse.

"Is there a Marriott?" he asked.

"There are two, actually. I'll take you to the better one, near the airport. I know that one pretty well—we play there all the time. As a matter of fact, we're playing there tomorrow night."

He locked onto my eyes in the rearview mirror for a full second, the first time we had really seen each other. There was something there, no, there was a *lot* there, but I had no context to help it make sense.

"OK," he said, "Let's do it," and sat back into the seat.

I hit the button, craned my neck around, nudged the gas pedal and we were out into the traffic and the slush, heading toward the Cermak Road exit about half a mile away. The snow had piled up since I had arrived. I turned up the wipers and cranked up the heat.

I usually let the fare know my intentions up front, and to let them have a say in which route to take. Hey—if you've got a preference or a plan, it's better you tell me now than after we get there. If I want to go back roads and you want to go Tri-State, and I just heard on the box that the Tri-State is all fucked up, I'm going to tell you. But it *is* your nickel.

"Here's the plan, and if you have a different preference, let me know, OK?"

I made a point of pausing here, looking back in the rearview. He looked up.

"We'll head a mile or two north to the Stevenson, take that west to the Tri-State, head north to DesPlaines Road, then about two miles east to the Marriott. There are more direct routes, but it's getting sloppy out there, and I think we'd do better to stick to the highways."

"Sounds sensible," he said, and off we went.

Cermak was a mess, only one lane open each way instead of the usual three. We were poking along in deep ruts, skidding whenever we hit a cross-rut. This kind of driving is like cross-country skiing: you can't really stop or go on command, but if you work at it you can control the sliding. It also helps to have a good car, and the Fat Man has made these as solid as possible—great tires, plenty of pull when you want it, brakes that, if you really want to stop, you can kick and they'll catch. I even heard a rumor that the Fat Man's own Marathon was a custom four-wheel-drive job, with a tranny lifted from an Audi Quattro.

The fare was looking out the window, his face close to the glass.

"Does this Marriott have the shuttle buses you mentioned?" he asked.

"Yup, to both airports—O'Hare every fifteen minutes and Midway every hour. They have all the amenities—decent restaurant, room service, indoor/outdoor pool. Cable, HBO, nice lounge. The other one is a Marriott Residence Inn, and you . . . you didn't look like you were ready to take up residence . . ."

He looked up at this, a wry grin creasing his face, just a tease of a smile, but something, finally. His left arm was still around that funny case. Either it's the world's worst-designed hidden-bottom case, totally obvious, or it's designed for something special, I thought. He turned away from the window and glanced at the case, his hand lingering on it.

Without looking up he said, "You said you 'play there'? 'Play there all the time'?"

"Oh," I said, "Oh, yeah. I'm with a band that has a regular gig there, on Fridays, every second or third one, like tomorrow, in fact, from nine 'til midnight."

"You're 'with the band'? What do you play?" he asked.

"I play piano, and I'm like their manager, their agent," I stumbled.

" 'Like their manager, their agent' . . . ?" he echoed.

"I was one of the original members, about four years ago," I said. "It started as a bunch of U. of C. students just having a good time. Man, some of the early gigs we had . . ."

" 'U. of C.'?" he echoed, again.

"University of Chicago," I spelled out. "We had a six-piece band, jazz, Dixieland, standards, that kind of thing. I played piano. Sorry, I already said that. We had a trombone player who had the time-sense of a Tourette's patient, a clarinet player who played in the key of H, a bass player who thought he should be playing lead and everyone else should be playing 'under' him, a drummer who, when he took a solo, sounded like someone kicking a drum kit down two flights of stairs, and this trumpet player who we found totally out of the blue and who had never played anything like this before in his life."

Vince, I said to myself, you're babbling. Take a fucking breath.

"What was this band called?" he asked.

"Man, we had a lot of names, 'South Side Strutters,' 'Chicago Dixie Kings,' 'Hyde Park Ramblers'—for an extra ten bucks you could call us anything you wanted. Lately, we seem to be called 'New Bottles.' "

". . . ?" He didn't even have to ask, just a twist of the head.

"For a while our trumpet player was calling it 'Old Wine, New Bottles.' You know, like playing the standards, but maybe in a different way."

"Sounds like fun."

"Yeah, it was. I'm too young to be talking about 'way

back when,' but we had a blast. Man, some of the gigs we played—" I reminisced.

We had pulled over the top of a ridge, and down below there was a car half-flipped in the median, an SUV, a Stupid Useless Vehicle, and people were stomping their brakes as they tried to get an eyeful, swerving side to side, their red taillights leaving trails like tracers in the night. I found a slot to the right of the pack and rode quietly around it. I found a clearing in the flow and quietly surged to fill it, then eased back, safely ahead of the fishtailing gawkers.

That's what real driving is all about: anticipation, timing, rhythm.

"So anyway," I continued, droning on in spite of myself. "We had a great time and then people started to leave and graduate and shit. We learned a lot of new stuff that all the new people brought with them. I'm not talking formal arrangements or anything. By this point everybody in the band could sight-read, but pretty soon, nobody would need to. People brought in their own styles, their own approaches. We started getting better gigs, better money. We evolved almost chronologically, that's the tautological logic of it, and pretty soon it was classics and swing and even three months or so of some Western swing—we found a sax player who thought he was a Texas fiddler—and then, of course, bop, the new thing, fusion, whatever.

"Now here we are, four years into it, we're all in the fucking union, and the only original ones still with the band are me and the trumpet player, and man has he changed some in that time. I mean, not who he is, I don't think that'll ever change, but what he can play is just in a different league. The rest of the guys have evolved around him. We've got a pretty tight, mellow group, maybe one more piece needed to complete the puzzle, but that's just the critic in me."

A typical Vinnie conversation—all poured out in a big one-sided rush and no one's paying attention.

"Like I said, I manage the band and act as their manager. I record most of the gigs and do the telephone thing with the clubs and the radio stations and the free papers like the *Reader,*" I continued. I added one of my stock lines, "I'm having almost as much fun doing that part of it. Suits my entrepreneurial nature," I added with a flourish.

I paused. Our exit was upon us. I hit the directionals, nudged right, and eased around a big slow curve and up to a red light.

"Well, it sounds like—"

"We're about two miles away, at this point," I said. "A straight shot."

He nodded.

I paused just a little too long. "Hey, sorry. I must have been on autopilot. You were saying something, all I caught was 'it sounds like . . .'"

"It sounds like you're having an interesting experience of the music business," he said, and with that comment, cryptic as it was, it was over.

We cruised east on DesPlaines, just plowing along. The snow up here was about seven inches deep, and piling up. I was thinking that maybe it was becoming the kind of night to deadhead *to* O'Hare, a rarely attempted maneuver, and see if I could pick up some scraps—people finally giving up, airport staff who didn't want to drive, whatever.

I was also thinking about why I was jabbering on and on to this perfectly strange stranger about my perfectly strange hobby, if that's what it was, and why I was feeling so this-way-and-that-way about it, when up ahead loomed the Marriott. I swung in along a path of lights glowing softly through a thick coating of snow. We pulled up under the canopy. I stopped the meter and gave him the total, about twenty-two bucks. He pulled the money clip and handed me a twenty and a ten, said "Thanks. Keep it." That half-smile again. I handed him a receipt, and he snaked it into his pocket. He tucked that case under his arm, pulled his coat closer around himself, placed his hand on the door handle, then turned and said, "Good luck with the music. And play your piano, every single day, no matter what," and was gone out the door. I could see him wave off the doorman, politely, as if it were some failing of his that he wasn't yet frail enough to need help; then he went in through the revolving doors and was gone.

Interesting fare, I was thinking, when one of the doormen blew his whistle directly in my fucking ear—me turning to face front as he swiveled to face me. I hear you, I wanted to shout. I fucking hear you.

I pulled forward a few dozen feet. I looked through the window and it wasn't snowing, it was raining. Big fat drops splattering on the windshield, increasing in intensity as I sat. I turned the wipers from intermittent to full. What was this shit?

Suddenly there was a knocking on the driver's window. I rolled it down two inches. It was the doorman again. "You can't park here. If you're going to wait you have to move it over to the cabstand there, on the other side of the circle," he said, swinging his arm.

"Yeah, I got you," I said, like this was news or something. "What's with this rain? Is it going to wash all this snow away? Wouldn't that be nice?"

"Not gonna happen," he said.

"Say again?" I asked.

"Temperature's dropping. They say it's gonna rain for an hour, then drop into the teens and freeze," he said. Curious—he sounded strangely happy telling me this. What, like he wasn't going to be outside in this mess chipping ice while I was sliding all over the roads? Where was the fellow feeling, the salaryman's solidarity?

"Sounds like lots of fun for all of us," I said, sarcastically.

"You weren't here in '78, were you?" he asked.

"You mean that blizzard, the one that stopped Massachusetts for a week?" I asked. "No, where I was it mostly missed us." Where I was was still practically in diapers, but for some reason I didn't mention that.

"Well, out here," he said, "it snowed about a foot, rained two inches, froze, and the temperature didn't get above twenty degrees for the next week. Highest murder rate in the city's history, that was. People killing each other over a fucking parking space. Lot of heart attacks, too, people trying to get their cars open with scrapers, picks, hatchets, acetylene torches . . . I remember in my neighborhood there were cars that didn't get opened until April. A fucking mess. 'The Deep Freeze,' the TV assholes called it."

Great.

"Well, sounds like fun for all of us," I repeated.

Some people do not respond to sarcasm, and he was one of them. He leaned back from the window, gave the car a rap, not too subtly reminding me that I had to move it along, and stepped back under the canopy.

I pushed a button to check the outside temperature: 33° with 96 percent relative humidity.

Hmmm . . . Maybe I should call the home base and see what they knew. I never liked to call in—it had something to do with autonomy—but this might be a good time to break with precedent.

And as I thought that, the cell phone on the dash rang.

I stared at it while it rang two times.

"Metro Car Service," I said, picking it up. "How may I help you?"

It was the Fat Man. I could tell by his breathing, even before he said anything.

"What you doing, sport? Where you at?"

"Just dropped off a fare at the O'Hare Marriott, trying to figure what to do next."

"Fixing to be a motherfucker out there," he said in that raspy voice of his. "Don't need no cowboy shit. Don't need my cars sitting in the shop. Be better if you go to ground, wait this out. You off tomorrow, right? Not driving?"

Friday was my usual day off, and, aw, he remembered, how sweet.

"Yeah," I said, "I'm off."

"That's good." There was a pause. "I got a place for you to put the vehicle, keep it from getting all iced up."

He then proceeded to walk me through a complicated set of directions back to O'Hare. Not the cabstand or the terminals, but the ass end of the airport, where the cargo terminals are. It was eerie: a couple of times he gave directions that were stunningly precise and timely. I drove for four or five minutes until he said "Turn left, now—no, not right, left, where that white van is coming from."

Finally I said, "What the fuck?" The Fat Man was always doing shit like this. I mean *always*. How the hell did he do it?

The car behind me flicked its lights on and off three times. Shit, he was right behind me.

"OK," I said. "I was *wondering* how I'd get a ride back to town."

He chuckled. "You think I'd let you hang at the airport, get your ass in all kinds of trouble?" he asked, rhetorically. "Where we going you can't get yourself into without I'm with you. Taxi Number One will get you home."

The Fat Man's personal cab is actually taxi number 1. Number 1 out of like 9,000. No one knows who he had to know to get that number.

We slogged on, not making good time but moving anyway. The rain on the windshield was starting to hit, splatter, and then spread into crystals. I checked the outside temperature again: 28°, 92 percent relative humidity.

We had somehow turned onto a runway, or a taxiing area. We pulled up to a little shack-like thing in the middle of nowhere, with a low slanted roof. The Fat Man, still behind me, honked three times and flashed his lights twice. We waited a minute. He did it again, and halfway through the flashing the side of the shack began to swing open over the top. There was a road inside, one lane with yellow stripes on each side.

"In you go, driver," said the Fat Man.

I carefully edged inside, and flicked the beams to high. It was a road, one lane, and it tilted down at about a forty-degree angle. I headed down, the Fat Man close on my tail.

The wipers started to squeak; I flipped them off. The sides of this tunnel, if that's what it was, were almost perfectly smooth, all concrete, gray. Not dirty and dingy and sooty like a real tunnel.

Finally we seemed to be at an end: a black wall with yellow diagonal stripes on it loomed before us. Behind me, the Fat Man honked three times and flicked his lights twice and the wall, which turned out to be a door, swung open, riding on rollers straight upward.

I nudged the gas and we rode up into a huge hangar, empty of airplanes but half-full of containers, the kind that come in on planes and leave on tractor trailers and ships. They were stacked three high and there must have been a few thousand of them, all with different names and colors, but all the same exact size. There was a big crane fixed to the center of the floor, but I didn't see any humans around.

The Fat Man rolled his window down and motioned me to come on back.

The snow on the cab was already starting to melt, which meant it was pretty warm in here. I opened the driver's-side door so the Fat Man would know I had gotten his message, then started to gather up all my shit: money, kit bag, coat, hat. I secured everything in my backpack and hopped out. I pantomimed locking the doors with a question mark on my face, and he nodded twice. I went around and locked everything up, even tested the trunk to make sure it was secure, and walked around to his right front door. It was locked. I looked over at him. He made a motion, waving me to the back door. I had heard that the Fat Man never allowed anyone to ride up front with him no matter what the size of the party or the amount of the tip. This was one small piece of confirmatory evidence. Or maybe I just smelled bad.

I got in the back.

On the way back to town, he stuck to the back roads. We did no more than thirty-five, ever, but he got us to Hyde Park in less than an hour and drove like the cab was a part

of him. Remarkable. We must have hit thirty or forty stop-
lights, and not one of them was ever red for us. I asked myself: Does he have some kind of transmitter in the trunk
that turns them green? With the Fat Man, you never know.

We drove on past a drug store with an old-fashioned
clock out front that read five o'clock, and it hit me. It had
been a long fucking day. I suddenly remembered the shooting, the blood, the cold wind. I shivered. That was tonight?
It felt like years ago.

I must have crashed, because the next thing I knew the
car was stopped and the Fat Man was flicking the right rear
door lock, like "Wake up! Wake up!" I jumped and saw that
we had stopped in front of my building. I looked at him in
the rearview: he looked fresh and cool and untroubled,
like he was sitting in his favorite recliner with a beer in one
hand, the clicker in the other, and the Cubs leading by five
in the ninth.

"Thanks for the lift," I said. Then remembering, "Oh,
where do I pick up the cab on Saturday?" Was I going to
have to drag my ass back to O'Hare again, try to locate the
hidden hangar?

"Be the same place it always is," he said. Not "if the
weather lets up," or "pending decent conditions." No "should
be" or "might be" or "probably will be." No use of the condi-
tional at all. The thing is, I believed him. What the Fat Man
says goes, always.

I pondered this, leaning back in the seat. I pondered
Roger Something-or-Other. I pondered the reluctant fare
and the runway bunker and the deep cold snow. My eyes
closed, my breathing slowed, and I fell into a deep sleep,
far away from the moment, a dark place where my dreams
were closed to me, and my thoughts were hidden.

CHAPTER 7
Ken Ridlin

1100 South State Street
Friday, January 10

The admin takes my arm, opens the door, wheels me around, walks me inside. The admin—Lieutenant Ali, David Ali—is six-foot-one, black, 180, thirty-six. Wearing a black suit, white shirt, black tie. Dressed like a Black Muslim. Which he used to be, back in the day.

Times change. People, too. Sometimes.

I look around the edge of the door, peek inside. It's a big office. A very big office. A very big *corner* office. Two walls of windows, shaded by thick vertical drapes. A small, understated portrait wall—the Man and the aldermen, the Man and the mayor, the Man and the governor, the Man and the president, the one before the current one. The requisite shelves of legal texts break the light into a contrast of blinding shards of light and murky swatches of darkness. The Man has been smoking a cigar—against all the regs. The haze hangs in the quiet air. I start to crave a cigarette;

even though I haven't smoked in years I can taste it, I can feel the warmth in my lungs.

Ali walks me into the room, his right hand on my shoulder, his left hand on my elbow. We take four paces over to the Big Desk. It's all dark wood, polished to a high sheen. There isn't a single piece of paper in sight. Ali nudges my right hand upward. From behind the desk Captain Hal Washington breaches, all six-foot-three and 350 pounds of him. I slow my approach, give him time to rise all the way up out of his chair. We do the Big Clasp. He wraps my right hand in his big mitt and squeezes. He places his left hand on top of both our hands. He's going for a kind of benediction effect. Then two manly pumps and it's done. His hands fall away. He motions me into a chair that Ali is already guiding into place beneath my knees.

"Ridlin, Ridlin, Kenny Ridlin, it's *good* to *see* you! How long has it *been*? Ten years? Twelve?"

I suddenly remember: He's always been one of those people who speaks in italics.

"You're looking good, Captain, if I might say—."

"It's *so* thoughtful of you to *lie* to me, son!" he booms. "I look like *shit!*" His laugh shakes the walls. I remember that voice, filling every corner of any room he is in. I remember that laugh, the big bass rumble of it, from ten years back, or is it twelve. It was actually eleven. If I want, I can remember every year, every month, every day, every minute. I push the thoughts down, out of mind. He continues: "But *you,* how've *you* been *keeping* yourself?"

Ali jumps in, picking up his cue—"That's why I brought him by, Captain. It seems that Ken here has been doing some excellent work over in Robbery—he got us a break in that Moralita thing. Ken got the lead that cracked the case."

I know enough to shut up, smile demurely.

"Why yes, I remember the case *vividly,*" the captain yells. Does he think I lost all those years because I had a problem with my hearing? "I followed it closely at the time, and when I was told about your, uh, break, I said, 'Ken *Ridlin?* Of *course.* Ken Ridlin has *always* been a *good cop,*' I said, *didn't* I?" he says, turning to Ali. "I've said that more than once, *haven't* I?"

"Just those words exactly, Captain." Ali volleys. "That's why, when Ken asked to be transferred back to Homicide, I brought you the paperwork, and you were excited at the news, and wanted to examine the files personally and—"

"*But*—" he butts in. "Not *'and'* but *'but'* . . . *But,* and I want to be honest with you, Ken . . ." He turns the big puppy-dog eyes on me.

When people say "I just want to be honest with you," they are about to lie in your face. This is something you learn.

"I had some . . . *concerns,* Ken," he lies.

He's leaning back in the chair. His lip is turning down. His jowls are resting atop his big right paw. His eyes are cast to the side. He looks ponderous, like an actual thought might be forming inside his head. It's a good impression, but it's just not possible.

"After all the, ah, after what happened and all back then, it's . . . ah, ah . . . it's a little *surprising* that you'd want to go back into this particular line of work. . . . There are so many options available nowadays. . . ."

His voice trails off in invitation. I refuse to give him a re-action. I think about a quiet spot I know up in Lincoln Park, under the trees, in the shade, with a gentle breeze. My happy place, they called it in the sessions. I retreat into it. I wait him out.

It doesn't take long. He hates the silence. He can't stand it. Never could.

"But of course it's *your* call, not mine. You know the de-partment has *always* wanted to *do the right thing* by you, Ken."

His mouth is open, as if he's waiting to taste my useless words on his fat pink tongue. He speaks again.

"I just had to make sure all the '*right people*' said it was OK for you to get back into the *fray,* so to speak."

This is all delivered in an empty spasm. All gesture, all protocol, all clichés, all quoting the quoting. It's the way he's always talked.

Except when he talked very very slow, which was worse, much worse.

"Captain," I lie, blandly, "I appreciate your concern."

It's a struggle to keep the tone out of my voice. He's looking toward me but a little off at an angle.

He looks toward Ali; then he looks back at me. Then he puts on the big wide smile.

He says, "So we talked to all the '*right people*,' and all the 'right people' said you were good to go. They couldn't figure out *why* you'd want to make this choice, but they felt you were . . . uh . . ." he raises his fingers in the air again, quoting, " 'sufficiently . . . uh . . . well-adjusted such that it should not significantly affect your day-to-day operational performance.' "

A wide empty smile creases his face.

I stay with the noncommittal grin, with my teeth clenched behind it.

"That's what they said, Ken."

I nod. Once. There is so much I could say, so little I dare to. He'll talk again soon. He can't help himself. The silence will make him crazy. He thinks the world would disappear if he stopped filling it up with himself.

"So you have my *blessings*, Detective. I know that Ken Ridlin will always be a *good cop*, and an *honor* to the *force*." No little quotation marks in the air this time, but still plenty of emphasis. As I try to consider whether there are any clichés he's left out, he pushes himself up out of the seat again. I'm remembering that he's a lot quicker than he looks. I rise from my chair. He leans over, grabs my right hand again, puts his left on top. Two short pumps again. Then he drops his eyes, stands back.

Ali wheels me toward the door. We take two paces. It's over. I start to relax. My muscles unclench.

Then that big voice blasts out again from behind my

back, "So, *Kenny*, what've we got you working on, to start? Anything *interesting?*"

Ali jumps in. This is his job: to interpret, to remember, to fill the void. "Ken is working that shooting last night at the 1812 Club, that jazz joint up on Lincoln, sir, you remember—"

He stops, turns, looks at us. His head angles toward the floor.

"Of course," he mutters. "We touched upon it earlier this morning."

"—Ken here was on his way home when he caught the call, and was the first one on the scene. We figured, since the swearing-in is later today, and since Ken has some history with the force, maybe we shouldn't let the red tape get in the way right off the bat, and maybe he should take the case," he says.

The captain looks at Ali. He's not giving much away. He swivels his neck to look at me, cocks his head. "Is that what *you* want, Ken?" he asks. He still has that big smile in his mouth. But now there is an almost wistful sadness in his eyes.

"Sure, sir, if you say so," I say. "Whatever you need me for."

He keeps staring at me. There is a pause. Then he leans his head back, nods. He looks away. As I leave he is reaching for his phone and sitting down all at once. His eyes are gazing at the portrait wall.

Welcome back.

CHAPTER 8
Ken Ridlin

1100 South State Street
Friday, January 10

Ali opens the door and nudges me through. I am considering how I feel about what just happened. I am feeling vindication, I am feeling apprehension, I am feeling relief.

Ali is feeling a need to get on with it.

"So, what do you think we've got here with this 1812 thing, Ken? You have a chance to think about it yet?" He pivots, turns me out of the foot traffic, backs me up against a pillar.

"It doesn't really add up," I say. "The victim is just getting into town. Here for a convention, some legal thing. He checks into his hotel, leaves his bag sitting on the bed, heads on up Lincoln to the club. He sits at the bar for twenty minutes, nursing a Scotch-and-soda."

Ali waits, patiently. I look at my notes, like I'm checking, and continue.

"He asks the trumpet player if he can sit in, one or two songs. He drops a name or two. They say, 'Sure, why not?'

He sits down at the piano. Plays one song, starts on a second one. Then bang, through the window. One to the head. A thirty-two, looks like."

Ali is looking far away, his forehead twisted up. "I don't get it," he says. "This guy . . ."

"Tremblay, T-R-E-M-B-L-A-Y, Roger," I say, flipping a page in the pad. "Male African American, thirty-eight, wife, two kids . . ."

"In from . . ."

"L.A., on the plane—"

"This Tremblay, he doesn't know anyone? Not meeting anyone?" he asks.

"Some convention appointments, but no, not really—"

"He doesn't have a record?"

"Not here or with the feds. We checked. Pure as the driven snow. A citizen."

"I don't get it," he says. "It sounds just like a mob hit, and they hit, who, some nobody?"

I shrug.

He puzzles it out. I let him take his time.

"Maybe the guy had some L.A. history, pissed somebody off. Maybe they didn't want to do anything in their own backyard. You interface with L.A. Homicide yet?" he asks.

"Left a message," I say. "It's early there yet." He looks at his watch, nods. I go on.

"He'd have to piss off somebody important for them to track him fifteen hundred miles just to whack him. It's easy enough to do him in L.A., make it look random, some drive-by."

I consider whether I should say this to a black man who holds my future in his hands. He is not reacting, except for a little nod of his head.

"There's something else, something you don't want to hear," I say.

He looks up at me, arches his eyebrows, waits.

"One of the patrons, in the club, says she sees a bag lady

walking by, slowly. Outside the window, at or about the time—"

He turns his whole body toward me. I can smell the coffee on his breath. "A bag lady?"

"Yeah," I say. "Footprints lead south to the end of the block, then west for a hundred feet. Looks like a vehicle was there. We cordon it off to run tire prints, footprints, but the storm covers them up before the lab people—"

He cuts me off. "Were there any other witnesses? Did anyone else see anything?"

"No. Nothing. The storm . . . the music . . . the excitement . . ."

We have wandered close to the entrance. I'm looking to escape, and I can see the way out but I know I'm not going to get there, not yet. Ali's got his hand on my arm again, squeezing my elbow. He dances me over to one side, leads me away from the doors, backs me up against a window. He stands still. He turns his head away from me and stares off into the street beyond the glass. He is running down a list in his head.

"What about the rest of the people inside—the musicians, the customers, the staff. Any probable targets?"

"Not so's you'd know it. The band is clean: the closest individuals to the vic were the drummer, the bass player, and the piano player. The real piano player, the guy this Tremblay was sitting in for."

"Any hits in the system?" he asks. "Any of them have records?"

"No. The band comes up clean. Well, except the saxophone player. Caught with some blow, few years ago, a recreational amount. Nothing else. All the customers come up clean, too," I continue. "The staff is just the manager, a bartender, and a waitress. They're nobody we know. It feels like someone professional was on this, but got the wrong guy."

He shakes his head.

"And the right guy wasn't even there," I add.

He mulls it over. "If the shooter is the 'bag lady,' and he's who we think he *might* be, then it's a mob thing, right? It's Joe Zep's guy, right? He doesn't work for anyone else, that's what the profile says, right?"

"Yeah," I respond. "If it's him, he's Zep's."

"Maybe . . ." he says, "maybe he screwed up . . ."

"Be the first time," I say. "But it feels like there's a lot we're missing. If we could—"

"Maybe this is the first crack in his armor," he interjects. "Maybe he messed up, left something we can use." He's on a roll, convincing himself. He doesn't need anything from me. It might spoil the line of his conjecture.

"This could be big, Ken. You have to stay on it."

I nod.

"You know who to liaison with on this, right? Mindich?" he asks.

"Yeah, already heard," I say. "We know each other from . . . from before." Mindich was there. He was there with the rest of them. He did nothing, he said nothing. Like the rest of them.

"Right," he says, "But you also liaison with *me* on this, directly, you understand?" I nod. He amplifies it a little. "I'm *in* this loop, Ken. I have an immediate *need* to *know*."

One thing he's learning from Washington is the italics.

"Right," I say, "anything I get goes right to you." I pause. "And to Mindich."

With that he looks me in the eyes. He holds the gaze for a second or two, then nods. He lets go of my elbow, turns, and walks past the revolving doors, doing all he can to avoid breaking into a gallop.

I gaze at the piled-up snow and ice outside the window. I stare at the people leaning into the wind. I'm not sure it's any colder out there than it is in here.

I shiver and pull my coat around myself and head out the door.

CHAPTER 9
Vinnie Amatucci

Airport Marriott—Tuning Up
Saturday, January 11

After sleeping away almost all of Friday, I got up early on Saturday morning to do my shift with the cab. The weather had cleared; the blinding sun was glaring off the ice and the wind had gone quiet, but the temperature was still in the teens and everything was still frozen solid. The side streets were still impassable, just no way to get any traction, but the main streets and the highways were actually not that bad. The airports were still shut down. What I heard was that they had expected it to melt so they could scoop it up in the morning, but then the temperature dropped, it all turned to ice, and they were fucked.

No one was going to going anywhere today, unless they really needed to.

My own car was back at the cab lot, where I had left it on Thursday, and without any wheels I had a hell of a time getting there. I finally made it, on foot and by bus, and old #691 was sitting there, clean as could be, just as The Fat

Man had promised. My own car was right next to it, and someone had dug it out as well. They had done a hell of a job; it was the cleanest it had been in years. I unlocked the cab, cranked up the heat, and took off.

I stuck close to downtown, and there was plenty of business. Most people still hadn't dug their cars out, and those who were lucky enough to have garaged them were the last ones you'd see taking any chances on getting them dinged up. A classic case of demand exceeding supply, which is always good news for those who provide the supply. For a change, my side of the coin had come up heads.

So I hit the hotels, the stores, and the office buildings, and the doors opened and closed, the meter started and stopped, and the money flowed in. No long trips, no big commitments, no airport runs, of course, just solid simple rides, with no letup, no driving from fare to fare, just one citizen getting out and the next one standing there waiting to get in. I was in the flow, and the other vehicles were other dancers in the dance, sharing the same choreography. Out and in and go and stop; it was as simple as it can get.

At about 4:00 I had a nice fat roll in my kit. I dropped the cab in the lot, booked back to my place, showered, and changed into some decent rags. By 5:15 I was back in my car, headed out to the Airport Marriott, and making decent time from Hyde Park to the Ryan to the Kennedy. My plan had been to get there by 7:00, and I made it with fifteen minutes of slack.

We weren't supposed to start until 9:00, but the early arrival gave me time to get things set up. The Airport Marriott was about the most unlikely place you could think of for a Saturday-night jazz gig: a cavernous room where the sound disappeared like rain in the ocean; a location that was too far off the beaten path to attract anybody; a clientele that was just passing through. And of course the Marriott itself, that bastion of white male Mormon capitalism, was not the kind of chain that featured jazz.

What the Airport Marriott had was Clarence, and

Clarence was a capital-F Fan. The story I had heard, true or not, was that Clarence and Paul Powell had known each other at the U. of C., and Paul had turned him on to the music, and Clarence had turned him on to weed (Clarence could always be counted upon to have the best source of herb in the city—always moist, fresh, consistent, and, at least for us, free). Now, a few years later, Paul rarely smoked anymore—it was way too frivolous for his serious side— but Clarence was still jonesing on the music. Clarence also had some kind of pull with the hotel chain, unusual for a very short, very gay, very black dude, and was able to book us on a regular basis. (The other theory I had heard was that he had a thing for Paul. Sometimes, seeing the look of rapture on his face as he watched Paul play, I gave this hypothesis more credence. You never know: maybe he appreciated Paul's chiseled ass more than his solid chops. But hey, different strokes, you know. Doesn't bother me.)

Whatever the reason, we had been booked there every other Saturday night for almost a year. The pay was solid, the sound system was top-shelf—Harmon-Karden/JBL studio components—the crowds were midsized but respectful, as pleased to be hearing us as we were to be seeing them, and it was an easy gig, in at nine and out around midnight, three short sets.

They have a pool there that's both indoors and outdoors. You start inside, swim under a partition, and you're out among the stars, the cold air on your face, the warm water cradling everything else. Even on a night like this, with the temperature dropping toward zero, you could still see people swimming outside, if only to be able to tell their friends back home that they had done it. I've done the pool thing—Clarence again—and it's sweet.

The pool was covered by a large dome that covered the pool and most of the lounge area that backed up against it, separated by a tall glass wall. The bandstand Clarence had constructed was just in front of that. This was acoustic hell, a place where beautiful notes came to die.

The basic rule of thumb on setting up the acoustics of any room is "dead in the front, live everywhere else." You don't want too many flat hard surfaces right behind where the music is coming from; it muddies the sound and also puts you inside a dead envelope where you can't hear a thing. On the sides and in the back, in contrast, you want a little bounce, to give the sound some warmth. It's the thing they try to replicate with ambient speakers in home theater systems, a little something to take the hard clinical edge off, to make it more natural.

This room was exactly the opposite. The glass wall at our backs was a virtual echo machine, and the high sloping ceilings and curved walls on the sides of the dome dispersed the sound every which way. We had convinced Clarence to put up some acoustic paneling behind us to soften the bounce so we could at least hear ourselves playing the notes we were actually playing, but for the rest of the room, we needed the sound system. Luckily enough, it was a powerful system, but a complicated one, and it needed to be both. I was glad to have some time to deal with it, because this space presented a challenging array of compromises.

Before I started in on the system, I got out my star wrench and my tuning fork and tackled the piano. The combination of the humidity from the pool and the alternating hot and cold drafts of air from the heating system and from the outside part of the pool created a perfect environment for fucking up a piano. This was an excellent one, a Steinway baby grand, but it had no chance in a room like this, and wouldn't stay in tune for more than a day.

I hit a middle A and compared it to the fork—not one iota of resonance. The piano was almost half a tone flat. High A was flatter, but Low A was sharp, not just in tune, but overshooting it. This was what you'd expect this crazy microclimate to produce. It was good that I had the time: this was going to take a lot of it. I rapped the 440 Hertz tuning fork again, and started with the A's.

Tuning a piano is an awkward process, especially a baby grand like this Steinway. If you wanted to be civilized, you would play a note, walk all the way around to tune the string, walk back to play it again, and on and on. Fuck that shit. The way I do it is to basically sprawl myself on top of the piano so I can reach the keys with my left hand and the tuning pegs on the sounding board with my right without moving. It must look a little weird, like I'm trying to hump this big black beast, but hey, this ain't some beauty contest; I'm *working* here.

At the same time, you can't help but get some looks when you're doing it: it's an announcement that something is going to happen. No one tunes a piano in a club on a Saturday night unless someone is going to be playing it. I was concentrating on my ears, but I could feel the looks, and I could also hear a spasm of quiet ripple through the room.

I don't have perfect pitch—that's why I carry the tuning fork. But I do have perfect *relative* pitch: give me one note, tell me what it is, and I can pick out what any other note is, pretty much every time. I've known a few people who supposedly had perfect pitch, and I mean *absolute* perfect pitch, the whole auditory genius thing, and I'll say this: they were all absolutely miserable motherfuckers: nasty, cranky, and depressed. We live in a noisy world, and to hear it all too clearly would probably fuck anyone up. My ear is good enough for tuning, thanks, but no more than that. Some failures are blessings.

There's something almost Zen about tuning up. It's solitary, you get in this zone, you work quicker and easier as you go, and the rest of the world disappears into the background. There's a guy named Mihaly Csikszentmihalyi, another U. of C. dude, who wrote a book about the Flow. A big best seller, rare for a serious tome. I signed up for one of his classes twice and never got in, but copped the book from Paul. I sense the Flow sometimes when I'm driving, like turning right not knowing why I'm turning right, but knowing that right is just *right* . . . and the fare is *right there*. I sense it sometimes in that moment after the light turns green and we all surge forward, and suddenly there is a pattern established, a current, a tide, and your foot eases off the pedal a hair and you slide right into it.

It also happens, sometimes, and I'm afraid it's only sometimes, when the band is really playing our asses off, playing things we hadn't even thought of considering, and it's all fitting together like some magical mosaic where all the pieces are slammed into place simultaneously.

But the flow runs deep, real deep, when I'm tuning. People have come up and tried to interrupt me, asked me what time the show starts. I just wave them off. I can't recalibrate myself to whatever channel they are on. Probably seems very arrogant, very off-putting. I admit it, it's my guilty little pleasure, my free rush, and I refuse to share a second of it with anybody.

Although that's not what I'm thinking in the moment, that's not what I'm feeling. All I'm thinking is A, C#, A, C#. All I'm feeling is A, C#, A, C#. And the way I do it, laying out on top of the piano, accentuates the kinesthetic part of it. As the strings get closer to harmony, the wood of the piano itself starts to resonate and I can feel the sound flowing into me, running up my spine, making me vibrate as if I'm part of the instrument. I always feel that while I'm tuning the piano, it's tuning me. I always pass gas, I always get half-hard, I always stop grinding my teeth. When I'm done, I'm always in a very peaceful but focused state.

A couple of years ago I stumbled into tuning pianos for money. Somebody saw me doing it before a gig and gave me a number to call and that led to other numbers. I liked it so much I had to quit: I lost all desire to play the damn things; it sucked all the initiative out of me. On this night it took me close to forty-five minutes, and I didn't begrudge a second of it.

When I got through with the piano, I started in on the sound system. Got the Uher out of my bag, set it down near the piano, popped in a closed-loop tape, hit RECORD, played some chords for about a minute or so, soft and then loud, soft and then loud, set it on top of the piano, turned it to PLAY, and set the volume at three. From there, it looped around and around. I turned to a mixing board that looked as if it belonged at NASA Mission Control, and pressed POWER. I walked around to each of the speakers, clockwise, putting my left ear about eight inches away, listened, and took some notes on a card. After I finished the last speaker, I went around in the opposite direction and did it again with my right ear, just to be sure, augmenting my written notes. Then I went back to the mixing board and started tweaking the equalization on each speaker.

I've been in people's houses and I've been in people's cars, and let me tell you, when it comes to their sound systems, most people don't know what the fuck they're doing. So much money, so little knowledge. In houses, the bass is always set too high and it makes the overall sound all cloudy. In cars, the back speakers are set way too high. Why would you have the speakers in the backseat louder than the speakers right in front of you? To replicate the sound of standing with your *back* to the band? And generally, people tune all the speakers the same way, even if they have a sophisticated system that lets them EQ each one individually.

But aren't the speakers the same? Yeah, the speakers are the same but the speakers' *environments* are different. This one's against a flat wall and the sound is going to bounce—turn it down a notch and edge down the treble. That one's against a curtain and next to a stuffed chair and the sound is going to get sucked up—crank it up a little but don't overdo the bass.

And that's the final idiocy I see out there. The bass. People spend hours trying to find the perfect location for that kick-ass four-hundred-dollar subwoofer. They move furniture, they cut niches in the wall, they hide it inside of tables, they even hang it from the ceiling. They're serious about it, spouting all kinds of theories, without having a fucking clue.

But here's the truth: it doesn't matter where you put it. Put it on the floor, hang it from the ceiling; place it up front, hide it in the back; orient it portrait or landscape or diagonally, like some Dalí painting. Your ear is going to localize the sound as coming from the floor. Period.

The subwoofers in the Marriott were up front and off to each side, because I don't like them sitting on the plywood bandstand. Plywood is a shitty resonating medium, because it's different kinds of woods glued together, so it doesn't have one dynamic profile but dozens. So we moved the speakers onto the hardwood floor, which is maple, a great resonating medium. It'd be perfect for a rock band or an action movie with surround sound—turn them up and you can feel that bass all the way up your spine. Us, we play jazz. The jazz drummer Jo Jones always said that if you can hear the rhythm section of a jazz band it means they're fucking up. You're just supposed to *feel* them, unless one of them is soloing. And I believe that. The trumpet and sax are up front, physically, and their sound is supposed to be up front, aurally. That's the nature of the music.

It took another half-hour to get the system right. I'd do a little more tweaking when everyone got here. After all, I had equalized it all to the piano, and this wasn't a solo piano concert. So when they got here I'd have them take a minute to get warm and tune up to the piano, and I'd fiddle with the dials again one more time, just a hair or two. But the way the system was at that moment, anybody could play into it and it would work.

By this time it was eight thirty-five. I took a water-based red Magic Marker and marked the levels on the dials, in case someone, particularly Jeff, fucked with them, then headed out to the bathroom to take a piss. No weed tonight, not until after. I wanted us to play well so I could wash that last scary gig out of my head. I looked around at all the glass in the walls and the ceiling. I didn't want to get all pot-paranoid and start hearing that glass breaking when it wasn't.

So it was Straight City for me, or as close to it as I come, at least for the next three hours. Please, I thought, no murders, no blood. Just let it be music.

CHAPTER 10
The Cleaner

Airport Marriott—Tuning Up
Saturday, January 11

8:00 P.M.: Getup tonight is Joe Businessman. Blue worsted suit. Dark blue socks. Cordovan shoes. Black galoshes over them. Blue button-down shirt. Maroon tie, cordovan belt to go with the cordovan shoes no one can see under the galoshes. Black-rimmed glasses, thick lenses, with a clear prescription. Toupee. Mousy brown. Mustache and Vandyke to match. Eyebrows dyed to blend in. Black gloves, black coat, black scarf. One word—inconspicuous.

Review the objectives:

> *Do not get caught*
> *Do not get noticed*
> *Leave nothing behind*
> *Reconnoiter*
> *Figure what went wrong*

Here to watch. Time to see for myself.

The boys? Tell them what happens? They say nothing. "Shit happens." Do they want to try again? Do they want to clear this up? No. They say, Back off. They will get in touch.

Me? Not happy. All this time, this never happens. Always get the job done. This job, when it comes in, it looks simple. Maybe it still is. See for myself.

Check the pain status. Three on a one-to-ten scale. Same place. Dull ache. The back is livable. Two of the striped pills, all ready. Two more handy if it gets any worse.

Park the car myself. Lock up. Keys in the right front pocket. Walk to the big glass door. Wait for the doorman to open it. Put the shoulders up. Put the head down. Pass on the coat check. Head for the lounge. Find a seat in the back, near the corner.

Hang the coat on the back of the chair. Leave the scarf on, the gloves on. Waitress wanders over, her own sweet time. Tall dirty blonde. Uniform that is maybe a size eight when she is at least an eleven. Do they have a size eleven? No idea. She looks past me.

I stare off at the ceiling, like what I want to drink is written there. "Ginger ale, please."

Do not give them too much of anything. Do not give them too little of anything. Be normal. Be average. Give nobody anything to hold on to.

She wanders off. Time to check out the room.

8:05 P.M.: Some sound in the air. Like a single note played over and over. Now the piano comes into my line of sight. It looks like a body is sprawled on it.

Then the body moves. One hand reaching into the guts of the piano. One reaching around for the keys. Guy is tuning it.

The drink comes. I lay a Jackson on the table, gloves still on. She swoops it up, fumbles for change. Drops it on the table. Gives me the big phony smile. Give her one right back. Leave the money on the table. One more soda, later, maybe. Whatever money is left is hers. Normal tip.

Pretzels and nuts and crackers on the table. Glass bowl. Do not touch.

Cannot see the face of the guy tuning the piano. Just hear the sound. Hypnotic. Easy to get lost in.

Know something about this. Studied music, when I was a kid. The clarinet. Couple a years is all. Remember a little bit about it.

8:10 P.M.: Early yet. Band starts at nine. Scan the room. Thirty-five people. A handful of couples. A scattering of middle-aged men, having a few pops. One table of noisy twenty-somethings. Talking too loud. This is not their kind of music—they will be gone as soon as it starts. Two bartenders behind the long bar, one male, chunky, five-ten, thirty-five-ish, one female, stringy hair, forty-five-ish, working steady. Three waitresses, including size-eleven-in-a-size-eight. One guy, the corner of the bar, clear drink with a wedge of lime, also scanning the room—the bouncer. Suit a little too tight around the shoulders. Hair a little too short. Neck a seventeen-and-a-half. Gray slacks, blue blazer, black mock turtleneck, gold chain. Does not appear to be armed. Makes two of us.

Tuning guy also dressed up—suit, shirt, tie. Hair a touch too long, beard.

Remove the gloves, tuck them into the coat along with the scarf. One sip of the ginger ale. Cold, nice, brings on memories.

8:15 P.M.: Tuning guy almost done. Plays a few chords, tweaks one or two strings. Plays some . . . what is the word? Arpeggios. Guy does a thorough piece of work—this I can appreciate. Not something I could do—had an ear for rhythm but not for pitch. One reason I stopped.

Turns around behind him, turns back to the piano, plays a few chords. Nothing to tap your foot to. Gets up, starts to walk around.

Thin, wiry guy, late twenties, early thirties, six feet or so.

The guy the papers said was the real piano player? Who was taking a break when I showed up? Could be him, doing double duty. Must not be very good. Doubt if Ellington tuned his own piano.

8:30 P.M.: Still waiting, watching. Amatucci, if that is who it is, still playing with the speakers. Same chords, over and over. Dedicated to his work. You can tell it is sounding better. The loud twenty-somethings are making wisecracks— "Hey. Dig the chops on this guy," "A freaking Elton John," "Did he go to Juilliard for this?"

8:45 P.M.: Waitress circles behind me. Reach for the glass. Take another sip. Place it on the table in the same wet circle it has already made on the coaster. She sees this. She veers off.

Time to count the house again.

Ninety-one patrons, staff of six. Make that seven. Guy in a tux. Black guy. Light-skinned. Slacks pressed like knife edges. Right shoes for it, what do they call them? Patent leather. A bow tie, a cummerbund, the whole rig. Looks at his watch twice a minute. Checks the room. He is counting the house, too. Checks in with a few tables, smiling, hey-how-ya-doing, can-I-get-ya-something? Shakes the hands, pats the shoulders, air-kisses the ladies. Maybe the lounge manager? Could be.

8:55 P.M.: Tuner is done, heads out of the room. Reaching in his right front pocket. Pack of smokes. Guys starting to come in with suitcases, instrument cases, whatever. Sit up in the chair, try to get comfortable. One good belch. Thank you.

One last look around the room.

Showtime.

CHAPTER 11
Vinnie Amatucci

Airport Marriott—The Gig—First Set
Saturday, January 11

Paul shows up about twenty minutes early and hands out copies of the set list to everyone, on three-by-five cards. I put mine down on the piano, like I'm in no hurry to see what we're playing, and say hello. He hangs up his coat, unpacks his trumpet, a gleaming brass King, a classic. He reaches into his case for some valve oil; he's like these people who put salt on everything before they taste it, whether it needs it or not. It's not the valves that need oiling, just his routine that needs to be fed. I look away and scan the list.

It's typical Paul. He tends to program the sets chronologically, from old to new. It's not in exact order that way, but it has that feel. The first set is almost all Dixieland, traditional stuff, a nod to the old days when that's all we could manage. I look up, and he's got the trumpet upside down, dripping oil into the three valves, two drops each, and pumping the valves with the fingers of his other hand, getting things loosened up, as if it needed it. If I know him, and I probably know him better than just about anybody, he's already spent half an hour cleaning and oiling the horn this afternoon. I'll tell you: If it weren't for the valve oil, you could drink champagne out of Paul's trumpet and it'd be so clean you could tell the vineyard and the vintage.

By the time I come out of this reverie, he's finished reoiling the valves, and he runs them, checking, and tightens number two, just a hair. He turns toward the felt backdrop, slides in his quietest mute, an old aluminum Harmon, and starts to warm up, long tones, in an ascending scale, then runs, arpeggios, then trills and tonguing drills, classical shit right out of the Arbans book, no melody, no tempo. He's not warming up his head, just his embouchure and his fingers. He knows enough not to tune up until he's warmed up, because until he is, the sound is a little pinched, and maybe a quarter-tone sharp. When he's ready he turns around, his head only, and looks at me. "Hey, Vinnie. What have you got?" This is a little of our code, my signal to play a B-flat. I strike one, he plays his C. I keep tapping it, slowly, and he adjusts the tuning slide out a hair, plays another C, moves it back in half a hair. I give him some octaves, he runs up and down the scale, looks at the tuning slide but doesn't touch it.

"Nice," he says. "I perceive that you've been working."

He knows. Ninety-nine percent of the crowd will have no fucking idea, but he knows.

Sidney wanders in, always looking as if he sees where we are at the last minute, carrying that big string bass as if it were a football, cradled under one arm, and his huge tuba under the other. He has his dazed smile on, which means he's a little nervous, which is good. When he's frowning or just staring steadily, it means he's somewhere else, engaged in some philosophical problem, some mental experiment, miles away. Not tonight.

Akiko had gotten there at 8:30, and had set up and tested the skins, tightening and tuning the heads. Then she disappeared somewhere until just before nine.

At about a minute before we're supposed to start, Jeff practically runs into the room, holding his sax case like a weapon, clearing the way before him. His eyes are wild, he's checking his watch. The guy is always late. He climbs up on the stand, no eye contact, but nods at Paul like he's ready. But he still has his coat on, still has his sax in its case. Paul looks him over, and then Jeff looks himself over, says "Shit," strips the coat off, flings it over by the wall, drops to one knee, takes out the sax, slides on the mouthpiece, clips on the neck strap, ducks his head into it. He looks back at Paul, like he's ready.

Paul hates this. Here's Jeff, late again, he hasn't tuned up, he hasn't warmed up, his breathing is still ragged from running in from the cold. He always tunes up on the fly, halfway into the first song, and Paul knows this is just wrong, it's an affront to us, to whoever's listening, to the music itself. Jeff hasn't even looked at the set list. That's wrong, too.

Paul is being cool with it tonight. He's standing with his horn held down around his belt, running the valves, and he gives a look at Jeff's set list. Jeff gives him a stare, like "Just start, man," but Paul stares straight ahead, waiting for him. Jeff finally picks up the card, looks it over, says "Hey, we got some old-timey shit here tonight," all sarcastic. He still thinks he's ready.

I jump in and play a B-flat. Jeff tenses his shoulders, looks like he's ready to turn around and glare at me. He slowly brings the mouthpiece up to his lips, slowly wraps his lips around it, closes his eyes, plays one long baleful G. Lots of vibrato, which is just fucking stupid if you're trying to tune up. He's sharp, but he makes no move to adjust it. I glance at Paul, who's still just staring off into space. I play another B-flat. Jeff half-turns toward me, then reaches up, pulls the mouthpiece out a hair, plays another G, straight this time. Pretty close. He doesn't remove the mouthpiece from his mouth, just mutters around it, "Let's play some fucking music, all right?"

Paul turns his head, taps his foot, counts out, "1 . . . 2 . . . 3," the "4" unspoken so he can bring his horn into position, and we start.

The first tune is the old spiritual "Just a Closer Walk With Thee." We start it like a funeral dirge, all modal chords, Akiko drumrolling on the edge of the high hat, Sidney humming way down low on the tuba. Then we start into it, with the tempo up to a walk, playing it straight at first. We play two choruses—there is no verse—then Paul nods at Jeff, who solos.

With Jeff, there's no transition. Jeff plays what he plays, and doesn't change much from tune to tune to fit the music. He thinks he's doing Charlie Parker/John Coltrane, all long runs and thousands of notes and the occasional soulful honk, but after a chorus or two you've heard what he's got and there isn't any more to learn, but he just goes on and on. After four choruses, Paul comes in on the change and vamps it over to me.

I start back toward the older feel of the tune, a little ragtimey, jumping my left hand with the bass. I'm OK with my right hand, but I really take pride in my left. I find a repetitive figure and work it rhythmically, then carry it over from the first chorus to the second. Now I'm swinging it in a more Earl Fatha Hines mode, doubled octaves on the right hand with the left laying down the rhythm. I take this through the second chorus and into the third, then the chords take over and get more dense. I start to invert the chords, vary the rhythm off the beat, then, as Paul starts to vamp, signaling a handoff over to him, and I surprise myself and kick it up a key, a run of triplet chords pulling it upward. Sidney is right there and rides on it, and Akiko pushes the tempo a little.

We didn't plan it, but Paul hears it coming. He's doing with a single note at a time almost what I did with the chords, finding the notes on the inside. Then he ramps it up into the upper register with a long run that doubles back. He's playing ahead of the beat, pushing it.

Coming into his last chorus he starts to soar, that big tone cutting through. He makes a circle with the horn and we all see it and chime in, except Jeff, who races to catch up. Now it's all contrapuntal, Paul riding on top with a solid punch, Jeff running underneath, The Professor striding along, Akiko kicking the pedal on her big bass drum.

Coming down the stretch Paul does a slowing staccato run that slows the tempo back to a dirge and pushes the pitch up to the actual melody. We finish the last eight bars almost in unison on the melody, then add a little coda with the original dirge again, Paul trilling modally, Jeff actually going along with it, then we wrap up and close it out.

Except that Jeff doesn't finish when we do, but has to add some little bop run, like an ironic comment. He does this all the fucking time. The crowd almost likes it this first time—by the middle of the set they'll be tired of it, and it'll turn from an ironic "I know this can get a little corny" to a sarcastic "Man, does this shit suck."

In the meantime, except for that, it's tight, and the crowd likes it, and responds. Jeff nods like they're clapping for him; the rest of us bow quietly, smile slightly.

As the applause dies down, we're right into "West End Blues," with Paul replicating the classic Louis Armstrong run at the start from the record with Kid Ory and Baby Dodds. Then "East St. Louis Toodleoo" and "Beale Street Blues" and "The Sheik of Araby." Finally it's "Muskrat Ramble," an old raver, complicated, at least eight sections to it, all arranged. When this works, it's a great way to close a set of the old stuff. All that complexity keeps circling back, but never coming back to the same place.

But this time it doesn't work. This is really not Jeff's thing, but tonight he's playing it like he hates it. He usually doesn't take a solo on this, but this time he cuts Paul off and dives in ahead of him, and doesn't take one chorus or two, which is all you want in this song, but drives on past three and four. He thinks he's Paul Gonsalves going twenty-three inspired choruses on some Ellington tune, but it's turning into some kind of free-jazz polyphonic poly-bullshit thing, no tempo, no melody, just honking and overblowing, rocking back and forth, his eyes closed. Akiko takes charge and signals the last chorus. Jeff barely hears her, but we overpower him and he fades to nothing as we finish. As the crowd claps, a little uncertainly, he's already jumping off the stand and heading out of the room. Fucking rude.

And that's the way the first set ends, not with a bang but a rebellion.

CHAPTER 12
The Cleaner

Airport Marriott—The Gig—First Set
Saturday, January 11

The band is not bad. The bass player, he is someone I could listen to. He has got these fingers? Knows right where he wants them to go? The drummer, she is a dynamo, but holding herself back. This I can appreciate. This is the kind of music my old man used to listen to. Brings back the memories. The trumpet player is the leader, they all look to him. Except the sax. The piano player, the real piano player, Amatucci, is not great, but he is pretty good.

Room is starting to fill up. One hundred and twenty-two. No familiar faces. The waitress is leaving me alone. I am applauding. Tapping my foot. Nodding my head. Nothing conspicuous. No more, no less than anyone. A big silly smile wants to break out. I am not letting it.

The sax player? A cokehead. No question. Seen them all, and he is the poster boy for it. Lost inside himself but wants to squeeze the rest of us in there with him.

Last song? Out of control. No music, just noise. Trumpet

is pissed, you can see it if you look. The sax runs off, soon as they are done. Got to get himself back to even. He is racing to the can for a couple a toots. To convince himself he is playing like a genius.

The crowd sees it. Sees an arrogant prick. He gets some looks.

Maybe enjoying myself too much, here. Lost in this old music. Nothing figured out.

Just waiting.

And then *she* walks in.

All by her lonesome. People are talking it up and then it gets quiet. Heads turn. Eyebrows raise again, like for the sax player. This time? Means something different.

What they see: a woman, hair reddish brown, wavy. A red slinky dress. Hugging every curve, and there are plenty of them. Not heavy, not thin. A perfect body. Long sleek legs up to here. A meaningful ass, something to grab on to. Full breasts, high up. And the face. High cheekbones, pointy eyebrows, dark eyes. A narrow chin, but not too pointed. A Roman nose. And the full lips, the same color as the dress. The crowd, they are imaging those lips on them. All the men, some of the women.

I do not see all this. Seen it before, plenty of times. I look at the crowd looking at her. I could stare, I wanted. Drool, I felt like it. Jump on the table, I had a mind to. No one would notice. She knows how they see her. And she is not even playing it up, not even a little. Seen her when she was. Could stop the whole Dan Ryan Expressway from a mile away. Not now. Not hardly trying.

Laura Della Chiesa. The Princess. The one and only offspring of Giuseppe Della Chiesa, the Boss of all Bosses of Chicago. My guy's little baby girl.

Like I said. Seen it before. Been some time. Christ, I remember bouncing her on my knee, up at the house. Remember her falling asleep in the crook of my arm. Could always get her to stop crying when no one else could. She probably does not remember that, not now. Seen her since

but she has not seen me. Makes it a point not to be involved. Never seen with our crowd.

I look, see if she has a handler with her, public place like
this. I reach down to tie my shoe, glance around from under the table. Take a good look. Nobody. Possibilities? He is
out parking the car. He is out waiting in the car.

Take one sip of ginger ale. Tapping my foot to the Muzak,
do not even know what it is.

A sudden pain, sharp, under the ribs. Wait. Two deep
breaths. Fish out two red-stripe pills, right coat pocket. Toss
them down. Another sip. Swallow. Count out two minutes.

She picks the seat at the corner of the bar. Next to the
bouncer. Conspicuous. But safe. The bouncer, he is turned
to stone. Cannot get his mouth to close. Cannot get his eyes
to blink. Laura is reaching into her purse. Dropping a bill
on the bar. OK. No handler.

She takes a pack of cigarettes from her purse. Camel
non-filters. That's Laura. Slides one out, taps it against her
watch. The bouncer and the bartender and the manager
are so quick with the flames they make a pileup. Almost set
her on fire. She puts it to her lips and leans toward the manager. Laura has a way of knowing. Knowing who is trouble.
Who is safe. The manager has got the tux. The patent
leather shoes. Gay, whatever. She knows it. He is leaning
over, trying too hard, laughing too loud.

It takes the bouncer and the bartender a couple of seconds to put out their lights. The bartender remembers it
when the match burns his fingers. He is red. Sweating. He
wipes the bar, massages his fingers with his towel. Asking
what he can get her, then jumping when she speaks. Almost knocking over the other bartender, the skinny one,
who comes in for a closer look. He snaps at her. She snaps
at him. Little domestic drama there. Like they have a past.

He has got the silver shaker. He has got the long spoon.
Martini. Stirred, not shaken. He is stirring it a little too
much, trying to impress. A real martini drinker would tell
him to stop it, he is bruising the gin, the vodka, whatever.

He reaches for a glass in the upside-down racks over his head, flips it right side up, almost drops it. She is chatting with the manager. He pours. Spears three olives with a pick. Slides them in. Bows. She turns her head. Picks it up, turns back to the manager, like she doesn't see any of it.

She *does* see it. Catches it all, but is not going to give him the satisfaction. Crosses one long leg over the other. It turns her away from the bartender, the bouncer. Toward the manager, who is talking like a man on death row. Telling his story, his one chance to get the words out. Her red shoe dangles off her right toe—how did it survive the ice and snow and slush?

Always was a heartbreaker. Stone cold just like her old man.

The bartender starts making himself busy. Wiping down the bar. Polishing the glasses. The bouncer still cannot move. Like if she looked at him his dick would fall off.

I pull my own eyes away, make like I am not looking. That would be conspicuous, not looking. I roll the ginger ale around the glass.

What is she doing here? Coldest night of the year. All the way out at the airport. On her own. Meeting someone? No one with her yet. Waiting for someone? Has not looked at her watch once, five-thousand-dollar black Movado like it's there for show. Just slumming? More likely she would be slumming at the Checkerboard Lounge on the South Side, with the brothers. Really rubbing her father's nose in it. But up here in the suburbs, with mostly white folks?

There is something missing.

Shit. Shit. Shit.

This changes everything.

CHAPTER 13
Vinnie Amatucci

Airport Marriott—The Gig—Second Set
Saturday, January 11

I step outside and get some cold air in my lungs, plus some tobacco. The thing with Jeff has me worried. I've looked at the second-set playlist, and there's a lot of trumpet-and-sax-together pieces in there, a lot of tight arrangements. It's a little more modern, which should be to Jeff's liking, but it has some harmony things, which he will hate. I don't know what's with the guy. He can play a little, but he always acts like it's an imposition. Even when Paul goes out of his way to program stuff that he likes, Jeff acts like, "Go ahead, *make* me fucking enjoy it." The guy's a head case, and tonight it's like it's the full moon and Mercury has gone retrograde.

I check my watch and head back inside. Paul is warming up his mouthpiece, Sidney is bowing his bass, Akiko is doing little paradiddles on the snare drum with her fingers. She seems up tonight, but contained as always—you wouldn't know it if you didn't know what to look for.

But no Jeff. Shit. Here we go again.

Paul has a thing about starting on time, not quite obsessive-compulsive, but it's there nonetheless. All these four years, I can't remember him ever being late for anything. The man has some kind of philosophical position about it, no doubt. It's all thought out with Paul, except the music itself. When he puts the horn to his lips all that recedes into the background. He never repeats a solo, hardly ever even repeats a phrase, which is rare, to tell you the truth. And it's not thought out at all; it just flows out of the moment.

He signals me to turn on the voice mike on the piano. He strides over, taps it twice, not to check to see if it's live, but to let the crowd know he's going to say something. They quiet down.

"Welcome to the Airport Marriott. We're 'New Bottles,' as in 'Old Wine, New Bottles,' and we're pleased to be here on this wintry night. We're also pleased that you could be here to share it with us."

A slight pause.

"I must have been having so much fun the first set that I forgot to introduce the members of the band. So, if you will allow me . . . On piano, Mr. Vince Amatucci . . ."

Akiko gives a drumroll and a cymbal crash. Bah-dah-BUM. Polite applause surges out of the crowd. I do a little bow from the piano bench.

"On the string bass, Dr. Sidney Worrell . . ."

Another flourish from the drums. Sidney acts like they're applauding for somebody else, looking around, his eyebrows crinkling, a hint of surprise on his face.

"On drums, Miss Akiko Jones . . ."

It would be impolite for her to give herself a little flourish, so I do the honors with some ascending chords. She bounces up and down in her seat, shakes her head, one hand turning one of the screws on the snare.

"On tenor saxophone," Paul looks to his left, sees no one there. This gets a chuckle from the crowd, but something more as well, something not as nice. "On tenor saxophone, has anyone seen Mr. Jeff Fahey?"

Sidney does a comic "OOH-wahh" on the tuba, and the crowd breaks up.

Paul is almost embarrassed to be caught making fun of one of his own and mutters, "I'm sure he has been unavoidably detained, and will be with us momentarily." Abruptly, he hands the microphone to me. He can't stand to announce himself. Quickly, I add, "And on trumpet, Paul Powell," stringing it out, like some ring announcer at a boxing match, undermining the effect his understatement was designed to evoke. Paul bows deeply, then reaches back for the mike.

"We'd like to showcase the musical talents of one of the band's original members. This is a composition for the piano by one of the greatest trumpet players—actually, cornet players—in jazz history, a man who played brilliantly before meeting an untimely end at the age of twenty-eight. Still revered by people who know the music, the man I'm speaking of is the late Leon Bix Beiderbecke, of Davenport, Iowa. The composition is called 'In a Mist,' rendered by our own Vince Amatucci. Vince?"

I don't know if I've ever heard Paul say so much in one breath. As for the tune, obscure but wonderful doesn't even begin to say it. I can't even remember the last time I played it. I remember the first time, though, about a month after the band started, when Paul brought me the sheet music and said, "Please indulge me, if you would. I just have to hear this in the air. I came across the sheet music the other day—it's quite rare—and have been hearing it from the page, and playing it one line at a time on the horn, but it's not enough. Could you . . . ?" It was a special moment, a rare glimpse of vulnerability, one of our first moments of bonding, and I feel a slight tightening in my throat as the memory comes back to me now.

The other band members are shuffling off the stage and I'm thinking all this and trying to remember what fucking

key it's in—it's in good old C, of course—and I look up and
see the guy from the cab the other night, the guy who
couldn't make up his mind, standing framed in the light of
the entranceway, that same weird suitcase in his hand,
leaning against the doorjamb, and I think, there's still no
Jeff, where the fuck is Jeff, and what is that guy doing still
here?

And all this takes maybe two milliseconds to rattle
through my addled brain, until I say to myself, "Not too fast,
Vince, do it justice," and start.

It's a strange enough piece, as if Debussy had smoked
opium and played whatever came out and then transposed
it upside down. I've heard the old 78 of Bix himself playing
it—playing it a little too rushed for my taste—but of course
he was really a cornet player, not a piano player, and self-
taught on both instruments at that. And I've read the stories
of how, when it came time to write it down for the publisher, he couldn't play it the way he had played it on the
record; he just had to improvise on his own improvisation,
until they just said "Fuck it," and had someone just tran-
scribe the record. Play it too slow and it's a dirge. Play it too
fast and you lose all the subtlety. Dense, packed chords, little runs, a rhythm that skips around. Classical and jazz, jazz
and classical melded into something else. And I try to shut
these thoughts out of my head, and let the lyricism of it
flow through me, and start to get there about the time I get
to the bridge, which is almost a funky bebop kind of thing,
fifty years too early. Then it just sings out, real stride piano,
the left hand dancing up and down the octaves, the right
hand belting out on top, before it cycles back to the chorus, this shy little rhythmic thing, subtly building, the
chords all sly and thick. Until the very end, when it slows,
and somehow darkens and brightens all at once, reaching
up into the stratosphere, almost as if he couldn't bear to
end it.

And I'm doing it justice, I think, and the crowd starts to
applaud, until someone who just can't wait for it to unfold

its curious logic starts clapping very loudly, yelling "Bravo, Bravo," which is really inappropriate for this particular piece of music and my own stumbling homage to it, and at the last second I realize it's Jeff, striding up to the stand.

CHAPTER 14
The Cleaner

Airport Marriott—The Gig—Second Set
Saturday, January 11

10:02 P.M.: Something is fouled up. You can tell. Trumpet is dying to start, you can see it. But no sax. Trumpet introduces the band. Buying time. Takes a little dig at the sax guy. Jeff Fahey, file this away. F-A-H-E-Y, F-A-H-Y, whatever.

Then the piano plays a solo. Strangest thing I have heard in a long, long time. Do not listen to much music, these days. Some you cannot help but hear. But not like this.

Piano guy does OK with it. Hey. What do I know?

Then at the end, Saxophone comes storming in. Making an ass of himself. Fully lit now. No pain. Showing up Piano. The crowd sees it. Trumpet and the others jump back onto the bandstand, get ready to start. Saxophone is standing in front of it. He and Trumpet are going at it. Trumpet all quiet, talking so you do not see his lips move, just the goatee bobbing up and down. This guy has some control. Can appreciate this. Sax is screaming, but he is facing away from the crowd. The words do not come through. Do not need to. Muscles in his neck as tight as cables.

Saxophone jumps onto the stage. Glares at them all, one at a time. Clips his sax on that string they wear around their neck. Runs his fingers over the keys.

An awkward pause. Saxophone turns to Piano, like he is telling him start already. Piano just stares back, then points at something.

Saxophone looks down. He is holding the sax but it has got no mouthpiece on it. Just this open neck. And, swear to God, he leans over and looks down into the hole. Like the top part maybe fell in there. Pats his pockets, getting frantic. Looks high and low. No mouthpiece anywhere.

Jumps down from the stand, unclips the sax. Turns back to the bandstand. Slings it over his head. Smashes it down on the edge of the bandstand. One time. Two times. Three times. Little pieces flying off. His face is purple. Drops the sax. What is left of it. Wrestles with the string around his neck, tries to tear it off. Ducks his head through it. Flings it at the bandstand. Aiming away from them. Knows if he touched Trumpet he would be toast. Something about Trumpet. One of those guys, if it came to it, he would not fight the guy, just kill him.

10:10 P.M.: Saxophone gets halfway to the door. I sneak a peek at Laura. Her head is down, but her eyes are up, watching. Just her cup of blood. Sax turns around. Heads back toward the bandstand there. Veers right, goes around the back. Tossing coats up in the air. Finally finds his. Heads around the front of the stand, sees his sax lying there. A twisted lump of metal. There is a pause there. He turns his back on it.

Turns toward the door. He is taking up the whole spotlight now, squinting in the glare. Starts to force his arm into one of the sleeves. Gets the wrong sleeve, the wrong arm. Whips it off. Knocks a round of drinks off a table up front. Big crash. Sticky liquor everywhere. Starts to look for the sleeve. Every eye is on him. Thinks better of trying to get it on. Slings it over his shoulder. His keys go flying, coming out of a pocket. There is a laugh from the crowd. Then it stops, quick. Like watching someone slip and fall on the ice. Can't help yourself.

He looks around. Daring the keys to be found. Sees something a couple of yards over to his left, on the floor. Now he is on his hands and knees. Finds the keys. Stands up. One schmuck applauds. The sound cracks the silence. Saxophone looks for the clapper but the spotlight hits him and he cannot see and he's got tears running down his face. He heads for the door.

There is a guy there. Leaning on the door frame. Some kind of suitcase in his hand. Tries to dodge Saxophone. They feint back and forth. Guy in the door stands aside and ushers him through. Like a matador. Cannot see his face. Average size, average build.

Saxophone almost rams into him, anyway. Gets past. Sprints out the door.

The room is silent, then a hum of whispers.

Trumpet leans in to the mike. There is a pause. The crowd settles. "That was Mr. Jeff Fahey, formerly on tenor saxophone . . ." There is a sadness in his voice, no anger at all. Cannot bring himself to hurt the guy. Even when he has been a total asshole.

Picks up a little card from on top of the piano. Turns to the band, tears it slowly in half. Tears the halfs in half. Lets the pieces flutter to the floor. Piano shrugs. What are you gonna do?

Trumpet picks up the mike. "Here's an old Duke Ellington standard, 'Mood Indigo.'" It is all wrong and it is just right. Makes the crowd take a big deep breath. Slows the old heart rate.

Yeah, life sucks. What are you gonna do? Play on.

I sneak another look at the guy in the doorway. Leaning on the frame again. Do I know this guy?

CHAPTER 15
Vinnie Amatucci

Airport Marriott—The Gig—Second Set, Third Set
Saturday, January 11

After Jeff implodes, and I hope it's the last time I ever have to see this shit, Paul calls for "Mood Indigo." The whole song is built on this trumpet and sax duet, the sax a minor third over the trumpet. I wonder how we're going to make this happen, but Paul just ignores the harmony part and plays the song as if the harmony didn't exist. It's just a naked melody and it sounds so different all alone. On the chorus, he plays the long tones of the melody, then adds little runs and obbligatos at the end, as if he's playing the melody and also playing another melody around the melody. After the first chorus, Paul hands me a few choruses, playing long tones underneath into a mute. I'm not sure what I'm doing, but it comes out lilting and longing and sweet.

Then I pass it off to Sidney for a rare bass solo, and he starts with the bow, long strokes like he's caressing your heartstrings. After one chorus with the bow he tucks it away and fingers the strings. He's getting deep, and he rides over the second chorus's end and pushes into a third. This is rare for Sidney, and even rarer still, he glides into a fourth, and all of a sudden the bow is in his hand again and he's stroking away, a throbbing sound in the low register, until at the end he brings it way down like a whisper, like a lover murmuring, "It's all right, take it easy, it's OK."

And even stranger still, Paul turns to Akiko. A drummer rarely takes a solo in this music, and never on a slow ballad or blues. Akiko has her brushes in her hands and doesn't hesitate. Paul makes a little signal and we go to stop-time, just the first beat of each measure, quiet and staccato, as Akiko deconstructs the rhythm a phrase at a time. I'm in heaven now—this is too much—and she's getting into it and the crowd is hushed and leaning in. And as I hear her wrap up her second and last chorus I feel a shadow move across my face and who's standing there, next to Paul, but the guy, the guy who was at Midway but didn't want to stay, the guy with the funny suitcase. And he's holding a cornet, an old-fashioned-looking one with that shepherd's-crook bend in it and he's standing there next to Paul.

Paul jumps in on top of Akiko's last few bars, bringing us back to the chorus, and here's that harmony thing, Paul on the melody and the guy with the cornet playing the harmony part on top. It's a little backward, tonally—the mellower cornet should be underneath the brighter trumpet—but nobody in the room knows this but me. Paul wags his fingers and they start trading fours. Paul improvises the first four bars, then the guy plays the next four, and back and forth they go. The guy has an uncanny ability to both blend with where Paul was taking the tune and also to kind of comment on it at the same time. He's got this beautiful tone that I can't quite place and then I flash on "In a Mist" again and it's like Bix Beiderbecke, who they say played like someone hitting a golden bell with a silver hammer. And that's the way this guy sounds, each note ringing out pure and rich, all honey and sunlight, and he's got Paul in this groove with him and it's like watching two old lovers make love—they know each other's moves and are responding before the other one even realizes it.

And it's building in waves, each wave a little bigger. We hit the bridge and the guy does an almost trombone kind of thing, two valves pressed halfway down and sliding up to the note as Paul lets the melody speak. Then into the last eight bars, and they're so together even their separate vibratos seem to shimmer at the same rate, and as it slows in the last two measures, they trade off, Paul holding a long note while the other guy dances around it, then the other guy holding one while Paul adds a little coda at the end, and we fade to pianissimo and it's over.

The crowd is half-stunned. They know they've heard something beautiful but gape for a full two seconds before they're willing to let go of it. And then they erupt, not just applause but this deep-throated roar of release, which pulls them out of their seats and up onto their feet. Clarence the manager has been drawn to the front of the stage as if by a magnet and his eyes are sparkling, his light-cocoa face flushed and shining. And he's not the only one; we've wrought some kind of cathartic release.

Paul grabs the mike, more animated than I've seen him in years. "I'd like to welcome someone I met last year and who just seems to have shown up here, out of nowhere— and, I might add, not a moment too soon—" which gets a big laugh. "Just a few minutes ago I was talking about Bix Beiderbecke, who composed the tune Vince started this set off with. This cat and I met last summer out in Davenport, Iowa, at the annual Bix Beiderbecke Memorial Jazz Festival. We jammed until dawn one night, and I haven't seen him since. Maybe if you are all very nice to him, he'll stick around. Would you please welcome, on cornet, Mr. Jack Landreau."

And the crowd gives him a nice hand. He and Paul shake, and we're all beaming, but he has no expression on his face. His eyes are cast down, shy almost, not smiling, not frowning—he could be waiting for a bus or doing a

crossword in his head. Paul whispers into his ear, and he
mutters something back. Paul turns to me and says " 'I Got
Rhythm,' in F, a little quick, give us an intro," and without a
pause I launch into four bars of lead-in and we're off. It
struts right out and the magic is still there, Paul and this guy
Jack playing like they've known each other for twenty
years. There's something bothering me about this song, but
Akiko and Sidney are wailing. Toward the end, Paul motions for Landreau to solo and he shakes his head emphat-
ically, twice, No, and holds up four fingers and they're
trading fours again, this time for four or five choruses, and
it's building with all the momentum of a freight train charg-
ing down a mountain, until the transition to the final
melody when he plays a curious lick and bumps us up a
key. Akiko pushes the tempo a little and it brightens, and
the guy, Jack, takes the lead line and bumps up the key
again, and then again, and we're spinning at the edge of
control until we run out of measures and abruptly stop, but
he plays on in a long eight-bar coda, bringing the key back
in steps to where we started and bringing the beat back to
a jumping stride and we all join in and wrap it as pretty as a
package at Christmas.

The crowd goes nuts.

It suddenly strikes me that the last time we played "I Got
Rhythm" was the night Roger Something got killed.

Was it really the last time we played? Only two nights
ago? Jesus.

The universe has somehow shifted. I have been trans-
ported to a different plane.

Paul turns and says "I Got the World on a String," and
we're off again, on a loose loping pace, and the magic is
still there. Paul seems less cool, less distant, like he's been
playing with a mute all these years and has finally let his
sound ring free. Then it's "Sing, Sing, Sing," the old Benny
Goodman raver, except this time it's nothing like that, a little slower with some bounce to it. Akiko has studied the
tapes and she has the Gene Krupa solo on the tom-toms

down, and it bounces right along. Then it's "St. James Infirmary," and about halfway through it strikes me that the guy hasn't soloed all this time, not once. He has stayed back, just filling in but leading from the back somehow, and I make eye contact with Paul and make a head wag to point to the guy. I'm finishing my own two choruses and Paul picks up the mike from the piano, says "Mr. Jack Landreau," puts down the mike and steps off the stage.

There's an awkward pause there, and the guy seems to take a step back. He looks up at the spotlight and seems to shrink. Akiko and Sidney and I vamp for a few measures, waiting.

Then he reaches down toward a table close to the stand. There's a black hat on it, a fedora, and he scoops it up and hangs it over the end of the horn and starts to blow softly, haltingly into the hat, a real old-school thing. He's going into a modal version of the key, all Middle-Eastern-sounding, weird and strange and soft. There's a melody there, but you have to search for it among the silences. This is something new for me, the way he uses the silence as well as the sound. Sidney and I pick up on it and work with it. Toward the end of the chorus Akiko even throws in a little vocal throat-warble, like the Arab women do when they're protesting The Great Satan—that would be us—and it's crazy but funny, and then he echoes the same noise on his horn—how does he *do* that?

The next chorus the hat comes off and his sound just opens up. He's playing this new take on the melody and then playing a counterpoint to it, like a duet with himself. I stop trying to figure it out and just go with it. On the turn, he builds to this beautiful note in the upper register and holds it. He's varying the loudness with his breath, which I can't believe hasn't run out until I see he's doing some kind of circular breathing thing, which I thought only reed players could do, for God's sake. This whole time he's standing stock-still, his head pointed down at a forty-five-degree angle. He's still holding the note, letting it shimmer, and the tension cracks as he arpeggios out of it and runs down the scale and back up again. Then hits it again, the same note, except it's now in a different harmonic context and it sounds different. Then some syncopated figures, quoting his modal approach from the first chorus, twisting it back on itself, then he quotes "In a Mist," a version of the chords at the start as they build up, like a humorous aside, and then down to the tonic and out.

The crowd is half-stunned, they can't applaud except for a few yahoos who don't know what they're hearing or why they're cheering; they just know it's expected. He holds the cornet close to his waist and waits. I jump in and take a short solo chorus while Paul steps back on the stage, and then they chase each other around the melody one more time until it's through.

I look at my watch and we're twelve minutes over with two fewer songs than we usually play and it feels as if we just got started—it's that aspect of the Flow when you feel, "Where did the time go, are we done already?"

Paul gives me a sign and I start in on "The Days of Wine and Roses," sort of our theme song—Old Wine, New Bottles, get it? But it's a song I love, full of sweetness and longing. Paul picks up the vocal mike and says, "We're 'New Bottles,' and we'd like to thank Clarence and all the folks at the Airport Marriott for having us. Once again, Vince Amatucci on the piano, Akiko Jones on the drums, Professor Sidney Worrell on the string bass, I'm Paul Powell, and I'd like to particularly thank our special guest, Mr. Jack Landreau, on cornet, for sitting in."

And with that the last chorus is upon us, soaring as the melody rises, and it's just magic again, and we wrap up nice and tight and they applaud loudly and we're off.

Paul takes Landreau by the elbow and they step off the stage, with me a half a pace back. The crowd starts to part as we head for the door and a space opens to reveal a woman, all dressed in red, looking absolutely magnificent, one goddamned hell of a woman, directly in front of us.

The crowd keeps parting and she holds her ground and we stop dead in front of her. She shakes Paul's hand and tilts her head up at an angle and gives him a soft kiss on the cheek, then turns to Landreau, curtsies deeply, raises his right hand and kisses it. He's staring at her, not looking away at all, and she's looking at his hand and then up into his eyes, and a quizzical expression crosses her face and it's only then that I see that he's missing the pinkie on his right hand, and has only nine fingers.

CHAPTER 16
The Cleaner

Airport Marriott—After the Gig—The Parking Lot
Saturday, January 11/Sunday, January 12

11:15 P.M.: I see the hand when she kisses it. All I need to see.

I pull on the gloves. Drain the ginger ale. Slip the glass into my coat pocket. Stand up. Get my coat off the back of the chair, the hand holding the handkerchief. Give the chair a wipe. Leave the change on the table, untouched. Give the table a wipe. Turn to leave.

I see something on the floor. Shining. Kneel down, retie one shoe while I look at it. Small, brass, with a pearl inlay. One of the keys from the saxophone. Must have come flying off when he smashed it. Scoop the thing up with my handkerchief. Tuck both into my breast pocket. Jam the hat on my head so the toupee will not come off. Head for the door, head down.

Go through the revolving door before anyone else has thought of leaving. Go straight for the car. Unlock it, get inside, start it up, crank up the heat. Leave the lights off. Keep my foot off the brakes. Waiting. Really cold. Let the engine warm up while all the other cars are starting up. When they are mostly gone, shut it off.

Know what I am waiting for. Know what I need to see: Who she walks out the door with. All the years I am doing this. Always comes a moment when things change and they cannot change back. That is the moment I look for.

11:40 P.M.: First one out is the string bass, big guy, hard to miss with the bass and the tuba. Guy is not wearing a coat. No hat, no gloves, not even a sweater. Steam coming off his bald head. Jesus. Heads over to some little Toyota, ten years old, the color of puke. Do not know how he gets himself in there and the bass and the tuba, too. But he does. Starts up, drives off. Rolls the window down as he goes. Makes me cold, just watching him.

Five minutes later, Piano. Stops in the doorway to light a cigarette. Looks around like he does not remember which car he drove. Stares at the stars in the sky. Pulls his collar up. Heads for an old navy blue VW. Fumbles for his keys, hands shaking. Gets in, smacks his head on the door frame, rubs it. Closes the door. Starts the car, lets it idle, warm up. A minute. Two minutes. Almost three. Fumbling around with something in his lap. Finally puts it in gear, takes off.

Who is next?

Nobody is next. Twelve o'clock. One o'clock. Two o'clock. My hands are frozen. My feet are numb. Cannot sit in a car with the motor on, middle of the parking lot. Cannot stay much longer with the motor off. The windows are getting frozen up. Hard to see.

Who is left? She is still in there, Laura. Can still see her car, the Mercedes, thin coat of frost on it. Trumpet? Do not see him come out. Drummer, do not see her come out. Would have spotted all the drums. The other guy, the cornet, do not see him come out either.

Too many to still be inside. Only eliminates two, and does not really eliminate them.

2:17 A.M.: Trumpet comes out, the black one. Powell. He

is bouncing, not gliding like before. Has a hop in his step. Heads straight to a black Taurus, not even locked. Gets right in, drives right off. See him buckling his seat belt, turning on the lights as he goes.

Down to two of them, and the worst two at that. Jones the drummer and Nine Fingers the cornet. It just cannot be easy, can it?

CHAPTER 17
Vinnie Amatucci

The Apartment—Hyde Park
Sunday, January 12

I wasn't driving today, and the band didn't have anything scheduled. Last night's magic was still with me, in the back of my head. And it was talking to me. Maybe I've been resting on my laurels, which is kind of stupid because I don't have any laurels to rest on—I'm a second-tier piano player in a second-tier jazz band. This is why I'm flushing my $100,000 education down the toilet, so I can be barely adequate? This is why I'm busting my ass driving the Fat Man's cab, because it gives me time to avoid practicing? Lazy, self-deluded, self-satisfied, and stupid.

After this first little lecture, I started to do what I've been settling for: I turned on some music to listen to other people play, as if I can learn what I want to sound like by listening to what someone else sounds like. The truth is, it can sometimes make it worse. When you listen, you pick up a few licks from whoever you're listening to, without even trying to. Even if it's Art Tatum or Earl Fatha Hines or Horace

Silver or Coltrane or Bird—the greats—it's someone else. But surprise, surprise: I caught myself at it and wouldn't settle for it, for a change.

So I plugged in the keyboard, unplugged the speakers, slipped on the headphones and played. I picked a few standards, played the melody, the accompanying chords, then a few choruses of solos on each tune. But I was just doing what I already know how to do. It didn't hurt to get the mechanism moving, but it wasn't what I was looking for.

So I went to the bookshelf and pulled out the old practice books. Exercises, chords, arpeggios, runs, octaves, triplets, the whole classical thing. It was a start, but it wasn't enough. So I started transposing it all into different keys. I'm most comfortable in the flat keys: F, B-flat, E-flat, A-flat, plus, of course, good old C-major. There's nothing inherently tougher about the sharp keys than the flat keys—the white keys are still white and the black keys are still black. But most of the tunes we play are in the flat keys.

By the time I got into A, four sharps, I started making mistakes, stumbling, and this pleased me, showed me I was outside my comfort zone. I'm not going to say "I played until my fingers bled." My fingers don't bleed from playing the piano, nobody's do. Whenever I fucked something up, I stopped, took the tempo way down, and played it again, slower, until it was right. Then I moved it faster until the tempo was where it was supposed to be. And after that, I did it a few more times until it sounded less mechanical, until it had some feeling to it.

I took a couple of handfuls of ice cubes out of the freezer, dropped them in a bowl, filled it up with cold water, and dipped my hands in there, slowly stretching, then making fists, for ten minutes, until they started to get stiff. Then I plugged the sink and started to run the hot water. I went back to the stretching and clenching in the hot water, resting every now and then, turning the water off when it started to get too hot. This wasn't punishment, it was work. A chiropractor recommended this to me when I sprained a thumb once. He called it "The Pump," and said the idea was to get the blood flow going to pump out the lactic acid that builds up and stiffens the joints and muscles. If you just use heat it feels good for a while but increases the swelling, leaves all that blood pooling. If you use just cold it feels good for a while but it traps the toxins. With any kind of muscular inflammation, he said, use some ice to get the swelling down, then go back and forth, hot and cold, as long as you can stand it.

This time I went for about thirty minutes, then shook my hands out for maybe five minutes. I could feel the tingle. The stiffness I had felt at the diner was gone, and I felt energized.

I went back to the keyboard. I picked a tune, the first thing that came to my mind—"All the Way" ("When somebody loves you . . .")—and started just playing the chords, very slowly, but with feeling. I have a pedal attachment for the keyboard, and I nudged that closer with one foot and started working that like a real piano, focusing on the dynamics of the sound. Then I took it up a key and did the same thing, then up another key. I started losing it at around three sharps but I gave myself another little talking to ("Come on, you lazy shit!"), and pushed through it into A (four sharps) and then B, not that anyone is ever going to ask me to play anything in five fucking sharps, but that wasn't the point. I was having trouble with the five, so I went back to the base chords, letting it come to me. It was painful at first, not physically painful but awkward. No rhythm, no dynamics, just getting my brain comfortable with my fingers on the keys. Then it started to come. I tried to shut off my brain and pretty soon there it was, and I let it ring out, strong and true, and then jacked it into six sharps! The ridiculous key of F#! And for just a minute it was there, like it was C-major and nothing but the white keys.

And then I stopped. I let the sound ring in my head, tried not to let anything else intrude. I flirted with the thought of going to seven sharps, C#, but I stopped myself. Don't finish satisfied, leave it incomplete, like some Tantric sex thing; that was my thought process.

I went back into the kitchen, got out the ice and hot water and did the pump thing for about twenty more minutes. I dried my hands, rolled a joint, twisted it off, and smoked half of it, feeling mellow and quietly righteous. I wolfed down some soup out of a can, then stripped and went to bed early, feeling rectified, purified, solidified.

CHAPTER 18
Vinnie Amatucci

In the Fat Man's Cab
Monday, January 13

I got up early this morning, drove my beat-up car to the cabstand, locked the car, unlocked the cab, got in and headed downtown to the Drake Hotel. It's Monday morning, and I have a regular customer I squire around town every Monday at 8:00. It's a great gig, really gets things moving at a nice pace, and I was looking forward to it. Sunday's thaw had opened up the roads, the planes and trains and buses were moving again, and the temperature was in the mid-thirties, sloppy but clear and crisp. The sky was deep azure with not a wisp of gray or a hint of white. The humidity was down in the twenties, and the blue reached all the way to the horizon.

I stopped for some coffee and a roll, got back in the cab, filled the pipe, had a few wake-and-bake hits, just enough to put a sparkle on things, and sipped my coffee a milliliter at a time. I put away the pipe, sprayed around some Ozium, lit a cigarette as I drove north on Michigan, and pulled in at the curb up the block from the Drake, at the top of what they call the Magnificent Mile. I had flipped on the NOT FOR HIRE light so no one could scoop me up, and, wouldn't you know it, a couple of people tried right away; the lines at the Drake were six cabs and ten people long, and a couple of civilians thought they were more important than everyone else in line and figured they'd shortcut the process. Hey, like it says, I'm not for hire.

The guy I drive on Mondays is a strange one, and I'm sure there's a story there, and I'm also sure I don't want to know exactly what it is. I figure it's one of those "I could tell you, but then I'd have to kill you" things. I think of him as "The Accountant." I started thinking of him that way the first time he climbed in the cab. He always wears a charcoal pinstripe suit, a white shirt, and a rep tie in subdued colors. In the winter he adds a black overcoat and a black fedora with a snap brim. He's maybe fifty, fifty-five, around there, and short. Not just short, he's small, maybe five-foot-two and not more than 130 pounds, with these thin little delicate hands, and a plain gold wedding band. It could mean he's married, but it's on the left middle finger, not the ring finger. Maybe there's some code to these things that I can't translate. He wears gold-rimmed glasses with no frames on the bottom, almost too expensive and contempo-Euro-trashy for the rest of the getup, and he's got a little mustache, clipped so short you wonder why he grows it at all, although he looks like he could muster a real walrus if he wanted to. He always wears a hat, even in the summertime, when he switches to a straw, and never takes it off, except to wipe his brow with a white handkerchief, linen from the looks of it. And when he slides it off you can see he doesn't have a lot of hair, and what there is of it is kind of gun-metal in color and slicked straight back. No comb-over, but "this is what it is; deal with it," and I have to give him points for that. He carries this big old satchel in a dinged-up cordovan color, like a teacher's bag, with the two sides cinching together at the top and two weathered brass buckles closing it, and he keeps it on his lap, with one hand on both of the handles. The satchel is accordion style, and when he arrives in my cab it's kind of thin, but when he leaves it's bulging. He always just looked like an accountant to me, so I thought of him that way, and one day, after about a month, when I asked him what kind of work he did, he stared off at the distance out the side window, stroked his little mustache, and said, in his clear high voice, "I would suppose that one might place me in the financial services category. I have a number of . . . clients . . . and I engage in my peripatetic rounds each week to visit with them briefly, so as to handle some fiduciary matters concerning their, ah, accounts."

That's the way he speaks, educated, but maybe too much so, like some people speak when they're trying to appear upper-crust. What tips it off is that he mispronounces the occasional word—like "perry-pa-TEET-ick" and "fi-DUKE-ee-ary"—the sign of someone who's read the word but hasn't heard it used. He always goes for the nine-dollar "Certainly, my young accomplice" phrase when a simple "Yup" would suffice. It's affected, in an almost British way.

He starts off at eight, like I said, and we drive around until almost twelve, when I drop him back near the Drake. We go all over town—Near North, up almost to Evanston, West Side, South Side, the Western suburbs, a couple of stops downtown. It's always the same sixteen or twenty addresses, only varying slightly, but each time he varies the route and we do them in a different order. It's nothing to him to go all the way north to Evanston, then all the way south to Calumet City, then up north again, then downtown, then west. I once turned to him at a stoplight and told him that I could save him a lot of time and money if I could plot the route for him, you know, link it all together in some kind of rational Grand Circuit, but he gave me a look that froze me, and then, chilling, said, "But then, dear boy, your remuneration would consequently suffer considerably, and we would *hate* to see that occur, now wouldn't we?" I hardly caught the words; it's the look that I remembered.

My guess? He's a bagman of some sort, a courier. The places are maybe gambling joints or whorehouses or dope dens, or they're the offices or the homes of the folks who run the gambling joints, the whorehouses, or the dope dens, and he makes the rounds right after the busy weekend rush to pick up money or chits or whatever it is that they've collected, including, probably, my own monthly contribution to my local weed purveyor. That bag looks pretty light when he slings it in ahead of himself into the cab at eight and awfully heavy when he drags it out behind himself after noon, so he's doing more picking up than dropping off. Unless it's some sort of ruse, and he's filling it up with rolled-up newspapers as part of some misdirection ploy. But I'll say it again: I really don't want to know. It's a great gig, perfect for the start of the week, and he's good company in his hifalutin way, chatting incessantly all the way about nothing in particular, and the money is great and he tips really well, way more than he needs to.

And to top it all off, we play our little game. We didn't start this until maybe the second or third Monday; he must have been sizing me up at first, the way I was sizing him up. But once we began, I couldn't stop.

I'm not sure what he calls it—I've never heard him give it a proper name—but I call it "license-plate poker."

Most of the Illinois tags have three numbers and three letters, not necessarily in that order. The are two roles in the game, the player and the scorer. The scorer picks out a car coming toward us or coming up alongside or dead ahead, and calls out the three letters on the tag, in order, like "TQM." The player then has thirty seconds to call out all the phrases he can think with those three letters, like "The Queerest Man," "Two Quaint Mensches," "Total Quality Management," "Tension Quiets Me," like that. The scorer calls "Time" when the thirty seconds are up, then the two switch roles. One thirty-second turn for both is a round.

There are a couple of side rules that we developed early on. You can't repeat any words in any one turn, but you can use variations, like singular/plural, or present tense/past tense. Words that start with a Q, a C, or a K are interchangeable (it's not the Q that's difficult, but the K, surprisingly), and in any string with an X in it you can use a word that starts with the sound "EX," like "exhibitionist," "excited," or "extroverted." You can be as vulgar as you like, and we sometimes get into some really nasty grooves. But you can't use names or foreign words unless they're part of what you might call the standard American lexicon, like in "GGD: Got Gehrig's Disease," or "ARJ: A Regular Joe." If the scorer challenges a phrase, you have to repeat it back in a sentence, and it's double or nothing. The Accountant never challenges me on my phrases; he learned that early on.

Most of the license plates in Illinois have three numbers and three letters. But some don't. Some cars have four and two, some have two and four, and some are vanity plates. With our rules, two-letter phrases pay the same as three, and anything more than three is double-your-money. So two-letter license plates are a license to steal—the number goes way up—and fours and fives and sixes can make you rich, but you have to work for it.

And, as that indicates, we play for money, a dollar a phrase. The scorer keeps count, out loud with his fingers held up, and counts out the money from his end at the finish of each thirty-second round. If the traffic gets really bad or we hit a nasty stretch of road, I'll ask him to hold up, and he's cool with that. And when he's getting near one of his stops, he does the same.

At first, he kicked my ass. He would hit four or five in a turn and I was averaging two or three. Not much, a couple of bucks a round, but if you play for ten or twenty minutes straight, like we sometimes do, that can add up. I quickly figured out that when I was totally wasted on weed I'd get skinned—"Wait a minute, wait a minute, uh, what were the three letters again?"—and if I was totally straight I didn't do any better, trying to overthink it. But if I was just a tiny little bit buzzed, the less-than-linear-connection factor kicked in, and the synapses hummed and popped, but not all of them at once, thank you very much. So I altered my preparation and quickly caught up. I also got the knack of seeing the right plates to keep his score down (I noticed he doesn't do well on phrases starting with vowels, for some reason). Now we each average around five to seven hits in a thirty-second round, sometimes more, sometimes less, but it pretty much evens out, with me usually a little bit ahead. If he gets way up he usually makes it up to me in the tip, so I don't get pissed and leave him to find another ride the next Monday. If I get ahead, I get all aw-shucks about it and he takes it like a gentleman, and even seems to appreciate it, like he's looking forward to getting back at me the next week. He likes the competition, and I get the sense that he's done this before, with other drivers, but they dropped out or he got bored taking their money. I always remember to bring change, maybe twenty or thirty singles, and he always carries a wad himself, in a money clip with the Franklins in the middle and the Washingtons on the outside.

I've heard this called a Chicago roll when I was in New York and I've heard it called a Detroit roll here in Chicago. I've also seen guys do it backward—a C-note on the outside wrapped around a wad of singles—and I've heard that called L.A.-style, which fits. Since I met the Accountant, I started carrying my money in a clip, not in my wallet, and switched the big fat wallet for a little leather credit-card case, and that's all I keep in it: a Visa, an AmEx, a Triple-A, and my driver's license. I also keep my roll Chicago-style, with the ones showing, but that's sort of related to the hazards of the profession: driving around all day with strangers, and especially picking up anybody who flags you down like I do, you do not want to tempt the mortals by rubbing General Grant in their faces.

I was musing on this when the door swung open and he hopped in, looking all bouncy and fresh and smelling of citrusy cologne.

"Good morning to you, young Vincent. And how are you comporting yourself this fine morning?"

"It's hanging good," I replied. "And you?"

"Splendid! What a magnificent morning, after all this un-remitting gray, I must say."

"Where to, sir?"

I call him Sir and he calls me Vincent—that's our routine. He somehow picked up that I'm having this problem lately with being called Vinnie, even though that's all anyone has called me since forever. What it is is that maybe I think I'm getting too old to be a Vinnie. Once you close in on thirty it sounds like the name of some guy who wasn't too swift and never made it out of the neighborhood. I didn't say this to him, but he figured it out somehow.

"Let us begin our appointed rounds . . ." he said, with a dramatic pause. "7232 North California."

That's north and west, so I hit the meter, put it in gear, and off we went. He generally doesn't like me to take the highways, but prefers the back streets, north and south, east and west. He never complains about the routes I take, not even a dirty look or a raised eyebrow. His confidence in my driving is implicit. He doesn't want me to hurry—I picked up on that the first time I raced a yellow light into the red and I looked in the rearview mirror to see him claw-ing the upholstery—so when he's in the cab I shift it down into limo mode and cruise it out as smooth as silk. He takes a very visible sensory pleasure in this, lolling back in his seat.

I cracked the window and lit a cigarette, something for which I got his permission long ago. He doesn't smoke, but he told me he used to, and that he appreciated the smell of it and the sight of someone enjoying it. I'm sure I wouldn't be so magnanimous; if I had to quit I'd want the fucking things banished from the planet.

He started in about the weather, and what a bad storm we had last week, and how it must have been good for business "for someone with your pecuniary interest," and I nodded and uh-hunhed and let him carry the ball for a while, just smoking and sipping my coffee. Traffic was a little thick, and the roads were puddling up with slush, but we were in no hurry, so I fell in line and just slicked my way out west, keeping an eye out for whatever, checking the scene. About twenty blocks from the Drake, he took his gloves off, pulled his big brass pocket watch out of his pants, reached into his other pocket for his roll, conspicuously enough, caught my eye in the rearview and waggled the roll a few times.

"Would you happen to be available for a friendly game of chance this fine morning, Vincent?" he asked.

"A game of chance?" I countered, doing my W. C. Fields: "Not the way *I* play it."

He chuckled at the reference as I got out my money clip and dug in my kit for a digital timer I keep around, for, well, for this and this alone. I smoothed the roll out, tucked it under my right leg, then set the timer on the dashboard.

"Care to go first, sir?"

"Oh, you're that confident of your abilities this morning, are you, young *Vincenzo*? You feel you can give me the early advantage and then compensate by the bye and bye, do you? I like that. I must say, I do like that. Certainly, I'll take a flyer. Why don't you call out some good letters for me?"

We were pulling up to a light, and a car nudged ahead of us. You're not supposed to go hunting for bad letters, just to take what the flow offers you. I played it straight. The car was right in front of us so I called them out: "JAP."

"Jewish American Princess, Just A Pal, Juice And Pizza, mmm . . . Jump Around Please, Join Another Party . . . mmm . . ."

"Time," I called. "That's five." I thumbed off five singles with my thumb, pushed them over to a pile under my kit. "I'm up. Call 'em out."

A car was headed toward us in the oncoming lane. It got closer and he called out, "TAL."

"Take Another Look, Thanks A Lot, That's A Loss, Tremble And Lose, Thin Ass . . . uh . . . Lover, uh . . . Try All Letters, Tempt Any Less, This—"

"Time. Seven. Quite a nice start. Now don't be too hard on me, my boy. Take pity on me." He peeled off seven ones, laid them on the seat.

The JAP was turning right in front of us, and that revealed "BTD." I called it out and clicked the timer.

"Beat The Devil, By This Date, Buy Those Dresses, Big Thick, uh, Dick, Bespectacled . . . Thin . . . Demon, mmm . . . Belay That . . . Demand . . ."

"Time." I counted off six more dollars. "Did you ever see that movie?" I asked.

"Fantastic flick," he answered. "Bogart, Lorre, Gina Lollobrigida, a cast of thousands, quite unappreciated in its own time. Huston at the helm, I believe, wasn't it?"

"I think so," I said, ready for another round. This is the way it goes. Some rounds would trigger off a reference, some strange synaptic association, and we would chase that around for a minute or two until the next set of letters presented itself.

"You call it," I said.

We stopped at a light. A car turned from the street to our left into traffic ahead of us. "XUQ, a rather infelicitous combination."

"Extremely Uncommon Quality, Exotic Unknown Quantity, Exhausted Ugly Queen, Excitedly Unbelieving Callgirl, Exhibitionist Under Cover, Extroverted Unlikeable Killer, Ex-Uncle's Kisses, Express—"

"Time. Well done, well done. Eight, on a difficult string like that! You are getting way too proficient for me, my boy."

"Me? I'm Extremely Un-Qualified."

It wouldn't have counted as a score—there was a repetition—but it worked well enough as a pun, and he threw his head back and laughed. He reminded me in that moment of the photos you see of Franklin Roosevelt, riding in the back of an open car, his great big head thrown back in a belly laugh so large you almost believed it was genuine. The gesture was fake, but the laugh erupting from within it was real.

We continued on like this until we got to California and turned north. He called time-out, looked out the window, and before we knew it, we were there. Our custom was to settle up on the game before he went inside, so we traded piles. I was up eight bucks, not a bad start.

In ten minutes, all with the clock on, he was back, and it was off to Highland Park, farther north. We played another few rounds, and he started hot but I caught him and passed him and was up another ten when we parked. This address was a house, a big shaded thing that looked like old money. He hopped out with his bag and I waited until he was inside, took a couple of hits off the pipe, opened the window, lit a cigarette, and waited.

Next was downtown, then the far South Side, then way out west to Naperville, then downtown again. We gave the game a rest for a while—it tends to take it out of you after a while—then played sporadically off and on until his last stop. Just before then, he said to me, "Let's try one more for you, now . . . CLP."

"Cunt Lover's Paradise, Clit Licker's Paradox, Come Like a Panther, Clever Lesbian Paradigm, Clumsy Loose Pants . . . uh . . . Can't Live Permanently, Can Love Perpetually, Crunchy Light Peanuts, Catastrophic Last Period, Certainly Lousy Penmanship, Clearly Lost Perspective . . . uh . . . Call Later, Perhaps, Crummy Little Pinch, uh . . ."

"Time." He edged closer to the front seat. "Well, now, Vincent, you seem to have established a new record of sorts. I count thirteen, that's correct, thirteen phrases in thirty seconds. I'm having trouble seeing how one of us might top that. In the beginning, you seemed to have been running with a theme of sorts."

"The lesbian thing?" I said. "Don't know what came over

me, sir. I will say that I have always identified with them, though. They love women, I love women. They like cunnilingus, I like cunnilingus."

"And a cunning linguist pervert you are, with thirteen all at once," he said.

"That makes fourteen," I said, and he opened his mouth wide and laughed his FDR laugh, his head thrown back, as he counted out the money.

On the way back to the Drake he was in a philosophical mood, going on about life, and existence, maybe owing to the fact that I was up twenty-nine bucks. I didn't join in but looked thoughtful, as if he were maybe on to something. Of course, if I had been *down* twenty-nine bucks, it might have been different.

A little after noon I dropped him east of the Drake. He paid up the toll, well over $240, plus a tip of an even sixty, thanked me for a "most pleasant divertissement," giving it a French accent that wasn't even close, then said "See you same time next week, young Vincent." He swung open the door, hauled the case out of the cab with both hands and was gone. I always make it a point never to look in the rearview mirror after him, never to wait around—the guy is a good customer and I'd just as soon keep him—so I pulled right out into traffic as soon as he shut the door and booked up the street back to Michigan Avenue South and headed for Jazz at Noon. Uh-oh, I thought. Jeff was usually there. Well, I'd deal with that when I had to deal with it.

CHAPTER 19
Vinnie Amatucci

Jazz at Noon
Monday, January 13

The joint was quiet, not many players were hanging out. I looked around the room carefully—there was no Jeff to be seen. Instead, there was a whole Dixieland band from downstate someplace, with the striped shirts and the arm garters and the plastic straw hats taking up the stage. They were pretty bad, except for the tuba player, a little bear cub of a guy who played his ass off, but they didn't know they sucked and wouldn't get off the stand. They must have planned this for months, their one trip to the Big City, and couldn't let go of it.

Then a hard-bop fool sax player I've met named Horace Starr got on the stand and he went a little out there. The tuba player was still up there—there was no string-bass player in the house—and he kept up just fine. Starr took like twenty-three choruses on some imitation Bird thing, the name of which I forget but which I started thinking of as "Idiocity," and in the middle of the twenty-second he started to scratch his nuts with a vengeance right there on the stand, and just couldn't stop, just like his playing. And through it all he played a chorus and a half with only one hand on the damned sax, just overblowing high notes, honking, squeaking. Three assholes in business suits sitting near me in the back, who couldn't see the scratching and thought this was artistry of the highest caliber, applauded like crazy. Horace finally had to resort to using both hands at his crotch and that was too much of a limitation even for him, so he hopped off the stand and headed for the door, still pawing away.

"Hey, Horace?" I called out to his fleeing form. "Get it looked at."

By this point it was 12:50 and still no Jeff, which was a relief. I had no idea what I would have said to him. The playing itself was pretty dispirited. People were soloing too much and trying to show off. Plus they had gotten into this stupid speed groove, with not a single ballad in over an hour.

These sessions usually go on until two or three o'clock, but by one o'clock I had had enough. Some things move you forward, some things leave you right where you are. This shit was moving me backward. I turned to get a waiter to settle up, and out of the corner of my eye I could have sworn I saw my mystery man, Jack Landreau, heading out the door, carrying that same weird case with him. I reached for my clip to throw down a five and run after him, but all I had was twenties—I had left my big wad of singles from the Accountant in the cab. I craned my neck trying to see him again, but I had to wait two minutes for the waiter to show up and another three for him to shuffle back with my change. I raced outside but by the time I got there, he was gone, if he had ever been there in the first place.

O'Hare's open again, I reminded myself. He's probably on his way to, where was it, Detroit? And as I thought that, a wave of disappointment rippled through me. I wanted to hear him again, to bring back that spark.

Outside, the sky had clouded over and the temperature had dipped. My mouth tasted like stale watery beer and fatty pastrami and my mood felt as sour as the aftertaste. I got back in the cab and sped out of there as fast as I could.

CHAPTER 20
Ken Ridlin

Near Fullerton and Halsted
Monday, January 13

In the middle of a shift in the middle of the day in the middle of a thought the call comes in and I head right over. I'm already in my unmarked, so I make a right and head up Lincoln. Five minutes is all. It's a one-bedroom apartment in an old building off Halsted near Fullerton. As I get close I hear the screech of the El overhead and to my right. Rents must be cheap here.

I pull up, park. We've got it cordoned off. I flash the badge and they wave me through.

Inside, Carter of Homicide is leaning on the doorframe, smoking a cigarette with purple gloves on. Three lab techs are scurrying around, taking samples, dusting for prints. There are no uniforms inside. A good sign. It's under control.

I come up around Carter so he can see me, and flash the tin again. It's not necessary. He's expecting me.

"Yo, Ridlin. Good you could make it, man. We got us one messy motherfucker, here." He looks at the cigarette. The ash is almost an inch long. He reaches over, hooks opens the right-hand pocket of his brown tweed jacket with his left hand, flicks the ash in there with his right.

I look again at the gloves.

"Purple?" I say. "This a fashion statement?"

"Nitrile," he says. "Purple nitrile. Got me a allergy to that latex shit."

I look around. The techs are swarming like flies around a lump in the corner. I see two feet on the floor, one wearing a blue sock and one not. The rest is blocked.

"What have we got?"

"Male vic, thirty-three years old, died of an acute drug overdose, far as we can tell so far."

"Yeah, so . . ."

The knowing glance—this is news? We get a few a day, and they're not homicides.

"I mean what you call a *acute* drug overdose. Somebody stuffed his nose with blow, highest quality Bolivian, beaucoup shit, and I mean stuffed. His nose was kept mostly closed—marks look like a plain old wooden clothespin, and, no, we ain't found no clothespins. His mouth was stuffed with a sock—looks like the one off his left foot—and duct-taped shut."

"So every time he breathed, he had to suck air in through his nose, and . . ."

"You got it . . . Hell of a way to go, you ask me. Higher and higher and higher and out. There sure be worse ways. If that's all there was."

He pauses, looks at me.

"But it ain't."

I wait. I let him tell it his way. You learn that on the job.

"He was, you know, tortured. For like hours. All his toes—broken. All his fingers—broken. Looks like all his ribs—broken. Somebody did not like this motherfucker, and somebody got real personal."

"Personal?" I ask. "Like sex crimes personal?"

"No. Pants are still on, for one thing. But he's got marks

all over him, look to be coming from a fork, one a his own, we think, matches the spacing. And I mean all over him. Not just marks, like he was poked. Marks, like, maybe a half-inch, a inch deep. Plus his eyes, his ears, his tongue, all, you know, removed."

"You find them?"

" 'Fraid so. Glass bowl in the kitchen. Washed and rinsed and cleaned. Like, you know, specimens, you know what I'm saying?"

"Time of death?"

"Hard to say, hard to say. Meat Wagon say none of the wounds was postmortem, he lived through it all, you call that living. Guess is, he started to lose it, to pass out, our guy stuffed some more blow up his nose and brought him around for some more fun. As for when? Maybe eight hours ago, maybe twelve, round there. Sometime last night, for sure. But he took a long fucking time dying."

"So somebody not only wants him dead, they want him to know he's about to be killed, they want him to suffer."

"Sure looks likes he did, too. Shit himself, more than once, premortem."

"Bleeding?" I asked.

"You know? That's somethin'. Not much at all, considerin'. I mean like the fork-wounds and the, uh, the removals. Our guy knew where to stick the fork, so it do hurt, but it don't spurt." He chuckles. I flash him the old cynical grin, the one I have honed all these many years.

He holds his notepad with the right hand because the left holds the cigarette, and flips it so the next page comes to the front. Nice move.

"They can't tell 'til they get him under the knife. But they think he aimed at all the major organs. Marks by his liver, both kidneys, spleen, pancreas, gallbladder, intestines. Lot around the pancreas, wherever that is, some reason."

He looks up.

"Best be taking notes, man. Gonna be a short quiz, end of this period."

He winks.

"The guy, the one with the fork, he had to know what he was doing," I venture.

I look over. Still can't see anything. Not that I want to.

He turns, steps out the door, the cigarette has gone out, toasted right down to the filter. He puts it in the pack that is in his coat pocket. He lights another one.

I watch. He wouldn't mind if I bummed one. Wouldn't think anything of it. There are cops who only smoke at homicide scenes. Covers up the smell. It'd be the most natural thing in the world.

"Trace evidence?" I ask. "Hair? Fibers? Prints?"

Carter looks me in the eye. "Look around you. Guy's a single white male, thirties, you ever see a single white male, thirties, got a place this neat? I mean, 'less he's a faggot?"

"Was he—" I start to ask.

"Nah, man. Pile of stroke books in the closet. *Penthouse, Hustler, Juggs,* like that."

I look around. The apartment, what I can see of it, is spotless. Not a thing out of place. Books lined up exactly at the edge of the bookshelves, stack of magazines all facing the same way, wooden floor looks like it was just polished. Even the rug shows vacuum marks.

"Are those vacuum marks?" I ask, pointing with my chin.

"Next-door neighbor thinks she heard one, 'very *a*-ty-pi-cal,' she says, for the vic."

"She notice when?"

"Not exactly." He flips open a notepad, reads. " 'All I know is it was still dark, ya know? I heard it, wondered what the fuck, went back to sleep. I hadda get up to go to work in the morning. I never hear the vacuum in there. I didn't know he even owned one.' " He closes the pad.

"Maybe he was just a neat freak," I offer.

"Neat freak? Look around, man. My baby's momma's momma don't keep house this neat, and she thinks it's gonna get her into heaven. We checked the drawers, kitchen, and bedroom. Fuckin' mess. Shit just stuffed in there. Silverware drawer? Knives where the forks s'posed to be, shit in there backward. Fridge smells bad, dirty clothes in the closet just laying there. No, the vic wasn't neat. But our boy sure was."

" 'Our boy'? Any evidence of the killer's sex?"

Carter looks at me again. His eyes are mournfully cynical. "I known some bitches in my time maybe wanted to do something like this to a man, maybe dreamed about it, you know? Of course, the men prob'ly had it coming, you know. But a woman couldn't do this. Maybe could neaten up this good, but the wounds? In your experience? You think? I ain't no profiler, but come on, man. Shit, had to be a dude."

"A professional?"

"Sure looks like it, don't it? Somebody who had hisself a plan, knew what the fuck he was doing. Also looks like some kind of message was being delivered, though fuck if I know what it was."

We look around. He continues.

"Hair? Fibers? Prints? Nothing. I mean nothing. He vacuumed, vacuum cleaner's gone. He swept up and mopped— no broom, no mop. No cleaner or polish under the sink, but you can fuckin' smell it. Can you fuckin' smell it?"

I sniff, sniff again. "Pine-Sol, and some kind of lemon wood polish . . ."

"Yeah, Pledge, whatever that shit is," he said. "Just try and find some in here. Zip. No towels, not one sponge, no garbage bags in the garbage cans. This guy cleaned up, and then he cleaned up the cleaning shit. Be surprised if we find one fucking atom off of this guy." He turns to me. "They find atoms these days?"

"Don't know about atoms. Maybe molecules, DNA, like that."

"Yeah, DNA. Doubt it. Doubt if he left behind the air he breathed out. Probably took that with him, too."

"What's the connection? Why'd you call me?"

"You mean, aside from I got nobody here to talk to except the lab rats, and they ain't big on conversation?"

The cigarette ash is getting longer. He hooks open the right pocket again, flicks it in. He reaches into his other coat pocket, pulls out a wallet, flips it open to a picture ID.

"That case you're working, the drive-by murder at that club last week?"

"Maybe more like a 'walk-by' than a drive-by, but yeah?"

"A 'walk-by' murder?" he says.

I shrug.

"This was your sax player. We found this, ran the name. One prior, but also got us a hit on your interview list. Computer flagged it. Your name came up."

He holds up a wallet. I'm not wearing latex gloves. My hands are in my pockets. I lean in, look at the ID. Jeff Fahey—the name is familiar. The lab guys are moving aside. I don't want to look. We take three steps over. I look.

I can't tell. His face is all contorted, plus without the eyes, the ears . . .

"You sure it's him?" I ask.

"Fingers are all broke but they still got prints. See, we anticipated your question. First thing we did. And we got a hit. One prior, 'bout ten years back."

"Cocaine possession," I mumbled.

He looks at me. "He shoots, he scores. What's the word? 'Ironic'?"

"That's the word."

"Nothing since. Stayed clean, or just got hisself a more reliable connection. Got a job at the Merchandise Mart, some kind of broker's assistant, some shit. Plays in this band, his off hours. Guess neither one paid too good, the look of this place."

"Or he stuffed most of it up his nose."

He nodded.

"The rest of the neighbors," I ask, "they see anything? Hear anything?"

"Aside from the vacuum? Nothing. Wait, one guy said he thinks he saw a cleaning van parked outside. He's on grave-yard shift, left around 10:45 P.M."

"Name? Plate number? Model . . . anything?" I say. "Pretty please?"

He consults the notepad again, flips another page. " 'White . . . not new . . . picture of a mop and pail, Some-thing-or-Other Cleaning,' he says."

"We could bring him in, let the hypnotist have a crack at him," I venture.

He looks at me. "You believe in that shit?"

"Doesn't matter if we believe in it. Only matters if the subject believes in it," I say.

He tilts his head. "Got a point there."

We stand still for a minute, two minutes, his eyes looking at the floor in front of him, mine flicking around the room. He steps outside, grinds the cigarette into the heel of his shoe.

Sparks flutter down onto the curled-up, yellowed linoleum. He lights another cigarette with a little pink dis-posable lighter. Keeping the smell of death away, as long as he can.

"Anything else I should know?" I ask.

"All I got, man," he says.

"One thing," I say. "He was a sax player. Played in this band, part-time. I see a music stand, I see some music on it. Where's his sax?"

Carter looks me in the eye. His eyes are dark brown in his light cocoa face, and turned down at the side like an old basset hound. The bags are starting to get deeper. Cou-ple of years they'll dominate his strong face.

"Man, they was right," he says, "you *are* good."

"Well, it's the obvious question."

"Maybe. Maybe there is one thing," he says. He reaches into his left coat pocket, pulls out a plastic evidence bag, holds it up so I can see it. "This be part of a saxophone?"

It's a little twisted piece of brass, with a circular piece of what looks like mother-of-pearl attached to it, the whole thing not more than an inch long.

"Yeah. A key. From a tenor saxophone." I turn to him. "Where'd you find it?"

He grabs me lightly by the elbow, leads me gently over to the corpse. Leans me down in front of it, blowing smoke all around us.

"See this mark here? On his forehead?"

I nod.

"Where we found it. Like, embedded in there. Like our guy hammered it in there with something—"

"His fist maybe?" I ask.

"Look at it, man. Only way he hammered it in with his fist is if he was some kind of karate man or somethin'. I mean, it was *hammered* in."

"So," I ask, "what did he hammer it in with?"

"Uhhh, a hammer?" he says. "And no, we didn't find no motherfucking hammer, and we didn't find no prints on the thing . . ."

He turns to me.

"You know what all this is?" he asks me. "You know what all this means, Ridlin?"

I turn. I look at him.

"It's a mystery," I say.

"See?" he chuckles. "Like I be saying. You *good.*"

Not this good, I think to myself. Nowhere near this good.

CHAPTER 21
Ken Ridlin

Interviews
Monday, January 13

I spend the rest of the day interviewing the members of the band. I start with Powell, the leader, the trumpet player. He lives in a high-rise at South 47th and Lake Park, all funny angles, very vertical looking. I park the car, announce myself on the intercom, he buzzes me in.

I take the elevator up to the 8th floor. The building is in pretty good shape—you can usually tell from the elevators. Here, they work, and they don't smell like piss. I show the badge at the keyhole. He lets me in, a tall African American male, thirty or so, a thick, well-trimmed goatee on a lean, carved face. He's got a great view from up here, facing east over the IC tracks to the lake, these big floor-to-ceiling windows inviting you to look out. From this view, you'd never know you're across the street from the southern boundary of one of the poorest and most violent slums in the city. That's Chicago, for you. Cross 47th Street heading north and half the buildings are boarded up, there are crack vials lying in the gutter, junkies skittering in the shadows. Stay south of 47th and you've got Elijah Muhammad's house, Muhammad Ali's old house, a classic Frank Lloyd Wright house, Robie, I think, and the U. of C., all part of Hyde Park, a racially mixed upper-middle-class enclave right in the middle of the ghetto. Clean streets, good schools, lots of shopping. What's the difference? It's the stupid race thing.

Powell leads me to a couch in the living room—it's a one-bedroom—and I sit facing the lake. He sits catercorner on a black leather recliner with his back to that magnificent view.

"That your favorite chair?" I ask. Got to start somewhere.

"Well, I'm not sure I would call any chair a 'favorite.'"

"I couldn't help but wonder. You got this great view here, the railroad, the lake, the boats, and your favorite chair is facing away from it . . ."

He lets himself think about that. I let him think about it.

"Well, this *is* where I sit when I'm in this room . . ."

"It sure is a great view. This was mine, I couldn't help staring out the window. Bet it costs a bit extra, having that view."

"Actually, no. If I moved out and someone else moved in, it probably would. When I first moved in it was a federal low-income housing project. I was a student, and I got in because of that. I'm no longer a student, but I've kept the place as the building transitioned to the private sector, so you could say I'm grandfathered in." He turns his head slowly, only his head, looks out the window.

"Did your favorite chair use to face the window, and you got tired of it?"

He pauses, his brow twists together a little.

"I don't mean to pry," I add.

"No, I was just thinking. No. Actually, that chair was always right there, virtually the same angle. Not always the same chair, but always the same spot."

I get the feeling I don't want this one to feel too protected. Your introverts? Your quiet types? You have to soften them up.

"Actually, to complete your 'investigation,' where I use the view is in the bedroom." He stands up, walks past me, turns a corner. I stand up and follow him. He waves me through an open door. There's a king-size bed on the left. There's another floor-to-ceiling window, with an even better view. And right in front of the window is a music stand, and behind that a white ladder-back chair.

This is where he practices. This changes the whole chair thing.

"I see," I say. I turn back toward the living room.

"What did you study," I ask, shifting gears. "Music?"

He was thinking about the chair, or the view, or something. "Excuse me?"

"I'm sorry. I was asking what you studied when you were at school. At the U. of C."

"Yes. Right. No. Psychology, not music."

"Were you going to be a therapist, a psychotherapist? Something like that?"

"No, nothing like that. I was studying cognitive psychology, how people think and reason and process information, how they acquire and utilize language. I was in a research program. I guess I thought I was going to teach, do research, something of that sort."

"Not something to help people? Not some therapy kind of thing?"

A small expression, almost a grimace, crosses the bottom of his face like a shadow. "Not to help people on an individual basis, no. Just research. We still don't know enough about how the brain works, the mind works, take your pick, epistemologically, to be very helpful to anyone, except on the most superficial of levels."

"Interesting," I say. I'm taking notes, and I use a moment to add a few words to my pad. Some people, it makes them feel important if you write it down. Makes them think it's serious. Must be working. He used a word, I can't even spell it, whatever it means.

"Well," I say, "the first time I met you, last . . . Wednesday . . . at the 1812 Club, I spoke with the members of the band, and one was the saxophone player—"

"Tenor-saxophone player." He cuts in. "Sometimes alto, but mostly tenor."

"Right, tenor-saxophone player, a Mr. Jeffrey Fahey."

I look up. His eyes show me nothing.

"I'm sorry to tell you, Mr. Powell, that Mr. Fahey was found dead this morning."

"Dead? This morning? How long had he been dead?"

"The coroner is still running some tests, but sometime last night."

He frowns. "Suicide?" he asks.

"Suicide, it's interesting you would say that. What would make you think that?"

"Mr. Fahey—Jeff—was rather self-destructive. He had a history you're probably aware of . . ."

"Yeah. All on file. But that was a long time ago—"

He looks away.

I pause, let some time run. "If you're suggesting that his problem with drugs—cocaine—was more recent than the ten-year-old bust we have on file, then maybe you better tell me what you know," I say, firmly.

He nods, shakes his head a few times. He looks up. "Can I get you anything to drink? I'm going to have a glass of water."

"Yeah, water's good," I say.

He gets up. I follow him into a tiny kitchen. It's very neat. The whole place is very neat, I notice, looking around. There's a rack over the fridge. A good single-malt Scotch—Macallan—Jack Daniel's bourbon, Tanqueray gin, Canadian Club rye whisky, bottle of red wine, bottle of white. All top-shelf brands. And all mostly full. We're having water. He gets ice out of the freezer, a jug of Poland Spring water out of the fridge, glasses out of a cabinet. He pours two, hands me one. Takes a sip, walks back to his favorite chair, sits down. I sit back down on the couch.

He takes another sip, clears his throat. "The last time I saw Jeff, he seemed to have . . . relapsed. This was not a rare occurrence, you understand. He acted . . . wild . . . out of control. Stormed off at the start of the second set, smashed his saxophone to pieces, left without it. It was, I don't know, shocking, in a way, although it wasn't surprising, if that's not too fine a distinction."

"Um-hmmm. See what you mean," I say.

"I always had this image of him as a sort of a man driving too fast on an icy road. He never learned to turn in the direction of the skid, if you see what I mean, never learned to turn much at all."

I nod, make notes.

"His playing was like that as well," he continues. "He would just go off, into his own thing . . ."

"Like a needle stuck in a groove," I finish. "Sorry," I say, "that must be pretty out-of-date."

He sits up straight, his eyes light up, he grins. He waves to a bookcase on the corner behind him where the northmost edge of the window meets the wall, and I see there are hundreds, no, thousands of records lined up there. Not cassette tapes, not CD's, but records, vinyl LP's, even what look like old 78's. I am drooling, thinking about what must be in there.

"I've transferred most of this to . . . newer media, but I still have the originals, so, yes, I take your reference. And yes, that's exactly what Jeff would get like, 'like a needle stuck in a groove.' Precisely."

I nod. I let him continue.

"When he was smashing the saxophone, that's the image that came to me, that he started it with one swing, and he could have stopped, with only minimal damage. He had made whatever point he was trying to make, but he couldn't let himself let go of it until the thing was in pieces, and I mean, in pieces. A sad thing, really."

"This was when? When he smashed his saxophone?"

"Saturday night, 10:09 P.M."

"Was this when you felt he might have . . . 'relapsed'?" I asked.

He looks down at the floor, then peers up at me. "I'm sorry to say that I've known a number of cokeheads, Detective. He was loaded. Not just a little." There is a touch of sadness in his voice, like he felt sorry for the guy. Like there was something he could have done. Seen a lot of cokeheads myself. Nothing you can do. Not a damn thing.

"So, I'm curious, why did he smash up his instrument? He was a professional player, semiprofessional anyway. Why throw it away?"

He pauses again. "I could answer you on a lot of levels, I suppose. The 'presenting issue' was that he found himself standing on the bandstand with his sax at the ready, but no mouthpiece plugged into the neck. I have no idea where it went. He was surprised by it, too, and frustrated, and took that frustration out on the instrument.

"Look," he continued, "you're going to hear that the two of us didn't get along. We didn't. I thought he might have a talent, and he was abusing that talent."

"He knew you felt this way?"

"Yes. Certainly. I tried to be positive about it, constructive, to phrase it more as a challenge. But he knew how I felt, how we all felt, for that matter."

"All of you?" I ask.

"Yes. Definitely."

"You said there were 'levels' to his unhappiness and you talked about two—his job and his playing. Anything else?"

Some people you just have to be patient, let them wrestle with it. Other people need structure. Powell is one of those.

"He drink?"

"Excuse me?" he asks.

"Well, some people with that problem, the powder, they go on to alcohol, or other things. Then there are the ones that just lose all interest in everything."

"Yes, anhedonia."

"Anhe—what was that?" I say.

"Anhedonia. 'An,' like 'anti.' 'Hedonia,' from the same

Greek root word as 'hedonism.' It's a well-known syndrome. When people, as you say, 'kick' something, and it doesn't much matter what it is—cocaine, alcohol, a lover—they often go through a period in which they cannot get pleasure from anything. Life is gray, dull, flat, uninspiring in all its aspects. That's one reason withdrawal is so difficult. Without the treasured object, life becomes lifeless."

"Huh," I say. "Have to remember that one."

Should be easy to remember, since I've been living it all these years myself.

"It's a cognitive coping strategy. You love something more than anything else, you love yourself when you have that something. Suddenly, you can't have it. So how do you stop wanting it? You stop wanting anything, turn off all desire. It dims the lack of possessing the object by dimming all joy."

"Hunh . . ." I say. "Interesting theory."

Theory my ass.

I change the topic, back to the night Fahey went crazy. Did he notice anybody strange at the club that night? Anybody the same as at the 1812 Club last week? Anybody else in the band acting funny? He tells me he didn't notice, he plays with his eyes shut, helps him hear the music better. As far as the crowd, the band, no, nothing jumps out at him.

I admire his view of the lake. I think about the better view in the other room, and the practice stand, and the chair. He plays with his eyes closed. He never sees it.

We go over some more details about the band, but there's nothing there. No agent—the piano player does all the bookings. No after-hours clubs. All of them except for him have straight jobs and have to get up in the morning. No other history with drugs from anyone in the band, except he drops some hints about some pot, but come on, nobody kills potheads.

And in a few more minutes we're done. I drain my glass of water, ask him can I use his bathroom, do my business, wash up, thank him for his time, and head for the door. He shakes my hand, genuinely enough. I notice he has already placed my empty water glass in a rack in the sink. A neat freak? I think. I look around. The place is very neat. This guy could maybe do the cleanup up on Halsted, but the murder?

Too early to be making any judgments, I think. Just gather the information, let the pattern form. Do not get out ahead of it.

CHAPTER 22
Ken Ridlin

Further Interviews
Monday, January 13

Because they are on the list, and because the list is where you start, I spend the rest of the day chasing down Professor Sidney Worrell, bassist, and Ms. Akiko Jones, percussionist. He lives south and she lives north, but it's not my gasoline.

Worrell is a professor at the U. of C. Teaches history of science, philosophy of science, like that. Has a big house in Hyde Park, near the college, half a mile south-by-southwest of Powell. He's a big man, big all over, not fat but just big, like a bear. A thick sandy beard covers his face. He's dressed casually, even for a philosopher: beat-up sneakers that used to be white, frayed khaki slacks, a blue oxford shirt, short-sleeved. He has got more hair on his forearms than I have on my whole body.

But I see right away that his guy cannot be our guy because our guy is a highly organized type and this house may be the worst mess I've ever seen. It's not dirty, not so's you would notice, but he has got stuff piled up everywhere.

Books, papers, magazines, the *Tribune,* music, records, tapes, CD's, you name it. There are floor-to-ceiling bookcases everywhere, but they're so jammed full you can't even see what they're made of. And most of the floor space is taken up with these piles. It takes him two minutes just to clear off a chair so I can sit down, moving the pile that's on it very delicately.

There's a woman buzzing around, small looking. When she scoots by, he doesn't acknowledge her; she doesn't say anything to him.

I look through the piles while he's rearranging. One pile has mostly philosophy books, but there's some art books, a chemistry textbook, and a string of comic books, of all things, thrown in. Another pile is more magazines, some architecture books and blueprints, and a few computer books. There's no logic to it that I can see.

When he moves the piles, he's very particular about where he wants them to go, and shambles around the place looking for just the right spot to put them down. Frowns, shakes his head. Places them down just so. Go figure.

The guy must be a genius, like they say he is, just to find anything.

When we finally get situated, his conversation is like he's reading me something off a page instead of talking to me. Very precise, very clear, unlike his surroundings. Every sentence is a complete sentence, and they all tie together into paragraphs.

We spend an hour going over it, starting with the background. Couple years back, Amatucci and Powell are both in one of his classes. Amatucci is in it because it was required for his major, Powell is in it just because he is interested. Takes all the tests, too. Gets an A, doesn't count. Worrell asks him about it, does he want to sign up for credit for the course after it is done. Powell says to him, "That's very thoughtful of you, but it won't be necessary. It was a very insightful course. Thank you for your time." Cool as a breeze off the lake. Following his own agenda.

Worrell is in some brass quintet in the college, and Pow-

ell shows up to play trumpet, of course. I ask Worrell what a
brass quintet was doing with a string-bass player in it. He
wasn't playing string bass with them, he says, he was playing tuba and euphonium.

"How do you spell that?" I have to ask.

"T-u-b-a," he says.

Serves me right.

He stops the interview to actually show me one, a euphonium, I mean, "a rather rare exemplar," he says, "of the
double-belled variety." It's like some little shrunken tuba
but with four valves instead of three and two horns sticking
out of it instead of one, the smaller one pointing forward
and the bigger one pointing up. The little horn looks like a
sort of midget mutant. He fiddles with the valves, gets them
working, and then plays something on it for me, some classical thing, and the guy can play the damn thing like you
wouldn't believe. It sounds about the same range as a trombone, baritone, except when you press the fourth valve,
then the sound comes out of the little bell, and it is way
higher, a countertenor. I look over, he has got an electric
bass in the corner, a cord running to some amplifier. I ask
about it. He says he plays with some rock band, too, and
string bass isn't their thing.

Neither is double-belled euphonium, I bet.

"As you may well infer," he says, "I'm a bit of a dabbler, in
music as well as in my academic endeavors. I seem to have
this predilection for blurring the obvious boundaries."

Turns out the guy has two PhD's, not one. One's in astro-
physics, the other's in philosophy. Even got an MBA, a business degree from somewhere, had "some entrepreneurial
notions early on around NASA" he puts it, "back when they
were actually doing interesting research." Couldn't stand
all the colonels. "I got on quite well with the generals, when
the colonels would let me see them, but the colonels were
decidedly second-order." Figures "a more free-form academic life" fits him better.

I bring the discussion back to Powell. Powell gets approached for this jazz band that needs a trumpet player. They also need a bass player, and he thinks of Worrell. Actually starts with them playing tuba, more old-timey style, but as the band changes he picked up the string bass, too.

He "picks up" the string bass. Jesus.

Guy's nice enough, but he scares me. Lot of horsepower there, though he keeps most of it under the surface, covered by the verbal folderol, which tempts you to dismiss him as some kind of twit. I think to myself: Do not make that mistake.

Says he wasn't aware of Fahey's cocaine problem. Wouldn't know what that might look like, unless he was doing it right in front of him. Not something he ever "dabbled" in. A brain like his, it would be like putting sugar in a Lamborghini's gas tank.

As I get up to leave, I trip over one of the piles and send it sprawling. His eyebrows get frantic, his breath runs ragged, his neck turns red. He stands with his hands on his hips and mutters that it's going to take him a while to get everything back in order.

I almost laugh out loud, but catch myself. I make my voice all serious again. "Now that you mention it, Professor, I'm a little curious. Nothing to do with the case, but, how do you keep track of all this stuff? How is it all organized?"

He looks up from the chaos at his feet to stare me in the eye. "The system is purely chronological," he says. "Everything is categorized by when I read it. I'm afraid I have a mind that works that way, sequential yet nonlinear at the same time."

I must look skeptical. He adds, "If you actually read through some of the piles, you would find that there's something of a theme to each one, however remote. And if you read through all of them, you would see a mosaic of all my little obsessions."

I believe him. Why not?

* * *

Akiko Jones lives in a small apartment up on the North Side, a little north and west of Fahey's place, and not too far from mine. Small four-story, the buzzers don't work, the lock on the main door is broken. As I check the mailboxes I watch two people push the door in and walk right up the stairs. I follow them in. The names are by apartment number, not by spelling. There's a Jones in B, and no other Joneses. Beyond the main door is a stairway leading up to the right. I open the main door, walk left, go past Apartment 1, Apartment 2, then right again, and there is a door there, no number on it. I open it, no lock, and there's a stairway leading down.

I walk down the stairs and turn right. I walk down a long straight hallway with storage lockers on both sides, closed and cinched with Master locks. I hear a faint thumping sound. Eventually there's a door, and the thumping is louder. There is a faint impression in the paint where a "B" used to be. I knock on the door. The thumping stops. A few seconds pass. I see her spy me through the peephole. I hold up the shield. Then I hear what must be a dozen bolts turning. She opens up a crack, the chain still on the door. A single woman, these days, you know.

I flash the shield again, she takes a closer look, shuts the door, unhooks the chain, removes the bar, lets me in.

She's dressed all in black. No shoes or socks. Thin black sweatpants, sleeveless black T-shirt. Her hair is also jet-black, short. The shirt is cut off just below her ribs, and her stomach is flat, muscled. Six-pack abs, just a hint of flesh to smooth the edges. Asian eyes, those folds at the corners. You could cut cheese on her cheekbones, sharp and distinct. Her complexion is a little darker than Asian, though. On her, it looks outstanding. You're not supposed to say this anymore, but she's a looker.

I scan the apartment as she relocks the door. Talk about your contrast. Unlike Worrell's, this place is naked. It's a studio, semi-separate kitchen on the left, open closet and closed bathroom door on the right. I know the type of place. Used to live in one, same layout as this. She has one of those futon things folded up on the floor next to the wall near the door. Looks like it doubles as a bed. There's a small table next to it, black lacquer, with a small lamp, a black candle, and a black digital clock. Across the room is a huge set of drums in front of a pair of tiny half-windows that face an alley. She plays facing in, unlike Powell. (As for Worrell, I get the feeling he plays anywhere he happens to be sitting when some instrument leaps into his hands.) Behind the drums is a stereo, cassette deck, CD, all stacked up, expensive-looking but small. All in black, of course. I'm picking up a theme here. I get the feeling there is something missing. I look around again, cataloging things. And it strikes me. No TV. No computer. Interesting.

The floors are wooden, with a high sheen on them. The closet is an open one, clothes hanging neatly inside. Again, mostly black, and some white. There are two baskets up on top, must be where she puts things she can't hang up, like socks and underwear and such. Walls are a stark white, no pictures or portraits or calendars or anything. Except that one wall, behind the bed, is covered with maps, all kinds of maps, like a collage type of thing. Mostly Chicago, but some L.A., a piece of San Francisco, a slice of Boston. Glued up or taped up or something, they cover the whole wall, the only splash of color in the place. No drapes, just thin white blinds covering the ground-level half-windows. And that's it.

She offers me tea and I'm glad of it. It's two blocks from where I put the unit to this place and I can still feel the late afternoon wind up the back of my neck. She gets down a black canister, puts the water on. Scoops out three spoonfuls of loose tea into one of those French coffee things that lets the beans and the water just mix together, no filter. No reason it wouldn't work for tea, I guess. When she reaches up to put the canister away, the shirt stretches away from her, and I catch sight of her strong left obliques and the lower edge of her left breast.

We go back to the main room while we wait for the water to boil.

Now the question. Where to sit down. She gets the stool from behind the drum set, brings it over next to the futon, asks where I'd like to sit. Futon's a little low. I'm worried I might not be able to get up. I take the stool. She lowers herself onto the futon, legs crossed, back straight. Those washboard abs are not just for show.

We start with background, "Where are you from, Ms. Jones?" and like that. Turns out her father's African American, her mother Japanese, met while he was stationed there in the army. She's the only child. "They were . . . only married a short while," she says. Moved to Chicago, South Side, they split, she stayed with her mother, hasn't seen her father in years, hasn't seen her mother in years either, though she calls on her birthday and Mother's Day and such. Doesn't sound like she dislikes either one of them, just doesn't need them. Gets me thinking. I look around, can't see photographs of either of them. Of anybody, it comes to that.

She got halfway to a degree in history at Baldwin-Wallace College in Ohio, then got into the music scene and dropped out. Knew right away she wanted to play drums—"Like, my DNA has that rhythm gene going on," she says. Plays in three different bands—two local rock bands I've never heard of and the jazz group. Answered an ad in the *Reader,* been with them almost two years. "It's good discipline," she says, "jazz. The rhythm is, like, more of a suggestion. It makes you listen different." Interesting. "Plus I had never used brushes before. The first time Sidney gave me a pair, you know, he had to show me how to play them."

Also works as a martial arts instructor in a dojo a couple blocks away. I ask how she got into that. "I guess I just have that Japanese kung-fu thing happening," she says. Kung-fu is Chinese, but I don't say it.

She is playing me. I keep my big dumb cop look on my face all the same.

We talk about Fahey. She takes the news of his death quietly. No crying, no wailing, just a little frown. I ask, did she know he had a problem? The drugs?

"Well, yeah, actually," she says.

"Since when, if I might ask."

"Well, he came up to me a couple of months ago during a break, said he had some friends coming to town, and asked me if I knew where he could 'score some,' quotation marks."

I let her continue, not taking notes. There are times you have to put away the pen.

"I didn't think he had any 'friends coming into town,' and I really doubted he'd go that far out of his way for them, if he did. I mean, it *is* still illegal, right?"

A glimmer as she says this. She is making a little joke, testing me, too.

"Not my department, but, far as I know, yeah, it still is," I say.

"I told him, like, no, I didn't know anybody like that, sorry, but he might try some of the clubs, the rock clubs. Truth is, I *do* know people like that. I'm not into it myself, but I didn't want to get in the middle of it with him."

"Why is that? I mean, aside from it being illegal," I ask, adding, "which again, is not my department."

"I didn't want to owe Jeff anything, and I didn't want him to owe me anything. That's a policy of mine, in general, but with Jeff, in particular."

"Why him in particular?" I ask.

She's been talking to me without looking at me. Now she brings her dark eyes up. "There was an evil spirit about the guy. Bad mojo. Bad karma. Bad vibes. Foul humours, you know?"

Translating for the old fart. "Foul humours" is from Shakespeare's day. A little before even my time.

"You're going to ask 'Is there anything particular you could point to that gave you that impression, Ms. Jones?' and I'm going to say, 'No.' It was just something about the way he was. Very self-centered. I mean, we were in this band, he was one of the featured soloists, but it was never enough. Paul would take four choruses, Jeff would have to take six. Paul would try to mix up the repertoire to add things he thought Jeff would like, like Charlie Parker's "Cherokee" and shit? Coltrane, Horace Silver, Monk, you know? But for Jeff, it wasn't enough. That's all he wanted to play. But what the band is about, it's like the whole history of that music. He came into it late, when it already was what it was, and expected everyone to cater to him, like it was his band. He was always late, he was always a little shit to everyone, he was always overdoing it. I'm sure he had a very small dick."

That's one part we never did locate, so I can't comment. This is the most she's said since we sat down. I hear the water start to boil. She starts to rise.

"Before you get that," I say, leaning forward. "He was a featured player, you played accompaniment. He played solos, and abused the, uh, privilege, and you had to learn to use brushes and stay in the background. Was there something personal there . . . ?"

The kettle is singing loudly. She wants to get up and get it, but forces herself to look at me, then look down, almost demurely. "That's very perceptive. Maybe you're right. Maybe there was some chord he struck in me that I didn't like."

She is squatting on the futon, her legs crossed, and she somehow stands up without uncrossing her legs, balancing on the outer edges of her feet until she rises to her full height. I think, How does she *do* that? She steps into the kitchenette to get the tea, and I creak off of the stool and follow her.

She moves the pot off the burner, turns the flame off, pours the water into the carafe where the leaves are, puts the lid on it. "It's better if we let this sit for a minute," she says.

She turns, opens the fridge, looks in. From my angle I

can see in, too. It's just about empty. There's two jugs of water, one of them half-empty, a small box of blueberries, a half-a-head of celery. In the door is some olive oil. No mustard, no ketchup, no mayo. No meat, no eggs, no cheese, no milk.

She turns, sees me looking. "You're asking yourself, 'What the hell does she eat?', right?"

I don't say anything but she can tell she's right. "Vinnie is always busting my ass about it. He calls me an 'airitarian.'"

"An airitarian?" I ask.

"You know," she says. "Like a vegetarian lives on vegetables, a fruitarian lives on fruit, an airitarian lives on air." She shakes her head. "Food just . . . food just doesn't do it for me, you know?"

"Well," I say. "I'm not a big eater myself—"

"I bet you used to be," she says.

I look at her. "Why would you say that?"

She looks me up and down, a cool appraising look. "You are a big American dude. What are you, six-four?"

"Well, close to that, about six-three or—"

"You look like you used to be even bigger. Not taller, of course, just bigger. Your clothes are hanging off you, even your skin . . ."

"I had the clothes altered. I'll have to tell that to the lady who did them. How can you tell?"

She gives that look again, no eye contact. "Must be Asian thing," she says, doing an accent. "We all supposed to be good at raundry," she says.

"That's Chinese, not Japanese."

She turns, grabs the plunger on top of the carafe, slowly pushes it down, a little at a time, very steadily. I watch, wait, enjoy the ritual.

She reaches up to a shelf, there's those strong obliques again, pulls down two mugs. Black, what else. Turns back to me. "I think I might have some honey somewhere around here, or a lemon, if I—"

"That's OK," I say. "Just black is good."

She nods, turns, fills both mugs, hands me one. We head back to the main room. I sit on the stool again, take a sip of the tea. It's strong, and good. I look for someplace to put the mug, set it on the floor between my feet. She lowers herself back into a cross-legged position, the tea in her lap all the way. Doesn't spill a drop. Jesus.

"Let's shift gears. Last Thursday at the 1812 Club, the guy who got shot, Mr. Roger Tremblay. You ever see him before?"

"No, never."

"He ever sit in with the band before that?"

"No, never."

"What was your reaction?"

"My reaction?" she asks. "Like, I freaked. I mean, it was so sudden, so out of place." She looks down, then looks up at me.

"Ms. Jones, this has all the signs of a mob hit, a mob hit gone wrong. You have any idea why anyone would want to kill anyone in the band? Any ideas at all?"

She looks away like she's thinking but she's already decided to say No. Then she says it.

"No."

Some people you have to circle around them gently. Some people you go right at it. Do I know which one she is? I don't.

"For example, is there any reason anybody would want to kill *you*, Ms. Jones?"

"No." It is a little too quick. I let her have some room.

"I mean, I'm just a drummer, a not-so-great drummer in a not-so-great band. Why would someone want to kill *me?*"

Now she is asking me the question.

She pauses, nods. "Like I said, I live a very quiet life, you know? Music, working out, more music, more working out. It's all I really do."

We sit in silence for a moment, sipping our tea. She has her eyes down, hidden from me. Oh, I think, we all have our little secrets. Most of them are just that, little secrets, ordinary, meaningless, of no consequence.

But I don't see any connection. That's something you learn: don't get too far ahead of the facts, don't start following your nose because chances are you might be smelling your own breath, nothing more. After all, it's the closest thing you can smell, and you're too used to it to notice it.

She drains the last dregs of her tea, gets up, asks me if I want any more. I stretch my stiff legs, stand up, say thanks but no thanks, and ask can I use her bathroom. She gestures to a door next to the closet. I head over as she walks to the little kitchenette.

After I close the door and flip the seat up, I notice that the bathroom is as empty as the rest of the apartment. The towels are white, not black, and the shower curtain is clear plastic. Interesting. So private, so closed off, yet when she's naked it's all right there to see.

I piss in the toilet, and carefully reach over to open the medicine cabinet. One small glass. A toothbrush, a tube of toothpaste, a hairbrush, all standing up inside it. Not a single aspirin, not a measly roll of Tums, no makeup, no moisturizer, no diaphragm or pills or rubbers. No creams, no emollients. Nothing else. What the hell kind of female keeps an empty medicine cabinet? What kind of person, it comes to that? Jesus.

I finish up and flush, and use the sound to mask closing the cabinet. I turn on the water in the sink and peer behind the shower curtain. Again, nothing. Soap, shampoo, conditioner, a disposable razor, that's it. This lady could pack for a weekend with nothing but a handbag, which reminds me, I haven't seen one of those either.

I run my hands quickly under the water, shake it off, and rub my hands on a hand towel.

When I come out, I grab my coat, hand her my card, and tell her to call me if anything comes up, if anything comes to her, anything at all. She nods. "Thanks for your time, Ms. Jones," I say. She nods again, a small figure dressed in black, coiled around her cup, and unlocks the door, opens it, and lets me out.

Outside the door I mime a few steps softly fading away, and stand near the doorframe. I hear all the locks, snapping closed. I count to three minutes. I wait for the sound of drums, but it doesn't come.

CHAPTER 23
Vinnie Amatucci

At the 1812 Club
Wednesday, January 15

After my third straight day of hauling the cab all over creation, I dropped it off, got my own car, headed to Hyde Park, washed up, changed, headed back to the car and drove uptown. A strange mood had settled over me. Like every block that got me closer to the 1812 felt like the temperature dropped five degrees. Like every block the wind speed increased five knots. Like every block the snow got five inches deeper. There were bright lights flashing in my rearview mirror. I checked the speedometer. I was driving fifteen fucking miles an hour.

Vince, I said to myself, either you are going to do this or you are not going to do this. You have to choose, one or the other. You can't fade into some Zeno's-paradox deal here, going slower and slower until it becomes an infinite regress.

Fuck it. It was too late to go anywhere else, anyway. And as soon as I thought this, there it was, up on the right. I pulled around the corner and parked in a space halfway up the block.

The place was packed. Every table was full, most with extra chairs pulled up, every barstool was taken, people were standing between the bar and the tables. There were even a couple of guys standing in the back, between the In kitchen door and the Out kitchen door. I recognized one of them, and did a double take; it was Horace Starr, fucking Horace Starr, holding a Miller longneck instead of his johnson: Whoa, progress.

I looked up on the stand and Akiko was already set up, already ready. I tried to wave to her, but I was stuck in the crowd, which was pushing me back through the door. I felt like I was being sucked under by a tidal wave, going down for the third time, when someone tapped me on the shoulder. I turned to look and it was Sidney.

"Ride my wake as I clear a path through the rabble, young Vincent," he said, in his jolly way. He picked his string bass up over his head, shouted "Make way! Coming through!" and lowered it to lance-height, pointing straight ahead. I grabbed the foot peg on the bottom, and we quick-timed it through the crowd and up to the stand.

Sidney jumped up, bowed to Akiko, and she returned it. I was still standing in what used to be the pit, floor level. I waved and she waved back.

"Has anyone seen Jeff?" I asked, looking around.

She came out from around the drums, he sat down at the bandstand, facing me.

"Were you working late on Monday?" he asked.

I nodded my head.

"Tuesday, too?"

"Yeah, trying to get ahead so I can take off for the weekend. And?"

They looked at each other.

"Jeff's dead," she said. "Somebody killed him at his apartment, they think Sunday night."

Sidney pulled on my sleeve, something a four-year-old

would do. "The detective, Ridlin, he never caught up with you?" he asked.

"Detective?"

"Paul didn't call you?" Sidney asked.

"I don't know. I was out, and I don't know if the message machine was on or off; I haven't checked since . . . Sunday, I think." I looked at the two of them. "Do they know who killed him? Why he was killed?"

"They don't have much to go on, it seems," Sidney said. "It's all rather mysterious."

We all stood around for a bit, letting the silence sink in. There was a strange feeling in the pit of my stomach I couldn't identify.

"What's with the crowd?" I asked. "Do they know it's only *us*?"

"So I can infer that you haven't read a paper since Sunday, either," Sidney said.

I shook my head, No.

"We've become something of a cause célèbre, my young friend," he said.

"Fucking *Tribune*," Akiko growled.

"My dear, imagine the impact on your self-esteem if the story had been broken by the 'Fucking' *Sun Times*, instead. Do be grateful for small but significant favors."

"And they mentioned that we were going to be back here tonight?" I ventured.

"Mentioned?" Akiko. "*Mentioned?* I'm surprised they're not arresting everyone who *isn't* here. They've made it into a 'civic duty' to support us in our time of need."

Just then a wave of quiet swept through the crowd, and the bodies parted at the door. The crowd separated and there she was, the brunette in the red dress, from the Airport Marriott, gliding into the room. She looked just the same, except she wasn't wearing the red dress. This one was yellow, the color of a pale glowing sun drawn by a four-year-old. It draped over her in some places and it fit her tightly in others, and she wore it like her skin. She slinked straight to the corner of the bar. A man, maybe thirty-five-ish, six-two and 250, with a round face and a thin brownish mustache and straggly mousy hair that desperately needed to take a meeting with Mr. Shampoo, saw her coming, ceremoniously offered his seat to her, and stood aside, his mouth open to the wind. She batted her eyes in thanks, then reached out for his arm as he helped her onto the stool. He was admirably steady, and remained fixed there until she settled herself, left leg crossed over right. The she patted his arm, said something quietly to him, and he took two paces back. A guy who must have been a friend of his, a shorter guy with a goatee and a receding hairline, grabbed him by the arm, then slowly wheeled him to the left and ushered him down the bar, people patting him on the back as he walked by.

As I watched them go, I caught movement beside me, and Paul was there, with Jack Landreau in tow, still carrying that ugly case. Paul looked serious, shook hands all around, and when he came to me, said, "You heard about Jeff? Man . . ."

"Just now."

"What? You heard just now? For the first time?"

I nodded. He took my hand again, then pulled me close for a hug.

When we broke it, I locked onto him, and said, "What're you gonna do, right?"

"Right," he said.

I turned and pointed to Landreau. "I thought he'd be out of town by now. He didn't seem to want to stay. What's the story?"

"I called him Monday night, after the police came to see me. He took a cab down to Forty-seventh, and we stayed and talked, played a little bit. Vince, the guy has played everywhere, you know what I'm saying? With everybody! Anyway, I told him we could get him some work, and he decided to take the opportunity."

"Is he still staying at the Marriott?" I asked.

"No, we moved him out of there on Tuesday. He's staying at Rolando's. You remember Rolando?"

"Rolando Fitzgerald, the guitar player?" I asked. "Sure, how could I forget?" Rolando had played with us for maybe a month, early on, back in the beginning. He was just money, a beautiful player—way too good for us then, and he'd probably be just a little too good for us even now, although, to give him credit, he never acted that way, not one little bit. "How are they hitting it off?"

"Jack called me this morning, begging me to come pick him up. Rolando kept him up playing and listening until dawn."

That was Rolando all the way, a man whose enthusiasms were all-consuming.

We were interrupted by Louie, the owner, who pointed at his watch.

"How's the piano?" Paul asked. "Do we need to tune up?" I slung my coat off my shoulders and draped it on the bench. I looked at the piano and remembered. Roger Something had had warm blood pumping through his veins and had spilled most of it on that piano. A cold wind stroked my neck and I shivered, involuntarily. I forced myself to look at it.

It was a different piano entirely, a Baldwin still, but a different model—they must have traded it in—and it was much better. Louie had put a new rug over the riser, a plush maroon, how ironic, and the window looked different somehow, double-paned? I reached out and played a simple B-flat-major chord, then some octaves.

Not bad. Not bad at all.

"Close enough for Indigenous African American Music," I said.

I settled in on the bench, and reached over to activate the sound system. I got my Uher and plugged it in, got a clean tape out of my pocket and put a minute of leader on the front of it, all the while tapping the B-flat so everyone else could get set. Sidney took a while, Paul was ready at the go, and Jack blew at his feet so quietly I couldn't tell if he was in tune or not.

I looked out at the crowd. Yellow Dress was still there, smoking a cigarette, sipping a martini.

I turned to Paul. He leaned in, and motioned the rest of us in as well. "No set list tonight, given the circumstances. We'll just make it up as we go. Start with 'A Closer Walk'?" He turned to Jack, said maybe five words in his ear, then counted us off and we were into it.

"Just a Closer Walk With Thee" is an old spiritual. We start it slow, like a funeral dirge, and play a chorus or two that way, then kick it up to an andante tempo and let it swing. Jack picked right up on the harmony thing with the slow dirge at the start, playing behind Paul, and we made the transition to the up-tempo without a hitch. And it was as if we hadn't stopped playing since Saturday night, we were still in that massive groove. After a group chorus, it was solos. Sidney took a beautiful one, a scant two choruses, but it was just right, like an appetizer that leaves you wanting more. Paul and Jack traded fours again like long-lost brothers, each one going right where the other one led him, then they handed it off to me. I took two quick and interesting choruses, and slid it back to Jack.

Who played a song. I don't know how else to put it. He improvised an entire melody that just happened to be based on the same changes as "Just A Closer Walk With Thee," and it just came out of his horn, straight, simple, and just there. Paul had been comping along, little blues riffs underneath, and he pulled his trumpet away from his lips and listened.

The second chorus, he improvised around this new melody, and the third chorus he twisted an improvisation around the improvisation, I don't know how, but it was understated and right. He used the same sign Paul uses to signal the last chorus, then in the last eight bars, cakewalked us into the slowdown back to the dirge, mournful and slow, and we were out.

The crowd loved it, and gave us a nice round of applause. Paul introduced everyone. I thought he might say something about Jeff—there was a pause there at the start—but he kept it simple and got through it. From there, we went into "Walkin' My Baby Back Home," then into "Singin' the Blues," an old Bix favorite, and it was just swinging. I hadn't realized how much smoother, how much tighter we could sound.

This guy Jack was right there, every measure, and his lyrical touch opened doors we had walked right by in the past. The whole two-trumpets thing was a little novel, to say the least, but the way he and Paul were playing together, it didn't really matter; they could have been playing goddamned pennywhistles.

Paul reached into his case and pulled out some sheet music—melody and chords for some song, "Spreading Joy." "Can you read this OK, Vince?" he asked.

"Gee, Paul, I really don't know."

Yeah, this is one of our little jokes. I used to take lessons as a kid, once a week, with a dweeby guy with nasty breath who came to the apartment on Thursdays—Mr. Colonna. And he would have me play the first four or eight bars of each exercise I was supposed to practice on my own, and then send me on my way. Of course, I wouldn't practice once; instead, I'd be out messing around. And when the next lesson came along, I'd just pick up the book and sight-read my way through it, seeing it for the first time. Fooled the poor guy for over a year. So my problem isn't can I sight-read, it's what to do when there's nothing in front of me.

This one was in F. The sheet was in Paul's typical geometric notation, and after looking through four bars I knew I had heard it, some Sidney Bechet two-soprano-saxes number, no doubt transcribed from something in Paul's estimable collection. Our Sidney—Worrell, not Bechet—saw his copy, set down his bass, held up his hands, ran outside—no coat, no hat; I don't think he owns one of either—and came running back twenty seconds later with this weird horn, a crazy-looking thing with two bells and four valves.

He flicked the valves a few times, blew hot air into the mouthpiece, turned to me, and played a B-flat. I played one back, and he was on the money. He turned and wedged his big bear body in between Paul and Jack. Jack gave Paul a look, like "Why not?" And we were off.

The song is basically this running passage going up and up and up, and then down and down in stages, with three horns playing in harmony through the whole run. Jack played the lead, Paul played a soprano voice a third on top of him, and Sidney played like a countertenor thing underneath them, until they got to the sustains, when he did something to switch the horn and went to a walking bass line, like a trombone. This went back and forth and round and round, chorus after chorus: simply magical. I was comping along merrily. Akiko was kicking the bass drum like it had offended her, keeping an almost military time on the snare. Toward the end, they got into this thing imitating Sidney Bechet's vibrato, which was just as wide as could be without fracturing, and for a while they all got it, perfectly in sync, and then we wrapped up with one glorious chorus, couldn't stop, put a coda on top of that, and a quick call-and-response between Paul and Frank, topped by Sidney all over that funky horn, and we were out.

The crowd went nuts, and Paul reintroduced the band and I segued into "Days of Wine and Roses" as he did, and all of a sudden there was this cop, a motorcycle cop, with the black boots and the leather jacket and the helmet pulled down low over his sunglasses, leaning over between the doorway and me, whispering to me and asking me if my car was license plate VLP-173. I said, "Yeah," and he said, "Follow me, there's a problem."

So I did.

And there was.

CHAPTER 24
Vinnie Amatucci

Outside the 1812 Club
Wednesday, January 15

The motorcycle cop turned left coming out of the door, away from the window. He twisted around inside his jacket, like he was digging in there for something. A few steps later he was hustling along. The wind was in our faces, snow was falling in fat flakes, and I was doing all I could just to keep up. All I could see of him was his back, leading the way. We got to the corner, turned left, walked up maybe fifty yards, and there was my car.

The driver's-side door was wide open, so I went over to it. There was a man in the passenger seat and he was holding a gun. The man was short, but the gun was long, and it dangled at a precarious angle from his right hand. Suddenly there was another man behind me, taller, wedging me toward the door. "Step in and sit down," said the one with the gun.

"What is this all—" I started to say, before the one behind me punched me in the right kidney. I doubled over in pain.

As I bent over, I could see the motorcycle cop just keep on walking down the block, and around a corner to the left, gone. What the fuck?

"All right, all right, you make a very persuasive argument," I said. The one behind me guided me into the driver's seat, but left the door open so he could crowd in and block me. The guy behind me was dressed in a nondescript manner, dirty chinos and boots and a ratty overcoat, a black watch cap on his head. The one in the car was dressed in a navy cashmere topcoat and a gold silk scarf and a bowler hat. He seemed to have tuxedo pants on under the topcoat; I could see the stripe. He was smoking a cigarette with one hand while he played with the gun with the other.

He said, "Place your hands where I can see them, please. One on top of the steering wheel, the other one on the roof of the car."

This seemed to be a somewhat odd arrangement. I mean, why not both hands on the steering wheel, or both hands on the doorjamb, or both hands on the dashboard or wherever? I was going to ask for some clarification, but he was waving the gun around in little figure eights a bit unsteadily, so I complied.

"All right," said the one with the gun, "let us proceed. We need you to tell us all you know about who—"

But he never got to finish the question, because right then the one outside the car shut the car door on my left hand, just reared back and slammed it, hard.

"We need fucking answers," the Big Guy said, "so don't fuck around with us," he growled. I didn't really hear him clearly because I was busy trying to scream. My mouth was in a big O and air was whistling out of it. There was no sound. But it was early yet.

"Excuse me, but what precisely are you doing?" the one with the gun asked, leaning forward and around me. "I'm in the middle of asking him the question, the very first question, and you—what, may I ask, are you doing?"

"This is just to show you we're not going to put up with any bullshit, here. We need fucking answers and we're fucking gonna get them, you got me?" the Big Guy said to me.

Pain had taken away my voice. I was holding my left hand up and away from me, too scared to even look at it. It was throbbing. I considered moving my fingers, but was too afraid to try.

"Well, now, there's the pitfall with your methodology right there," the Little Guy said to the Big Guy behind me. "Now he can't even talk because you went and broke his hand before I even asked him the first question. Do you see this? Are you paying attention? All he can do is nod. Do you have any idea how hard it is to get information from somebody when all he can do is nod? Do you? Do you? Are we supposed to just randomly ask every name we can think of and watch him nod yes or no? Does this sound professional to you? Does it sound efficient?" He turned to me and said, "The things I have to put up with. You wouldn't believe . . ."

He turned to the Big Guy. "Are you getting any of this? Is any of this sinking in?"

"I guess so," he replied.

"He guesses so," the one with the gun said to me. "He guesses so. I mean, it should be obvious to anyone, even a four-year-old. The thing with the hand is supposed to be a *threat*—'Tell us what you know or we'll break your hand'— but he can't even wait for the first question. That's not how you use a threat. I mean," he said, leaning around me so the Big Guy could see he was now talking to him, "I mean, what are we supposed to do now, threaten to break his hand *again?* Is that it? Is that how it's supposed to work?" he asked, glaring now.

"I was just," the taller guy said, "I was just trying to emphasize the seriousness of the situation, that's all."

" 'Emphasize the seriousness of the situation,' he says," talking to me. "Can't he understand that the time to do that, if there even *is* a time to do that, is after the victim—that would be *you*—fails to *see* the seriousness of the situation, not before he even knows what the situation *is?* I mean, am I right or am I *right?*"

It seemed as if he expected me to nod. I nodded.

"Of course I'm right. Even," he leaned around me again, talking to the taller man, "even the victim here knows that. I mean, Jesus H. Christ, even the *victim* knows that."

I started to find my voice. I groaned.

"All right, that's enough of that," he said, pointing the gun back in my direction. "I'm beginning to think I liked you better when you were mute with pain."

I bit down on my tongue, trying to suppress another groan.

He turned in his seat until he was facing me. The gun was hanging off his fingertip, and he had gone back to waving it around. I was worried it was going to go off and blow both of us up unless he got control of it.

"No nodding now, and no moaning, we need real answers. Are you ready?"

"Yes," I said.

"All right, then, who is it?"

"Who is it? I don't know what you mean. I mean, who is *what?*"

"You know what we mean, who is it, who's the one?"

"Who's the one?"

"Yes, who's the one? Who's the one she's with? Who is it?"

"Who's the—she *who?*" I asked. Realizing how incoherent it was, I added, "I'm really trying to answer your question, but I don't know who you mean. The anaphoric reference was ambiguous. Just tell me who you mean and what you want to know, and I'll—"

The little guy with the gun made a motion at the taller one, like a twitch of his head. Nothing happened. The taller one stood there not comprehending. The little one made the motion again, more exaggerated this time. The taller one frowned. The little one with the gun made the same twitch, very slowly, and the taller one threw his head back in an epiphany—ah-HA!

And slammed the door on my hand again.

I screamed. With this second slam I had found my voice again.

The little one with the gun brought its muzzle up to my right ear and cocked it, quite distinctly. "That will be enough of that," he said. I stopped screaming, and started slowly waving my hand up and down as I bounced in my seat.

The little guy with the gun turned to the bigger one. "We went over this, didn't we? We went over this yesterday, and we went over it today, and I could have sworn you had it down, I—"

"What?" the taller one said. "That's not what you wanted? I mean, it was obvious, the guy was not understanding the seriousness of the situation, just like you said yourself, he—"

"No! Like *you* said. *I* didn't say it, *you* said it. I *hate* when you do that, quoting something you said as if it's something I said, when *I* didn't say it at all. He wasn't questioning the seriousness of the situation, he wasn't sure what the situation *was*. The evident pain from the first incident clearly distracted him, and he—"

"What?" asked the taller guy. "That wasn't what you wanted? What was wrong?"

"I was giving you the signal to get his attention a little bit, to slap him, or—"

"Whoa. Stop right there. There is *no* signal for me to 'slap him or something' because I do not go around 'slapping people or something,' that's not what I do. Guys who go around 'slapping people' are—"

"All right, all right, slap, hit, punch, what is the difference? I just wanted—"

"It's a big difference. I do *not* slap people. 'Slapping' is not something—"

"All right! All right! I got it. Punch. Hit. Smack. Is that better? Hmmm?"

He turned to me. "All right, back to you. We know she's been coming to see your little group here, and we know she's been seeing someone in your little group here, and we need to know, and, believe me, we *are* on a 'need-to-know basis' here, we need to know who it is. That she's seeing."

I tried to take this all in. I turned to the taller one. "Please don't get me wrong. I fully understand the seriousness of the situation. I'll tell you anything you want to know, trust me. I'm just a little unsure of what he's asking me. So don't hit me, don't break my hand again, I'm trying, here." I turned to the little one with the gun, trying to get my breath.

He looked at me and then looked around me to the bigger one. "You see? You see this? He's comprehending the seriousness of the situation, as *you* put it, not as I put it. Sometimes all it takes is some solid questioning to clear up any misunderstandings. It doesn't always take breaking their hands. It's like I was telling you the other day, it's just like what I'm *always* telling you, *every single time—*"

"Stop it! Fuck you! Shut up!" The taller one screamed, then leaned right across me and shot the shorter guy right in the middle of the forehead. The Little Guy slumped back in his seat, a big dollop of blood rolled down his forehead and between his eyes and down the side of his nose, and that was it, he was dead. I froze solid. I had the strange thought, "thank God this is my car and not the Fat Man's cab."

The taller one started hopping around outside the car, waving the gun, looking up and down the street.

"Look," I said to him, trying to make my voice as calm as possible. "I don't know who you are. I didn't even see your face, right? And I'm looking away from you even now, right?" I let this sink in.

"I can't identify you, I don't *want* to identify you. There's no sense in making this any worse than it already is. Please don't shoot me, I'm asking you, you have no reason to, it won't help me understand the seriousness of the situation,

I think I already understand the seriousness of the situation . . ."

At that point I forced myself to shut up, and what I heard was my heartbeat, up around 190, pounding in my ears, and nothing else. I edged a look to my left, and saw he was running back up the road as fast as he could go, and had already covered half a block, which was pretty impressive, considering the ice and the slush.

I looked at my left hand and almost gagged. Fingers were pointing where fingers are not supposed to point. There was a crease across the back of my hand that hadn't been there five minutes ago, and it was in the wrong direction. I held my left hand up while I patted my pockets with my right hand, looking for the keys. I found the ring, isolated the car key, slipped it in the ignition, turned it to Accessories, turned on the lights and the emergency flashers and leaned forward onto the horn. And that's all I remember because at that point I let go and passed out.

CHAPTER 25
Ken Ridlin

Cook County General Hospital
Thursday, January 16

It is three o'clock in the morning. I have been talking to
Amatucci for half an hour after waiting here at Cook County
General for three. His story is all fouled up. Not like he is lying. I don't think he is lying. But the situation he is describing is all fouled up. Fouled up and getting worse.

Lieutenant Ali pokes his head in. I point at my watch and
hold up one finger. A minute later I head out of the room.
We walk down the hall to the waiting room and sit on two
spring-strung vinyl-covered chairs. There's no one there but
us. He wrestles his coat off, rubs his eyes. He looks terrible.
His dark skin has a gray pallor. His brown eyes are bloodshot.

I remember hearing about him, that he is a wild-ass, back
in the day. Runs with the Muslims' security squad, busts a lot
of heads. Then he leaves town, comes back, takes back his
former first name, and joins the force. Go figure.

"Thanks for the call," he says. "I asked to be in the loop and you reached out. I appreciate that. What have you got?"

"We have the outline of our story," I say. See, cops know, there's always a story. "And it sounds like a messy one."

I pat my pockets like I am looking for a smoke. I don't smoke anymore. He sits back. I sit back. I pull out my notepad and start to spin it out.

"Amatucci is just finishing the first set inside when this motorcycle cop pokes his head in, says to follow him, there's a problem with his car."

I pause. He arches one eyebrow, the left one.

"A motorcycle cop? In the middle of a snowstorm in the middle of the winter?"

"Yeah, I know, I know. Wearing sunglasses, even. At night."

He squeezes his eyes together, shakes his head, sits back.

"Amatucci didn't get much of a look at him, except his uniform, which was a real one, far as we can tell, and his back, which he says . . ."

I flip open my pad.

"He says he saw his back so clearly he could pick it out of a lineup of thousands."

"A lineup of thousands of backs," he repeats.

I nod.

"And there was no problem with his car?" he concludes.

"Sure there was. There was a little guy sitting inside it with a gun. And a taller guy coming up behind him. They interrogated him, if that's the word for it."

"What do you mean?" he asks.

I think about how to put it.

"Good help is hard to find . . ."

He nods, waits.

"They start this interrogation by slamming the car door on his hand."

"His hand? Man . . . He's the piano player, right? Which hand?"

"Left hand. They had him place his right hand on the steering wheel and his left on the doorjamb, like he was straphanging . . ." I say, pantomiming.

He nods his head. "How bad is his hand fucked up?"

"Seven or eight broken bones, some dislocations they had to pop back in, a few splinters they removed. Pins, they put some pins in. Don't think there's any nerve damage, far as they can tell. But they're not saying, you know how it is."

"Well, it's only his left hand—"

"That's the thing," I say. "He is *known* for his left hand."

I let this sink in.

"Ah, Jesus," he says.

Are Muslims supposed to say "Ah, Jesus"? Don't they say "Ah, Mohammed," or "Ah, Allah," or something?

"Anyway," I continue, "Amatucci is frozen there in pain and the two interrogators start arguing back and forth. The taller guy outside reaches around Amatucci and pops the little guy one in the forehead, nine millimeter, then runs away down the street."

"Good help *is* hard to find," he says. "Who are these losers?"

"The dead vic was Charles W. Cantrowicz, a.k.a. Charley Canty, Sir Charles, Little C, Canty the Dandy. He's a known associate, not made. The taller one we think might be a guy named Santo DiUllio, formerly of New Jersey. Amatucci didn't get a good look at him, tried *not* to get a good look at him, in fact. Might have saved his life. But Canty and DiUllio were a team, small-time B&Es. Did some time together in Joliet. We've got an APB out on him."

"Amateur hour," he mutters.

"Our institutions are crumbling," I say. "If you can't count on the Mafia to do things right, who can you trust?"

He nods his head.

"The actual interrogation, what there is of it, is worse. They keep asking 'Who is it?' and "Who is she with?' "

" 'Who is it?''Who is she with?' " he repeats. "Who the fuck is the 'she'?"

"That's the question, all right. Amatucci was spotted by an off-duty who called in the EMTs—and I got called as well, and by the time we got back to the club most of the patrons had left. But we did get one description of a woman. She was there, watching the band."

I turn my head, look at him. He looks back. He is tired.

"There's nothing that ties her to the band . . . yet. We're trying to get a sketch, circle back to the other places they play. See if she's been seen there."

He nods. Waits. Finally asks, "One particular woman? Help me out here, Ken."

I flip open the pad.

"Woman comes in, two minutes before they start, walks directly to the front corner bar stool, commandeers it, and locks in on the band for every note in the first set. Doesn't take her eyes off them for a second. The break comes, around nine forty-five, drags on a little, they're getting fidgety. Then the cornet player talks to the trumpet player, puts down the cornet—"

"Wait a minute. I don't remember a cornet player in the last incident report, and I would remember because I don't know what the hell a cornet is."

"Same as a trumpet," I say, "but shorter with a rounder tone."

I immediately regret the "rounder tone" part. I don't want to lead him in certain directions.

"The cornet player is new, he sat in with them on Saturday when Fahey was last seen in public—"

I have put this wrong.

"I don't have any reason to mean it that way . . ." I say.

He waves it off.

"Anyway, he showed up again tonight, last night, and played cornet with them the first set. Crowd was impressed, what I hear."

He is sitting hunched over, letting me tell it.

"So after Amatucci doesn't come back, they're out a piano player—"

"Trumpet, cornet, bass, and drums might be a bit thin,
unless they were playing some modern shit—" he deci-
phers. I'm surprised—he knows the music, a little.

"They don't really play that much modern, uh, stuff, from
what we understand. Anyway, the cornet player sets down
his cornet, sits down at the piano, and off they go."

He looks around. He notices I'm waiting. "Yeah? And?"

"Turns out he was even better on the piano than on the
cornet, and the people who our people talked to loved him
on the cornet."

The lieutenant sits up, yawns, looks at me, "And the
name, rank, and serial number of this prodigy would
be . . . ?"

"Landreau. Jack Landreau. Nothing turns up so far in the
system. I haven't had a sit-down with him yet."

I let that hang there. I'm trying to tell him something
without telling him anything.

"It gets worse," I say. "The woman . . ."

"The 'Who's she with?' woman?"

I shrug.

"Maybe. They're getting set up for the second set, her cell
phone rings. She picks it up, listens for five seconds, drops
a twenty on the bar, and leaves without her change, the
back way. The time is 10:38."

I seek his eyes.

"The woman," I say. I look at him. "How long have I been
doing this, asking what someone looks like . . . ?" I ask,
rhetorically. I flip to the next page in the pad:

"Exquisite body . . . Incredible legs . . . Extraordinary
cheekbones . . . Magical eyes—"

"What is this? Poetry night?" Ali asks.

"It gets better. Height: five-foot-two, five-ten, five-six, five-
nine, five-five, five even . . . Weight: 110, 100, 125, 130, 115,
120, all over the place, right? But: Eyes: café au lait." A little

pause here. "Four of the six people I talked to said café au lait, two said light brown. She walks in and the place freezes, every eye on her. At the level of evidence—" I hedge.

"Evidence?" he says. "Evidence is this: How many women we know of with that general description and those café-au-lait eyes could walk in and stop the room? And make everyone remember her for a month?" He is rubbing his forehead.

"Well, it's a short list . . ."

"But we both know who's number one with a bullet, don't we, Ken?"

I look away. What can I say?

"If it's 'Laura on the Loose' again, we are both fucked, I'll tell you that right now, Ken. It's fucking Laura Della Chiesa, man! Shit!"

He crosses his hands under his armpits. I sit there slumped forward.

We both squirm for a moment.

"Do we know 'Who's the one? Who's she with?' In the band?"

"No, no one seems right for it."

"But you'll talk to the cornet player."

"Tomorrow." I look at my watch. "Today."

He's been slumping backward, and now he pulls himself up, slowly comes to a standing position. I unfold myself from the chair. He stretches, then looks me in the eye.

"Oh," Ali says. "The chief says to ask you about the Riddler."

He lets it hang there. I wonder what would happen if I just got up, turned on my heel and walked away.

"What'd he tell you?" I ask him.

"Some."

"I guess," I sigh, "we do need someone on the inside . . ."

I wait for him to let me off the hook. He lets me twist instead.

"Hell, Lieutenant. I haven't played in years, I don't know . . ."

"What was it?" he asks. "Sax of some kind, wasn't it? Which one? I see you as an alto man."

"I played most of them," is what I say.

He wants to ask me why I stopped. I want to tell him to go fuck himself if he does.

He doesn't.

He picks up his coat. "Let's keep her name out of it for now, if we can, but let's also make sure it's her." That's the trick, for sure. "And since you agree that it makes sense to get access to the inside, to have a presence . . ."

How delicately put. I grunt, looking away.

"Maybe what's his name, the bigger guy—"

"DiUllio," I fill in.

"Maybe DiUllio will turn up. Maybe he'll even turn up alive, confirm that the Don ordered this, tell us what the fuck they were after."

"It's always a possibility," I say.

"Yeah," he says. "As to the motorcycle cop . . ."

"I know," I say, "it's not his kind of assignment, unless . . ."

"Unless . . ." he says.

"Unless he can pick out Amatucci from prior contact."

He nods and shakes his head, both, little figure-eights. "It's starting to add up, isn't it?"

"Starting to," I say.

But it's not the adding up that matters. It's the subtracting. It's the facts that tell you: It can't be this, It can't be that.

He rouses himself first. He looks at his watch. I look at mine. Three fifteen.

As he walks down the hall, I ask myself: would I recognize his back out of a lineup of thousands of backs?

CHAPTER 26
Ken Ridlin

Small Group Practice Room—University of Chicago
Thursday, January 16

It's noon and Amatucci is still in the hospital. The doc started talking about inserting some more pins, and I cut him off right there. I really don't want to know.

I drive down to Hyde Park, park north of South 59th Street, and walk over to the practice-room complex. This is where they usually practice, once a week, every Thursday. Powell told me it was a leftover from their old days as a band made up of students. No one had classes at noon. And as for Thursday, if they did it on Friday the brass players would be all played out for that night. If they did it on Wednesday, the subatomic particle physicist clarinet player would forget everything they had practiced before the weekend gigs.

For my purposes, it works—private, secluded, comfortable for them. I can hear them inside, tuning up. I take a deep breath, grab the doorknob, and walk in. I'm carrying a black case and a manila folder, and I set them down on top of the beat-up spinet piano. Everyone is present: Powell, Worrell, Jones, and the cornet player or piano player, Landreau. They stop playing.

Powell reintroduces me around. We all shake hands. Introduces me to Landreau for the first time. Six-foot-even, 175, trimmed salt-and-pepper hair, brown eyes, no distinguishing scars. Check that: We shake, and I notice he's missing the little finger of his right hand.

This stops me. How do you play the piano without the little finger of your right hand? Do you learn to play the piano, then lose the finger, then decide to relearn it all over again? Do you lose the finger early, then decide to learn to play with only nine fingers anyway? My brain is spinning as this sinks in, and for a second I forget where I am and why I am here.

I sit down on the piano bench. I figure I'll start with the truth and improvise from there.

"You people have a problem. A bigger problem than you know. You've got three victims in just over a week, and it's not over."

I pull out the morgue picture of Tremblay. Place it on the music stand on the piano.

"First, Wednesday the eighth. Roger Tremblay. 1812 Club. Sitting in for two songs. One thirty-two-caliber slug in the back of the head."

Landreau is looking on intently. He wasn't in town yet for Tremblay. I'm guessing they didn't tell him: "Hey, the last guy who sat in? He got shot in the head."

"Tremblay has all the earmarks of a mob hit, except for the victim himself, who had no connection to that world. No gambling, no vice, no dope, no loans. A citizen. Right now, we're treating it as a hit gone wrong. Mistaken identity."

I pause, look at them.

"Which means he was aiming at one of you, or at Amatucci."

GET UP TO
4 FREE BOOKS!

You can have the best fiction delivered to your door for less than what you'd pay in a bookstore or online—only $4.25 a book! Sign up for our book clubs today, and we'll send you **FREE* BOOKS** just for trying it out...**with no obligation to buy, ever!**

LEISURE HORROR BOOK CLUB

With more award-winning horror authors than any other publisher, it's easy to see why CNN.com says "Leisure Books has been leading the way in paperback horror novels." Your shipments will include authors such as RICHARD LAYMON, DOUGLAS CLEGG, JACK KETCHUM, MARY ANN MITCHELL, and many more.

LEISURE THRILLER BOOK CLUB

If you love fast-paced page-turners, you won't want to miss any of the books in Leisure's thriller line. Filled with gripping tension and edge-of-your-seat excitement, these titles feature everything from psychological suspense to legal thrillers to police procedurals and more!

As a book club member you also receive the following special benefits:

- **30% OFF all orders through our website & telecenter!**
- **Exclusive access to special discounts!**
- **Convenient home delivery and 10 days to return any books you don't want to keep.**

There is no minimum number of books to buy, and you may cancel membership at any time. See back to sign up!

YES! ☐

Sign me up for the Leisure Horror Book Club and send my TWO FREE BOOKS! If I choose to stay in the club, I will pay only $8.50* each month, a savings of $5.48!

YES! ☐

Sign me up for the Leisure Thriller Book Club and send my TWO FREE BOOKS! If I choose to stay in the club, I will pay only $8.50* each month, a savings of $5.48!

NAME: _____

ADDRESS: _____

_____

TELEPHONE: _____

E-MAIL: _____

☐ **I WANT TO PAY BY CREDIT CARD.**

☐ VISA ☐ MasterCard ☐ DISCOVER

ACCOUNT #: _____

EXPIRATION DATE: _____

SIGNATURE: _____

Send this card along with $2.00 shipping & handling for each club you wish to join, to:

Horror/Thriller Book Clubs
1 Mechanic Street
Norwalk, CT 06850-3431

Or fax (must include credit card information!) to: 610.995.9274. You can also sign up online at www.dorchesterpub.com.

*Plus $2.00 for shipping. Offer open to residents of the U.S. and Canada only. Canadian residents please call 1.800.481.9191 for pricing information.

If under 18, a parent or guardian must sign. Terms, prices and conditions subject to change. Subscription subject to acceptance. Dorchester Publishing reserves the right to reject any order or cancel any subscription.

JOIN NOW!

"I don't see how—" Worrell begins. I hold up a hand to silence him.

"Next. Sometime Sunday night Fahey is killed in his apartment on the Near North Side."

"Excuse me," says Worrell, "but I must confess that I am a little curious about exactly how he died. Are you at liberty to divulge that? Unless it's confidential police business—"

"He was tied up and gagged. Someone filled his nose full of cocaine. Every time he took a breath, he snorted some more in. Died of a heart attack. Massive."

His eyes pop. "A most curious exit strategy," Worrell says.

"Before you start making any plans, understand he was tortured along the way."

"Tortured?" Worrell asks.

I slip a morgue picture of Fahey onto the music stand, next to the picture of Tremblay. It's not detailed enough that you can see much, but you can see he doesn't look right. Powell and Worrell peer in. Jones is still staring at the corner. Landreau is looking at me, not the photo.

"His fingers—broken. His toes—broken. His ears, his tongue, his eyes, removed."

Powell looks ashen. Worrell stares even more intently, leaning in more closely.

"And you are deducing that the same person killed both Tremblay and Fahey, one with a gun and the other with torture and illicit drugs?" Worrell asks. He is in the mentor role, speaking for his young charges.

"We have reason to believe the killer was the same in both incidents," I say, vaguely, "despite the differences in method."

"Is there anything you can—" Worrell presses.

"No."

They frown, but nod their heads.

"Then last night, Wednesday again, 1812 Club again. A man posing as a motorcycle cop lures Amatucci out of the club during a break with a story about car trouble. He leads him to two other men, waiting at his car, who attempt to interrogate him. The two men get into a fight. One shoots the other one, takes off. In the course of the, uh, interrogation, they break all the fingers of his hand—"

"Which hand was it?" Worrell asks.

"Left," I say.

He winces. "What's the prognosis?" he asks. Landreau has turned away, lost in himself.

I place a picture of Amatucci, asleep in his hospital bed, next to the other two. His left hand is hanging up in the air, wired and bandaged and hooked up to some tubes.

"I was there this morning," Powell interjects. "They're not saying, because they really don't know. Some dislocations, some broken bones, some bone chips. They operated last night—reset the breaks, cleaned up some debris, put some pins in his fingers to stabilize them so they'll heal straight. They called in some orthopedist from Evanston, a specialist. He's aware that Amatucci is a piano player, and is doing all he can so he'll still be one. But it's going to take time, and work, and luck."

"These people," Worrell asks, "were they Mafia as well? As far as you can tell?"

"Yeah," I say. "The one who's dead, we have an ID on him. Spent time in the joint. The other one is his jailhouse buddy. We're trying to track him down."

They're not sure what to say. Finally, Powell weighs in.

"You used the word 'interrogated'; what do you mean when you say they 'interrogated' Vinnie?"

I can hear the quotation marks he puts on the word. I probably put them on it myself when I said it.

"I use that word loosely. It was done loosely. But the gist of it was, *'Who is it? Who is she with?'*"

Their foreheads crease, except for Jones, who was already scowling. I don't catch a flash of recognition from any of them. I wait for Worrell to jump in with a paraphrase.

"'Who is it? Who is she with?' Detective, I fail to see the

meaning in this. To what, or to whom, does it refer?" he obliges.

"Well, that's what I'd like to ask all of you," I say, bouncing it right back.

I am thinking that this is an unlikely quartet of prospects for Laura Della Chiesa. I am also thinking: Who knows? I mean, I think of some of the women who have slept with *me,* for God's sake . . .

I take out one of two remaining items in my manila folder. It's a composite sketch of the woman in the yellow dress who was at the 1812 last night. It does look a lot like Laura.

"Who is she?" I ask, turning it around. They stare intently.

"She was at the 1812 last night," Worrell says. "She arrived just before Paul and Jack, made quite a stunning entrance. She sat right up front, and wore a rather dramatic yellow dress. She seemed to be enjoying the music. I didn't see her at the end, though. Who is she?"

"Who is she?" I echoed.

"I saw her there, too," Powell says. "As a matter of fact, she was at the Marriott last Saturday, too, in a red dress."

"Is there anything she did that made her especially memorable?"

He grinned. "Detective, there's nothing she did that *wasn't* memorable. Her mere presence left quite an impression. I wasn't watching her during the sets, but I was aware of her. And at the end, when we left, she bowed to me, even kissed Jack's hand." He looked up. "Hard to forget."

"Kiss of death?" I ask myself. Don't get ahead of yourself, I think.

"Anyone else remember her there?"

Worrell says, "Yes, of course," and Jones nods.

"None of you knows this woman?" I repeat.

They shrug. I reach into the manila folder one more time. We've made up a photo array, Laura, taken from one of her many bookings, and five other brunettes, in a tic-tac-toe arrangement. I slide it out of the folder and place it on the stand, next to the other pictures, on the right. In putting it there I nudge Tremblay's picture off the stand. It flutters to the floor.

"Take a minute and look at these pictures and see if any of them look familiar," I say.

"Lower right," Worrell and Powell say in unison. "That's her, that's the woman in the red dress, yellow dress, whatever," Powell adds.

"Quite an exquisite specimen," Worrell adds. "Who is she, if I may ask?"

I turn to Landreau. "Is that her?"

He glances sideways at the photo. "She looks very familiar."

"Ms. Jones?" I ask.

She looks over, lazily. "I don't know if I saw her, if I saw anyone. We Chinese people are a little nearsighted."

"But my dear, you must have seen her," Worrell gushes. "An absolutely fabulous creature—"

"Can't say I did. Can't say I didn't," she says. "I don't spend a lot of time staring at chicks in bars."

"Who is she?" Worrell asks me.

I look them over. Nothing.

"If it's her and she's been seeing someone in the band, or someone even *thinks* she's been seeing someone in the band, then who she is is a goddamn nightmare. She's Laura Della Chiesa, and her father is the head of all organized crime in Chicago. If they think she's with one of you, all of you are in danger."

I stop myself. Don't want to oversell it.

"Which brings me to the next point," I say. I stand up, pick up the case I have set on the piano, sit back down on the piano bench, and open it. I start taking out the pieces of my old soprano sax and assembling it while I talk.

"It's been decided downtown that there should be a police presence on the inside. We've been too late too many times with this thing. We could plant a bartender, but we'd have to plant one in every place you play, and that could get obvious. Same with waiters, waitresses, customers. And none of them would have access to you offstage. So it's been decided that the best plant would be someone in the band. And I've been nominated."

"You've played before?" Worrell asks. "I mean, jazz, this kind of music?"

I look at him, nod. I turn to Powell. "Probably way before your time, I'm afraid. I used to play under the name of Kenny Riddles . . . some people called me 'the Riddler.'"

"I know that name," Landreau blurts out. "Played the reeds, all of them."

I turn to him. "Didn't you say you were in Detroit? I never played in Detroit. Only here. Only in Chicago."

He blinked. "Word travels," he said. "Even to Detroit."

"How long ago?" Worrell asks.

"Long time. Eleven years ago," I say.

"If I may ask, why did you stop playing?" Worrell presses.

"Maybe when you hear me you won't have to ask," I say.

"Not what I heard," Landreau says.

I ignore him. I know better.

"Amatucci says you have two jobs up in Wisconsin this weekend. If we can find a way to work it, I need to be there," I say.

Nobody protests.

"When does Vince get out?" Jones asks. It's the only thing she's said since I arrived. "I'm worried that whoever came after him might, like, try it again."

"He gets out this evening, and that's probably a valid concern," I say. "Should he be staying here or going to Wisconsin?"

Jones turns to me. "You, you're like 'on duty' when you're with us, which means you're getting paid by the city, right?"

"That's right."

"Then I propose that we keep giving Vinnie his share, for as long as it takes. He can, like, stay here and heal up and focus on being the band's manager for a while."

They all mutter their agreement. One for all. All for one.

"Where is he going to stay in the meantime?" she asks. "I mean, we can't let him lie in that rat hole in Hyde Park."

She turns to me. "Protective custody?" she asks.

"Afraid not," I say. "It would make sense, but . . ."

"I could put him up," Powell says. "The couch folds out."

Jones consider this. "I'm the only one with an unlisted phone and address—the rest of you are in the book, except you," she says, turning to Landreau.

He nods. She looks at Powell, at Worrell. Worrell says, "You know, I don't believe I know where you actually do live, my dear."

"See? Like I said," she says. "OK. When we're done here, I'll swing over to County and pick him up, and meet you all up there tomorrow night."

They fall to discussing directions to Wisconsin, and talking about who is going to ride in what car. I let them settle before I go on.

"In the meantime, if I'm going to be on the inside, it has to work for you. I said I was *'nominated.'* You get the final vote. So we ought to take some time while we have it, go over a couple things, you know, musically. Like I said, it's been a long time."

So we practice. We start with some simple things, old chestnuts, then work up to more complicated modern pieces. I actually know these better. They were big back in my time.

I look around during the second one, and can't believe it's Landreau at the piano. Not just the fingers—that is amazing enough. But the expression, the body language—it's a whole new person. While we are talking, it's like he's frozen in ice. Now, playing the beat-up old spinet, his face is all lit up, his posture is ramrod straight, there's energy coming off him in waves. I take a quick solo, a single chorus, and he is looking at me, very directly, with light filling his eyes.

At the start, my head is all wrong, my fingers are behind

the beat, my embouchure is tight, my sound is pinched and pale. And I realize how good they really are as they carry me through it. But then we go on and I get flashes, and the old spirits come to visit. A certain vibration starts to hum in my gut. And it's not all bad. For stretches, it's almost good. And a feeling comes back that I thought had been gone for good, and flickers in and out of the present like a strobe light, making everything shimmer.

CHAPTER 27
Ken Ridlin

Solo Practice Room—University of Chicago
Thursday, January 16

After the rehearsal, I signal to Landreau and we walk to a solo practice room down the hall. Jones has left to pick up Amatucci. Powell has also left, points unknown. Worrell is still practicing. Says he doesn't teach his next class for another hour.

I close the door behind us. There are two places to sit—a folding metal chair and the piano bench. I take the piano bench. It's where he would be comfortable, and I don't want him comfortable.

"Just some basic information. Let's start at the beginning. Place of birth."

"Billings, Montana."

"Mother's name."

"Sandra."

"Sandra Landreau," I say.

"Sandra Kerrey, Sandra Fitzgerald, Sandra Mayo, Sandra Gold, Sandra Jefferson . . . My mother married frequently."

"Kerrey was her maiden name? With one 'e' or two?"

"K-E-R-R-E-Y," he says, then pauses. "Well, at least that's what she told me."

"You grew up in Montana?"

"In Montana, Cleveland, Detroit, Kansas City, Pittsfield, Massachusetts . . ."

"Her occupation?"

"She really didn't have any marketable skills," he says, with an ironic smile. "Her occupation was getting married, getting divorced, getting alimony."

"When you listed her names, I didn't hear Landreau as one of them," I say, as delicately as I can, like I made some mistake in not hearing him.

"My father was in between Fitzgerald and Mayo, a French detour in the middle of her Irish period." There is a pause. "She never married him, unlike most of the others."

"Brothers and sisters?"

"None, surprisingly."

"Aunts, uncles, cousins?"

"There must have been, but I never met them. She wasn't close to her family."

"Any contact with the Landreaus?"

"No. I was never sure there even *was* a Landreau."

"No curiosity about it?" I ask. "A lot of people these days spend years trying to track down, uh, lost relatives, whatever."

"Curiosity? A little. Obsession? Not really."

"How about yourself? Married? Kids?"

"Neither," he says.

"Residence?"

"Twelve-twenty Division Avenue, Apartment 5."

This is his Chicago flop, where Powell is putting him up with a friend.

"No, I mean permanent residence."

He's sitting, bent forward, his elbows on his knees. He looks up at me.

"Permanent residence? None. For tax purposes, I list a P.O. box in Davenport, Iowa."

"P.O. box number . . ."

"Eight-zero-six," he says.

"Music is your only source of income?" I ask, then immediately retreat. "Look, I could care less. Informational purposes only."

He nods. "Mostly music. What I make I put in the market."

"You one of those day-trader guys?"

He shakes his head. "Hardly. I have a broker, she handles all of that. I send her money, she invests it. We talk maybe twice a year and maybe make some minor adjustments. She keeps enough cash in my account, pays the bills. She has a key to the P.O. box and power of attorney."

He pauses, then reconsiders. "I pay on time, pay estimated quarterlies in advance, pay state taxes every place I play, even report tip income. Mr. Straight and Narrow."

The guy has the smallest paper trail I've ever seen. He could do all of this off the cuff, not declaring a dime. They'd never catch him. But he doesn't.

I have a sudden thought: It would also be the perfect cover for our assassin, the bag lady, the motorcycle cop, whoever. All the travel, anonymous hotels, all cash income. Just mix in a couple of aliases, it would be airtight.

"Her name? The broker?"

He gives me a name, Melissa Yeo, a phone number, an address.

We talk about how he got stuck in Chicago, the plane, the storm, like that.

"Talking to Amatucci," I say, pushing it, "he feels this is your first time in Chicago."

"It's not on my regular rota."

That's not what I asked.

"I would think that Chicago would be a regular stop, all the clubs here and all."

"No. Never has been."

"Any reason?" I ask.

"Just hasn't been on the list," he says.

The more I look at him, the more familiar he looks to me.

Am I recognizing someone, slowly, in stages, or just getting used to the way he looks? Slow down, I think, slow down.

"What about this time? Plan to stay around?"

He pauses, looks away. "If I could, I'd be on the next plane. This situation . . ."

"But . . ." I say.

He looks toward the wall. "It's Paul. He's good to play with. There's something special there . . ."

"So how long?"

"As long as it works. That's what I do. I go someplace, get some work, meet some players, and stay as long as it works. As soon as it stops working, I go someplace else."

"You prefer that, or does it just work out that way?" I ask.

"It started that way by chance, but right now, I prefer it, yes."

"A couple of weeks, a month or two, a year?" I ask, trying for a time frame.

He looks at me again. "As long as it works," he says.

I change gears. "The picture, the woman. You know her?"

"No. I'm sure I've never seen her before."

"You sure?"

"She looks a little like someone I used to know, and if I had seen her I would have remembered the resemblance."

"This 'someone you used to know.' "

"She's . . . she died. A long time ago, at about the same age as the woman in the picture."

I finish some notes in my pad. Close it. Stand up. Stretch. He gets to his feet as well.

"Oh. Just out of curiosity. How'd you lose the finger?"

He looks down. "An accident, when I was young," he says, and sits down at the piano I have just abandoned. A wave of arpeggios slams my back just before the door shuts behind me.

CHAPTER 28
Vinnie Amatucci

Jones Apartment
Thursday, January 16

I don't remember much about what happened after the bigger one shot the smaller one in the head. There was a lot of pain, I do remember that, then I passed out. I remember only flashes of the ride in the ambulance, the bumpy trip to Cook County General. I remember X-rays, and the heavy lead apron, and some test where they rolled me into a long narrow tube, a CAT scan or an MRI, one of those. I remember the banging noises, as if they were whacking the tube with hammers, and I remember another set of noises like the grinding of gears. I remember them telling me to hold my breath, over and over, for what felt like longer and longer intervals. Then I was out of the tube and shivering on a gurney and begging for a blanket. I remember them putting the intravenous drip in my arm, and I remember the drugs, oh, do I remember the drugs—the good shit, morphine. I remember that once the drip was working, they wheeled me all around the fucking hospital, for what felt like hours, as if we were in a time trial, an endless gurney journey. I remember they rolled me into a very bright room, and I remember squinting and asking where I was. Then I was out for a long time.

A little later, I remember the detective talking to me, the same one I talked to at the 1812 a week ago, the tall one with the loose skin, but I don't remember what he asked me and I don't remember how I responded. And then I must have gone out again. Then I remember waking up again later this morning, feeling an itch on the left half of my scrotum, going to scratch it, and being unable to move my left arm. I remember looking up and seeing my hand, covered in plaster, hanging in the air in front of my face. Then I remember more X-rays, and more drugs, and being gone again for a long time, until it was dark outside. I don't know what time it was; there was no clock in there and they had taken my watch—it had been on my left wrist.

And I remember Akiko coming to the hospital, and signing forms, and talking to doctors, and wheeling me out to her heap of a car.

And after that I don't remember a thing for a long time. Nothing. I was still on medication, but they had switched me to pills instead of the intravenous drip, some kind of Percocet or Percodan instead of that good sweet morphine, and the pills were really atrocious, miserable shit that just made me want to lie down and close my eyes and watch the time slip away. I felt as if I were watching my IQ drop by ten points a minute.

And then I was remembering all of this. I felt no urgency about trying to remember; it was just my brain exercising itself, like an involuntary spasm. It was just listing and sorting and categorizing and linking, going on about its business as if I weren't involved at all, just a machine clearing its circuits.

But at this second, I am not dreaming. I open my mouth, lick my lips. They are dry, and taste a little metallic. I must have breathed in when I licked my lips, because now I could smell something. It is salty, with a sweet undertone of musky perfume. It is familiar somehow, but on this one I could do the listing and the sorting but not the categorizing or the linking. I can't complete the sequence. I can't quite place it.

Then a sound. A sigh, a breath, released. A long breath. Then a giggle, no, more like a chuckle, like "Huh, huh," like that. Female. A low, husky female voice.

I stretch my neck, left and right, forward and back. I let out a breath and let my head lie back. My eyes are still closed.

I remember my left hand, and decide to do another empirical test—I try to wiggle my fingers. I can't. I mean, I can feel them moving a little, but they only move a millimeter and then they are bumping into something. And they hurt. My kinesthetic sense tells me my hand is on my chest, my stomach, somewhere around there. And I am lying down, flat on my back, which is curious, since I never sleep on my back.

I breathe in again and there's that smell again. It is time to stop teasing myself. I turn my head to my left. I open my eyes.

And then I blink twice. I am in a darkened room, lit by candles, on a bed, and there is a woman lying next to me, a woman I don't know. Long wavy hair, almost black, but with an auburn glint in the candlelight, high chiseled cheekbones, a smooth forehead, big deep-sunk dark eyes, the lids molded to her eyeballs with a thin dark crescent of a crease at the top. I can see them because she is looking at me, her eyes half-open. Her mouth is open slightly, and she sucks in a breath, sharply.

I move my eyes and see that she is naked, with extraordinary breasts, a flat stomach, not six-pack abs but no flab at all, and a trimmed bush of pubic hair, with Akiko's face pressed up against it, her eyes closed, a look of concentration on her face. I look back up at her face—the brunette—and realize I *do* know her. It's the woman in the red dress, the yellow dress, whatever, the one who made the big entrance at the 1812 Club last night, if it *was* last night, the one who parted the crowd at the Marriott last weekend. She is looking at me but not really seeing me, her breath is ragged, getting faster. Her face is flushed, the red creeping down to her chest, and then she looks away from me, rolls her eyes back, and she comes.

Big-time. In waves.

I see her muscles tense. I see her back arch. Her left hand is on her left breast, holding it. Her right hand reaches down and she grabs the back of Akiko's head and pulls her closer. She shudders again, once, twice, her upper teeth raking her lower lip. She tries to grab a handful of Akiko's short hair, can't, and pushes her face away, muttering, "Enough, stop it, you know I get ticklish," and rolls over toward me.

I hear a rustling, and I see Akiko slide up her and lie on top of her, craning her neck up to kiss her, except as she does so she kneels on my left hip and I jump a little, involuntarily. She says something like "Oops, sorry," and the brunette says, "I think our guest is awake."

Akiko looks at me. There is a look on her face I can't decipher, not that it is blank, but more like there is more there than I can take in all at once. She sits up—she is naked, too—and says, "Sorry, Vince. I thought you were, like, out of it, all those pills. Did I wake you up? Sorry."

The brunette doesn't let me answer. "No, you didn't wake him up. He's had his eyes open for a couple of minutes."

So she *did* see me watching her, she just didn't let it stop her.

Akiko asks, "Are you OK? How's the hand? How are you feeling?"

I look down at my hand. It's in a cast and the cast is in a sling, and the sling is strapped tight to my chest. I can feel my hand inside all this; it is sore as hell, as if I don't have bones in there, just shards of broken glass.

"Shit," I say, remembering how it got that way. "Shit."

"Can I get you anything?" Akiko asks.

"Water," I say. "I'm really thirsty." My voice is full of gravel.

She hops up, and knees the brunette in the thigh as she does. "Ow," the brunette says. "We've got to do something about those knees of yours." Akiko says "sorry" again and walks around the corner, out of sight. I hear the refrigerator open and close.

A few seconds later she's back, with a tall glass of water, the condensation already covering it. She looks at me, and sets it down on the floor. She turns to the brunette. "Help me get him sitting up." They each reach a hand under an armpit and slowly ease me up. Akiko picks up the water and leans over me and holds it up to my lips. I try to sip it and spill a cold gulp of it down my chest. She says "sorry" again, and I realize that I have never heard her use that word once in the two years I have known her, and now I have heard her say it four, five times in the space of a minute-and-a-half. You never know with people. You never fucking know.

She holds the glass up again and I drink again, and then gulp some more until I pull my head back and shake it side to side: no more.

"I could get you another pill," she says. "You're not due for another hour or two, but hey, who's counting?"

I squint. I'm thinking about it.

"Does the medication help?" she asks. "Is it taking the pain away?"

"That's not the way it works," I say. "The pain is still there, but I'm gone. Far, far away."

She turns to the brunette and they giggle.

"Are you sure you don't need another?"

"What I need," I say, "is to take a piss, real bad."

I'm still half covered up. They pull the covers back, swing my legs over the side. The bed isn't a bed, it's a mattress on the floor, a futon. With my one good hand I can't seem to get any leverage to stand up. I flop around for a minute until they get on both sides of me and pull me up to a standing position, one foot on the futon, one foot on the floor. I feel a little dizzy and they keep holding me until my head clears a little.

Then they start to walk me toward the bathroom, one step at a time, and I realize they're both naked and I'm naked, too. I also realize I have a hard-on, an impressive piss-hard-on, pointing just about straight up.

The brunette notices, too, and as we get to the bathroom, says, "Are you planning on doing a handstand or do you want me to aim that for you?"

I can't tell from her tone of voice if she's joking.

"If you can help me sit down, I think I can manage it from there," I say.

They do, and then look at each other and leave, closing the door. My hard-on subsides a little, I manage to get it under the lid, and eventually I start to piss and keep pissing until I actually have to check to make sure it's piss and not blood. I'm not counting, but it feels like I've been pissing for well over a minute. I finish up, give it a shake or two, lean forward, get my feet under me, and stand up. I reach behind myself and flush.

I hesitate. I look for my clothes; they're not in sight. I walk out of the bathroom, a little unsteadily, and they start applauding.

"You really *did* have to go," says the brunette.

I make it back to the futon, and manage to plop down on it, not too gracefully. I reach over and pull the sheet over me.

Akiko gets up, walks to the kitchen again, comes back. She has my kit bag in her hand, and tosses it over to the brunette.

"I thought you'd want me to save this for you, keep it from the cops. It was in your car." She turned to the brunette. "Why don't you do this? I'm not good at it."

The brunette takes out the little black film can, finds some papers. "Open the other zipper," I said. "There's a pipe in there." She does, finds it, loads it up. A couple of flecks land on her stomach. She picks them off, drops them in the pipe, tamps it down with her pinky. "There should be a lighter in there, too," I add.

She turns toward me. "I like a man who comes prepared," she says, then reaches over, places the pipe between my lips, flicks the Djeep, and fires me up. I take a good hit and immediately start to cough my brains out, a good twenty seconds' worth. "Good shit," I say, quoting the old joke. I suck on the pipe again. It's out. She flicks the lighter again, I take a hit and manage to keep it down this time.

I reach up with my right hand and pass it over to her. She takes it, takes a hit, then another, and passes it to Akiko, who shakes her head and hands it back to me.

"I forgot," the brunette says. "Miss Purist. Sound mind in a sound body." She goes to light me up again. She leans to her right, and her right breast nuzzles against my rib cage as she leans in. I take another hit, and a second one while it's still going, and pass it back to her. A slow soft buzz is starting to creep into my head, different from the pills, familiar and warm and welcoming. A whole minute has gone by and I haven't thought about my hand.

She hasn't moved, she's still leaning against me. Akiko is now spooning her from behind, her left hand resting on the brunette's left hip, as we pass the pipe back and forth. There is a languor in the room, and it's not just the weed. And what is with Akiko? All her hard edges are gone.

And I notice there's something else in the room as well— Mr. Hard-On has reappeared. The brunette notices, too, and arches one eyebrow.

"Looks like you're feeling a little better," she says.

"Don't mind him," I say. "He has a mind of his own, hasn't listened to me since we were twelve."

Akiko leans up on her elbow. We've lost her; she doesn't know what we're talking about. She finally sees what has come up and makes this expression, her hand going to her mouth to cover a giggle, her eyes lowered.

"Typical," I say to the brunette. "We get high and she gets the giggles."

The brunette half turns, gives her a little scowl, slaps her on her hip. "Don't you know anything?" she says. "You are *not* supposed to giggle at a moment like this. You're supposed to say 'Oh my God! I've never *seen* one that big!'" She mimes the whole thing, her mouth wide open, her eyebrows raised, her hands on the sides of her face, and now they're both giggling.

"It would be a lie," I say, "but it *is* the protocol."

"Besides," the brunette says, as if reading my mind, "size doesn't matter, as long as you know what to do with it. And besides, this one is quite nice."

"That's what you're supposed to say," I say to Akiko. "Whether it's true or not."

"Sorry," Akiko says.

It strikes me that I'm intruding here, and maybe my discomfort starts to show. The brunette picks up on it. "I'm sorry to involve you in our little thing, here, but I just had to see her, and you were out cold, and—"

"Hey. No problem. I'm the third wheel here. By the way," I ask Akiko, "how did I get here? What am I doing here? And where is 'here,' anyway? Not that I don't appreciate the gesture and all."

"The hospital was going to release you and the cops weren't ready to put a guard on your place, and we were worried that the other guy, the guy who took off, might come back, so we're at my place . . . *Mi casa es su casa,* at least temporarily," Akiko says.

"Don't think I don't appreciate it," I say, "but while we're trading aphorisms, *two's company, and three's a crowd.*"

"What, you didn't like our little show?" the brunette asks.

I start to blush. Usually I'm the last to know, but this time I feel it, a dense heat flowing from my neck to my hairline and beyond. "Don't get me wrong. It was quite, uh, stimulating, the little I caught of it, but—"

"Fuck it. Two's company, three's a threesome." And with

that she reaches down and takes my cock in her hand.

"Pleased to meet you, too. And your name would be . . . ?"
I ask.

Akiko sits up. "Sorry," she says again. I am seeing a whole
different side of her. "I'm a terrible hostess. I kidnap you
while you're in a drugged and helpless state, I kneel on you
and wake you up, I spill water on you, I fail to act impressed
by your manly equipment, I neglect to introduce you to my
friend. . . . I'm just being a terrible person tonight."

"You did capture my supply before the authorities could
grab it and smoke it up themselves so I could return to a
drugged but not entirely helpless state, I'll give you that," I
say. "But you're right, you haven't introduced me to your
friend."

The brunette shrugs, turns away from her. I see it clearly
then: There is a decision to be made and she is not going to
be the one making it.

Akiko starts in. "Look, I'm not just being impolite. We
talked about this," she says, including the brunette, "and I
wasn't sure you would want to know. It's complicated—"

"Complicated?" I say. "How many syllables does it have?
Any glottal clicks? Lots of velar fricatives?"

She rolls her eyes at me, and squints sideways at the
brunette.

"Hey," I say, "your friend is lying here naked with her
hands on my family jewels—"

"To be precise," the brunette says, "these are the family
jewels," she says, reaching down to squeeze my testicles,
"and this," she says, circling the head of my cock, "is the
royal crown."

Part of me wants to brush her hand away. Part of me
wants to leave it there. That part is temporarily winning.

"What's the big mystery?" I ask the brunette directly. "Are
you some sort of a secret agent? Some kind of mystery
woman?"

"Can you keep a secret?" Akiko asks. "I mean, *really* keep
a secret?"

"Sure," I say, none too convincingly.

Akiko looks me in the eye. "Her name is Laura. This trouble with the band, you know? It's all about her."

I try to let this sink in.

"Hi, Laura, my name is Vince."

She shakes my dick like she's shaking my hand, and this time the two of us giggle while Akiko is being serious.

"Don't you want to know what it's all about?" Akiko asks. "After what's happened? After what they did to you?"

I turn to the brunette and take back the pipe and the lighter with my right hand. I get it between my teeth, take a couple of hits, hold the smoke in a good long time. I finally let it out. "If you want to tell me," I say.

"Let's tell him later," the brunette says. "One thing you have to learn about these things," she says, giving my erection a little tug, "is that talking is not their strong suit, and another thing is that you never let one of these go to waste, not if you can help it."

"*You* never let one of those things go to waste," Akiko corrects her.

"That's right," Laura says, "*I* never let one of these go to waste."

There is a look here, a moment in which some meaning has been passed.

"Hey," I say. "You guys have something going on, and that's great. I don't need to get in the way or anything." I make a move to arise but the brunette still has hold of my cock, firmly.

"Yes, we've got a thing going," the brunette, Laura, says, "as you could spy with your own little eye. But it's not an exclusive thing. She likes girls. I like girls and boys—"

"And probably donkeys—" Akiko cuts in.

"And probably donkeys," Laura echoes, "but there are no donkeys here at the moment while there *is* what seems like a perfectly serviceable dick, right here in my hand."

I jump in. "Hey, excuse me, I think I just missed my stop, so if you want to let me off at the next block I'll just—"

"No," Akiko says to me. She turns to Laura. "We *have* talked about it. It could be, what was your word, Vince, 'stimulating,' like watching us was stimulating for you." She looks me in the eye. "Was it really stimulating?"

"Oh, you have no idea, even as half-conscious as I was, as I am."

"And you only got to see the very first act," Laura says, "mere foreplay." And with that, she lets go of me, rolls over on top of Akiko, and kisses her deeply.

Ah, shit.

CHAPTER 29
Vinnie Amatucci

Jones Apartment
Thursday, January 16

This time it's the brunette, Laura, who takes the lead. She gets on top of Akiko, resting on her elbows, and kisses her deeply, their lips melting together. She slides up, dips down to nuzzle an ear, slides up some more. Her left breast is close to Akiko, who twists up to reach for it. Laura hovers just out of reach until Akiko arches up and clamps a nipple between her lips. Laura scoots away, sliding down and burying her face between Akiko's small breasts, then licking her way up the inside of each one. Her hands mold Akiko's breasts, her thumbs strum across the hardening nipples, lightly. She gives each a tiny lick, then swoops down between Akiko's thighs. She starts in, licking at a slow pace—teasing her. Her face comes up to look at Akiko, and it's glistening. Then she leans back down. There is no teasing now.

Akiko squirms, her breath ragged. Laura knows exactly what she is doing; this is no fumbling first time. Akiko makes a sound, then a gesture with her hand. Laura shakes her head vigorously back and forth. Akiko reaches for her, and Laura slaps her hand away.

"Come on up here," Akiko says.

"Well," Laura says. "I'm kind of busy at the moment—"

"Come up here," Akiko says, "please?"

Laura stops, pulls her head up, looks her in the eye. "Shut up and come for me." And swoops back in.

And with that, Akiko throws her head back, tilts her pelvis up and abandons herself. It happens quickly, no more than another ten seconds, then a yelp and a shudder and a growl deep in her chest and she's over the edge. Laura doesn't let go, but burrows deeper, and Akiko continues to spasm, her yelps turning into deep moans, her hips bucking up and down until she finally grabs Laura by the hair and drags her off. "God," she says, "you are too good."

They chuckle at this, two deep belly laughs, and flop against each other loosely.

After a minute or so, Laura turns and looks at me. I'm harder than ever, and feel as if I could have come any time during this without even touching myself. But the moment was somehow too sacred for me to sully it.

Laura gets up, grabs my feet, and pulls me down on the bed so my ass is on the edge and my feet are on the floor. She kneels down between my knees and pulls her hair back from her face with her left hand, over her shoulder. Then, using only her lips, she engulfs me with her mouth, just the tip at first, then more as she slides down it until it hits the back of her throat. She pulls almost all the way off me and then does it again, and again, her tongue sliding between her lips to snake around the root of it.

I arch up, but there's nowhere to go. My cock is buried as far as it can go without going up her nose. She bobs up and down a few more times, then stands up, and says, "Bad angle."

She pushes me up the bed, turns around, and nestles down on top of me in a sixty-nine, her sex just out of reach of my tongue. I'm about to complain about this when she grabs my cock with her lips again and slowly, agonizingly, slides her lips all the way down to my balls.

I've heard about women who can do this, but never experienced it and it's all I can do to keep from exploding. I want to buck up, but her hands are flat on my thighs, her teeth are close to my scrotum. She pulls up and descends again and I'm in bliss, practically crawling away from underneath her.

She pulls off for a second, says, "Don't fucking move." I want to say 'Yes, ma'am,' or at least salute. I'm thinking of how to say it when she slides all the way down again, and I groan.

I look up and Akiko has crawled up toward the head of the bed and is licking Laura from her ass to her clit in long slippery strokes. I want to help but I'm pinioned under the both of them. I try to move my arm but it's the wrong arm and the cast bangs against someone's thigh.

Broken hand? What broken hand?

Two more deep strokes and Laura kneels up and turns around. "Fuck me," she says. "I need you to fuck me." She's on her knees now, positioned with her knees on the end of the bed, her magnificent ass arched up in the air.

I somehow manage to lever myself up off my back and stumble toward the edge of the futon. I get my legs under me and turn around.

"Akiko, get me a condom, quick," she says.

Akiko looks bewildered for a moment, shakes her head, and spreads her hands palms up.

"Oh, shit, of course not," Laura says. She turns to look at me. "Put it in my ass," she says. "You'll have to put it in my ass."

"Hey, that's OK, really," I say.

"Now," she says. "Now."

Well, if you put it that way.

I kneel behind her. Akiko has slid beneath her, in a sixty-nine again, and is working her fingers, spreading the moisture around. I dip the head of my cock into her pussy for lubrication, pull it out, get one foot on the bed for leverage, grab my cock with my right hand and place it against her. She stops wiggling and I slowly ease the head in and wait. Her ass clamps against my cock and the pressure stops me from coming on the spot. I stop dead and wait. She slaps Akiko's ass, once, loudly. "Stop it," she says. "You're distracting me. Wait until he gets it in."

She starts to relax around me and I take the cue and slide in another inch, and wait. She's breathing deeply now, long inhalations and quick exhalations, willing her body to relax. It does, and I slowly slide all the way in and wait there.

She is tight, so fucking tight. I slowly slide halfway out and then all the way back in again and it's easier this time and she starts to back up against me in a regular rhythm, slow and steady at first. Her head droops down and buries itself between Akiko's thighs. I can feel a slight change in angle and realize that Akiko has done the same.

We start with long slow strokes, but she screams out, "Fuck me, goddamnit! Fuck me!" and we're off at a gallop. It's a different sensation; all I can feel is her sphincter, just a narrow ring squeezing me, and nothing beyond it. She's tight, and she's hot, and I'm pounding away for all I'm worth. I have my right hand on her hip, and try to get some purchase with my left, ignoring the cast. She's slamming back into me, rocking hard as I push in faster. My strokes get shorter and quicker and I can't even think about holding back, I can't even think about thinking.

Then she stiffens, pauses, Akiko has worked her magic down below me. As they both start to spasm, I throw in four more fast hard thrusts before I stop dead still, all the way inside, and I come. My dick is jumping and her ass is pulling and the both of them are rocking and we all collapse into a heap on the futon, trapping Akiko underneath, my balls against her chin until we roll over onto our sides.

I'm covered with sweat. We rock gently back and forth slowly for a minute until I flop over onto my back. I'm seeing stars and hearing violins and have lost all sense of time until I feel a warm wet washcloth wrapped around my cock as one of them washes me up, and that's the last thing I remember until I drift off, dead to the world.

Later I wake and it's dark and I don't know what time it is and Akiko is pushing something into my mouth—a pill— and holding a glass of water to my lips. I mutter something and crash again, totally beat.

A few hours later I wake up for a minute, and think to myself, Man, what an amazing fucking dream. Then I realize that my right arm is asleep and try to move it and realize it's under Laura, and we're all three of us on our right sides spooning, my softened dick nestled in the crack of her ass, her soft thighs against Akiko's firmer ones. I flex my hand until the feeling comes back, and fall asleep again and don't feel a thing until morning is streaming into my eyes.

I sit halfway up and see that they're dressed and sitting cross-legged on the bottom of the futon, sipping coffee from big black mugs. They look over at me.

I rub my eyes with my good right hand and stare at the cast on my left. I look over at Akiko and say, "What did you mean when you said that all the trouble in the band, Laura was behind it?"

And slowly, a little at a time, as if they're talking to a troubled three-year-old, they tell me. I listen, and my dick shrinks to microscopic size and my brain expands exponentially as I think: Oh shit. Oh shit. Oh, shit.

CHAPTER 30
Ken Ridlin

On to Wisconsin
Friday, January 17

Powell picks me up in his beat-up old Ford. I've got a gym bag with some clothes in it, plus three cases—an alto sax, a soprano sax, and a tenor. I also own a clarinet, and a baritone sax. I don't have the chops yet for the clarinet. I don't have the wind yet for the baritone.

Powell pops the trunk, I load in my gear. I open the back door, but Landreau is in there, fast asleep.

"Come sit up front," Powell says

Powell is quiet, like he doesn't want to wake Landreau. His driving is quiet, too—smooth and easy. The roads are a little slick, but he's comfortable. No nervous small talk.

We head toward the expressway. Amatucci has given him directions—290 North to 52 North to 12 North to 50 West. He hands me a three-by-five card. It's a list of songs for tonight. He explains that this is a private gig at a house. Someone they meet at a club date, says he'd love to have them up to his place at the lake sometime. Yeah, right, they say.

Last month he calls to set it up. Amatucci takes the call, almost hangs up on him, quotes him way too much money. The guy doesn't flinch, asks, "Would cash be acceptable?" Faxes down a map, mails down an envelope with half the cash up front—must have picked up something in Amatucci's tone of voice. They're locked in, it's all set.

It'll be three fifty-minute sets. Music for a hundred people. Background noise. Easy.

The list doesn't follow Powell's usual past-to-present pattern. Not much real old stuff at all. Nothing real new, either. All '30s and '40s and mainstream '50s, no bop, all standards. A couple of unusual choices—"Something in the Way She Moves," by George Harrison of the Beatles, "New York State of Mind," by Billy Joel—like that.

I look at him. "Chicago Style?" I ask.

He nods. "After a whole hour-and-a-half of rehearsal, we're not going to do a lot of complicated ensemble arrangements," he says. "So, yes, Chicago Style."

What he means is, we'll start each tune with an ensemble chorus, usually the trumpet or the sax playing the lead, then take solos, two or three choruses each, three or four of us on each song, and then wrap up together with the ensemble melody one more time. I don't know how it got the name "Chicago Style." Maybe in New York they call it "New York Style." I wouldn't know. It's the easiest way to go if you're a pickup band. If you don't know the tune, you can comp in the background and skip the solo. Nobody gets embarrassed. This is for my benefit.

"Any tunes you don't know?" he asks.

I look at the card again. "All depends on what key they're in," I say. "I'm not much on the sharps."

"Ask Vinnie about the sharps, sometime when you have an hour," he says. "He'll give you a whole dissertation on it. We get into anything you don't know, just lay low. We'll cover."

I nod.

"So," I say, changing direction, "why did you leave the U. of C.?"

He squints, then says, "I left because I was done."

"Just got tired of it? Had enough?"

"I did get tired of it, yes, but I finished anyway."

I must look lost. He says, "You must have me confused with Vince. He hasn't completed his doctorate. He's ABD."

"ABD?"

" 'All But the Dissertation,' " he translates. "He has all the credits he needs, just has to write his thesis. I was at the same point he's at: I didn't see the point of going any further with it. But I just couldn't walk away. I don't know why, exactly . . . so I finished."

"Dr. Paul Powell," I say.

I'm not mocking him, but maybe it comes out that way.

"There are some people who think of me that way," he says.

"But no thought of pursuing it, doing something with the degree?"

"Well, that would mean either a research job or a teaching job. I did both as a grad student, and I can't say anything negative about either. But after I got into the music, both prospects seemed a little . . . pale."

"Never going to get rich being a musician," I say.

"I was never going to get rich being a college professor, either."

"Got a point there," I say.

"Is that why you quit playing? To make the big money with the cops?"

He's so quiet I have to keep reminding myself that he's sharp. He's so calm I have to remind myself he can sting.

"As long as I have the basics covered, money by itself is not a priority for me," he says.

Landreau is snoring softly in the back. "Your friend said pretty much the same thing."

He glances back there. "I wouldn't doubt it," he says.

"What do you know about him?" I ask. "Beyond you met him in Iowa and played together a few times?"

He pauses, thinks. There are still some people who do

this, though they're rare. He glances back at Landreau, who's still asleep. He turns to me.

"I know he's the best musician I have ever met in my life, and I've played with a lot of people, names you would know. He knows any song you can name, he can play every one of them in any key you can think of, at any tempo you want. He can play every style from Dixieland to swing to bebop to free jazz to fusion. He has a beautiful lyrical sensibility; whole new songs just flow out of him every time he plays. He has a dynamic sense that I can't even fathom. And until the other day I never knew he could do it on the cornet and on the piano as well, maybe even better."

" 'Aside from that, Mrs. Lincoln,' " I quote the old line, " 'how did you like the play?' "

He almost chuckles. "Detective, you got me; I'm in awe."

"What about outside the music?" I ask.

"I don't know much. Troubled childhood, dysfunctional family. He has some formal training from somewhere, but I don't know where or when. I don't think he's married, don't think he has any kids, don't think he does anything but practice and play, play and practice."

"And sleep," I say.

Powell glances back at him in the rearview mirror. "Actually, he doesn't even do very much of that. He once told me he read something about Thomas Edison, the inventor, and how he never slept, and only sleeps about twenty minutes at a time every couple of hours."

If that's true, I think, time's almost up.

"What do *you* know about him?" Powell asks. "You must have been checking."

I wonder how much to tell him. I also listen to hear if Landreau is asleep.

"Far as we can tell?" I say, quietly. "He doesn't even exist."

Powell looks at me.

"He gave me his mother's name and address, long deceased. It checks out. Found a birth certificate, matches up pretty well. Except he looks maybe five years younger than the certificate."

"All that sleep deprivation must be keeping him young," he says.

"Could be," I say. "Except the certificate also says he has blue eyes, not brown."

"That could be developmental," Powell says. "A lot of babies, Caucasian babies, are born with blue eyes which turn brown or green within a couple of weeks."

"You know," I say, "I heard that from somebody. Didn't really believe it."

"You can believe it," he says. "It's true."

"Well," I say, "that could explain the blue eyes, then."

I hesitate. I'm not sure why I'm laying out my hand for him. It's a gut thing, feels right.

"One thing it doesn't explain," I say.

Powell waits for me.

"We found the birth certificate, like I said," I say. "We also found his death certificate, and that checks out, too. Jack Landreau died a few months after he was born. Died as an infant, crib death, what do they call it—?"

"SIDS," he says. "Sudden Infant Death Syndrome."

"Right," I say.

Powell ponders this. "Any chance of a mistake?" he asks.

"Well," I say, "it *is* government work. But still . . ."

"Why would somebody, I don't know, change names like that?" he asks.

"This used to be a pretty standard way of getting an alias. Go to the library, look up birth certificates, cross-reference them with deaths, find somebody who died young. Get a copy of the birth certificate. Tell them you lost yours. The feds have a database of all births, and they have a database of all the deaths. Two different systems. Take the birth certificate, get a Social Security number, use that to get a driver's license. Get that, you can get anything—credit cards, whatever. No chance of running into the real Jack Landreau—he's dead."

"You've been very clear about the 'how' of it; I was asking more about the 'why' of it."

"Thought *you* might be able to help with that," I say.

He thinks again.

"I would imagine that people who do that are hiding. People who do that are running from something."

"But what is he running from?" he asks.

I look at him. "Do you want to ask him?"

He turns to me, shakes his head, once. No. We fall silent, The miles pass.

There is a stirring in back. Landreau sits up, rubs his eyes. "Where are we?" he asks.

"On our way to Wisconsin," Powell says. "We're almost there; it won't be long now."

So we keep driving. The roads get narrower and slower and eventually there we are. It's a huge house, looks the size of a golf clubhouse. A big porch, all the way around, dark hunter-green canvas awnings covering it.

Worrell and Jones are already there, and they join us. It is foggy and dank and cold. We walk around to the side facing the lake. Nothing much to see until it parts and maybe half a mile away we see this house, all long horizontal lines. Landreau whistles, Powell stares.

"What an amazing structure," Powell says. "I wonder if it's a real Frank Lloyd Wright or a knockoff. Too bad Vinnie isn't here—he knows them all by heart."

"I imagine that would be a much more commodious place to play than this monstrosity," the professor says, jerking his head over his shoulder at the country club.

And a voice comes from behind us and says, "I'm afraid you gentlemen will never get the opportunity to discover that for yourselves."

We turn. There is a guy there, mid-fifties, clean-shaven bald head. Dressed in tails, of all things, little white vest. Is this the owner? No. There is something about his look.

"You must be the entertainment portion of the evening, am I correct?"

We nod.

"I was informed of your arrival, and told I should transact with a Mr. Amatucci . . . ?"

This is the butler, the majordomo, whatever.

Worrell jumps in. "Mr. Amatucci is temporarily indisposed and will not be joining us, unfortunately. But we have secured a more than adequate replacement." He pauses. "I am curious—why did you say that we would never have the pleasure of playing there, in that glorious house? Is the owner not a fan of indigenous music?"

The butler probably doesn't know what "indigenous" means, but makes a quick recovery.

"I only mean," he says, "that the owner of that house never mingles with our little community up here, and jealously guards her privacy. Some call her "The Lady of the Lake." I would imagine that you might be a trifle . . . loud . . . for her tastes."

The little snot.

"We'll try not to disturb her," I say, "you show us where to go."

CHAPTER 31
Ken Ridlin

To Milwaukee
Saturday, January 18

It is nine o'clock when Powell comes bouncing down the stairs. He sits. We wait for Landreau. His bag is sitting there but he's not around. Ten minutes later he shows up, coming in from outside. Has on a hat and gloves, and steam is coming off him.

I put my coffee cup down on the table, and it makes a little clink.

Landreau turns to Powell, mutters something. Powell grins.

"What?" I ask. "What is it?"

Powell looks at Landreau, who shrugs. Powell turns to me and speaks.

"He was telling me it was a G," he says.

"A G?" I repeat. "What's a G? What do you mean?"

Powell reaches past me and picks up the coffee cup, flicks his finger nail against it. "G," he sings, "G, G, G."

I turn to Landreau. "You one of those people with perfect pitch?" I ask him.

He looks at me. Squints. "Nothing's perfect," he says.

I'm not sure what to say to this. I reach over and pick up my cases.

"Should we wait for the others?" he asks.

"Sidney has already left," Powell says. "He took off with Akiko at dawn."

"We might as well head out, if you're ready to go."

I look at Landreau. He shrugs, picks up his case.

The trip to Milwaukee is uneventful. Mostly back roads, four lanes, forty miles an hour. No traffic. The weather is cold. The roads are clear. Nice scenery, trees hanging low under a cloak of snow. No one talks, we just look out the windows.

We get to the club way too early. Jones has already been there, setting up her kit. There's a string-bass case, locked to a radiator with a cable and a padlock. All present and accounted for.

The place is called The Joint, and could be called The Cave. Under street level, just a little light filtering in from the half-windows. Strong smell of beer and cigarettes. Music posters on the walls—Clapton, Creedence Clearwater Revival, Guns N' Roses, Beck. Beck? What the hell?

The gig is just OK. Not like last night, which I can't even find the words to talk about. We're playing OK, but not great. The crowd is into it. They applaud for every little thing, even the parts that don't really work. The piano is flat. Powell and I have to adjust all the way open to get close to it. Throws everybody's intonation off. The crowd doesn't notice. Landreau notices. He has a look on his face like he's got bugs stuck in his teeth.

The crowd is couples in their thirties, forties, and fifties. No singles to speak of. There seems to be a pitcher of beer on every table, no mixed drinks. The food is bratwurst, knackwurst, weisswurst, and hot dogs, and they all come with sauerkraut and french fries. I look a little closer.

There's not a soul in here less than fifty pounds overweight, men and women both.

Powell tries to do what he can, but the rest of us are stuck with our feet in the mud. Landreau? He plays beautifully, he can't help it. The crowd doesn't really notice. He gets less applause after his solos than even I do. That's just wrong.

After the first song, whenever someone else solos I'm scanning the crowd. No Laura.

We play a set. Take a break. Play another set. More applause. The worse we play the more they like it. It's Saturday night—they want to feel like they're getting their money's worth. And they're getting beer-drunk, happy and sentimental. I look at all the bottles lined up so pretty behind the bar. Sparkling in the light. Singing their songs in color. I look at the glass of flat ginger ale on the floor next to me.

The last set, I lean over to Powell, "Let's play some blues, just jam." He nods. Powell calls out "C-Jam Blues," an old Lester Young sax classic. I start with the tenor and Powell comes in on the trumpet. I take it back, on the alto, hand it to Landreau. Take it back again on the soprano. A chorus, another chorus, another chorus. I have stopped thinking about my fingers. Jones is working the drums, Worrell is slapping the bass. Another chorus. We go on and on and on. I swing my sax in a circle. They all join in, pushing to the finish.

Wild applause. Almost deserved.

Powell vamps into the band's theme song. Introduces the band. We each play a half a chorus, then we're done.

Manager comes up and gives Powell a fat envelope. He opens it. Counts it. They shake hands. Powell turns to the band, divvies up the cash. Except for me. Which is right. We pack up.

Coats on. Handshakes all around. We're all in a better mood than a few hours ago. It's the music is what it is.

And then we're into the cars and into the night. Back to Chicago.

No Laura. Not a glimpse. But there was the music, and that will have to carry me for now.

CHAPTER 32
Ken Ridlin

Back to Chicago
Saturday, January 18

After the gig, we're ready to go. Last second, Landreau jumps up, says he's going with Worrell and Jones.

I have the thought: is he going to skip? Back to Detroit? Iowa? Slip away?

No. It comes to me immediately—it's just a definite No. He's staying, for now. The fact that I know this but don't know how I know it gnaws at me.

We watch him walk away; then we're gone.

We wind through the city streets. The wind is howling. Everything is shades of gray. It's quiet, cold, dark. I let Powell drive for a while, get settled in. Then I interrupt.

"What can you tell me about Amatucci?" I ask.

"I could tell you a lot, but we're only going to Chicago, not Los Angeles. What do you want to know?"

"Whatever," I say. "Background."

He pauses, gathers his thoughts. I remind myself: he does this.

"Born in New York, got his BS at Columbia—"

"That where he gets his BS?" I say. "He sure has plenty of it."

He pauses again, tightens his mouth.

"I mean," I say, backing up. "The guy can sure talk, and about the craziest things. Night I saw him at the hospital, he is going on and on about the thermometer, the battery thing they use now, on that rolling stand, and how it figures out the temperature with electricity. I mean, details like you wouldn't believe—"

"Ohm's law?" he asks.

That stops me. I turn to him.

"He give you the same rant?" I ask.

"Did he say more than two sentences?" he asks.

"You kidding? He goes on for three, four minutes—"

"Then it's the truth," he says. "When Vinnie just says something brief, it may be a fact, it may be that he's bullshitting you, it may be that's he's testing you, it may be that he's just trying some idea on for size."

He pauses, lets this sink in.

"But when he goes on for more than two sentences, he knows exactly what he's talking about; he's researched it, he can cite references."

"Really?" I ask.

He nods.

"He got his BS at Columbia, Phi Beta Kappa, summa cum laude, with two majors and a 3.9 GPA. And he got all A's here in graduate school and I never saw him study for a single minute."

"Two majors?"

"Mechanical engineering and psychology," he says. "A somewhat unusual combination."

"I'd say," I said. "How'd that happen?"

He's one of these people who drives sitting straight up. He shifts in his seat, sits straighter.

"He was always interested in the way things worked; gadgets, gizmos, appliances, machines of all kinds. He won a number of engineering contests in high school. He got accepted at MIT, Purdue, Rensselaer, all the big engineering schools, but he got a scholarship at Columbia, and his folks pushed him to stay close to home. He took a class, sophomore year, called 'Invention and Inventors,' and what interested him was not just the machines but the fact that they had all been invented by people, most of them very curious people. He started to get interested in those people: How did they do what they did? What separated Thomas Edison from his siblings? Ben Franklin from his brothers? Cyrus McCormick from his peers? One Intro Psych course and he was hooked. He couldn't get enough—child development, sensation and perception, physiology, cognitive, disorders. He kept up the mechanical engineering all the while, and ended up with credits enough for both. Next, graduate school at the U. of C., strictly cognitive psychology. That's where we met."

"So what happened?"

"What happened?"

"What happened that he hasn't finished?"

"Epistemology," he says. There is no pause this time.

"E-what?" I ask. I have heard this word before, but can't place where, or what it means.

"Epistemology. The study of how we know what we know."

I look at him. He must be able to read my blank look.

"How do you know I'm driving this car?" he asks. "You have what you think is the objective sensory evidence of your eyes and your ears and your kinesthetic sense. You can see the world moving outside the window. But it could be a dream, a hallucination. Take it further: how do you know I don't have a dead body stuffed in the trunk, or two kilos of heroin under the seat?" He pauses. "Assumption, interpretation, implication, deduction. No direct evidence."

"Yeah . . ." I say.

"Epistemology looks at the sources of our knowledge, and our beliefs, and the deeper you look at the former, the more you see the latter. We don't experience the world, we create it. The field Vinnie was in was cognitive psychology, and epistemology messed him up. He got to the point where he saw that most of what we know about ourselves is just metaphor, simile, analogy. Emotions are 'like a teakettle.' The mind is 'like a computer.' Even the whole notion that there is something called a 'mind' and not just an actual physical brain, three pounds of hamburger between your ears. He had ended up studying and testing the metaphor, not the brain itself, so there was no 'there' there. All the research he was working on was all assumption, interpretation, implication, deduction. No direct evidence. No sensory data. Just abstract theory."

I nod.

"It stalled him. Here he was, studying how we process information, how we interpret the world, and he's seeing that the basic data we all start with is not data at all, but a chimera, a dream, a shadow on the wall of a cave."

"Plato," I say.

He looks at me, cocks an eyebrow.

"Cook County Community College," I say. "They've heard of him, even there."

He nods. Pauses.

"Meanwhile, we had started the band, and epistemology does not apply. With music, you know going in that it's all opinion, you know there's never going to be any direct objective evidence of whether something you play is good or not. You've got the sensory evidence of your ears, and the social evidence of your peers, and sometimes they're just wrong. Vinnie was good enough that he saw he could get better, and he has. And he doesn't have to know how he knows he's getting better, he can hear it. So he got deeper into the music, and backed off on his thesis."

I think about this.

"I can kind of see what you're saying," I say. "It's like he's doing something he thinks is important, is true, and it gets pulled out from under him."

There is a pause. There's not much traffic, but he's keeping it at the speed limit.

"So why the cab? Even without the degree, must be something better he could do," I say. "The Merchandise Mart, finance, teaching, whatever?"

He looks straight ahead. Then glances over at me.

"What he's trying to do is to see how far he can go with his music. Driving a cab gives him the flexibility to work on that. It's his way of not letting himself get interested in anything else. You mentioned teaching; he's done that. This sounds like heresy, but he put a ridiculous amount of thought into it; three or four versions of a one-hour class outline were the norm. It was taking him twelve hours a day to prepare for one hour; he had no time for anything else. It seems to be part of his nature to be prone to sudden enthusiasms, and to immerse himself completely in them."

"Well." I say, "This city, learning it so you can go out and drive a cab and make money, is more of a lifetime thing than some 'sudden enthusiasm.' "

" 'A couple of hours with a map, then two days of driving around, systematically,' that's what he told me," he says. "Vinnie studied a map one night, then drove around to associate visual landmarks with the street names, and after that he had it all. I believe him. I've been in that cab. He doesn't keep a map in there; he has a better one in his head."

We're both alone with our thoughts. The miles pass.

"On the way up," I say, "you said that Landreau must be running from something."

He nods.

"Any idea what he's running from?" I ask.

He turns to me, shakes his head, once. "We're all running, in our own way. Running from something, running toward something."

"Everybody?" I ask. "You think?"

"Well, some people aren't running. They're standing still."

"Standing still? They're not running from anything?"

"They're hiding," he says.

I look at him.

" 'Fight or flight,' " he says. "It's been in the gene pool since before the beginning."

I think about this. "So, if you're running you may be running away from something or running toward something, but if you're standing still you're hiding. Is that it? Is everybody who is standing still hiding?"

"Well, not everybody," he says.

"The rest of them, what are they doing?" I ask.

"They're not doing anything," he says, "not a damned thing."

I look over at him. Waiting for the rest of it.

"The ones who are standing still and aren't hiding, they're dead."

Yeah, I think. I ask myself the question: Which one are you?

I answer my own question: Which one am I *not*?

CHAPTER 33
Vinnie Amatucci

Hyde Park
Sunday, January 19

I've been staying up ridiculously late the last few nights, doing absolutely nothing but staring at the TV, flipping through some old magazines, smoking some weed. My real agenda was to get more depressed. The hand still ached, but it was steady, with not as much throbbing as before, not as many sharp pains when I bumped the cast into something. It was almost worse like this, because for long stretches of time I almost forget about it, and then when I crashed it into something I would get surprised and pissed off all over again.

I had a little breakfast and a lot of coffee and laid around reading the Sunday *Tribune*, the words going into my eyes and out of my head, with no traction at all. At around two o'clock I caught myself reading an article in the Sunday magazine that I had already read at ten o'clock in the morning, and threw the paper down in disgust, accompanied by a fit of wild fucking cursing.

I was pissed at myself, because this was all I had been able to make of my stupid life. I was a first-rate cabdriver and a second-rate piano player. In other words, nobody. I was about to turn thirty, far away from home, with no friends but the guys in the band, still without the god-damned dissertation done. I had nowhere to go and no big shiny degree to fall back on.

I was pissed at Landreau for showing me just how second-rate I was. I was pissed at Paul for believing in how good I might be.

I was even pissed at Akiko because she was madly in love. Not that I envied her Laura—Laura was the most beautiful, sexy, exotic woman I had even met, and she scared the shit out of me. I was pissed at Akiko because she faced it, straight ahead, and she held on.

I was pissed at the thought that the guy that got away would come back, or that they'd send someone else. I was hunkered down, dug in, making time pass.

There's a time to be constructive, and a time to lay back and lick your wounds. I was licking my wounds.

And the rest of the day passed that way, in a blur. I took the pipe back out of the drawer, even turned on a football game on the tube, the play-offs. I got a little buzzed, I lay on the couch, I watched the hours roll by.

Waiting it out, whatever *it* was.

That night, in my sleep, she came to me.

I was in my apartment, in bed, knocked out on Percocet—I had been saving them for sleep, to quiet the throbbing that started in my hand and migrated to my chest. It was two in the morning, maybe three, when the covers were slowly pulled back and she slid into my bed. Her body was warm and she smelled like vanilla. The lights were out and the shades were drawn. I couldn't see a thing, but I could picture her perfectly.

I was lying on my left side, with my mangled left hand stretched out in front of me, and when she slid under the covers, she backed up against me, in a spoon position. She pulled the covers up over the both of us, and backed in closer, fitting my forearm into the curve of her neck.

She sighed a long sigh, and wiggled her perfect ass against me. Her skin felt like heated silk, smooth and pure and perfect.

I was hard almost instantly but didn't dare move an inch; I just lay there, breathing her scent, feeling the warmth at her core spread through me.

She breathed deeply once, twice, and backed against me tighter. I was dying to push toward her, that primordial hump reflex pounding in my temples, but I lay as still as death, afraid to lose the moment. My right hand, my good hand, was resting on her hip, and I fought my desire to reach out and stroke her, to rub along her flank, to trace my fingertips down her leg. I could feel her calves slide against my shins, feel the hollows of her knees rub against my kneecaps, feel the arch of her spine tickling the hairs on my chest.

It was pleasure, absolute pleasure; it was torture, sheer torture.

Oh, God, Laura, I thought, Oh God.

And with that the covers were flung back, she sat up in the bed, turned on the light, swung her legs over the side, and reached for her clothes.

It wasn't a dream at all. And it wasn't Laura.

"Akiko?" I asked. "Akiko? What are you doing here?"

She was holding a black T-shirt in her hands, wrestling with it. She had it half inside-out, half outside-in. She twisted it twice more, then threw it down in disgust. She leaned forward, put her head in her hands, squeezed her short hair in her fists.

"I don't know, Vince, I wish I fucking knew, you know?"

"I mean, how'd you get in here? I mean, I thought I— wasn't the door locked?"

She held her chin in her hands, her head down. "Cheap locks, Vince. Took me no more than twenty seconds, didn't even leave a mark. You ought to get them replaced. Really."

"What happened? What is it? I was asleep," I said.

"Well," she said. "You called out her name—'Oh, God, Laura. Oh God'—like that."

She was turned away from me, her shoulders bouncing up and down in a slow rhythm. I reached a hand out, my right one, and touched her back. Her skin was tight against her spine.

"I was asleep, I was having a dream."

She half-turned, half-faced me. I caught a trace of a smirk; then she turned back away. "It's cool, Vince. You're right, you were only having a dream." She muttered. "Maybe so was I. I have, like, no fucking idea what I was thinking . . ."

I sat up and wrapped my arms around her, tried to quiet her. She began to shake and I kept my arms tight and my mouth shut. Sometimes there's nothing you can say, and anything you could say would just make it worse. She kept rocking, but she wouldn't let the tears come out, couldn't give voice to the pain. So I held her until the quaking stopped and her shoulders relaxed and her breathing slowed to a regular rhythm. We slowly settled back into the spoon position we had started in.

After a few minutes she half-turned toward me and said, "I'm sorry, Vince. I'm freaking out. I haven't seen her since, well, since that night you were at my place, and I'm scared she's dumped me. Run off. Gone back to men. Gone on to someone else, whatever."

"Let me see if I'm following this. You came here, broke in, to see if she had 'gone on' to *me?*"

She shrugged. "Well, yeah, I guess. Sort of."

"And you had to get naked and get into my bed to look *really really closely?*"

She pulled her arm back and smacked me—right on my cast. She shook her hand back and forth. I shook my cast back and forth. We both howled. It took us a while to settle down.

"So, does this mean there's a side of you that I haven't seen?" She didn't even shrug this time. "I mean, do you have some kind of dark and sordid heterosexual past I don't know about?"

She looked up at me. "My feelings are all jumbled up. I wasn't thinking, like, at all."

I hadn't been thinking too clearly myself lately, so I was in no position to push the point. Some time passed. We let the implications trail out.

"And besides," she said, "I've been with men . . . a couple of times."

"You have? Really?"

"When I was like, younger."

"And . . . ?" I asked.

She shrugged.

"So," I said, trying to lighten the mood, "how do you want it?"

"What?"

"Well, how do you want it? Straight-up missionary style, woman on top, doggy style? Should we start with a little foreplay, some oral perhaps—"

She smacked me again, reached around and back-handed me in the head. Unfortunately, my head is at least as hard as the cast. We both howled again.

"Does this mean you really don't want me for myself?"

She started to protest, but I cut her off.

"No, I mean, here I thought you wanted *me,* and now I discover I was just supposed to be some transitional sex object, some *tool* . . ."

"Come on, Vince," she giggled. "Cut it out."

"God, I feel so, I don't know, so *used* . . ."

She chuckled again, but then she turned around, put her hand gently on my face. "Vince, you know I really love you. You're a friend."

"Oh, that's right. I keep forgetting, you're only supposed to fuck people you really despise—"

"Stop being sarcastic," she said. "You know I love you like a brother."

"Geez," I said, "you really know how to make a guy's dick go soft."

She rolled her eyes, then moved her leg up against me. "Liar," she said.

I started to protest, but she cut me off. Then she rolled over onto her back, spread her legs, turned to me and said, "OK, go ahead. Let's do it. Fuck me."

"Always the romantic," I said.

"No, really, go ahead. I can do this, really. I thought about it, kind of, on the way over. Might even be, uh, you know, interesting."

"Flattery will get you everywhere. But that wasn't flattery."

I pushed her right leg closed and leaned up on my elbow. I leaned down and kissed her gently on the lips. Her eyelids fluttered three times. She tasted like vanilla, and honey. I leaned back, took a breath.

"Look, Akiko, the one you really want is Laura, and, as you can tell, I'm not Laura. You and I, we could have a great time together, but at the end you'd still want Laura, and you'd feel bad for having me instead. Am I right?"

She looked into my eyes, and saw I was telling the truth, at least the truth as I saw it. She squinted.

"I mean," I said, "don't get me wrong. You're a beautiful woman, plus of course smart and charming and intelligent and a great percussionist and 'gee, that really looks great on you' and all that . . . But you're right, you're my friend. Another time, different circumstances, I would make love to you as well as I know how, fuck you like I meant it, and I would mean it. And you're right, it might be interesting. Very interesting. But right now?"

There was that shrug again.

"I do love you, Vince. Sorry I doubted you, suspected you, whatever." She twisted toward me, her black eyes searching mine. And we had a moment there, a genuine moment.

She smiled, rolled onto her knees, reached over, turned

out the light, and curled back up against me. The room was cold, and she was warm, and I tucked the covers in around us. We sighed, and started to sink down in together. Mr. Dick was still standing at attention, and I shifted to try to get him out of the way. She reached behind herself, grabbed it, gave it one squeeze.

"Hey. Don't be embarrassed. Don't forget, I've seen it up close and, like, personal."

I nodded against the back of her neck.

"Besides," she said, "it's kind of, like, flattering, you know?"

And she giggled.

Yeah, I guess, I thought. And with that we drifted off to a restless but gentle sleep. Still friends. More than ever. Even if one of us had a hard-on.

CHAPTER 34
Vinnie Amatucci

In the Fat Man's Cab
Monday, January 20

Akiko had disappeared sometime in the night, but her scent fluttered up from my bed as I flipped the quilt roughly into place. I slipped into the shower, got dressed, and wedged into my car. It was twenty-two degrees on the way to the cabstand to pick up the big black beast. The sun was a dim rumor in the sky, hidden behind a smear of altostratus clouds. I clicked open #691 and slid in.

It was time to get back to work. Driving one-handed didn't figure to be a problem—I do it all the time. I tossed my stuff in the front, started the engine, let the cab warm up enough to cut the frost on the windshield, and headed downtown. It was Monday, the Accountant's day, so as I drove north I kept the NOT FOR HIRE sign lit up, and I got slightly lit up myself—just a couple of hits. As I stopped at a light on Michigan Avenue across from the Hilton, a citizen standing in front of the hotel tried to flag me down, to make me make a U-turn and pick him up. I pointed to the sign on the roof, and he gave me the finger.

I cruised up Michigan, turned right at the Hancock and then left and left again, and as I rounded the corner, the Accountant was standing there, reading the paper, which he had neatly folded in half vertically and then into thirds horizontally, like people used to do on the subways when I was a kid in New York, so they wouldn't take up too much of the communal space. Now they just sprawl out all over the place, and are less likely to read a newspaper than to deposit some bodily fluids on one. But not the Accountant, he's old school. Just seeing this little gesture restored my faith, such as it is, in humanity, such as *it* is.

I pulled up to the curb and popped the locks. He took a few seconds to finish whatever he was reading, then folded the paper, tucked it into his coat pocket, smiled and got in the cab.

"Why, Vincent, it's so good to see you this morning, prompt as usual," he said.

There was something else in his tone—a little weak in the upper overtones; something in his body language; a crease of worry on his forehead; a hunch of doubt in his shoulders—but I didn't say a word, except, "Where to, your Lordship?"

He settled himself in, unbuttoned his coat, placed his briefcase in his lap, took off his gloves and wrapped his hands around them, squeezing them a little too forcefully. Finally he looked up at me. His eyes bugged out, and he leaned forward.

"What in God's name happened to your hand?" he asked.

"Uh, a little mishap," I said.

"Sticking your fingers where they don't belong, eh?" he leered.

"Something like that," I said.

He paused, gave me a serious look. "Can you drive?"

"No, actually, I pushed the car up here from South Twentieth and State. Luckily, I can do that one-handed."

He guffawed his fake laugh, but still looked serious. "Are you sure?"

"Quite," I said. "You are in the competent hands—*hand*—of a trained professional."

He looked at me for a beat, he nodded, then his face looked away and turned darker.

"Well, today it's going to be a long day indeed. Serious errands, portentous tasks—"

" 'And miles to go before I sleep,' " I quoted.

With that, he looked at me, blankly. Not a Frost fan, evidently. "Well, not so many miles today, not so many . . . Sometimes it's not the distance that counts but what you do at journey's end . . ."

I must have shown something on my face that looked to him like concern, because he piped right up: "But never fear, lad, you will be well-compensated, as is the custom of our little weekly tête-à-tête."

"Whatever is on the meter, sir," I said. "Be assured that you will be driven in comfort and class, or at least as well as this classic carriage and my one good hand will allow."

Now we were falling into the old comfy repartee, and it eased him noticeably. He gave me his chin-thrust-out FDR look, called out "Onward, then!" and I punched in and off we went.

I got all the way to a stoplight before I politely asked where the fuck we were going.

The first stop was down on the South Side, down in the Nineties somewhere, off Cottage Grove, where we were the only white folks in sight—not that there's anything wrong with that, except that there is—and we got there in less than twenty-five minutes. It was a storefront, a mix of Checks Cashed, Lottery, Grocery, Bakery, Beer and Wine, Premium Cigars, and Convenience. He was in and out in less than a minute. Then, unusually, we went still farther south, only about ten more blocks or so. This was an apartment building, semi-middle-class, and again, he was in and out in a flash. Then we headed up north, to the suburbs where the richer people hide from people who use check-cashing stores, first to an office building, then a fenced-in house. Again, in-and-outs, both of them, quick work. Then we started south again.

On the way, he cajoled me into playing some license-plate poker. We went back and forth for a while with me getting hot on a six-spot with QCR—"Quite Chilling Really, Quilt-Clad Reprobate, Quaint Condom Replacement, Quirky Cub Reporter, Queer Clock Robber and Quince Cooking Recipes," and him getting stumped on KJV, with only two references, and me picking it up on a challenge and adding "Killed Juvenile Victims" and "Kilt Just Vanished."

He wasn't taking much joy in it, whether I beat him or let him win. So I made some excuse to stop—I was at the tail end of "BBU" and I dropped a lit cigarette on the floor and said I had to locate it before we Both Burned Up. He got the joke, but didn't laugh, just gave me a tight little grin, so I changed the topic and we settled up on the money that had passed so far; I was up about twenty bucks.

As soon as I let him off the hook, he turned to look out the window and got a pensive look on his face, not sad, really, not angry or morose or troubled, really, just, like I said, pensive.

Or maybe he was trying to pass some gas; sometimes it's hard to tell them apart.

We went out to the West Side, past Greek Town, another quick in-and-out, then downtown, a little longer stop. When he came out he was checking his watch.

He hopped back in, shivering from the cold, and reached into his coat pocket, took out a flask and took a long pull on it. I made like I didn't notice, and in a few seconds I got a whiff of Scotch. He screwed the cap back on, wiped his mouth with his sleeve, showing a crack of what lay underneath his thin veneer of class, but then he saw me seeing him.

"Care for a little spot, a wee taste, a morning eye-opener?" he asked.

"Little early for me," I said, "and I'm kind of 'on duty' here. The cops don't like drunken cabdrivers."

"Cops?" he said, looking around.

"Just speaking hypothetically," I said. "But you go ahead; after all, you're not driving."

He nodded, looked at the flask, took another swallow and tucked it away. He reached into an outside pocket and fished out a roll of mints, popped one and commenced to suck away, looking out the window.

It took him close to a minute to realize that we were parked at the curb, not going anywhere. I let him take his time—I get paid whether we're moving or not—and I had a sense I didn't want to spook him.

He finally roused himself and called out an address out on the West Side again, south of Midway Airport, on Cicero. The way he said it was very precise, every syllable standing on its own, all alone. I drove up to the light at the corner, stopped for the red, and flipped the directional on; the Expressway was only two blocks away.

He immediately looked up and said, "Back streets, if you please, Vincent, back streets." He glanced at his watch again. "This next appointment is a scheduled one, and we have plenty of time."

I nodded, flipped the turn signal off, and headed straight through the intersection. It was mid-morning, traffic was light, and within about twenty minutes we were getting close to the address. As we did he leaned closer, put his hands up on the back of the front seat, and said in an almost conspiratorial whisper, "I'm afraid I'll be having some company at this appointment, a gentleman I have met only once, and who, frankly, I had no desire to meet again. But the vicissitudes of this business . . . This gentleman is someone who is extremely, uh, reticent, very private in his dealings, and it might be better for you and also for me if you parked around the corner and let me walk over from there."

As he said this his eyes were darting all over the place, even though we were still more than a mile away. Before I knew it, his hypervigilant state started to infect me. I noticed myself slowing imperceptibly, eyeballing every parked car, checking every pedestrian. I didn't want him to see me doing this, so I took a breath and locked my head facing straight ahead. But my eyes were doing the lateral tango.

And I blew it totally. I totally lost track of the blocks and instead of pulling over one block before the address I drove right by it—shit! I tried to act nonchalant about it and pulled around the corner after our stop, and even though my eyes were focused front, I saw somebody, a door or two down from the storefront we were aiming for, leaning up against the building. Middle-aged, middle-sized, nondescript, dressed in gray, an average face with a big Fu Manchu—and maybe it wasn't even him, hell, I had no fucking idea, just that there was a man standing near a building where we were supposed to meet someone.

I was panicking inside but tried to cover it by playing dumb on the outside. I cranked the wheel to the right, pulled over in a no-parking zone, and popped the locks. I put a stupid grin on my face, half-turned and asked, "Will this be close enough, sir?"

The Accountant didn't make one of his wise-ass remarks, didn't even nod. His face had turned red, his jaw was set, and he flat-out glared at me for a second before pulling his eyes away. Shit. Then he grabbed his briefcase, opened the door, slid out, and slammed it shut.

I hunkered down in the cab and waited, going through the old coulda-woulda-shoulda. My armpits were sweating and my hands were cold. This was a nice weekly gig, good money, good times, and I didn't want to blow it. But more than that, whatever he did on our little forays, the Accountant was a good guy, a fop and a jerk, but still a good guy. He had never stiffed me, never said a nasty word, never treated me like the help. I had a sense that I might have gotten him in some kind of trouble, and that was twisting me around inside.

I tried to sit still.

I checked my watch: five minutes had passed, much longer than his stops usually took. There was nothing I could do but wait; if I moved and he came out looking for me and I wasn't there, it'd be worse. If I got out of the car and walked around to stretch, it'd look like I was spying on him. Shit.

I looked at my watch again: ten minutes gone. My mind started to race with the possibilities. Calm down, Vince, I told myself, the guy's probably just there for show. We're not talking Al Capone here, not talking big-time drug dealers; there's no briefcase in the world big enough to hold that kind of money. Besides, I didn't even know if any money was involved at all. I had no evidence, no proof, not a single scrap of facts to go on. This whole scenario about mob activity or collections or whatever was all in my head. Let it go, I told myself. All the weed is making you paranoid.

My injured hand started to ache, deep under the cast where I couldn't rub the pain away.

And all of a sudden there he was, stepping in through the back door, his briefcase under his arm. He slid in very slowly, very carefully, like a much older man. His right hand was cupping his balls. He reached across with the left to close the door, still keeping the jewels under cover, reached into his right breast pocket with his left, took out the flask. His face looked ashen. He held the flask between his knees and unscrewed the cap, brought the flask to his mouth and took a long drink. Not a sip; I'm talking a couple of swallows—you could see his Adam's apple bobbing up and down. He kept drinking until it was maybe halfway empty, then brought it down into his lap again, the cap still off. He was breathing hard.

I wanted to say something, but what the fuck could I say without betraying some knowledge or suspicion of what he was up to, of what our little journeys were all about? I didn't want him to think I knew anything, I didn't want him to think I had seen the guy—I hadn't, well, not much, anyway. What the fuck was I supposed to say?

We just sat there, with the motor running and my brain racing.

Finally, I glanced in the rearview mirror, raised my eyebrows a notch, and said, "Everything OK, sir? Anything I can do?"

He kept looking out the window. Finally, he slowly turned until he was facing front, stretched his neck, and in a low voice said, "Mission accomplished. Let's head home, shall we?"

So we did.

Neither one of us said a word on the way back. I wanted to apologize for getting him in trouble, but that would have acknowledged he had gotten in trouble. I mean, what are you going to say? "Are your balls all right? Did he punch them or kick them or squeeze them?" I kept thinking of things to say, then editing them and saying nothing, feeling the silences like weights.

Every now and then he'd raise the flask up to his mouth and take a little sip, staring out the window. The color slowly came back into his face. As we hit downtown he took the last pull on the Scotch—the aroma was unmistakable by that point—found the cap, screwed it back on, tucked it away in his pocket. He took his hand away from his balls, stretched his legs, stretched his back. His face had regained some color; his posture had loosened.

He remembered the briefcase, which had slid off his lap and onto the seat next to him. He pulled it back onto his lap, patted it reassuringly. He took off his hat, set it on his lap, and reached into his pocket for a comb. He raked it over his head two, three, four strokes, slipped it back into his pocket, and carefully set his hat back on his head, just so. And just like that the mask of his persona slipped back into place. He glanced at me in the rearview once, then twice.

Finally, after what felt like a lifetime, we pulled up to where we meet, down the block from the Drake. Wrapping his scarf and coat tightly around himself, he looked at the meter, pulled two fifties and two twenties and a ten out of his pocket, and handed them forward. Then he added the twenty he owed me from our game, and fifty more.

"Somehow," I said, despite myself, "I get the feeling that you shouldn't be tipping me today. I know it's none of my business, but—"

"Ah, Vincent," he said, a wistful tone in his voice, "you have performed admirably, as you always do, and I wouldn't think of committing a failure of remuneration."

I opened my mouth to protest but he waved me off. He paused before he spoke.

"Hush hush, now. There are some days that are better than other days, but every day is better than no days at all." He paused again. His voice was small, distant. "Our lives, dear boy, are fraught with . . . challenges, some great, some small. I have mine, you have yours, and it is better for us both not to compare our struggles. But, whatever they may be, my lad, they all pass away. Over time. They all pass away."

I turned and looked at him, and we had a second of eye contact.

"Take care of yourself, sir," I said.

"I always try, Vincent. I always try. And you take care, too. Watch that hand!"

With that he opened the door, and leaned forward, testing himself to see if he could move all right. He slid out and walked around to my window. I opened it and looked up at him.

"Same time next week, my boy?"

I nodded, expectantly.

As he walked away I knew that I had done something; I just had no idea what it was.

CHAPTER 35
The Cleaner

The Meet; Near North Side
Tuesday, January 21

11:14 A.M.: Here they are. Cadillac stretch. Black. Car pulls up, almost goes past me. Pulls over. Backs up. Right rear door swings open.

It is the both of them. The Old Man on the left, the Nephew in the jump seat. The Old Man smiles. Leans forward. Reaches over to shake my hand. The Nephew elbows him aside. Has something in his hand. Metal detector. Wand thing like they use at the airport. Scans me. Up and down. "Sorry," says the Old Man. "You know how it is."

The Nephew motions to me. I scooch forward, raise my arms up to the divider. He gives me a pat down. Up and down. The groin. Around the back. The ankles. A halfway decent job.

Turns to his uncle. "Looks clean."

"What do you expect?" the Old Man says. "This is the last person who would hurt us."

"Still," I say, "cannot be too careful." Saving face for him.

Zep? Still has that spark in his eye. Tanned, trimmed, well-dressed. The Nephew looks like hell. Bags under the eyes. Skin all blotchy.

Old Man looks me over. "You're looking good, my friend," he says. "But I don't remember the mustache. I don't know if it becomes you."

Turn toward him. Pick up the corner of the mustache.

"Hah!" he laughs. "It's fake! Talk about security, this man wears a disguise to see his oldest friend in the world!"

"You, I know," I say. "Mr. Chase, I know. The driver up there, I do not know."

The drivers are the lowest of the low. Trade you to the cops for a pack of smokes. Zep raps his knuckles on the privacy shield, three times. The car moves out into traffic.

I take a chance. "How sure are we? Our information?"

The Nephew glares at me. "We got this from a reliable source, a very fucking reliable source. A friend of ours from Detroit was in town. I can't imagine he could get it wrong."

We sit in silence for a minute.

"So," the Nephew says, "we contract for a hit, something goes wrong, we need to know what the fuck happened. There needs to be accountability, you know what I'm fucking saying?"

Look over at the Old Man. He gives a tiny nod.

"My instructions: shoot the black one in the back row, near the window."

I look up. They nod. I did not misunderstand.

"Walk by. Scope it out. Two black ones in the back row. Check again. The drummer, she is female and more like Asian. Piano player is black. He gets it. Later I hear he is not the one."

"Some civilian," the Old Man says. "Some conventioneer, a lawyer, I heard."

"Then we bring in the reinforcements," I say. "Ask me, lead them to a source of information. I lead them to a source, safe place. Good setup."

"Couple of stupid shits," the Old Man says. "You look up

the word 'stupid' in the dictionary, their mug shots are in there. Not our best caliber. But hey, you did your job."

"We don't know if they fucked up," Chase adds. "We don't know that for certain. We're not exactly sure what situation developed, what they got—"

"What they got? One got a bullet in the head, the other got a train out of town," Zep says.

"So, was it the woman?" I cut in. "The Afro-Asian woman?"

"Are you sure she's Asian? Are you fucking positive?" Chase grills me.

"Name is Akiko Jones," I say.

"Hey, those people will name their kids anything: Douchebag Johnson, Gonorrhea Smiff, what do they know?" the Nephew says.

"Looked her up. Martial arts instructor—"

"That doesn't mean dick. I studied martial arts myself. Aikido, karate, judo, I—"

"Father is African American, in the army, overseas, a quartermaster," I continue. "Mother is Japanese," I say. I have to wait for a second.

"Is she the one?" I ask. "Did the backups get anything?"

"Look," the Nephew says. His tone changes. "We are not prepared to fucking say at this time. And it's not your fucking business anyway, is it?"

There is a moment of silence. The Nephew is breathing hard, working himself up.

"Then you have to go whack the other one, the saxophone player. What's the deal with that? He's not in the back row, he's not black. He's not 'Afro-Asian.' He can't be the one—"

"It was not him," I start.

"Of *course* it wasn't him. He doesn't match anything about the description. Not a fucking thing. Who the fuck told you to go and whack him? I'll tell you who. Nobody!"

"I did not charge you for that one. That was no charge."

"No charge? No fucking charge? Do you hear what I'm hearing!"

The pain is a five now. Turning from dull to sharp. I try to breathe.

"It won't be tied to us," the Old Man cuts in. "The cops have got nothing, nothing at all."

"That's what you say," the Nephew says.

"No," the Old Man says, "that's what the *cops* say." Gives the Nephew his cold hard stare. The one he's been saving up. "You know our source at State Street. Our source is unimpeachable. He says they got nothing, they got nothing."

Shuts the Nephew up.

"Why don't you run it down for us? Give us a sense of the players."

"Powell: trumpet player. He is black, but he stands in the front row. He is the leader. Serious, quiet. Does nothing but the music. Fahey: White, not black, and up front, not in back, saxophones. Worrell: He's white, sits in back, plays bass. Professor, down at the U. of C. Amatucci: Italian American, from New York. Sat in back, at the piano, but not that night. Does not seem shook up by it. Still driving a cab, broad daylight. Works for the Fat Man—"

"The Fat Man?" Zep asks. "Marcus Hanson?" His eyebrows are raised.

"Yeah, what—"

"Nothing," he says.

I look at him sideways. He knows things that he cannot tell me how he knows them.

"Jones: drummer. She is Afro-Asian. Sits in the back. With the drums. Looks mostly Asian, short straight hair. Teaches at some martial arts place. She is female. Landreau: white, maybe forty-something. Shows up in town *after* the first hit," I say. "My source says he knows Powell. Supposed to play very good."

"What is this, some music review in the fucking *Tribune?*" the Nephew says. " 'Supposed to play very good.' What does that have to do with anything?"

"A lot older, he . . . Plane gets forced down in a storm. Got here too late."

The Old Man leans forward. "One more for you to look out for."

We both turn his way. He always likes this part of it.

"Ridlin, Ken. White male, early fifties, six-three, thin. Really thin." Looks at me, eyebrows arching, waiting. "Remember him?"

"The Riddler," I say.

"One and the same," the Old Man says. Has a little grin on his face.

" 'The Riddler'?" the Nephew asks. "What the fuck is this? Did I just walk into a fucking Batman movie? The Riddler? How come you never told me about—"

"Just happened," the Old Man says. "The cops just put him onto it."

"Been thinking he is out of it," I say. "Since that time . . ."

"He was," the Old Man says. "*Way* out of it. A couple of years ago, he gets back in. The cops send him to Siberia. He works his way back up, now he's back in Homicide."

"Ridlin," I say.

"Who the fuck is Ridlin?" the Nephew asks. "You going to fucking clue me in?"

"Like I said," the Old Man says, "I just got the word, from our guy downtown. Ridlin goes way back. We had some, uh, dealings with him, back when you were still in diapers. This guy, he had it out with your father, once upon a time. Frank, well, Frank held his own. Like always. But Ridlin? A straight arrow, old school. They just put him on it, inside."

"Inside?" the Nephew asks.

"The new saxophone player?" I say.

The Old Man nods.

The Nephew's head is swiveling. "What the fuck? What does it mean?"

"It means," the Old Man says, "that the cops have put a cop in the band. He used to play saxophone, back in the day, and now he's on the inside. It means it's going to be harder now. We go in there blazing, now we have someone who will shoot back. And not just anyone, but a decorated detective . . ."

"With something to prove," I add.

"Oh, yes, my friend, with a *lot* to prove," he says.

The car goes around the block again. The Old Man notices. Picks up a phone, presses a number, speaks. "Could you please find somewhere else to drive? We're being a little obvious here, going around the same block, over and over."

Pauses. Listens.

"What am I, Traffic on the Twos? I don't care where you drive, just drive somewhere else." Slams the phone down.

Driver makes an immediate left.

The Nephew speaks up. "Here's what we do." We listen. "This band, they're playing again tomorrow night, at the Casbah. You know the place?"

Surprise. He is doing some homework. I nod.

"We let Laura out tomorrow night. She's been all cooped up, she's going to want to see whoever it is. You go there, wait for her to show up and see who she sees."

"Not what I do," I say.

"That's true . . ." the Old Man says. "That's the way it's always been . . ."

"What the fuck?" the Nephew says. "We'll pay you your normal rate, just to look and report back. The same money you get for a hit. That's fair, isn't it?" he says, asking the Old Man.

"It's not about the money . . ." The Old Man and I both say this. At the same time.

"It would mean exposure," the Old Man says. "One reason our friend here has been able to help us out in this way for so many years is that he does not do anything but what he does. And no one ever sees him do it, except maybe the vic, and the vic doesn't live to tell about it. What you're talking about, he could be seen. We have other people. Send someone else."

The Nephew is not happy.

"I am so tired of this fucking shit," he says.

"Number one, he knows the players, right? He won't get confused or give us some cryptic shit about 'the black one in the back.' He can just say 'Powell,' or 'Jones,' or whoever. Number two, he's supposed to be so good at disguises, right? So he can do it again, a different disguise. And number three, I mean, this isn't some stupid coke deal. This is a *family* thing . . . I say we use the best we've fucking got and keep it close to us."

The Old Man is staring out the window. He is not going to back me up on this.

"So," the Nephew says, "it sounds like we have a fucking plan."

"How are you going to make sure she gets out?" the Old Man asks.

"What, Laura? Don't worry about it, that's my end." He turns to me. "You just make sure you're there to see who she runs to."

Nothing I can do. Trapped in this.

"So you'll do this, and report back, what, Thursday, same time, same place, we'll pick you up—"

"No," I say. "Different time, different place." Least I can do. "Say, two in the afternoon, bus shelter at Fifty-first and Lake Park, southwest corner."

Least I can do. But this is not good. This is not good at all.

CHAPTER 36
Ken Ridlin

At the Casbah
Wednesday, January 22

Powell is already here when I walk in. He's standing on the stage, in a corner, with his back to the room, a Harmon mute in his trumpet, playing long tones. You can't hear it, because he's playing along with the tune that's on the Muzak, which is some pop thing, all dynamics and no soul. He's being very unobtrusive, playing pianissimo. It's harder to play soft than it is to play loud, especially on an instrument like the trumpet. This is something I know from before. If you didn't look closely, you would think he was just standing there, holding that horn up to his lips, not playing, but maybe just warming it up. Maybe not even warming it up but just getting the feel of it. Maybe not even getting the feel of it but just resting it in his hands. When you look closely, you can see the muscles in his embouchure tightening. If you look really closely, you can see his chest rising slightly as he breathes in. Impressive. Myself, I must look like I'm gasping, drowning, going down for the third time. Powell is not drowning. He's swimming. No, he's not swimming, he's floating on his back. No, he's not floating, he's on a raft, half-asleep, gliding with the tide. That's how good his breathing is. On my best day, back when I could play all night, I never had breathing like this.

Powell is standing by the piano, pointing toward it. As I get closer, I see a head, dark hair, over the edge of the piano, slowly bobbing up and down with the downbeat. It's Amatucci, leaning over. He's playing simple chords, as softly as Powell. I cannot hear him; I can see his hand moving, his right hand. His left hand is down in his lap. They are playing together, the way they have for years.

The stage is on the left as you come in, in the front right corner as you face the front of the building. Opposite it is a long wide bar. No wood, just a kind of rough sandstone texture, curved, swooping in and around. The lights behind it are all indirect. You can't see the lights themselves, just the glow on all the pretty bottles.

Along both sides are little alcoves with semi-hidden tables, places to have a quiet drink, places to have a private romantic moment. You can only see in from directly in front of each—from the side they are shadowed by the arches.

In the center of the room, small round tables are scattered about. I watch a waiter swerve his way through them, a tray of drinks on his upturned palm. And then I notice it—there is no floor, just sand, maybe half a foot, I think. Everywhere. Oh, man.

I look up. In a sort of closed balcony there are tiny spaces that look like caves. I see a woman's hand at one of them, lolling over the curved ledge, but you can't see inside them at all. Very private. Very dark. Flickers of candlelight.

If Ford's Theatre had been built this way, they never would have caught John Wilkes Booth. Caught him? They never would have seen him. I keep scanning, at the spiral staircase leading to the balcony, at the tables tucked under the overhang, at the mess in the middle.

I don't know what I'm seeing.

Of course, I don't know what I'm looking for, either.

CHAPTER 37
The Cleaner

At the Casbah
Wednesday, January 22

8:30 P.M.: Strange place. Little slice of the desert, middle of the Near North Side. Table upstairs, little booth, alcove, whatever. No straight lines. Arches the color of clay. Sand on the floor for Christ's sake, six inches deep. Sand all in my shoes.

Pain is about a two. For a change.

The waiters? Waitresses? All wearing poofy white shirts, no collars, all buttoned up. Poofy black pants, tight around the ankles. On their heads? Those little caps, look like an upside-down thimble. What do you call them? A fez. With a tassel on top.

The clientele? All dressed in black. Not a necktie in sight. Air kisses for the women, knuckle bumps for the men. Heavy jewelry, all around. Paradise for phonies.

Ridlin shows up last. Same face. Looks like he has lost half his weight. Powell introduces the band. They start right in. Modern jazz tonight, place like this.

9:15 P.M.: Scan the room. Check each one, one at a time. No Laura.

First set finishes up. Band splits up, Powell to the bar, talking to Amatucci. Jones screwing with her drums. Worrell comes up the staircase, the can. Landreau sits there, the piano.

10:00 P.M.: Second set. More of the same. Grows on you. Crowd starting to get into it. Talk is down, dinner mostly over. My foot is tapping. Old habit.

10:22 P.M.: The front door opens. She walks in and stops the freaking room. Again.

Laura.

Wears a little gold number. A black coat over her arm. She walks to the bar. Seat opens up, like magic. Slings the coat down, perches. Next to Amatucci.

Powell still staring at the floor. Eyes closed. Worrell playing a solo. He is sneaking peaks. Ridlin looking straight at her. Jones looking up at the ceiling, eyes half-closed, flailing away with the brushes. Landreau? Sees her at the door. Tracks her all the way to the bar. Leans forward. Squints. Then there's Amatucci. Sitting next to her. Looking at the band.

Laura reaches over. Places her hand on Amatucci's arm. There is a cigarette in her other hand. He sees it, gets a lighter out. Snaps it on, holds it up. She leans in, lights up. Nods at him.

Whole time, he does not look at her. She does not look at him. Usually a moment, when the flame touches the tobacco, the woman looks up. The whole point. Not this time. She stares at the lighter. He stares at the cigarette.

Great. The high probables? Do not even see her. The low probables? Are all staring.

Powell introduces the band again. I am watching Laura. She applauds the same for each one. Powell introduces Amatucci, at the bar. She gives him the same smile, the same applause.

I told them. This is not what I do.

Introductions are over. Remember this one, the old days. "Night In . . ." something. Middle-Eastern-sounding. "Tunisia." "Night in Tunisia."

Perfect. It is "Night in Tunisia," in the Casbah. She is here and they are here and I am here. And what I am supposed to see? Is invisible.

Band plays the hell out of it. Got to give them that.

Laura is looking at each one of them, when they play. She is rocking on her bar stool.

Maybe it is none of them. Maybe she likes the music.

Coming to the end now. Powell plays a phrase. Holds the last note. Then seven crashes on the cymbals, and a pause, and they all end with two short choppy notes.

Crowd goes nuts. I am looking. Laura is standing, cheering. Crowd sees her standing. They stand. Powell waves the horn over his head. Crowd roars. They walk toward the bar.

They come up to Amatucci. Handshakes all around. Laura jumps in. Starts kissing everybody. Kisses Jones. Kisses Worrell. Kisses Ridlin. Leans over, kisses Amatucci. Kisses Powell. Kisses Landreau. Gives him a big hug.

There is someone else. Coming up behind them. Female. Long fur coat. Floppy black hat. Grabs Landreau by the shoulder. Hauls back her right hand and slaps him hard. Across the face. He reels back. She pulls back to slap him again. Freezes.

Looking for her face. Cannot see her face.

Landreau falls back. The woman grabs Laura. The hair, a good handful. Pulls her off the barstool. Pulls her to the door. Waiters diving for cover.

The woman turns. Hat falls off. Stares back at Landreau. Her face? A mask of shock.

Aw, Jesus.

Aw, shit.

CHAPTER 38
Ken Ridlin

At the Casbah
Wednesday, January 22

The crowd is buzzing, my head is throbbing, my eyes are blazing. We have maybe ten minutes left on the break. I turn to the band, say, "Let's go. Everyone outside. We need to talk."

I've got my serious voice on, and they comply. It takes all of a minute to get them rounded up and out the door and into the alley.

Amatucci lights a cigarette. Worrell pulls out a briar pipe and sucks on it, unlit. Powell has his hands in his coat pockets, Jones has her hands in her armpits. Landreau leans up against the bricks, watching his toe draw circles in the snow.

"So what the hell was that?" I ask.

No response. I expect a wisecrack from Amatucci, but even he is mute.

"So what the hell was that?" I repeat. "Talk to me."

They are looking away. Shifting their weight. Looking at their shoes.

"You don't want to talk?" I say. "Then you get to listen. That was Amelia Della Chiesa, the long-lost wife of Joe Zep, the Boss of all Bosses for the whole damn city. She was dragging her little girl out of the bar, the little girl that one of you is screwing. The Don, he knows that one of you is screwing her. And now that *she* knows it, I'd be surprised if it isn't on the front page of tomorrow's *Sun-Times*."

They still do not want to talk.

I turn to Landreau. "And you, she turns specifically to you, and slaps you in the face. Is it you who's screwing her?"

He shakes his head, but he's avoiding my eyes.

I know he's all wrong for it, but I hate the attitude. I grab him by the shirt and push him against the wall, get in his face. "This is the cop speaking, not the saxophone player, you hear me?" He nods, looking away. "Is it you? Are you the one who's screwing her?"

He looks me in the eyes. "I have not had intercourse with her or her mother. I swear."

What? Where does that come from?

Amatucci reaches in, grabs my arm. "Leave him alone," he says. "It's not him."

"OK, smartass," I say. I drop Landreau, get in Amatucci's face. "You want to play, too? How about you? Have you been screwing her?"

He looks at me, and says, "Yeah, I fucked her."

I step back. Is he being sarcastic?

"Vince," Jones pleads. "Vince . . ."

"It's true. I fucked her. She was something else, man. It was truly incredible. She was without a doubt the best piece of ass I've ever had in my life, and I'm not lying."

I'm counting. That was five, six sentences, not two.

"Shut up!" Jones yells. "Shut up shut up shut up!"

I turn toward her. She is shivering. I notice she is wearing black jeans and a T-shirt, and it is only fifteen degrees out.

"What, is he lying?" I ask.

She looks at Amatucci, looks back at me. "No. Yes."

I wait.

"Yes, he slept with her. Once. At my apartment, the night after his hand got broken. He was loaded on meds, half out of his mind. And he woke up and found us there, Laura and me."

I stare at her. Landreau leans forward. "She's my lover," she says. "We've been together for six months. They—they were coming after *me.*"

CHAPTER 39
Ken Ridlin

After the Casbah
Wednesday, January 22

The rest of the gig? Well, let's just say that we finish it. The last set is terrible. Amatucci is sulking at the bar. Jones is playing the drums like she has two broken wrists. Powell doesn't want to solo, Landreau is a million miles away, sneaking glances at the door. Worrell is sawing at the bass like he wants to cut it in half.

Me? I'm playing my ass off, best I have played in years. Story of my life.

So it drags on and on, and soon enough Powell introduces the band one last time and thanks the crowd. And we are done.

I immediately turn to them and say, "Is there a place we can talk?"

They fumble around. I get the feeling I'm not about to be invited into anyone's house.

Amatucci turns to me, says, "I've got the cab. It's a big old Checker International, seats seven in a pinch."

I look at him.

"Hey, I'll even leave the meter off," he says. "What the Fat Man doesn't know . . ."

I nod and we all pack up.

Amatucci is helping Jones with her kit, one-handed. I tuck the soprano-sax case under my arm, grab the tenor and alto cases with the same hand, and pick up her bass drum. Worrell is standing by the door, his bass under one arm, his tuba under the other. Landreau picks up the high-hat bag and the snare. Powell grabs the tom-tom. Usually, she won't let anyone touch her stuff.

We're outside in the snow and it is still fifteen degrees but the wind has come up and it is like a knife in the back of the neck. Amatucci's cab is parked in a cabstand right out front. There are three or four couples lined up, waiting for a taxi to show. They see us start to load up, and don't know whether to applaud us or curse us. We're the band they were just cheering. We're also the people who are taking their ride. One guy has a cell phone in his hand. Amatucci slings the drums he is carrying into the trunk, taps the guy on the shoulder, motions for the phone, opens it, taps in a number. He talks, they all listen. He turns the phone off, hands it back to the fat guy, says "Five cabs, five minutes."

He turns to me: "I called Checker. It seemed the decent thing to do," he says.

We load up the cab and pile inside, Amatucci in the driver's seat, me in the front passenger seat, the others in the back.

We go three, four blocks. I signal to pull over. He does, rounding a corner onto a side street, easing into a loading zone. He kills the headlights.

"Vince, do you have a cigarette?" Powell asks.

Amatucci flips one out of his pack, passes it back to him.

"I didn't know you smoke," I say.

"Smoke? I don't smoke," he says, taking a light from Worrell. Worrell himself has got his pipe out, and spends a minute firing it up, tamping it down, and firing it up again. Jones tries to wave the smoke away and they both crack their windows and try to aim the smoke outside. Amatucci is fumbling with something in his lap, one of those little pot pipes. He fills it up carefully, one-handed. As he's about to light it, he turns to me. "Gonna bust me for this?" I just turn away and crack my window. He takes a couple of hits, passes it to Jones. She takes one hit, another, passes it back. He offers it to Landreau, who declines, offers it to me. There was a time, well . . . I tell him "No, thanks."

"So," I say, to no one in particular, "tell me about it."

Jones exhales, looks at me. "We met in a bar. I was playing there with one of my other bands. She asked me out for a drink, and it kind of went from there."

"How long?" I ask.

"Six months, so far."

"She has a long history with men," I say, "not that it matters."

"Maybe they were all the wrong men."

She looks me in the eyes.

"I guessed that part about her, like, right away. Looking the way she looks, it's a pretty easy guess. I guessed it was a history with the worst kind of men, too. I even insisted she had to get tested before I would sleep with her."

I look up.

"Made her wait a whole week. Got her hotter than shit." She almost giggles, then frowns.

We all have a question we want to ask.

"Oh, she passed," she says, answering it. "Not that it matters."

"Then why—?"

"Being willing to take the test passed the test. It meant I wasn't just another conquest, you know, just a one-night stand."

"And she's been with you, uh, exclusively—I mean—"

"Except for that night we were with Vince, yes." There is a pause. "I mean, who knows? But she says so, and I don't have any reason to doubt her."

Worrell turns to her. "You knew who she was, Akiko?"

Jones nods. "Well . . . soon enough."

"You must be very much in love with her," he says.

She lowers her eyes. "I must be."

I flick my eyes to Landreau. He's spooked, I can see it. He's ready to run. O'Hare, Midway, Union Station, Greyhound—east, west, north, south—Detroit, St. Louis, Minnesota, Cincinnati. Slide back into "Where do I stand and what key are we in?"; "Do you want me on piano or cornet?"; "Chicago Style or New York?" I so much as blink at him, he's smoke.

I turn to back to Jones.

"Look, I make no judgments. You fell in love, and a person is allowed to fall in love."

Amatucci starts to say something. I hold my hand up. "Let me finish."

They settle back.

"Here's the thing. That show the two of them put on is gonna complicate things. The Don is gonna hear about it. He can't sit there and let his invisible wife go public like this. In his mind, she's showing him up and he is gonna be pissed. And when he's pissed, he calls that guy—"

"Who is this guy?" Amatucci asks. "Do you even know?"

They all look up, nod.

"There's a guy they have been using for years for contract killings only. He is a professional, the best of the best. We have him down for over fifty killings. Here in Chicago, around the Midwest. They send him out, he does the job, he disappears."

"So who is this madman?" Worrell asks.

"We have not one eyewitness description. And I'm not sure I'd call him a madman."

"He could be quite psychotic, but just highly organized in his psychosis," Powell adds.

I nod. That's exactly what the police shrinks say.

"He's coming for us," Landreau says. First thing he says in a while.

"Maybe yes, maybe no. We'll just have to be ready."

"Ready?" Amatucci asks, all excited. "Ready for what? For a guy who looks like I don't fucking know what and is going to shoot us I don't fucking know how at around the time of I don't fucking know when? What the fuck are we supposed to do?"

I look at him. "When and where is the next gig?"

Amatucci reaches into a little calendar, turns it so he can read it in the orange smear of the streetlight.

"Friday night. 8:00 P.M. The Nickelodeon Club, Calumet City."

"Oh, Vinnie, you didn't . . ." Powell moans.

"What? What is it?" I ask.

"The club. He doesn't like it. It creeps him out," Amatucci says.

"Why is that?"

"Me, I think it's kind of cool, in a *retro nuovo* sort of way."

"We'll try to use it, somehow," I say. "Let me see if I can set something up."

We discuss logistics, how we're going to get there.

I turn to Landreau. "In the meantime, no one leaves town. That means you." He looks down at the floor, defeated. "You'll be watched."

"By you or by 'him'?" Amatucci asks.

Well, yeah, that's the question.

CHAPTER 40
Ken Ridlin

At the Airport
Thursday, January 23

It's O'Hare, and it's midweek, mid-morning, medium-busy. I park in front of the NO PARKING AT ANY TIME sign, pull the PO-LICE BUSINESS card out of the glove box, set it on the dash. I hop out, lock up, walk inside. I go up to an airport rent-a-cop, flash the tin, ask for the security office. I don't get out here much, don't remember where it is.

How do I come to be out here? I get a call. Put out a mid-level alert last night, "Be On the Look-Out," wanted for questioning, unarmed suspect, like that. And he walks right into it and damned if some Wally Wackenhut doesn't see him.

There are some people we are BOLOing for a dozen years. We have pictures of them posted everywhere there's a space that'll fit an eight-by-ten. We run mug shot reviews with everyone from the baggage handlers to the pilots. Do we find them? Not a trace. This guy? One phone call, a general description, a name, the next morning someone nabs him the first minute he walks in, middle of the second-busiest airport in the world. Go figure.

Up a flight of stairs to the security office. The door is locked. I press the buzzer, hold the tin up to the little quartz window. The door opens. A fat rent-a-cop with a flushed face is sitting on a bench by the door. Reading the paper. The *Sun-Times*. "Detective Ridlin?" he says. I nod. He lumbers up off the bench, drops the paper, brushes some powdered sugar off his shirt, sticks out his hand. We shake. A cop thing.

Like he's a cop.

"Good to see ya," he says. "Officer Mumble Mumble" something. I'm not listening for his name. "We've got your perp right over here, in Holding."

He's not a perp, but Officer Mumble Mumble is having a moment of cop glory, and I'm not going to spoil it for him. Probably the dumbest luck ever. Maybe our guy bumps into him and makes him drop his doughnut, and he looks up at him looking for trouble and, what do you know, it is the guy on the poster. Or maybe he has a girlfriend in the airlines office and our guy shows up on some flight manifest. Or maybe he trips over him on the way to getting a fresh cup of coffee, goes to apologize, wipes the coffee off his shirt and wipes his hand right across the BOLO he is keeping there since the shift-change meeting at oh-seven-hundred.

Who knows? I'm being cynical but I am impressed and surprised. A needle in a haystack, and this guy reaches in and pulls it right out.

"This the one?" he asks. We round a corner and there he is, Landreau. His left hand is cuffed to a metal bench, that funny-looking case is at his side, the clasps and zippers all undone.

I nod. "He's the one." I turn to the cop. "Very nice job, Officer . . ." I look at the name tag on his chest, "Officer Verdoliak. Very nice job."

"We checked out the case, found a trumpet in it, some clothes and shit like that. ID, money, a ticket, but no weapons, no drugs."

"No," I say, playing to him, "he's too smart to be carrying when he's on the move like this. You did good."

The rent-a-cop looks at me, all expectant, a puppy waiting for a treat. I've already thrown him a couple of kibbles. "If he had slipped through our hands . . . well, there's no telling what could have happened. Thanks again."

I'm kind of hinting that he can take the cuffs off now and release him into my custody. He's still wagging his tail, begging for more. "Is he dangerous? What's he wanted for?"

I take him by the left bicep, all fat and soft under my fingers, and wheel him around like I'm getting him out of Landreau's hearing, like I'm passing a confidence. I lean up into his face, place my lips close to his ear. "Oh, you have no idea what this man is capable of, no idea. Of course, I'm not at liberty to divulge the details," I say, "police business and all, you know how it is, but you saved a lot of people a lot of trouble here today, a lot of trouble." I step back, reach my left hand out, grab him on the right arm. I am holding a folded-up twenty in my palm—that was going to be my move all along, he's a rent-a-cop. But it strikes me that if I offer this man money it will ruin it for him. He is having a moment of authentic glory, here, as far as he knows. Doing his civic duty, living out his childhood dream.

I curl up the twenty in my pocket, fish out a pen and a scrap of paper, and make a point of writing his name down, getting the spelling right. I'm having trouble reading the name tag because his chest is heaving so much, but I do it, spelling it out to myself out loud, "V-E-R-D-O-L-I-A-K." Then I stash the paper and pen back in my pocket, reach out for the big cop handshake again, and say, "Nice work, Officer Verdoliak. I'll take it from here."

He shakes my hand twice. I reach behind me for my own cuffs, snap one end open, clip it on Landreau's same left wrist, snap the other end on my own right.

Officer Verdoliak is trying to act like he does this every day. He fumbles the keys out of his pocket—thank God he doesn't drop them—and reaches down and unsnaps Landreau from the bench, pulling the cuffs loose as he does so.

I nod to Landreau. He picks up his case with his free hand, straightens back up.

Verdoliak stands back a step, straightens his spine, and damned if he doesn't rise up into a salute. I'm the cops, I think, not the marines; we don't do this, except at parades, and this isn't some stupid parade—it's a charade. My right wrist is cuffed to Landreau, so I bring my left up. Sacrilege. I flip him a condescending-officer one, the old "Carry on." He snaps his hand back at me, eyes straight ahead like he's seen in the movies, nice and crisp.

Touching, really.

There's a way to walk with a man cuffed to your wrist so it doesn't look like cop-and-prisoner or like two gay guys holding hands, and I know how to do it but Landreau doesn't, so it takes us a while for him to fall into step. Speaks well for his pedigree: the only way you get good at this is with practice. Lots of practice. He hasn't had any.

We move through the sparse midday crowd and head to my car. I fumble for my key with my left hand in my right pocket, fish it out, get the passenger door unlocked awkwardly; these are not usually left-handed activities for me. I hand Landreau into the car, uncuff myself, and relock the cuff on a bar in the middle of the bench seat. He is passive throughout this. I lock and close his door, walk around, open my door, slide in. I fasten the seat belt, give him a look, and he reaches up with his right hand, grabs the metal piece, and brings it down and into the buckle all in one motion. It should be awkward—no one does it that way, right hand reaching up and to the right and pulling it down and to the left—but he makes it look smooth. Like this is the only way to do it.

I shouldn't be surprised that the guy's got some physical

dexterity, but his grace at doing this catches me somehow. I start the car, stash the sticker, check the traffic and accelerate into the road.

We are silent as I weave through all the drop-offs and pickups and focus on getting us back to the highway.

"So," I ask, when we get there, "where were you heading?"

"I hear Hawaii is nice this time of year," he says.

"Your ticket said Rock Island."

"It's in the right direction," he says.

"What's in Rock Island?"

"Used to be a railroad," he says. "They wrote a song about it, in the key of G."

"And now?"

"Just an island. It's rocky," he says.

I turn to him. "Right next to Davenport, Iowa, isn't it?" I say.

He turns to me, raises his eyebrows. "Wow, you caught me," he says, dry as toast.

"So, you're doing, what? Heading back to pick up some cash, maybe a new identity, then back into obscurity?"

He doesn't say anything. He is staring straight ahead.

"Come on, what's the story?"

"The story?" he asks. "I don't do stories, I do music."

"You *do* do music. Got to give you that. Never heard anyone play like you do, ever."

He stares straight ahead.

"But you also do stories," I say. "Big whopping stories."

"Stories?" he says. He shakes his head.

"You gonna deny it?"

"Am I under oath?" he asks.

"With a cop, you're always under oath, or you should act like it. See, cops . . . The whole job is stories. Man gets shot? What's the story? Burglar makes off with the goods from some locked apartment? What's the story? I know bars, cop bars, you could walk in there any time of the day or night and hear a thousand stories. Each one told just so, the details lined up in a row."

He's still staring straight ahead.

"But the thing is, we like *true* stories. We'll listen to some shit from each other, sure. Cop gets shot two times, before you know it, it's three times, four. But from a citizen? No. You get a nose for them, hearing enough bullshit. And the thing is, your story? It's a bullshit story."

He pauses, his mouth scrunches up tight. "All right, so maybe I wasn't going to Hawaii."

"The least of it," I say, "where you're going."

His forehead wrinkles, just a little.

"Me? I'm more interested in where you're coming from."

He pauses, looks out the window.

"I've never found it helpful to live in the past," he says. "It always leads back to the same place. You can't do anything about it. The present, or the future, maybe there's more than one road in front of you. Going back, it's a one-way street."

"With you, it's a one-way street in a cul-de-sac. It's a dead end," I say.

"What are you saying?"

"I'm saying you're not Jack Landreau."

"You've seen my ID—driver's license, Social Security, credit cards . . ."

"All part of the story. A bullshit story. A good bullshit story, nicely told, but still a bullshit story."

"Why don't you take me downtown, run my fingerprints—"

"Already did," I say.

He raises his eyebrows.

"They took them off the horn, this morning, you being otherwise detained."

"And?" he says. "What did you find?"

I look at him. "Nothing," I say.

"Nothing?" he asks.

"Nothing. You don't exist."

"You mean I don't exist in any police files. I don't have any kind of a record."

"That's right."

"So, who am I?"

I look at him again. "You gonna tell me?"

"I'm Jack Landreau."

"No, you're not," I say. "He's dead. You're not dead. Not yet."

CHAPTER 41
Vinnie Amatucci

In the Fat Man's Cab
Thursday, January 23

The ride that took me out to the airport was a quick one, and the other ride that took me right back downtown came almost immediately. I stayed busy into the midday mini-rush, racking up the miles, watching the meter turn. The temperature had risen all the way to thirty, the sun was bright in a high blue sky, and I felt as if I might be starting to thaw out a bit myself. Until I got a fare back toward Hyde Park.

Not that I minded that. I mean, I do live there, and at midday the traffic can be light and the business can be decent, if you can catch the flow. It can also be lots of students riding their bikes in and out of traffic, lots of fools crossing the street in the middle of the block, lots of jerks driving their own cars three blocks from their apartment to the store. It all depends.

The problem wasn't the fare; she was great—a woman in her mid-thirties, well-dressed, fashionable in a conservative way. As soon as she got in and gave me the address, she pulled out a book and dove into it. I could have taken her up to Evanston and back and she wouldn't have noticed. But I'm not that kind of driver.

The problem was this gray Chevy Cavalier in front of me, maybe twelve years old, a small gray head poking over the top of the steering wheel.

I was headed south on Michigan Avenue when she pulled out in front of me, without a signal. I slammed on the brakes and stayed behind her, in no hurry, but she started to slow down erratically as we got down toward the south Twenties, so I pulled out to pass her, and she started wandering into my lane, almost clipping me. I dropped back, cut the wheel and started to pass her on the right when she wandered over into the right lane again, no signal, no warning. "Jesus," I thought, "How many driving instructors did you have to fuck to be allowed behind the wheel?"

I got into the left lane to weave my way east, put the blinker on and waited. The arrow went green and I had just started my turn when the gray Chevy came out of nowhere, cut right across me, and turned left from the right-hand lane. Very creative, I thought. Extra points for degree of difficulty. I slammed on the brakes, and the brunette in the back jerked forward.

"Sorry," I said. "We seem to have an adventurous driver in front of us."

She looked up, said, "There's no hurry," and went back to her book.

We were now on a two-lane street with nowhere to pass. No sense blowing a decent tip just to feed my pride. I reached for the switch on the dash and brought the partition up, not for the passenger's privacy, but for mine. I had a right turn coming up, so I put my signal on and coasted to the corner. The Chevy got more than halfway into the intersection and jerked her wheel hard to the right, careening across my path on two wheels.

"How many box tops did you have to save up to get your license?" I wondered. "Was it Cheerios? Or, let me guess, Fruit Loops?"

It was as if she were following me from in front, going where I wanted to go, but not aware of it until almost after each turn. It was making me just a little bit nuts. "Who gave you these directions? Ray Charles?" I thought.

Chill, I thought, chill the fuck out. The fare's address was only a few blocks ahead; there was no sense pushing it. I ratcheted it down a notch, set it at thirty-five, and cruised up to the fare's building. I lowered the privacy window, put it in park, and punched the meter to OFF. She reached into her purse, pulled out a twenty, said "Thank you. Keep the change," and stepped out into the cold. I tucked the cash into my kit, watched to make sure she was in past the door, pulled out the pipe, gave a 360° glance around, and fired up, two long hits.

Better. A little better. If a little is good, a little more can be better, so I had a little more.

I thought I'd head down toward 51st Street. There was a shopping center there; maybe I could pick up a grocery shopper, or a bus rider who was tired of waiting in the wind. Maybe I could pick up some lunch. I checked my watch; it was almost noon.

I pulled back into traffic, headed east, and who was there, straddling both lanes, but the gray Chevy. She was in the middle of the road and she was backing up. Backing the fuck up!

I hit the brakes, pulled over to the curb next to a hydrant, and stopped to wait her out. "Free entertainment," I thought. "Not for the first time, and definitely not the last."

A city bus came roaring up from behind us and she yanked it into drive. The bus swerved around her, edging into the oncoming traffic, leaning on his air horn. She jerked it into reverse again, and got diagonal. If she kept this up, she was going to be broadside to the flow of traffic.

She sat there, not moving, for close to twenty seconds. It

was pure dumb luck that not a single car came by. Finally, she lurched into the oncoming lane, got straightened out, and started twitching back to the right. Not all the way, mind you, but a little. I pulled out behind her, giving her lots of room. She kept making turns, all at the last minute, with no signal ever; a right, a left, straight two blocks, a left, a left. "What the fuck is this?" I mused. "Slalom driving?"

Two more blocks and damned if she didn't turn right into the parking lot of the shopping center I had been heading for, a strip mall off 51st Street, across Lake Park from the elevated tracks. She wandered down one lane, headed down another the wrong way, found two spaces open together, and pulled in diagonally across both of them. I had been planning to park next to her; instead I pulled into a space facing 51st. I got out, closed and locked the door, walked over, and, wearing my best hundred-watt smile, rapped on her window.

She looked up at me in surprise, then rolled the window down.

"Afternoon, ma'am," I said. "If you don't mind my asking, what the fuck?"

She was looking up at me, her brow wrinkled like I was speaking Martian.

Sometimes you wonder if there's even a point.

I reached in the window. She jerked backward, her hands curling up in front of her. I smiled, leaned in, and pointed at her directional lever. I smiled at her, said, "Now, this little stalk here is called a directional signal. You push it to the right, a little blinky arrow comes on pointing right," I demonstrated. "You flick it to the left, a little blinky arrow comes on pointing left." She sat there, mesmerized by the flashing lights.

"Some drivers use this to let other drivers know where they're going."

She was still looking up at me.

"But not you," I said. A half smile was competing with a look of confusion on her face.

"Well, you won't be needing this, now will you?" I reached for the base of the lever, got it in a nice tight grip, and yanked it out by the roots.

It was kind of beautiful, the snap of the plastic as it broke free of the housing, the sight of the wires all red and green and black as they pulled free, the frozen look of horror on her face, her hands coming up to her open mouth, as I came away with the stalk in my hand. She looked at it carefully, as if it was the first time she had seen such a thing. Maybe it was.

I held the stalk aloft, examined it in my hand, and turned toward her one more time.

"Have a nice day," I smiled. "And happy motoring."

CHAPTER 42
The Cleaner

In the Black Limo
Thursday, January 23

●

11:05 A.M.: In the bus thing, what do they call it? Kiosk, that's it, on 51st Street at Lake Park. Wind is off the lake. Pain is about a five. Not good. Dull ache. Sharp pangs now and then.

My car is parked, a lot uptown. Take a bus down to here. Disguise: workingman. Scruffy beard. Work boots. Plaid ball cap with earflaps. Big thick safety glasses. With the side shields. Thirty extra pounds under the shirt. Thermos. Greasy paper bag.

11:07 A.M.: Here they come. A big black limo. Step forward, to the curb. They don't even slow down. Go past, turn right, around the corner. What the hell? Look to see if they pull over, better spot for a pickup. No. They keep going.

11:11 A.M.: Here they come again. They stop at the kiosk, wait. Hear the door locks click open. Slide in the back, close the door. Off we go.

The Old Man, the Nephew. Both again.

Old Man looks me over. "We went right by you, the first time." He chuckles to himself.

Turns to the Nephew, "What did I tell you? Is this guy the best or is this guy the best? I've been knowing him all my life, and even *I* can't tell it's him. Jesus Christ."

The Nephew gets right to business. "What do you have to report about last night?"

Like we are having some meeting. Like I am vice president of something.

Turn it around.

"What was she doing there?"

"She was *supposed* to be there?" the Nephew says. "That was the whole fucking plan—"

I cut him off. "Not Laura. Her mother."

The Old Man slides forward. His eyes coming out of his head. "Amelia?" he says.

Nod.

"Fuck," the Old Man says. "Fuck fuck fuck. What *was* she doing there?"

"Wait a minute," the Nephew says. "Walk me through it, step by step."

"Band plays a set. Starts another. The middle, Laura walks in. Takes over a section of the bar. They finish the second set, she is cheerleading. Amatucci, the piano player, at the bar, is near her. Between sets? They come over to see him, get a drink, whatever. She hugs them all, kisses them all—"

"This is getting ridiculous," the Old Man says. "We start this out as a simple little thing, and now look at what we've got."

" 'She kisses them all'?" the Nephew says. "Every one of them?" I nod. "Then what happened?"

"Middle of hugging the last one in line? Amelia walks in, reaches over, belts him, grabs Laura by the hair, hauls her out of there. The end."

"The right hand?" the Old Man asks. "She's got a hell of a right hand, that one. 'Coulda been a contenduh.' Wait, who'd she hit?"

"Piano player," I mutter, "Landreau, the new guy."

Zep is watching, too close. The way he does. Sees something.

"Do you know him?" he asks.

It is all coming down now. All coming down. A ringing is starting in my ears.

"Could be I know him. Could be I do not."

"What makes you think you might know him, my friend?" the Old Man asks.

He is looking right at me. He is waiting. He will wait all day, he has to. It is what he does.

"He is missing a finger, right hand. He has got nine fingers."

The Old Man stares harder. Lips are set tight in his face.

"My friend," he says, real quiet. "Which finger?"

Cannot stand to look at him. I look down.

"This one," I say. Wiggle the pinkie.

He sucks in a breath. Sits back in his seat. Looks out the window.

A taste of metal, rising in my throat. A sound of wind, rushing through my head. A knife slicing in, behind my eyes.

It is all coming down. Feel it all coming down.

CHAPTER 43
Vinnie Amatucci

In the Fat Man's Cab at 51st and Lake Park
Thursday, January 23

I walked into a coffee shop to get myself a little caffeine, just to restore the natural balance. The guy behind the counter was Indian, or Pakistani. He handed over the cup, said "A dollar forty." I love the way they do that retroflex "r," with the tongue circled up toward the back of the soft palate. I reached into my pocket and slid two dollars onto the counter. He handed me the change, I left a quarter, picked up the coffee, and shuffled toward the door.

"Have a nice day," he called after me.

Right. And realized I was still holding the turn indicator. Fuck.

I looked around for the gray Cavalier, and it was gone. I looked for a fleet of black-and-whites, their blue lights flashing, a phalanx of cops kneeling facing the door, pointing shotguns at me. They weren't there either.

OK, I thought. You seem to have survived this little episode of temporary insanity, Vince, now it's time to reestablish contact with the mother ship.

I walked up to the cab, set the coffee on the roof, tucked the indicator under my arm, and reached for the key. I pulled it out and opened the driver's-side door. I pulled the turn indicator out of my armpit, and for some reason I looked up. Landreau was standing by the passenger door, and right next to him was Ridlin, the cop.

"Hey, Vince," Landreau said. A little smile played at the corners of his mouth.

"Yo, what are you guys doing down here?" I asked.

"Looking for you," Ridlin said.

"Looking for me? Holy shit. A whole city, a couple of million people, a couple of thousand taxicabs, and you're looking for me and you find me? Holy shit!" I was amazed at the mystery of it, the beauty, the grace.

"I called the Fat Man," Ridlin said.

So much for the mystery, the beauty, the grace. I *knew* that cab was tagged with some kind of GPS device. The Fat Fuck knew right where I was, at every minute of every day.

"OK, here I am," I said. "Why are you looking for me?" I said.

Ridlin looked up and into my eyes, then down at the indicator, then into my eyes again.

"You're not breaking any laws here, are you, Vince?"

"Me? Breaking laws?" Shit, that was an intelligent riposte.

"What's the story with that?" he asked.

"Story? This?" I asked, indicating the indicator. "I found this when I pulled in, on the ground, and was going to dump it in the trash."

I looked over at Landreau. He wasn't looking at me, he was staring past the front of the cab, toward the bus shelter on the sidewalk, and his eyes were bugging out.

I looked at Ridlin. He looked at me. We both looked at Landreau. What the fuck?

CHAPTER 44
Vinnie Amatucci

On 51st Street
Thursday, January 23

Landreau stopped staring at whatever he was staring at, and ducked his head down, turned away from the street, and started yanking on the door of the cab, trying to rip it open. It was locked, and I had the key in my pocket.

"Vince," he whispered, "open the door. Open the goddamned door." He looked panicky, flushed, but the strange thing was that he was whispering, as if someone might overhear him. What, like Ridlin wasn't going to hear him?

"Jack," I said, "take it easy. What am I going to do, spirit you away while he's standing here with a gun in his pocket when all I have is," I looked in my hand and there it still was, "this . . . turn indicator?"

"Open the door, Vince," he said. "Please open the door." He had his back to the street and was leaning way over, still yanking on the handle. I had never seen him like this.

I got the keys out, clicked the clicker, and I swear he was inside before I heard the click.

Ridlin looked at me, his brow furrowed, his mouth hanging open. He reached quietly into his coat and took out his gun, all oily menace, and let it hang from his hand. He turned slowly around, looking at the lot, scanning every car, every pedestrian, every housewife pushing a cart. His head was turning like a gun on a turret, slowly sweeping. Oh, shit. Here we go again. I took two steps over to the cab, pulled the door open, and slid inside. Landreau was still down in the seat, almost on the floor, breathing hard.

"Jack," I said. "What the fuck is it?"

He shook his head back and forth, three times, hunkered a little lower.

"Look, man, you've got Ridlin spooked. He's stalking the crowd like a lion looking for which gazelle to cull from the herd. He looks like he won't be happy unless he shoots somebody."

He wasn't responding. I took a shot.

"Jack, you saw somebody, somebody who scared the shit out of you. Who was it, man? You've got to tell me and you've got to tell me now."

He was holding his right hand against his chest. His eyes were wild, darting around.

"Talk to me, Jack!"

And he started snapping his fingers. There was a pattern to it, a rhythm:

SNAP-two-three-four
SNAP-SNAP-three-four
SNAP-SNAP-SNAP-four
SNAP-SNAP-SNAP-SNAP

It was one of those old-timey stop-time things, the kind of thing you play when you're comping behind someone who's playing a solo.

I looked around for Ridlin. He had wandered maybe twenty yards away, still stalking. I reached into my coat and pulled out a cigarette and a lighter. I took one drag to get it going, tucked away the lighter and took another, a deep one, all the way to my toes.

And as I exhaled I looked toward a group of people waiting for the bus in the kiosk. There was a guy dressed like a workingman, with a scruffy beard. I didn't know him, but something about him looked oddly familiar. I looked more closely. He was tapping his foot:

TAP-two-three-four

TAP-TAP-three-four

TAP-TAP-TAP-four

TAP-TAP-TAP-TAP

It was the same rhythm.

I looked over my shoulder at Landreau; he was still in the cab, snapping away. I looked to my left toward Ridlin, he was still stalking. I tried to both whisper and shout at the same time: "Ken!" It came out sounding like one of those guys with a hole in their throat, all hoarse and glottal. But it worked; he stopped in his tracks. "Ken, now," I said. He started retracing his steps, walking sideways.

"What?" he said.

"Landreau . . . he was hearing a rhythm, and he started to snap his fingers . . ."

Ridlin looked like he wanted to take my temperature with the back of his hand, the way my mother used to. I rushed ahead.

"Listen, I know it sounds crazy, forget it. But the guy over there waiting for the bus is tapping the same rhythm with his foot." I nodded my head subtly in the workingman's direction.

"Which guy is—"

I could hardly hear him. My head was filling with a loud rushing sound. I turned.

It was the bus. It had pulled up and the doors were open and they were all filing into it.

"Shit," I said. "Shit shit shit."

"Get in the cab, Vince," Ridlin said. "Follow that bus."

CHAPTER 45
Vinnie Amatucci

In the Fat Man's Cab
Thursday, January 23

We both dove into the front of the cab. I tried to fish the keys out of my pocket with my left hand, but of course that hand had a cast on it, and I jammed my stupid thumb on my pocket and yelped. I quickly switched to my right, patted my coat pocket—not there—patted my shirt pocket—not there—and finally reached into my jeans and found them. I thumbed the ignition key away from the others, jammed it at the ignition and missed entirely, scraping it along the plastic trim, cursing up a storm. The second time it went in, but it was crooked. I took a deep breath, pulled it out slightly, guided it home, cranked the engine to life, threw the shift into reverse, and looked up, my left foot on the brake, my right feeding it some gas.

"Vince, he's getting away." Ridlin said this calmly, just reporting the facts as he saw them. I looked around and saw that I was turned the exact wrong way. My path would take me out the northern side of the lot, turning east; the bus had started facing east but had already turned south on Lake Park.

"Shit shit shit."

I raised my left foot off the brake and slammed my right foot onto the gas, and backed up, and kept backing up. At the end of the one-way row, I swung into a diagonal sliver of a space, switched to drive, cranked the wheel all the way left, and blasted south down the northbound row. Up ahead there were four cars lined up to exit the lot.

"Hold on," I said, "evasive maneuvers."

I swung the wheel left, gave a quick glance, squeezed between a parking sign and a concrete bench, miraculously missing both, and bumped over the sidewalk and over the curb and into the street, a spray of sparks kicking up where my muffler kissed the one and then Frenched the other. I lurched again and I was on South Park southbound.

"Oncoming traffic on the left," Ridlin said. I leaned on the horn and hit the gas again while I lurched the wheel to the right. I heard brakes and breaking glass over there, almost turned to look, but caught something out of the corner of my right eye. It was the first of the four cars leaving the lot that I had so skillfully exited, and he was now in the street, heading straight toward me, about to hit me broadside. I hit the horn again, jerked the wheel to the left, mashed the pedal down, and swerved around him, cutting into the northbound lane, and scaring a white Buick there over toward his right. As he moved, I jerked the wheel again and fishtailed us into a more-or-less straight position.

Okay, I thought. Not bad.

I looked up and the bus was all the way down to 53rd, and had pulled over to drop off and pick up. The driver was now edging back into the street, swinging the big behemoth into the center lane to avoid the parked cars in front of the bus stop. I stepped on the gas.

I zoomed past 52nd and accelerated through a yellow light at 53rd and kept pouring it on. Nearing 54th I caught up with the bus.

All I could see were the passengers on the left-hand window seats. That left the center seats and the right-hand window seats out of my view, unless I drove down the sidewalk. That could be fun, I thought. In the meantime, I started to scan the passengers.

"Vince, look straight ahead," Ridlin said.

A northbound car was stopped in the middle of the road with his left-hand turn signal on. Fine. Understandable. But it wasn't facing true north, it was facing north-by-northwest. It was the fucking gray Cavalier! She had begun her turn and stopped, her nose poking into my lane.

"No, not again!" I screamed. "Just fucking pick a goddamned lane!"

I was parallel with the bus, and he wasn't about to move out of his lane for something as small as a cab. Shit.

I pulled the wheel left and jumped the center divider, swerved all the way toward the curb of the northbound lane to avoid an oncoming Ford, then passed the Cavalier in the center lane, jumped the divider back and pulled up parallel to the bus, leaving a trail of sparks behind.

I honked at him like crazy, and Ridlin flashed his badge. We edged just in front of him and Ridlin was out of the cab before I had finished braking.

CHAPTER 46
The Cleaner

On Foot in Hyde Park
Thursday, January 23

12:35 P.M.: I do not know how they make me but they make me. It is Amatucci. He is calling out to Ridlin. Pointing his busted hand at me and I am wishing the bus would come.

And what do you know—it does. Get on. Drop the fare. See them jump in the cab. Going the wrong way—this Amatucci has got himself a pair of brass ones.

I need to disappear. What are they looking for? Workingman, beard, plaid coat. Without those they have nothing. Means leaving behind evidence. Hate to do that.

Half-block south of 53rd. Next stop a block away.

Shrug off the coat. Take off the hat. Pull out a black watch cap. Pull the cap on, down low. Roll up the coat and hat. Jam them under the seat. Leather jacket, now. Different look. The beard must go. Not where citizens can see my actual face. After.

Driver starts to pull over. Two people outside getting on.

When the door is closing, jump up, step forward, down the two steps, outside. Facing away, my head low on my chest.

The bus edges out into traffic. I walk alongside it. One car, two cars, a van. I get behind it, squat down. Reach up, find the corner of the beard. Work it free. Ditch the beard under the van. Look through the windows for that big black Checker. There they go. Swerving in and out of traffic. I look away and head north to the corner, west along 53rd. Need to get out fast.

This is not good. I am wearing my actual face, and I never go out with my actual face.

CHAPTER 47
Vinnie Amatucci

At Akiko's Place
Thursday, January 23

That night I ended up hanging around Akiko's place. I'm not sure how she heard that I was cooped up at the police station all day, but when I walked out the door, she was sitting there in her beat-up old Buick, waiting for me. I walked around to the police lot and got my cab, and she followed me to the Fat Man's stand. I got into my own car, she took off. I gave her a five-minute head start and drove up to her place, throwing up a couple of amateurish evasive maneuvers along the way.

I was starved, and, of course, she had almost no food in the place. She finally scrounged together a fried tofu, lettuce, and tomato sandwich on some kind of multigrain bread and I wolfed it down. It wasn't bad, considering it was tofu, but by that point I would have eaten the linoleum off the floor. As soon as I was done inhaling the food, I walked her through it.

They had taken down the IDs of everyone on the bus,

put a CTA police officer at the wheel, and driven us all downtown for questioning. Landreau and Ridlin and I took the Fat Man's cab. The main question was who got a good look at the guy, and what exactly he looked like. They had two sketch artists there, a male and a female, circulating among the crowd with these computer tablet things, and the first one, the guy, would draw what he heard you describe; then the woman would eventually come along and draw what she heard you say. It was a little weird; you'd think you had nailed it with the first one, and you'd look at the drawing and say to yourself, "Yeah, that's him," and the second artist would come along and would do something entirely different, and it would also look right somehow, even if it didn't look much like the first one. Another lesson in the subjectivity of experience.

I kept having this feeling that he was familiar from somewhere, but all my drawings of him were mostly of his back, because that's most of what I saw from my angle. I'll tell you, I never knew how many different ways you could draw a back—how broad are the shoulders, how narrow is the waist, how long are the arms, and do they turn out or turn in or hang straight?

I had a clear image of the coat, and could visualize every color, every line, and spent a lot of time describing it, which turned out to be pointless because he had ditched it and the cops had found it. I also kept reaching for an ephemeral sliver of an image of his face, something that felt like it was there, just out of reach, but after a while, I just couldn't say. I mean, the guy had a coat on, he was facing away from me 90 percent of the time, and I was mostly preoccupied with Landreau freaking out and Ridlin stalking the parking lot. But I would let them draw what they drew and then say, "No, not like that, more like this," and they'd go back in and change it and I'd say, "Yeah, well, not quite so exaggerated," and they'd change it back a bit. It was all computerized, so there wasn't any erasing, in the traditional sense of the term, but they could do it freehand, like an actual artist would, using the tablet and a stylus. They each started out in pure black-and-white, and added shading and color later on, building it up a layer at a time.

We were all supposed to be sequestered and neutral, but there was no room to isolate all forty-something of us, so you couldn't help but overhear snatches of conversation. Some people were very definite about it—"No, No, No. Not like that at all. His nose was much more plain than that,"—while others were a little less sure—"Well, that could look like him, I mean, in a certain light, at a certain angle . . ."

You could see that the artists were making multiple passes at people with a purpose. It's all basic psychology. Some people do better at recall; they can tell you what they saw, or at least what they *remember* they saw, without much prompting. Others are better at recognition; they might not consciously remember anything off the top of their heads, but if you give them three drawings, they can say, "Well it definitely *wasn't* Number 2." It's as basic as the difference between fill-in-the-blank and multiple choice.

As to Landreau, he wasn't denying he recognized the tapping, and he wasn't confirming it either. I had the sense that Ridlin could have pressured him—thrown him in an interrogation room with some unfriendly detectives—but he didn't. I think he was as spooked by Landreau's reaction as I was.

When we got to the end of the first round, the two artists huddled together in another room and the cops went around and got us all coffee and soda and whatever. We waited a while and they came back in and showed us what they called a "consolidated version" of the guy, and I have to say, it looked surprisingly familiar, even the face, and that was kind of eerie.

Then Ridlin walked in carrying a plastic bag, and showed us the beard, which they had found somewhere near the 53rd Street stop. He couldn't take it out of the bag—they were still checking for fingerprints or fibers or DNA or whatever—but it looked right. So he posed the question to the sketch artists: what does this guy look like without the beard and mustache?

They went off to their side room again, while Ridlin went around to everybody, trying to find out if anyone had looked out of the window and seen him taking off the beard. No one had. I was a little stunned, myself—it had looked real enough to me. But, like I said, I had only had that one fleeting glimpse of his face. The sketch artists asked a few people to come into their side room, one at a time. I wasn't one of them.

After another hour, the artists came back in with three drawings of what they thought the guy might have looked like without the facial hair. Actually, by this time, they weren't drawings but electronic portraits, done up in color and laser-printed on nice glossy stock. They passed sets around to everyone there, and we all started to debate which one looked the most like him. For some reason, they made no pretense of sequestering us this time around. They hadn't even randomized the letters they used to label them—it was just A, B, and C, and everyone had the same A, the same B, and the same C.

None of the pictures were pictures of his back.

For me, C resonated, somehow, just a little "click" from my unconscious when I saw the picture. I didn't know why; it just did.

Most of the rest of the group liked B, and hardly anyone thought it was A. Ridlin thanked everyone, gave us all free passes for work and vouchers for bus fares and lunch, and we all dispersed. All except Landreau, who stayed there with Ridlin.

As I finished the telling, Akiko went to the kitchen to pour some more tea. I was wishing for a cup of coffee, but she didn't have any. I was also wishing for a coat hanger to reach inside my cast and scratch the back of my left hand, which was making me crazy. I glanced at her open closet, and there were lots of hangers there, but they all looked like wood—cedar, in fact. Why you would hang a collection of black T-shirts on expensive cedar hangers is beyond me, but that's Akiko. I went into the bathroom, took a leak, washed my hand, and then had some trouble zipping up; one-handed, it's not easy.

As I was working my way through this maneuver, I heard a key turn in the main door, then another key, then heard the door open, and close.

I dropped to my knees, looked through the bathroom keyhole, scared of who I might see. Was it him, the Godfather? One of his henchmen?

I heard Akiko scampering in from the kitchenette, then heard her stop in her tracks, then walk forward two steps.

It was Laura, in the flesh, and her flesh was as lovely as ever. They embraced. I made a show of turning the water faucet on and off and then rattling open the bathroom door.

She looked at me, up and down, and said to Akiko, "Well, look what we have here."

"Nice seeing you again, too," I mumbled.

"Vince was at the police station this afternoon, all day," Akiko cut in. "They think they got a look at the guy, like, the one who's been stalking the band? They had two sketch artists there and they had a whole bus full of people trying to make up a drawing of him. So I met him there and he followed me back here."

Laura arched her eyebrows.

"I didn't think it would be safe for him at his place," Akiko said, her eyes cast down toward the floor.

"Was Vince the one who identified him?" Laura asked.

I jumped in. "Actually, it was Jack Landreau," I said.

"Jack Landreau?" Laura snarled. "And you believed him?"

I looked at Akiko; she was looking at her shoes.

"As it turned out, the guy who he, uh, identified, got on the bus. We got in my cab and chased the bus, and by the time we caught up with it, he had gotten off."

"Let me see if I'm following this. A man gets on a bus, and then a man gets off the bus, so that man must be some kind of mass murderer? Because Jack Landreau said so?"

"I wouldn't add the 'must be' in there," I said. "But between when he got on and when he got off, he ditched his coat and his hat in the bus—"

"Sounds like he was forgetful, not dangerous—"

"And he ditched his false beard and fake mustache, too," I added. So there, bitch.

I couldn't figure out why she was being such a shit—the tone of voice, the attitude. It was all-of-a-sudden-Hello-and-go-fuck-yourself. What, did she think I had something going with Akiko, by myself? Right. First, Akiko is jealous because she thinks I have something going on with Laura, then Laura is jealous because she thinks I have something going with Akiko. That's me—all the women think I'm such a stud that all the other women must be fucking me. Give me a fucking break.

I didn't say this, but moved over to the futon and flopped my ass down. I reached into my kit bag and started to fill the pipe. My thoughts were getting a little yang, and it was time to yin them out a little.

"Can I get you some tea?" Akiko asked her.

"Sure," Laura said. "Japanese gunpowder?"

Akiko nodded.

Laura looked around, then came and sat down next to me. I made a point of not looking at her, but out of the corner of my eye I noticed that she was wearing all black, just like Akiko. I also noticed that hers was silk and fit a lot tighter.

"Are you sure that whoever it was didn't follow you over here?" she asked.

I looked over at her. "I didn't think that with forty people trying to draw his picture, he'd be waiting for us outside 1100 South State Street, but, just in case, I had Akiko make a show of following me to the cabstand where I left the cab, and got back in my car. I waited ten minutes, took a very indirect route here, parked a couple of blocks away and walked in the back way."

She raised her eyebrows.

"Seriously?" she asked.

"It probably wasn't perfect," I said, "but still . . ."

She nodded.

I reached out to her with the pipe, "Would you care for some, uh, tea?" I asked.

"Why, Vincent, you are so chivalrous," she said. She took the pipe, I fired up the lighter and held it for her, and she took a long hit, and then another. She didn't smoke it delicately, but sucked it down in great gulps, and held it in like an experienced pothead, not exhaling until there was almost none left to trickle out.

I took a hit myself, then passed it back. She took the lighter as well this time, and fired it up. I had no doubt that she would be equally practiced with a line of cocaine or a spike of heroin.

"How about you?" I asked.

"How about me?"

"I would imagine that the people watching you have more resources at their command than the one guy who may be watching me. How'd *you* get away?"

She took a hit, passed it back, nodded. "You're right about that," she said in a low dope-whisper. "The last time, I think they *wanted* me to get away. I really should have known better. This time, they didn't, so I had to use all my wiles."

I must have given her a look, because she jumped right in. "No, not *those* wiles. But I did have to get creative—slipped out with the help, went by foot to a CTA stop, took the train west for a couple of stops, switched to a bus, walked here kind of backward, and came in over the fence."

I gave her an approving glance.

"I have *some* experience at this," she said. "You could say I had a sheltered childhood."

"I'll bet," I said. I grabbed the pipe and took another hit. It wasn't the pot that was confusing me; it was her. I felt awed by her, and attracted to her, and a little bit scared of her. Not just by her father, the mob and all—yeah, that was scary enough—but by her, all by herself. Usually, once I've been with a woman, that way, these kinds of nerves seem to go away, especially when it's been good. Not with Laura.

Akiko came back with the tea. She hooked a little table with her foot and dragged it in front of the futon, placing the tray on top. She knelt next to it and poured the tea. It felt like some kind of Kabuki moment. It made me a little uncomfortable—I hadn't rated a table, just a mug—but Laura seemed at ease with it. She slumped back on the futon, letting herself be served.

When Akiko was done pouring, she came around the table and sat down on the other side of Laura. She took her hand, then, and it struck me that they probably hadn't been together since the night I was there last, and that had been, what? A week? They had seen each other at the Casbah, but that had been in public, and it hadn't ended too well. Laura made no move toward Akiko, but let herself be caressed a little.

"So, what does he look like?" she asked. "This guy?"

I held up a hand, my bad one, reached into my coat with my good one, and fished out the sketches of "The Workingman." I laid them out on the little table, in order, first the Beard, then A, which nobody bought, then B, which most people liked, then C, my own personal favorite, kind of fanning them across.

I looked over toward Laura to grab back the pipe. Her hand had gone up to her chest, her mouth was open, and her face was turning white. It was the same gesture her mother had used at the Casbah.

Akiko put down her teacup and knelt in front of Laura, holding her hand, the one pressed to her chest.

"Laura, do you know one of these men?" she asked.

Laura turned slowly and looked at her, and nodded slowly, swallowing.

I picked up the four pictures and riffled through them. "Which one, Laura," I asked. "Which one do you know?"

She glanced past the Beard, past A, looked for a minute

at B. When her eyes settled on C, her hand went back up to her chest again, and the rest of the color drained from her face.

"He looks much older," she said, "but I guess he would. And there used to be a scar through the middle of his left eyebrow, but I guess it grew in or he had it fixed or . . ." her voice trailed off, almost wistfully.

"Laura," I asked. "Who is he? How do you know him?"

Se looked at the picture again, then turned to look at Akiko.

"It's over, baby. I'm so sorry. He's going to kill us all."

CHAPTER 48
Ken Ridlin

At Headquarters
Friday, January 24

You would think I just figured after all these years out how the Chicago Fire really started. Not just how it starts but who starts it. Not just who starts it but why. Not just why but with which match. The whole HQ mobilizes to handle the witnesses on the bus, the way we do. A Red Ball. A Full-Court Press. An All-Hands. Different people call it different things. It's a routine, and we fall into it like a bone-tired man into a soft feather bed.

Me? I am pissed. If I really stay with Landreau, back at the lot, work him, give him some room, get him to talk, maybe I nail this guy. Maybe I crack open a couple dozen of unsolveds. Maybe I get back to where I was, once. But no. I have to play the hero. Pull out the gun. Scan the area. One minute of quiet conversation, he tells me. Maybe. But I couldn't give him ten seconds.

Now Landreau is all tucked away. Babysitters. Safe house. Even found him one with a piano. A baby grand no less. So you know he's gonna find his way back into *his* comfort zone. He's already halfway there, all clammed up, nothing to say. You tell him he freaked out, he says, "Did I? Hunh . . ." You ask him about the guy he sees, he just looks at you, shakes his head. Like that. Nothing. It was all there, right on the surface. Now the waves have washed over whatever it was and it's back at the bottom of the ocean. Under pressure. Where he keeps it.

The whole thing backfires. Now our guy knows we are onto him. Now he's more cautious. If it's me? I go to ground. Wait until we get lazy again and move on to something else. Which we always do.

They always tell you this—think like the criminal. Put yourself in his place. You can't, really. He's in his place. You're in your place. If you could think like a criminal, you'd get every one of them. And if they could think like us, we'd never catch a single one of them.

Lieutenant Ali? Yeah, he gets all involved again. He gets a whiff of anything, he's all over it. He thinks he's a detective again, the poor guy. Comes in, heart pumping a mile a minute. He's "concerned," there's a word for you. That's code for "pissed off." He can't tell me he's "pissed off," because I broke a major lead. He can't chew me out because we're standing in the bull pen and every five seconds someone comes up and pats me on the back.

So he says he is "concerned." Concerned that maybe I am not keeping him and the captain in the loop. "It's not just the result, it's the process," he says. His face is all beagle-eyed, his forehead is creased, the body language is something he must practice in front of the mirror.

But I swear to him he is in the loop, this just kind of happens, you know the way things sometimes just happen, Loot? I always call for my backup as soon as it is feasible. At the time, I'm not wanting to spook the perp.

Are we allowed to say "spook"? Not that I mean anything like that by it.

He wants to know about the next opportunity, the next

time the band will be in public. He gets all sensitive when I mention tomorrow, at the Nickelodeon. More puppy-dog eyes. On my way back into the force, they gave me the same training, and I could never get it right. I either looked the way I felt or I looked like I felt nothing at all, which sometimes I guess I don't. But Ali must have aced it. I feel his concern. Don't I trust him, he asks?

Don't make me answer that. Not on the record. Not to a so-called superior officer.

I look him dead in the eye. This is something I know how to do, training or no training. I say I have it rated as an improbable target. This place, the Nickelodeon? It's not really advertised here in town. It doesn't fit with the kind of joints the band plays. It's an out-of-the-way place. So out-of-the-way it's over in Indiana, and that means jurisdictional disputes, and that means—

He cuts me off.

"And that means, Ken, that you *need* me even more than you would if it were in-state."

"If it *were* in-state"? Where do they manufacture these guys? Is there a kit you can buy?

"I can get jurisdiction, if I hurry. You, alone, you're just some guy with a gun. You're not even a police officer to them down there."

I nod. That's stretching it. But it's what he's supposed to say. Now he has to do what he's supposed to do. He rushes off to "get on the horn." He'll have to get back to me, "coordinate the operational aspect."

Jeez. I mean, we always talked cop talk, but when did it stop being English?

As he is striding away I'm shaking my head back and forth. We're going to have Chicago cops, plainclothes mostly. But the uniforms can smell something like this like they can smell a doughnut shop two miles away. They'll be crawling all over it. We're gonna have the Indiana Staties. Because we have them we're gonna have our own Staties. And the Calumet City locals—that's gonna be their price for letting us operate on their turf. I'd be surprised if we don't have the Park Service Smokies in this before we're done.

It is going to be a royal snafu. It is going to be cops looking at cops. A real patron gets in the club? It'll be an accident. I feel like I should call Powell, tell him to start working on our arrangements of "Oh, Danny Boy."

And the perp? Are you going to tell me he doesn't see this from a mile away? The guy we're looking for? Saw it the minute he got on that bus. Knows what's going to go down. He's home making himself a new beard, in a different color, or a new mustache, thicker or thinner. He's growing his hair out, or cutting it short. He's putting on a few pounds, or he's on a diet. Before this, I make the Nickelodeon as a high-probability site, for all the same reasons I'm telling Ali it is a low probability—out of the way, out of the profile, out of the state. We could have baited him, could have sent him in feeling confident. Now? Now it's going to be poison.

By now he's laying low. And if he knows about Calumet City? He wants no part of it after yesterday. He's too smart. He knows too much about us, about the way we have to do this kind of thing. He will be sitting on his ass and drinking a cold one and watching the Bulls while a hundred cops in a hundred uniforms will be freezing their balls off in the snow.

He won't come. He wouldn't dare.

Would he?

CHAPTER 49
Vinnie Amatucci

On the Way to Indiana
Friday, January 24

I picked Akiko up in my car at her place, and we drove toward Indiana and the Nickelodeon. We were both silent for about a mile, until one of us couldn't stand it anymore. That, of course, would have been me.

"So, what did Laura say after I left?"

She paused. I waited.

"She thinks . . . Oh shit. She thinks Jack Landreau is, like, her father, and they're trying to kill *him*, not me."

"Her father?" I said, my clueless brain trying to sort through it. "How could Jack be her father? Jack's never even been to Chicago until a couple of weeks ago, remember?"

The light turned green and I slid forward.

"Vince, think about it," she said. "He says his home base is like three hours west of here, in Iowa, right? And he's like the best goddamn musician any of us have ever heard anywhere. Any tune, any style, any key. He plays Detroit, he plays Cleveland, St. Louis, Cincinnati, even Rock Island,

and he never plays Chicago? Aside from maybe New York, where else would anyone *want* to play? I mean, especially this kind of music, the old stuff, you know?"

She had a point there. Facts are one thing, logic is another.

"The only reason not to play here is if he's scared of coming here. And the only reason he'd be scared would be if he had, like, a history or something, you know?"

She looked at me.

"Laura thinks she's that history."

I was trying to sort it out but it wasn't parsing at all.

"But Akiko, we've been over this with Ridlin, remember? This whole thing started *before* Jack got into town. I'm the one who picked him up at the airport, a couple hours *after* Roger What's-His-Name got shot, remember?"

"I know, Vince, I know. I tried to tell Laura that, but she wasn't listening. And she wouldn't say why she thinks he's her father. She can be, like, stubborn, you know?"

"I guess."

"But she sounded so sure of it. And she's usually not like that. I mean, she doesn't make stuff up, she's not, you know, melodramatic or anything. Believe me, that's like one of my requirements, you know?"

Two plus two were somehow adding up to 1003; we were missing an exponent somewhere. I was trying to think linearly but it kept slipping away from me laterally.

So I slipped sideways with it and changed the subject.

"Akiko," I said, "did she say any more about the guy in the parking lot? Number C?"

She looked straight ahead.

"Well," I asked, "did she?"

She turned toward me, her face half in profile. "Every now and then she would glance at that picture, like she couldn't stay away from it, and every time she did her face would turn all white and she would, like, shiver. I kept asking her who it was, did she know him, did she recognize anything about him . . . ?"

"And?"

"She's like, 'Yes, I know him. He's not even going to spare me, we're all going to die.' "

"That's it?"

"That's enough, isn't it?"

It was, but it also wasn't. This is my problem: I need to know the "why" to believe in the "what," and I didn't know anything about the "why" of it.

We finally broke free of the traffic when we merged onto Lake Shore Drive. My shoulders were knotted tight. As we were slingshotting around Soldier Field she must have noticed this. She reached behind me and started to knead the spot where the neck flares out and that wedge of muscle angles down. At first, her fingers felt like knives going in, but she backed off a notch and I relaxed enough to let her in. She had some serious skills. I let my head rock back, put my right hand on her leg, steering with my cast propped up against the wheel, and we cruised south that way. There was a sudden sense of peace, of quiet within the chaos. The stop-and-go noise of brakes and horns was behind us, lost in the high-pitched wind-noise of the highway. For just a moment, there were no words, there was no thinking, there were no reasons, just two people trying to comfort each other in small ways.

If only for a moment.

CHAPTER 50
Vinnie Amatucci

At the Nickelodeon
Friday, January 24

It felt like we drove for hours and hours, as if we were going to India, not Indiana. The weather had turned colder, the sky the color of concrete. After we got off the expressway, we turned right and left and left and right, weaving slowly and steadily. We never seemed to go slower than thirty, we never seemed to go faster than forty. It was monotonous, but I could feel my pulse pounding in the throbbing of my hand.

I was in the lead in my old Jetta. We had picked up Paul at his place on 47th and Sidney at his place farther south. Akiko sat next to me, her hand resting on my leg. Sidney was instantly snoring in the back right corner, while Paul leaned up against my seat as he quietly called out the directions.

I knew that we had been to this club before, a couple of years ago, but I didn't have any memory of it. Someone else must have driven; I was like the passive rat, pulled through the maze in all those Intro Psych experiments who has no memory of how to get back to the cheese. So Paul navigated and I drove. It was all I could do.

We entered an industrial area, the faceless stucco buildings matching the gray of the darkening sky. Everything was painted in nameless colors, dozens of layers thick. The horizon was crowded with buildings, two and three stories tall, with faceless names like QuanTech, DyPro, Questronix, RoMac, places where they could have been making absolutely anything in the world, or nothing at all, where there could have been hundreds of workers scurrying around or one solitary watchman snoozing in a chair. The rights followed the lefts, and we never seemed to go straight for more than a couple of blocks. Every now and then I would glance in the rearview mirror, and see Ridlin's Crown Vic behind us. When I glanced at the parked cars lining the road I did a double take. Cop cars. Lots of cop cars, of all kinds. Ridlin must have called in the cavalry. And there they were, in force, parked by the side of the road, sitting in pairs at the bus stops, walking up and down the sidewalks.

Ahead of us was an empty space with overgrown grass three feet high in the abandoned lots along the side. You could see the wind, blowing the grass almost sideways in sinuous waves. We slid slowly forward until a narrow street parted the grass and we saw a building straight ahead, with a large neon sign that said "Nickelodeon."

It was a large squat structure, a rambling mess that had seen better days. There was a porch around three sides and an awning out the side, facing a parking lot occupied by fifty or sixty cars. The whole building looked as if it was listing slightly to the left.

We parked near the building. The cars were mostly busted-out old Detroit iron with Bondo and duct tape on the side panels, except for one gleaming black Cadillac limo with Wisconsin plates and smoked windows.

I looked beyond the building and there was nothing. We had reached the end of the road.

We were on some kind of promontory, jutting east into the lake. Off to the north you could see the lights along the shore poking out of the haze. On a clear night you could probably see the bright lights of downtown. Now it was just clouds and haze and a dim orange glow.

We walked in through the side door under a sign that said EMPLOYEE ENTRANCE. I helped Akiko unload her drum kit, grabbing the big bass drum with my one good hand and tucking her largest Zildjian cymbal under my left armpit.

Paul opened the door and we walked into a blast of heat and light and aroma; it was the kitchen. It was as bright as the surface of the sun, and I squinted in the glare. Dozens of Hispanic men in spattered white jackets and sweaty red baseball caps were scurrying around. The smell that assaulted my nostrils was grease, in all its forms—burgers, fries, pork, melting cheese. I usually like it greasy, but this was too much even for me, and I could feel my throat starting to close. I reached up to wipe the sweat off my forehead and dropped the cymbal onto the floor with a deafening crash. The six of us stopped in our tracks, every neck in our little conga line craned toward me, but none of the kitchen workers missed a beat; it was as if it was a sound they heard every day, all day long, and they were used to it. I set down the bass drum, scooped up the cymbal, wedged it back under my arm, then picked up the bass and moved forward.

As we stepped out of the kitchen, my eyes blinked again to adjust to the dark, and I stopped in my tracks, unsure of my footing. The song playing in the background was coming through a tinny sound system with way too much treble; it was Louis Armstrong scat-singing "The Heebie Jeebies," a classic. Whatever medium it was on must have been a classic as well; there was more static than sound. Then someone bumped into me from behind, then someone bumped into them, sending them ramming up against me again, and I staggered. And dropped the fucking cymbal again, sending it to the floor with another loud crash. It spun around and around in ever tighter circles and rang at an ever-increasing pitch, getting right up to the fingernails-on-a-blackboard level before sizzling to a stop.

The sound silenced the crowd. And then, in the same instant, the lights came on, the music on the sound system was cut off in mid-phrase, and a torrent of strange sounds came at us from everywhere.

Finally able to see, I looked around. The room was hexagonal, and in the middle was a circular stage, rotating slowly in a clockwise direction. And arrayed around the outside of the hexagon was a collection of every kind of old-style player-instrument you could conceive of, and some I couldn't, all running off electric current: player pianos; player violins, their bows sawing across the strings and building up little cones of dry rosin underneath them; player saxophones and clarinets, their mouthpieces hooked up to mechanical bellows rising and falling in a cyclic rhythm; player trumpets and trombones and baritone horns; player drums of all kinds, and off in the northeast corner, an enormous player organ, pumping away. They were all playing "When the Saints Go Marching In," they were all playing out of tune with each other, and they were all playing at slightly different tempos. It was cacophony, and it was all coming back to me now.

I looked around: Akiko looked stunned. Sidney was cackling loudly, his hairy face thrown back so far you could see his molars. Paul was smiling a faint little smile. Landreau had dropped his case at his feet and was frozen, his head down and his hands covering his ears, his mouth open in a silent scream. Ridlin was into his scanning mode, checking every patron.

We stumbled up onto the bandstand. Some folding metal chairs, bent and bruised, were set up for us. It took a minute to get all of Akiko'a drum kit in one place, and once we had, she held up a hand, politely asking us all to back away.

I stretched up to a standing position and as soon as I heard Landreau play a C-major chord on the chipped hulk of a spinet piano, I groaned. To say it was out of tune would be putting it mildly; it was nowhere near the key of C, but hovered in a different universe of sound altogether. He looked at me plaintively; I reached into my jacket, found my star wrench and brandished it over my head.

"Sir Vincent to the rescue with his mighty scepter," he said.

Paul looked over at me. "We don't have a lot of time," he muttered.

I looked at Jack, looked inside the upright's lid, and said, "I can maybe give you three octaves, right in the middle. No deep bass, and don't go reaching for any high notes."

He seemed to grimace for a second, then nodded.

So I set to it. Because it was an upright, I could reach right inside and do what I needed to do. I had left my tuning fork in the car and didn't want to take the time to run out and get it, so I started struggling to find an A in my head, wandering around the pitch. Landreau tapped me on the shoulder, and said "Just a bit higher." I turned the wrench a quarter turn. "Keep going just a little more," he said. Another quarter turn and he said, "A little too far, down a hair," then, "Wait. Stop. That's it." From there it was a straightforward process. But there was one note, a high F, that wouldn't seem to hold. I'd adjust it and it would slip back down. If I couldn't get this one, the whole job would be fucked.

I looked inside; the gear looked stripped, all shiny amid the dust balls.

I looked around in desperation, then turned to Akiko and said, "No gum-chewing in class, young lady." She eyed me quizzically. I put my hand out, made a "gimme, gimme" motion, and she took her gum out and dropped it into my palm. I reached into the guts of the piano, screwed the F to where it needed to be, left the wrench on, and wadded the gum against the gear, holding it there until it dried out a bit. Then I slowly wiggled the wrench off, stood back, counted to ten, and tried an F-major chord. It had held.

"My work here is done," I said to no one in particular, and headed toward the edge.

I was stopped by Paul's voice, saying, "Well, not entirely." He was standing holding a microphone in his right hand, keeping it at arm's length in obvious distaste.

Of course, I thought, how could you play on a rotating circular stage without amplification? A big guy with a curly blond beard and a ponytail waddled up onto the stand, and walked over to where I was crouching.

"I'm Egon," he said. "I'm the manager here." We shook hands.

"Help me out, Egon," I said. "Where is the sound system?"

In the middle of the stage, by a large pole, was a tarpaulin that looked like someone had just dumped it on the floor. Egon lifted the tarp and a cloud of dust wafted up. Below it was an ancient soundboard. He pointed to the side, where the power switch was. I leaned down and blew on the board, and another cloud floated up. Next to it was a small block of wood, obviously handmade, bolted to the pole. There were two rusty toggle-switches on it, and a popsicle stick was taped to the bottom of the right one, limiting how far you could throw the switch. I looked up at Egon.

"What's the popsicle stick for?" I asked.

"That there's the switch that controls the stage's rotation. There's your regular speed, like now, and your OFF, which is up, and your high speed, which is down. We rigged it so that stick blocks you from high speed. Trust me—you don't want to go there," he repeated. "The one on the left is for all the player pianos and shit," and turned his back and hopped off the stage.

I looked at Paul. He made a point of looking at his watch. I looked at my own; we had maybe five minutes before we were scheduled to start. "I know you'll do what you can," he said. "Maybe we can make some adjustments between sets."

I did what I could to get the levels right, to bring the piano up and the trumpet down, to clear some of the mud out of the bass, and to round off the tinny treble. Paul usually carried a small mike that clipped onto the bell of his horn. I rooted around in his case and found it, praying that it would connect up. I held out the connector of the little mic, and brought it closer and closer to the cord coming from the board, my arms out straight and pointing inward, like Dr. Frankenstein preparing to summon the lightning into his laboratory.

"Please," Paul said, "I can't stand the suspense."

With a flourish, I brought the two together. I made myself shake for a few seconds, then dropped the connection to the floor and headed to the bar.

There's no way I was going to sit there listening to them play without me while I was stone-cold sober.

The bar wrapped all the way around the north third of the hexagon, between the entrance and the kitchen door, and it was magnificent—an old mahogany-and-brass classic that had felt the weight of a million elbows perched on its edge. A heavyset barkeep came up to me, I said "Jack on the rocks and an Old Style draft," as I settled into a rickety red vinyl barstool.

Akiko was busy with her drums. Paul was blowing into his horn to warm it up. Sidney was playing trills, of all things, on the tuba. Landreau was touching the piano tentatively, the way a man might reach out to touch a leper. Ridlin's reed was in his mouth, getting moist, but he was turning his head, sweeping the room.

I decided to take a peek myself, and it was a motley crowd indeed. It looked as if everyone already had a half a dozen drinks in them. Most of them were males, most of them were obscenely fat, most of them were wearing greasy ball caps with a sharp break in the bill, and all of them were loud, laughing, slapping each other on the back. There were maybe a dozen women in the room, and they all seemed to be smoking as if this would be their last one for a month, taking long slow concentrated drags, barely letting any out, then taking the next ones, as if they felt they had to inhale smoke with every breath of air they took.

I lit one myself, and self-consciously coughed. I found an ashtray on the bar, already full, nudged some dead butts out of the way, and set my own carefully down. As I started to turn away, the barkeep set down my shot-and-a-beer and swept the ashtray off the bar, freshly lit cigarette and all, dumped it somewhere behind the bar, and banged it down empty front of me.

I thumbed another one from the pack, lit it, and held onto it.

I went back to looking around the room, checking out all the player instruments, when I saw her. She was sitting in one of the hexagon's corners, in a dark space, out of the light, a glass of red wine sitting in front of her. She was wearing a long black dress, closed all the way to her neck, with a string of dark gray pearls in the front. She looked fabulous: rich, slim, elegant, sexy, sophisticated, demure. In a place like this, she stuck out.

No, not Laura; her mother, Amelia Della Chiesa. She was almost as tall as Laura, but less voluptuous, with a little less flesh in the bust and the hips, as if time had carved the excess off her. Her cheekbones were sharper, her hair more severely styled. Her skin was that same flawless olive tone, and polished smooth. She was holding a cigarette, cocked at an angle. Every now and then she would reach out and flick it over the ashtray, but I didn't see her actually inhale it. She was sitting very still, her right leg crossed over her left, not moving a muscle. And she was staring, but wasn't making any attempt to hide it. It was a bold, frank stare, unwavering, unblinking.

She was staring at Jack.

No one else caught her interest; her eyes didn't flinch. She was taking in every gesture as his fingers roamed across the middle half of the keyboard I had managed to salvage. Her eyes were cool, her back straight. I couldn't see lust; I couldn't see disdain; I couldn't see anything. Whatever was going on inside was way down deep, for herself alone.

As I stared I heard the band start its final tune-up, and they quickly jumped into the same song we had heard on the sound system on the way in from the kitchen, "The Heebie Jeebies." This hadn't been on the playlist; it must have been one of Paul's last-minute improvisations.

It was hard to tell that we hadn't practiced this tune in years. Sidney remembered it from our early Dixieland days and played it on his tuba, and Akiko knew the old Baby Dodds drum routine well enough, and Jack and Ken jumped right in and made it work.

The crowd applauded madly.

Paul took a minute to introduce the band, even pointing to me over at the bar, and they went right into "West End Blues," another Louis number, starting with the famous sixteen-bar obbligato way up in the stratosphere on the trumpet. After that was "Skid-Dat-De-Dat." And then right into the ballad "When It's Sleepy Time Down South," a beautiful tune, all minor-key regret and major-key resolution, and they did a fabulous job on it. I looked over at Amelia and the expression on her face was rapt and yet surprised.

They played the final chorus on "Sleepytime" and before I knew it my shot was gone and my beer glass was empty and they were done, an all-Armstrong set, and a nice one.

The crowd gave them a big ovation—some of them even stood up and hooted—and all of a sudden all the lights came on and all of the player instruments came on all at once, playing "When the Saints Come Marching In," and we all held our hands over our ears until it was over.

CHAPTER 51
Ken Ridlin

At the Nickelodeon
Friday, January 24

Halfway through the first set I see her, sitting at a table in the corner in the darkest spot in the room. At first I think it is Laura, with her hair pulled back, watching Jones play the drums. But the stage rotates a notch and I see it is her mother, Amelia. She's not watching Akiko play the drums, she's watching Landreau play the piano.

We're in the middle of "When It's Sleepy Time Down South," all minor keys with lots of sharps, and I don't like lots of sharps and I haven't played this tune in years, and Powell hands the solo off to me as we get to the bridge and I have to concentrate just to stumble my way through it and I lose sight of her as I focus on the music.

We come down to the close and the set ends and the crowd applauds and I look for her again. The stage is still turning. I am feeling dizzy and nauseous and weak. I lean back in the chair to feel the forty-five tucked into the small of my back, and it comforts me. I rub my right foot against my left ankle to feel the thirty-two tucked in the holster there, and it strengthens me.

For a second, I see her again, just a glimpse. Then the crowd stands and we are borne off the stage and I lose her again. In seconds I find myself in front of Amatucci at the bar, and a beer is placed in my hands and I look at it, the light shining through it all golden and warm. In a second a ginger ale replaces it. I take a sip and look around and we are all there.

Except for Landreau. I find Amelia's corner and she is gone as well.

CHAPTER 52
Vinnie Amatucci

At the Nickelodeon
Friday, January 24

By one in the morning the place had finally emptied out and Akiko had finished packing up her kit. Ridlin herded us over to a booth. He took one of the police drawings and held it up.

He asked us if anyone had seen him tonight, and we all said, no, we hadn't. I had been looking for him, but I hadn't seen anyone who even fit the general physical parameters. Ridlin took the drawing, set it down on the table. A breeze lifted it away. He put it back down on the table, smoothing it out with his long fingers, and placed his ginger ale on top of it.

"The latest thinking over at headquarters is that the focus may have shifted, from Ms. Jones to Mr. Landreau," he said.

Passive voice, I thought. Not "I think," not "We think," not even the protective coloration of "They think," but "The latest thinking." I glanced at Paul. He had caught it, too. Passive voice. What he sometimes calls the "Present Irresponsible" tense.

"Shifted?" I followed up. "Why?"

"You were there at the bus stop. The man who was there may be the man we have been looking for. Who identified him? Landreau. We think there might be some history there."

Sidney leaned forward. "History?"

Ridlin waved him off. "Nothing I'm at liberty to say. Jones may still be a target, but Landreau may be a target as well. That's why we're keeping him in town. He may know something he's not saying. But now he's disappeared."

"I mean, like, 'disappeared'? He didn't leave alone," Akiko said.

"I don't know if that's better or worse."

"Do you *know* if Jack has, you know, a history with her, with Laura's mother?" Akiko asked.

He said nothing.

She said nothing. It was a standoff, each one trying to see how much the other knew.

I was also acutely aware that I didn't know how much I knew myself. I had seen Landreau freak out and ID the guy in his semi-autistic way at the bus stop. I had heard Akiko's interpretation of Laura's wild theories about Jack and her mother. I had seen Amelia, unable to take her eyes off him. But I didn't know if she was staring at him with hate or lust or disdain.

When you have no data, it's easy to speculate. In fact, if you have half a brain, it's hard not to.

Ridlin interrupted my reverie.

"But we don't even have a clue where she might be hiding out."

Akiko spoke up in a quiet voice. "Yes, you do, you just don't *know* you do."

Ridlin looked over at her. So did the rest of us. She does that a lot, waits and circles and then pounces; it's like a linguistic version of her martial arts discipline.

"What do you mean, 'he knows but he doesn't know he knows'?" I prompted.

"You all do," she said, "except for you, Vince. You weren't there."

We all leaned in. She had the floor.

"Remember the gig up at Lake Geneva?" she asked. They all nodded their heads.

"We went outside and looked over the lake, and it was cold and foggy and beautiful? There was a house there, a house on a promontory—"

"I remember it," Paul said. "Modern. Plains style, very Frank Lloyd Wright, all horizontal lines. I remember wishing Vince were there so he could tell us if it was a real Wright."

"In Lake Geneva?" I repeated. "No. No way."

Akiko looked down at the floor, then looked up, but only halfway. There are some stories you can tell and look someone in the eye. This wasn't going to be one of them.

"We went up there once," she said. "Laura and I. She's like, 'Field trip!' so off we went. This was back in, I don't know, October, November. We drove and drove and got there and it was dark. There's a road, on the other side of the house from where we were, where you can see it? The road sticks out into the lake a bit and you look over a little cove and there it is. It's like the same sideways view of the house that we saw, but like, from the other side. So she had me pull up this little road, almost to the water's edge, and kill the lights. Laura likes to—well, she's adventurous, OK? She was telling me about this fabulous house with this incredible view, and how the bedroom ceiling was all glass, so you could see the stars, and the walls were all glass, so you could see the water and the woods. She was pulling me out of the car and I'm like, 'But Laura, we'll get caught, someone will see us, I am *not* breaking into somebody's house, no *way*, I don't *care* how cool the view is,' and she's like, 'No, it's OK. I have a key.' And she was dragging me out of the car and just then the porch lights came on. She grabbed me and pulled me down behind a bush. A door opened, and a woman came out onto the deck. She was standing there, smoking a cigarette, looking out at the lake. Laura kept shushing me, begging me not to make a sound. Finally, the woman went back inside, and turned out the lights. We waited maybe two, three minutes, freezing our asses off, and then scrambled into the car and she said 'Drive!' and I did. She had one of those looks on her face, so I backed out of there and did a U-turn and said, 'But I thought you had a key,' and she said, 'I do,' and held it up, in the light of the dashboard. 'I thought you said you knew her,' I said. 'I do,' she said again. 'So?' I asked. 'Why aren't we going in?' She looked back at the house, and said, 'I didn't know she was home. I thought she was at her other house, on Saint Barts. We can't go in there if she's home.' And I said, 'Why? Who is she?' And she's like, 'She's my mother. She's my long-lost mysterious mother, and we have to stop talking now.' And that's, that's how I know where she lives. In Lake Geneva. In that house."

I was stunned. There was nothing to say.

Until Ridlin picked up his ginger-ale glass from on top of the picture of the killer.

The glass had left a ring on the paper, right about where a mustache would be, and that pulled the image together for me. It was a different mustache from the one with the beard at the bus stop. With the beard it had been straight and bushy, almost British sergeant-major-ish. The wet line on the picture was curved, like the bottom of the glass, and it ran down his chin like a Fu Manchu and I slapped the table and yelped, "Holy shit! Holy fucking shit!"

Ridlin looked at me and I looked back at him. "Do you remember that I said I thought the picture of this guy looked familiar, like I had seen him somewhere, but I didn't know where?"

"Yeah?"

"And I couldn't figure out why because at the bus stop all I saw of him was his back, and that was kind of familiar in a kind of a strange way, but how the fuck do you recognize somebody's face when all you saw of him was his back?"

He squinted, like he was trying to remember something.

"Now I know where I saw him. He was wearing a mustache, like a Fu Manchu, like in this picture, in the shape of the water stain."

"Who is he, Vince? How do you know him? Where can we find him?"

I thought through his three questions.

"I don't know who he is or what name he goes by, but I have a regular customer with the cab who I think works for the Mob—I think he does collections—and he had this guy show up someplace where he had a problem collecting. It was on the West Side, out on South Cicero, and I missed the address and went too far, and when my customer saw that I caught a glimpse of this guy he freaked out. I mean he fucking lost it."

"I'm not following," Ridlin said.

Paul jumped in. "What Vince is trying to say is that he doesn't know the guy, but he knows a guy who knows the guy."

"Is that right, Vince?" he asked.

"Yeah," I said. "I don't know him and wouldn't know where to find him, but my guy, my regular customer, does. He's like a leg-breaker, but my guy was surprised as hell when he showed up, like he was the leg-breaker to end all leg-breakers, if that makes any sense."

"That's exactly what he is, the leg-breaker to end all leg-breakers, although using him like that, I don't know . . ." Ridlin said.

Ridlin knitted his brow together, and drummed his fingers on the table.

"So, what are we going to do?" I asked.

" 'We'? " he asked. " 'We' are not going to do anything. You two are going to come with me and make a full report down at HQ, and they are going to take it from there."

"No, we're not," I said.

"That's right," Akiko said. "No, we're not. By the way," she said, turning to me, in a stage whisper, "how come we're not?"

"Because it's gotten personal," I said. "These guys are personally coming after us, and they're going to keep coming after us until they get us. Think about it," I said. "We have a chance to get our hands on both Amelia and the mob's favorite all-purpose assassin. What kind of fish could we lure in with that kind of bait?"

"Vince, you're talking crazy," Ridlin said. "It's totally outside of policy. I can't just—"

I cut him off.

"Look, you can tell us all about policy later. I'm sure it'll be fascinating. But think about it. What do you think we might be able to trade for if we had both of them? They want to make it personal? *We* make it personal. They take a pawn, and then our rook? We take their queen and threaten their bishop."

"What are you talking about?" Ridlin wailed.

"Chess," Sidney said. "He's talking about chess."

"These people don't play chess," Ridlin said. "They just kill you and then they go get something nice to eat."

I looked at him. "Are you talking about the mob or about the cops?"

"Come on, that's not fair. I can control the cops," he said.

"Like you controlled them tonight?" I said quietly. "They were everywhere, man."

He looked hurt.

"Sorry, but you gave it to your people, and they took over from there. They do what they always do, and he—you know, *He*—he saw it coming and he didn't come near this place, right? And while everybody was looking for him, Jack and Amelia slipped the hook, right?"

"Vince does make a compelling point," Sidney said. "There are times for a frontal assault and times for a more indirect approach. One could quote Machiavelli on this, or Lao Tsu for that matter."

I figured Sidney as a Machiavelli man—he had had that kind of classical education—but the Lao Tsu was something of a surprise. Akiko was nodding. I figured her for Lao Tsu but not necessarily Machiavelli, although, after all the maneuvering she had done to be with Laura, I was entertaining second thoughts.

"What's your plan?" she asked Ridlin. "To keep dangling us like bait and wait for this shark to circle in so you can catch him before he kills us? That sucks."

Ridlin wasn't dangling us, he was dangling *her*. Sure, I had gotten bitten, and it looked like Jeff had stumbled into his path and gotten chewed up. There was always the possibility of collateral damage, but it was still really about Akiko.

Unless, of course, it was really about Jack.

"I don't know about you guys," I said. "But the waiting is making me a little nuts. Every time we go out in public, my hand starts to twitch. My eyes feel like I haven't blinked in a month. Even if I see the guy, what the fuck can I do? Start snapping my fingers like Jack? I can't do shit, except hope that you get him before he gets one of us. I mean, no offense, I'm sure you're doing all you can, but it leaves me feeling passive, and I just fucking hate that."

"One does want more of a sense of involvement," Sidney said.

"A proactive approach," Paul said, "preemptive."

Akiko nodded. "Let's get them playing defense for a change. See how they feel."

There was a chorus of murmurs all around. Ridlin said nothing. He could easily quash this train of thought with a word or a look. He didn't.

"So what do we do?" Sidney asked, to no one in particular.

"We sit down and we plan it out, every step," I said. "I think the first thing we do is shake them off our trail, go somewhere they wouldn't think to look."

"Quite," Sidney said. "But where?"

We all thought for a minute, until Paul spoke up.

"No one looks in a dead woman's unmarked grave."

We locked eyes. I think I even grinned.

"To Wisconsin," I said.

"Now just hold on," said Ridlin. "If he saw the, uh, presence here, and held off because of that, he'll maintain his perimeter and try to pick up the trail on the way out, evading the surveillance."

"Like, what the fuck does *that* mean?" Akiko asked.

"He'll be looking to ditch the cops and follow us when we leave," I translated.

"No problem," Paul said. "I know a back way. No one will know we're gone."

"A back way?" I grinned. "More complicated than the way we came in?"

He smiled and arched his eyebrows. This I had to see.

CHAPTER 53
The Cleaner

In Calumet City
Friday, January 24

9:30 P.M.: Drive down in a stolen Calumet City taxicab. In blackface. What you call irony. Got on a tiny mustache, one of those shiny caps with the little brim.

The cab is for shit. Shakes like it's got the Parkinson's. Check the pain. It is not good tonight. A six, maybe a seven. Which reminds me. Take two of the blue pills, one of the red stripe. Reach for the bottle of water. Take a deep gulp. Another.

Checked the maps. This is a one-way deal. Easy to get in, couple a turns. Then you have to turn around. Come back out. Be better it was a loop. Be better I had a passenger to drop off. Cab going to a club. Dropping someone off. Could take a look around. But no. No one to trust.

Deserted down here. Not an area a real hack would be cruising for fares. Nothing to do about that. I get stopped? Got papers, decent ones. Got a forty-five under my leg, nice shiny one. The papers do not work? The forty-five will.

So. Just cruise in, see what is what. No good? Gone.

11:30 P.M.: Does not take long, see what is what. Streets smell of cop. Flop sweat and powdered sugar. Cheap beer and hard-boiled eggs. They are all over this. Chicago PD cars pulled over everywhere, two guys each. Uniforms with radios standing on the corners. Plainclothes on the benches in the park. Huddled at the bus stops, radios in their ears.

They trying to make it this obvious? Keep driving.

1:20 A.M.: Head north. Pull off at Java Jive coffee joint. A drive-through. Park. Think this through.

A beat-up old Jetta pulls up at the pickup window across from me. I look over.

I catch a quick look. It's enough. It is them. It is Amatucci and Jones, sitting in the front seat. Powell in the backseat. They get their order. Off they go. But they stop up ahead. A car pulls up behind them, a Crown Vic. Ridlin, following. The Professor, in the back.

Do I follow them? Do I stay here? Is this a setup? The cops trolling? Using them as bait? They would not have two separate cars as bait. It would be all of them together.

Ridlin moves ahead, and both cars head into the street.

Take off after them.

CHAPTER 54
Vinnie Amatucci

Driving North
Saturday Morning, January 25

After a few blocks of gliding through the tall grass, we weaved through some turns too sudden to track and some straightaways too short to notice. We were not going anywhere near the Skyway, but weaving through the neighborhoods below the far South Side. It was two o'clock in the morning, and if I had been cruising on the highway I'd have been getting a little sleepy, but with all the twisting and turning, I was wide awake, my knuckles white on the wheel.

The plan was that Akiko, Paul, and I would ride in my car in the lead, with Paul navigating for us, while Sidney rode with Ridlin. He insisted on it, vehemently; it's probably the only time in his life he'd get to ride in the back of a cop car. Ridlin would drop off Sidney in Hyde Park—he had an appointment in the morning he couldn't miss—then Paul would switch to Ridlin's car, and we'd all head to Wisconsin.

Ridlin was right on our tail, no more than a few lengths

behind. Paul had promised we wouldn't be seen, and on this route, the citizens were locked up tight in their beds, and even the criminal class, who own the night down here, was staying out of sight.

The miles passed in a blur of three-story tenements and strip malls. We doubled back and headed south for a few blocks. Then another left, east, and I looked in the rearview. Ridlin was right behind us. Then another left, north again, and Ridlin was still there.

But so was someone else.

I edged out toward the double yellow line in the center to sneak a peak. It was a late-model Chevy, with something sticking up on the roof. Did Ridlin call in the reinforcements, after he had agreed not to? Or was this something else entirely? I started to grip the wheel a bit tighter.

Another left, and I slowed down as I headed into the turn, forcing Ridlin to brake quickly. This time I stared in the side-view mirror all the way around the turn, and took a long look.

"Uh-oh," I said. "I think we've got trouble."

"Trouble?" Paul asked. "Vinnie, I would have thought that an experienced driver like you would know exactly where we are."

"I do. But so does someone else," I said, glancing back again. "At the next turn, take a look at the car behind Ridlin's and tell me if it's a police cruiser or a taxi."

I made another right, hard, then slowed down. Ridlin caught up and then braked, and the car behind him came careening around the corner, trying to keep up.

"It looks like a cab, Vince," he said. "But what's the problem? Lots of cabs work the night shift—you do it yourself."

I glanced at him. "I know a stretch near here where the light isn't so bad. When we get there, I'm going to drift into the center. I want you to look behind us and see what kind of cab it is. It looked red, white, and blue to me, but I need to be sure what company it's from."

"Vince, what is it?" Akiko asked.

"What's this about?" Paul chimed in.

"Will you do it?" I asked him.

He stared at me a second, then nodded.

"And while you're at it, can you try to see if the driver is, you know, black?"

He squinted, but nodded again. Akiko had grabbed my leg, and was squeezing it hard.

I saw a stoplight up ahead near a well-lit strip mall. It was green, and I slowed down. We were getting closer, and closer, and yes, thank God, it finally turned yellow. I had almost rolled into the intersection but I stood on the brakes and jerked to a stop. Ridlin stopped behind me, his Crown Vic nose-diving, and the cab stopped a dozen lengths behind him. Paul turned around in his seat. So did Akiko. They were both looking hard at whatever was back there.

The light turned green, and I flipped the blinker on and inched around the corner, with Ridlin tailgating me. The cab hesitated when he came to the intersection, his wheels barely rolling. Eventually, he turned right as well.

"Red, white, and blue," Paul said. "All-American Taxi, number 1751. And yes, it looks like the driver is black."

"Shit shit shit!"

"Vince, what is it? What's happening?" Akiko's voice had a little tremble in it.

"He's been behind us since Calumet City, but he doesn't know what he's doing. He's following too close. And, like I said, he's black."

"Yeah, so?" Akiko said. "Half of the cabdrivers in the city are black, aside from the Arabs and the Russians."

"He's black, and he's driving for All-American. All-American doesn't *have* any black drivers, not a single fucking one. And they don't pick up black passengers, not ever. They wouldn't be trolling down here, even in the daytime. I think he's following us . . . I think it may be him, the guy in the picture, the assassin."

Paul frowned. "I didn't know that," he said. "About All-American, I mean."

"When do you ever take cabs, unless you're deadheading with me?"

I stepped on the gas and we jumped. Ridlin was right there with us. The cab was taken by surprise, and was slow to react. We raced ahead for five or six blocks and got it up to sixty in a thirty-mile-an-hour zone.

I jammed on the brakes. Ridlin fishtailed to a stop behind us, the cab slowed after that. I touched the gas, crawled forward. Ridlin moved with us as if my pedal were connected to his accelerator. The cab was slower to react, but accelerated to catch up. I braked again, sped up again. Then I edged a bit to the right and pulled over. Ridlin pulled in behind me, and the cab slowed to a stop a half a block back. No one moved. My pulse was up around two hundred, so I counted to twenty, trying to breathe. Still, no one moved. Green lights, no traffic, no cops? That tipped it. Any self-respecting hack would have said "Fuck it" and blown right by us.

I thought—what's my play, here? Do I hope that I'm just being paranoid and drive normally until he drops off on his own? Do I try to lose him with some evasive maneuvers? Do I somehow make it obvious to Ridlin so he can go into attack mode and fucking shoot him? Shit. I stepped on the gas again, grinding through the gears. By now Akiko had a death grip on my leg, her eyes wide as she scanned the scenery flashing past us. Paul was leaning forward between the two front seats, swiveling to look forward and backward, in flashes.

"Do you know if Ridlin carries a cell phone?" I asked.

"A cell phone? He's got to," Akiko said, "but I don't know the number. What about Sidney?"

Paul chimed in. "No. He won't go near them. He's worried they'll rot his brain."

I reached for my own phone and flipped it open.

A woman's voice came on the line, "Nine-one-one emergency."

"Hi. I'm at—" I glanced at the signs as we zoomed past

them—"Torrance and 105th, heading north. Can you tell me where the nearest police station is?"

"Can you tell me what the problem is, sir?" she asked.

"Can you tell me where the nearest police station is?" I repeated.

"What seems to be the problem, sir?" she said. She sounded tired and bored.

"Listen," I shouted, "the problem is I need a police station and you won't tell me where the fuck it is! Are you gonna tell me where the fuck it is, or are you gonna tell me your name so I can report you, if I ever fucking find one?"

I was talking too fast and too loud, but maybe she heard the panic in my tone.

"Stay on Torrance until it merges into Colfax, go up Colfax to Ninety-fifth you know, Stony Island Avenue, and take a right, it'll be a block to the east on your right," she said, annoyed. "Now, sir, would you please tell me—"

"Thank for your kind assistance," I said, and clicked the phone off.

"Vince, why are we going to a police station?" Akiko asked. "Ridlin's right behind us. And besides, I thought we didn't want to get the cops involved in this."

"Ridlin doesn't know what's going on—he probably thinks I'm just fucking around. And if the guy in the cab catches up to us we're going to need *somebody* to get involved. Better the cops than the coroner."

I continued to step on it, hitting green lights all the way. Akiko still had her hand on my leg and was starting to cut off the circulation. Ridlin was right on us, but the cab had dropped back seven or eight lengths.

Then Akiko screamed, "Vince!" and clawed at me. I looked ahead and a woman pushing a shopping cart was stepping out into the street between two cars not fifty feet ahead. I yelled "Shit!" and jerked the wheel to the left, leaning on the horn at the same time. My car swerved and shuddered and I missed her by no more than an inch. Paul was breathing on my neck, his hand clamped on my shoulder. I swerved

back to the right and looked in the mirror to see Ridlin miss
her and the cab behind him miss her, too, as she stood
there frozen in the road. I turned my eyes ahead and
stepped back on the gas.

In less than a minute, we bent onto Colfax and in a couple of blocks we were at Stony Island, and we screeched
around the corner on two wheels, with Ridlin riding our
ass. Up ahead I could see bright lights in front of an old
stone building. I coasted to a stop a hundred yards down
the block. Ridlin shuddered to a halt behind us. The cab
was still on Colfax, pointing north. We all waited for a
minute, unable to breathe, until the cab took off at speed,
heading north.

I waited for another two minutes, then put it in gear and
creeped ahead. We circled back south, then west, moseying around the side streets. Paul was still calling out directions, but he didn't have to; I knew where we were. Akiko
had let go of my leg and was slumped back in her seat, the
adrenaline flushing from her system all at once. I headed
back to Stony Island and turned west and within three minutes we were at the Midway, the southern edge of Hyde
Park. I was trying to breathe, but my pulse was pounding in
my ears. We stopped at a red light and Ridlin and Sidney
drew even with us. Ridlin rolled down the passenger-side
window, looked over, made a corkscrew motion pointed at
his head. I shrugged.

Two blocks later we both turned left and rolled up to Sidney's building. It was dark, not a light on anywhere. And I
wished I could say the same for my brain, still racing with
possibilities that I had no way to confirm.

CHAPTER 55
Ken Ridlin

On the Lake
Saturday Morning, January 25

We are meeting in the lot behind the house on the lake where we played last Friday night. I'm there first. With Powell in the backseat, stretched out. Sleeping there since two minutes after we get on the expressway, after we drop off the Professor, his place in Hyde Park.

We're in Wisconsin. Again, I have no jurisdiction, the second out-of-state move in twenty-four hours.

It is foggy. A light drizzle coats everything. The temperature is just above freezing. I turn the car so it faces the road coming in. I put it in park, kill the lights, crack the window a quarter-inch. I lean the seat back an bit, put my elbow on the window ledge, put my head in my hand, and close my eyes. I'm too jacked up to sleep, but my eyes feel like they're full of splinters.

I look at my watch. Four o'clock. I crane my neck to the right. Powell is still asleep. I lean my head back in my hand. I take a deep breath.

There is a sound right next to my left ear. Knuckles, rapping on the window, driver's-side door. I jump, pick my head up off my hand. My left arm is numb. I look at my watch. Six o'clock, a little after. What?

I turn my head to the left. Amatucci is standing there in his navy peacoat, the collar up against his ears. He wiggles the fingers of his right hand at me. I look beyond him. Jones is there, shifting from foot to foot, her eyes cast down on the asphalt. I blink and try to get my eyes to focus. It feels like I'm scraping my corneas with sandpaper. Jones stands still for a second and I see Laura Della Chiesa standing behind her. She's dressed to kill, even at this hour of the morning.

Amatucci holds up two brown paper sacks.

"Bacon-and-egg sandwiches and coffee," he says. "Breakfast of champions."

I rouse myself, try to open the door. It's locked. I fumble for the switch, flip it up, and spill out into the parking lot, my left arm hanging limp at my side, my left butt-cheek tingling.

"You're late," I say, for no reason at all. He hands me a sandwich and a Styrofoam cup.

"We made a little detour," he says. "Picked up some hitchhiker by the side of the road."

I look at him. "Hitchhikers can be dangerous," I say.

"Especially that one," Powell mutters. Amatucci hands him a sandwich and a cup. "Decaf for you, as always," he says to Powell. "There's cream and sugar in the bag." I notice I am starving. I take a big bite. I take a big gulp. It tastes like the best thing I've ever eaten, even if the sandwich is soggy and the coffee is lukewarm.

We fall silent while we eat. I have the same thought I had when Amatucci first laid out his plan: It's a great plan to get them all in one place together, and it's a place we get to choose. And once we get them all together, something will happen. I don't know what, but something. That's a hell of a start. But after that—nothing. I look up at them. They're wrapping up the breakfast things, stashing them in a garbage bag Amatucci has produced from somewhere.

"Let's do it," Jones says, somehow reading my mind. "Figure it all out later."

CHAPTER 56
Ken Ridlin

In the House on the Lake
Saturday Morning, January 25

We walk away from the house toward a road that will take us north and east. There is slush underfoot. We are all wearing the wrong shoes for this except for Jones, who always wears these black sneaker-boot kind of things. Within a hundred yards my feet are soaked and frozen. We walk single file, except for Jones and Laura, holding hands in the back.

After another hundred yards, there is a single lane winding through the trees. I stop, look back at Laura. She nods her head.

It's only forty yards but it takes us two minutes to slog through the mud. After a turn, the house reveals itself. It looks just as impressive from this angle, silhouetted against the lake.

We come to a set of five stairs, leading up to a wide half-covered porch that wraps around the house. We all stop.

Akiko and Laura come up behind me, step to the front. Jones gives Laura's hand a squeeze, and Laura turns toward the house, puts her foot on the first step.

Before she can move, the door opens. Her mother, Amelia, steps outside. She is wearing a green silk bathrobe, tied loosely in front. Landreau steps out from behind her in a black terry-cloth bathrobe. She reaches over and takes hold of his hand.

Jones steps up and grabs Laura's hand. We all stand there.

"Hello, darling," Amelia says, "you set off the motion sensors."

"Sorry to wake you," she says.

"We were already awake," the mother says. She turns to Landreau and smiles. "In fact, we've been awake all night."

"Yeah," Amatucci says. "So have we."

"I'll make some coffee," Landreau says.

Amelia turns to him, kisses him lightly on the lips. She turns to the rest of us. "You'd better take those shoes off— you don't want to be tracking mud in the house."

We move up toward the porch. Jones lets go of Laura to untie her sneakers. Amelia comes up to her, holds out her hand. "You must be Akiko," she says, saying it Ah-KEE-ko.

"Yes," Jones says, "Akiko," saying it AHH-kee-ko.

"Ah, AHH-kee-ko," Amelia says, correcting herself. "Why don't you and your friends come in and warm up."

As we step into what seems to be a vestibule, I turn to her. "We're really sorry to have to impose on you, ma'am."

She turns. Looks at me. "No, you're not. You're here to get Jack, aren't you?"

"Actually," I say, "we're here for you."

She raises her eyebrows, turns and looks at Laura.

Laura lowers her eyes. She is oddly deferential. She nods her head up and down, twice.

"We're here to try to help your daughter, and her, uh, friend," I say.

"Yes," she says. "And it's going to take both Franco and me to help you do it, isn't it?"

Amatucci is standing there.

"Franco?" he says.

"It's a long story," I say.

CHAPTER 57
Vinnie Amatucci

At Amelia's House
Sunday, January 26

Jack's story came out, eventually: the musical prodigy, the symphony star, Amelia's engagement to the Don, their affair, his finger. Ridlin told most of it, Amelia occasionally filled in the gaps, and the rest of us sat there with our mouths hanging open. Jack himself said nothing to confirm it and not a word to deny it. Mostly he sat slouching behind Amelia, his gaze resting longingly on the white baby grand piano in the center of the room.

The Akiko/Laura story got told, mostly by me, without either of them contributing much to it. I somehow got located sitting between them on the couch, the two of them holding hands across my lap, as if I weren't there. It posed a real dilemma to my lap, which I fought by talking nonstop. Typical.

Then we went over the plan.

At one point, Amelia turned to Laura, and asked, "Is this who I think it is?" Laura mumbled, "Uncle Josef?" and

Amelia held up her hand. "They don't call him that anymore."

Ridlin sat up when she said this.

"What *do* they call him?" he asked, looking straight at her.

She paused, looked straight at him.

"They call him 'The Cleaner.' "

I looked at Paul, and his eyes met mine. Nice. You got a mess? Call the Cleaner.

Then she dropped another bomb.

"And you'd better expect the Nephew to be there, too. That's the way it's supposed to work now."

"The Nephew?" I asked.

"Gianni Della Chiesa. Johnny Chase," Ridlin said. "New front man. Supposed to be making all the decisions. Our sources say different."

"So do mine," Amelia said.

Paul jumped in. "I don't really read that section of the paper. What should we expect him to bring to the dynamic?"

Amelia looked at him, then looked away.

"Chaos," she said. "That's all he brings. Chaos."

Ridlin turned to Amelia and asked if she saw any angles we could use, maybe talking to her ex, reasoning with him, maybe using the Don against the Nephew, using the Nephew against the Don. With every alternative she just shook her head. We talked and talked but there were no great insights. Ridlin was set on grabbing the assassin, and we never really pushed him on it. Akiko was firm on her need to confront them head-on, and for Laura to be there with her. Laura herself sat there as calm as a cat on a rock and did everything but purr. Landreau was fidgeting, but fighting it. Ridlin and Paul and I kept at it. We would find these little threads, and we'd pull on them, but they'd break off as soon as we tried to tie them together. We couldn't seem to get past the setup. Every next step seemed to involve someone shooting someone else.

We broke for coffee, and everyone but Ridlin wandered away.

I stepped up to him.

"Can I ask you a favor?" I said, sotto voce.

He shrugged.

"Let's find a way to leave Paul and Sidney out of it?"

He stared at me.

"I mean, they can't really help, all they can do is get hurt. It's not their fight."

"You wanna be the one to tell them?" he asks.

I looked down. "My idea was to tell them we'll all meet up someplace, but the wrong place, far enough away that once they figure out it's bogus, they won't be able to get to the real spot on time," I said. "You know; my specialty: something lame but simple."

"I see your point," he said. "What's the Professor gonna do? Hit Joe Zep with his tuba?"

I nodded.

"OK, we'll do it the way you want."

Akiko and Laura came down the stairs, Amelia swung out of the kitchen with coffee and some pastry, and we all got back to talking, but it went nowhere. Around midday, we all crashed. Amelia and Jack excused themselves. Paul leaned his head back and fell asleep immediately—he's always been able to do that, and I have always hated him for it. Laura and Akiko fell asleep leaning on my shoulders, and I slumped down and crashed in between them.

Around three o'clock, I heard a sound and roused myself. I limboed out from between the two women without waking them. The sound was coming from outside, so I slid the door open, stepped out, and eased it closed behind me. It was Paul, playing long tones on his horn into a mute, the sound rippling out across the lake. I stood there, pulled the pipe out of my pocket, took a couple of hits, and let the sound wash over me. There was no melody, just long individual notes, each one starting crisply, then dropping down to pianissimo, building steadily in intensity, then slowly fading away until at one second the note was there and at the next only its echo remained. It sounds easy to do, one simple note at a time, but it's not. I studied the French horn when I was a kid before taking up the piano, and it was precisely this exercise that made me switch; it took enormous control, and I didn't have it, and I didn't have the patience to develop it. It can be boring to listen to, but at that moment it filled a deep hole in my soul. My hand had been aching all day, and suddenly it stopped. I felt my breath go a little deeper, my shoulders drop a little lower.

He must have sensed me there, because he turned around, without breaking his concentration, raised his right pinkie from the horn and wiggled it at me. I gave him a little nod, and he turned back toward the lake, and continued for another few minutes, working steadily up in his register until it must have required a phenomenal effort to hold each note. But each note was like a rounded little pearl, fat and shiny and hard, even the high ones. Paul wasn't one of those screechers—"hernia trumpet," he called that style—with him every note was full and ripe. That was because he worked at it, constantly, just like he was doing right now. But listening to it, it didn't sound like work.

That's the thing about technique: when you really have it, it doesn't sound like technique.

When he was done, he opened his spit valve, blew the moisture out, and turned around. A cloud of steam was coming off his head in the cold air. He twisted off his mouthpiece, slipped it into his pocket, and tucked the horn under his arm.

"So what do you think, Vince?" he asked.

"I think you've never sounded better."

"That's not what I was asking," he said.

I lowered my head. "Yeah . . ."

He turned to me. "Maybe if we just shot the Don and shot the Cleaner and walked, let Ridlin explain it all away . . ."

"And the Nephew," I added.

"And the Nephew, of course, we can't forget the Nephew," he echoed.

Paul is usually a complete pacifist; do your own thing, live and let live. I had had the same thought but had kept it to myself, and was shocked to hear it coming from him.

"What, you have a gun?" I asked.

"No, but I'm sure I could get my hands on one," he said.

"You? Where?" I asked.

He looked at me. "I live on Forty-seventh, remember? All I'd have to do is walk one block to the north and wait for someone to offer me one. It wouldn't take five minutes, I'm sorry to say."

"Hey," I said, "I live off Fifty-ninth, all I'd have to do is walk south across the Midway and be in the same kind of neighborhood."

"If you walked south of the Esplanade, you'd get a gun, all right," he said. "Someone would stick it right in your ribs."

"And you? Nobody would jack you?" I asked.

"Yo, yo, yo, you be forgettin', man," he said. "I'm a 'person of color,' dawg, or, at least, I could pass for one in the presence of my brothers."

"As long as you didn't go flappin' yo' motherfuckin' gums, blood," I said.

He chuckled. "Word," he said.

" 'Word'?" I echoed. "I didn't know you knew that one."

"I must have read it somewhere," he said, a slight smile creasing his face. "Which means no one uses it anymore."

We had always been tight, he and I, and I hadn't been sure if the recent craziness had affected that. My attention had been on Akiko, on Laura, on Ridlin. Shit—my attention had been on *myself*. Paul's focus had stayed on the music, where it had always been.

I shifted my weight, and changed the topic. "Would you really kill someone so Akiko and Laura could be together?" I asked.

"Check your premise, Vince," he said. "I doubt they'll be 'together' all that long," he said. "Laura, from her history, doesn't seem to be the 'together' type."

I nodded. There was truth in that, for sure.

"But would I kill someone so that Akiko could have the *right* to be together, with whomever? If the one I had to kill was himself a killer, who had killed Jeff and that guy Roger Tremblay, and almost killed you?"

I nodded again. That was the question, when you got down to it.

"It'd be a 'righteous shoot,' as they say," I said.

"And add one more condition to it: would I do it if I were assured I could get away with it? I'm afraid I have to admit that I probably wouldn't go to prison for twenty-five-to-life so Akiko could get herself some choice Eye-talian pussy," he admitted, and I loved him for it. "But if I could walk away, clean? I'd consider it, Vince. It's Akiko, you know? And besides, it's a 'rights thing,' you know, and I'm kind of predisposed to be 'down with that.'"

"Yeah, when you put it that way . . ." I said. And as I thought this, my resolve to keep him as far away as possible from this mess only strengthened.

"But—"

"Yeah?"

"But I can't see walking away from it, not unless a whole lot of people happen to die. And I'm trying not to think of scenarios in which a whole lot of people happen to die."

"Yeah," I said. "Myself, every thought that goes through my head seems to push me one way or the other. I can't seem to find the middle way, that Taoist line, anywhere in there."

"That's because you're trying to find it by thinking," he said. "That's not Taoist, that's Confucian, or maybe just confusion."

I laughed. "Yeah, OK, I hear you. So what do you do? I mean, what the fuck do you do?"

He took the trumpet, raised it to his lips, blew some more spit out of it.

"I was doing it before you interrupted me," he said.

"Yeah," I said. "Sorry. That's what I've been missing. I can't slide back into the music like I used to be able to."

He looked at me. "Why not?" he asked.

I held up my left hand, knocked the cast on the porch railing. "Can't fly on one wing."

He looked at me again. "Why not?"

"Why not?"

"Hey," he said. "I'm just saying. It's not like your right hand is perfect and a little practice would mess it up. It's not like there aren't any options. I mean, Jesus, look at Jack."

"Yeah," I said, "but he's Jack, he's from another fucking universe, and I'm only me."

He looked at me, paused, looked back down.

"This might be a good thing, Vince. We've talked about this before—how everything has always come easy for you, how you sometimes have to handicap yourself, just to keep it interesting. You know—creating an impossible double major at Columbia; picking an insane thesis topic even your advisors don't understand; driving all around this crazy city in that Black Maria totally stoned; always having to fall in love with the one woman you know is totally unattainable . . ."

"Yeah, well," I muttered, thinking, "make that the *two* women who are totally unattainable," and adding, out loud, "That's me, making the simple shit difficult."

"You can also make the hard stuff easy. But this is a *real* handicap. Might be interesting."

It was bracing to hear that he was thinking of options, not obstacles.

Stop, I told myself. Be patient. There's still plenty of time for them to kill you and relieve you of having to commit to anything.

CHAPTER 58
Vinnie Amatucci

In the Fat Man's Cab
Monday, January 27

I left Lake Geneva at four-thirty in the morning with Ridlin and Paul trailing close behind. Ridlin would drop Paul off at the first CTA station, and he would supposedly meet up with us later. Before we left, Ridlin sat us all down and said that we would all meet at short-term parking at O'Hare, that he had a place, "a safe-house kind of place," somewhere out in DesPlaines. We were supposed to park facing outward with our lights on at a certain level in a certain row, and at 5:00 P.M. we were supposed to turn our alarms on for one minute, and keep doing it every five minutes until he drove past, at which point we would caravan over to his "secret safe-house location." He told this with such detail and conviction that he had to nudge me on the way out to the cars to remind me it was all just bullshit.

The weather was still dry but had turned warmer. Most of the slush had dried from the highways, and the interstate felt like a dark gray corridor meant for only us. I kept the needle at sixty-five—I didn't see the need to burn that much adrenaline; I had a feeling we would be needing plenty of it later—and cruised along, alone with my thoughts. Ridlin was a precise six-and-a-half lengths back.

Three or four times I thought about filling up the pipe and getting a little buzz on, and every time I talked myself out of it. My rationalizations were classic—you ought to make it like any other day driving the cab; you need to relax and be cool so you don't spook the Accountant; it will force you to concentrate because you'll know you're stoned—all bullshit reasons that would have sufficed at any other time. But today I wasn't buying it. I would feel my hand reach for the pipe, hear the comforting sound of "why not?" in my head, but my hand would stall and wander back to the wheel.

We came in from the west, and I swung north onto Cermak from the Stevenson, dropped Paul off, drove up fifteen blocks, hung a right, looked for a space and parked my car. I cleared out my stuff, locked up and walked to where Ridlin was waiting for me. I threw my stuff in the back of his car and got in the front. He hung a U-turn and we got back on the Adlai and in twelve minutes we were on 21st Street.

By the time we got to the cab lot, dawn was still just a rumor. A dim blue-gray light was sifting into the eastern sky over the lake, but it was earlier than seven.

"We're early," he said. "So," he said, "what are you going to do now? Pick up a few fares on the way to the Drake? Make a few bucks?"

"Can't take the chance," I said. "If some citizen wants to go to the airport, I can't blow him off—I could lose my license. I always meet my guy at eight; so we'll just have to wait."

He nodded.

"You know," I said, "what I'd really like to do is zip over to my crib, change clothes, maybe grab a quick shower. I feel like the slime is getting grime on it."

"We got time?"

"If we hurry," I said.

He reached over and opened the passenger door. "So let's hurry."

We headed down Michigan to the LSD, headed down that to 47th, headed down Lake Park toward 59th, and headed west to my place. It took maybe ten minutes; I must have dozed a little, because the feel of the car braking roused me.

"You got fifteen minutes," he said. "Don't fall asleep in the shower."

"Right," I said. "You want to come in and make yourself some coffee?"

He shook his head. "I'll wait here."

I bolted from the car, unlocked the lobby door, ran up the stairs, unlocked my door. I tore my clothes off, cranked up the hot water. I got a large Baggie out from under the sink, taped it over my cast with some adhesive tape, and jumped into the shower, trying to hold the cast aloft to keep the water out of it. If you ever get a little complacent, try this some time—shower or shave or cook or do any of a number of everyday activities with only one hand. On this occasion, I couldn't manage to hold on to the soap, and every time I dropped it, trying to bend over and pick it up with my good hand while holding my broken hand aloft to keep it dry was a nightmare. After about the fourth drop, I said "fuck it," and just stood there and let the water stream over me as I watched the soap get smaller and smaller at my feet.

Finally, I roused myself, toweled dry, and got dressed. I threw some clean shirts and underwear and socks into a gym bag. I walked over to the desk, opened the top drawer, took out half a carton of cigarettes and my last Baggie of weed, and added them to the bag. I went back into the bathroom, combed my hair, brushed my teeth, and stopped to look around one more time. I checked my watch: twelve minutes.

I went back to the drawer and opened it again. I rooted

around in back until I found it: a gun, a short, slim, silver twenty-two-caliber Smith&Wesson.

I've been robbed twice driving the Fat Man's cab. The first time, the guy took off and damned if he didn't walk right in front of me, and, I'm sorry, you do that and I'm going to run your ass down. Which I did. I broke his leg, it took half a day of paperwork, and it was worth it. The second time, I talked the guy out of it. I'm serious. There had been a whole string of cabbie murders that year and he was even more nervous than I was. I turned my rearview mirror up to the ceiling so he could tell I couldn't see him, and started to talk about how the cops were going to want to pin all that shit on somebody, anybody they caught messing with a driver, and how he didn't want to be doing anything stupid to bring shit down on himself, and how I certainly wasn't going to turn him in, but you never know who saw him getting into the cab. Just talking and talking and not even taking a breath. And when we stopped at a light at Central and Division, he opened the door and bolted. And left his gun on the back-seat. I thought about all the paperwork and decided to eat the fare and keep the gun. I had had it ever since.

I checked the clip. It was full. I slid it into my cast; it was tight but it fit. I slid it back out again and realized that the safety had been off. Shit.

I flicked the safety on, tucked it into the gym bag, zipped it up, and bolted down the stairs.

Ridlin was asleep in his seat, with the car still running. I knocked on the window, feeling a flash of déjà vu from just twenty-four hours ago. He roused himself, popped the locks, and I crawled into the front seat beside him. He turned the key twice before realizing the engine was still on, then put it in gear and headed north.

The sun was coming up over the lake, and it poked be-tween the buildings as we drove. When we got to the lot, I hopped out, said "Follow me," opened up the cab, got it started, and got the heat going. I turned on the NOT FOR HIRE sign and pulled into traffic.

Two blocks shy of the Drake I looked at my watch again; we were still four minutes early. I pulled over in a loading zone and the phone on the dashboard rang. I looked at it, tried to will it to stop ringing. It wouldn't. I picked it up.

"Metro Car Service," I said.

It was the Fat Man; I could hear his breathing before he even spoke.

"Well, Mr. Amatucci, what you got going, this fine motherfuckin' morning?"

"Oh, you know, same old same old. I've got my regular customer this morning."

"You got nothing special going on?"

"Special?"

"No particular plans you got yourself pursuin'? No little projects you cookin' up?"

What the hell? I thought. It's one thing to have the car wired and bugged, but how could he know what was inside my head?

"No," I lied. "Nothing special."

"Hunh," he said.

There was a pause. Did he know I was lying?

"Hey, listen," I said. "I've got to run; I don't want to keep this guy waiting."

But he didn't seem to get the hint.

"Well, you listen up, youngblood. It don't work to be gettin' ahead of yo'self, to be tryin' to do too much, you know what I'm sayin'?"

"Uh, hunh," I said, knowing it all too well.

"You get into somethin', you call me, you hear? I'm here all day today, tomorrow, too. You call if you need somethin', whatever, you got it?"

"Right, Chief," I said. He hates when I call him that.

He didn't say anything. There was a long pause, then a deep breath on the other end. "Aw'ight, then," he said, and hung up.

Weird. The guy is just fucking weird.

I looked back in the mirror; Ridlin was still there. We had

argued over this part of the plan, but he wanted to make sure I made the pickup. He also wanted to see the Accountant for himself, for reasons he never really made clear. I had protested but he had just kept shaking his head back and forth, persistent bastard, and I had finally given up. I flashed my lights at him two times, flipped the directional on, and headed back into traffic.

Two left turns and I saw the Accountant standing with his big briefcase on a dry spot of pavement just east of the Drake, his nose tilted up to sniff the wind. I slid up to the curb, popped the locks, and he flipped the briefcase in ahead of himself and slid in behind it.

"Why, if it isn't Mr. Vincent Amatucci himself, the esteemed driver in his sleek black chariot, here to accompany me on my trail of tears with his skill and wit," he said.

"Good to see you, too, sir." I said. "How was your weekend, if I might inquire?"

He looked up at the ceiling of the cab as if the answer was written there, and said, "Outside it was cold and clammy and damp, so I stayed inside where it was warm and cozy and dry. And you, Vincent? How was your brief sojourn?"

I noticed he pronounced it "so-your'n."

" 'My sojourn'? It was brief."

He patted the bag on his lap. "Well," he said, "let's see if we can get your week off on a good start."

My silent response was: Let's fucking hope so.

I said out loud, "Where to?"

He recited an address on the North Side, and I dropped the flag, hit the signal, gave a glance and headed into traffic.

It was about a twenty-minute ride, so within three blocks I asked if he'd be open to a little wager to pass the time. "I thought you'd never ask," he said. He pulled his roll out of his pocket, peeled off a pile of singles, and said, "Let the games begin."

"You first," I said, and called out the letters of the car in front of us, "TTL."

He reeled off a handful of acronyms: "Toe The Line, Two-Ton Lineman, Take This, Lamebrain, Ten-Toed, uh, Loser, uh, uh, Track That, uh, Track That, uh, Letter—"

"Time. Five," I called. I counted out a pile of five ones.

He called out the next one: "SST." Clicked his watch.

"Well, of course, Super Sonic Transport, but maybe that's a given?"

"Twenty-two seconds, my boy, twenty—"

"Right," I said, "well, there's, uh, Senegalese Sensimilla Treaty, uh, Saxophone Sounds Tranquil, uh . . . Some . . . uh, Some Sweet . . . Some Sweet Twat . . . uh, Special . . . uh, Special . . . Special . . ."

"Time! That would be four." He cocked his head and raised one eyebrow, his left one. I wondered: how do people do that? Do they sit in front of a mirror and practice it? How long does it take? Does it hurt?

And on we went for most of the next ten minutes.

I took a left off of Lincoln, went two blocks west on Belmont, made a U-turn and pulled up at the doorway of number 655, a bar that looked as if it had seen better days.

He said, "Be back shortly," and slid out the door, the briefcase trailing him.

I looked straight ahead. More than once in the past he had come back in ten seconds or twenty, just to "check on something I may have dropped on the floor," and when he'd see me staring ahead and paying no mind, it made his heart flutter. It was part of our routine.

Except this time I took a chance, reached for the cell phone, and dialed Ridlin.

"Ridlin speaking," he answered.

"Just checking in—" I said.

"Hey, thanks for getting back to me on this thing," he said.

There was someone else with him.

"We are on schedule," I said. "Status quo," I said.

"Uh-huh . . . Yeah . . . OK . . . I'll pull the paperwork, take a look at it," he said. "Why don't I get back to you later?"

"Gotcha," I said, "you can't talk right now," and clicked off.

As I did so, the right rear door opened.

He hopped in headfirst, this time dragging the briefcase behind him. It took both his hands to drag it up onto his lap. He was beaming. It was really full.

"5555 South Cottage Grove," he said.

"Oui, mon Capitan," I said.

I pulled into traffic and headed east toward the Drive. It was eight twenty-five.

CHAPTER 59
Ken Ridlin

1100 South State Street
Monday, January 27

Am I thinking they're not going to track me down? Am I expecting they'll just let me run around off the hook forever?

I drop the tail on Amatucci east of the Drake. When I swing over to my apartment to change, they're waiting for me on the stoop—two uniforms, announcing their presence from a hundred yards away. I could just keep on driving—they're busy yakking away, not even bothering to look up—and they'd never know they missed me. But I pull over, stop the car, get out. I look them over—fat and skinny, like Mutt and Jeff. Fat is maybe five-nine, early thirties, 235, a jowly face with a mustache he trims crooked. Smells like Newports. Skinny is six-one, 170, late twenties, black hair cut in a short Afro, his brown eyes way back deep in his dark face. They got their orders—take me straight to Captain Washington if they see me. Still in their twenties, they're already lazy, already cynical. In this job, it doesn't take much.

"Which one's riding with me, and which one's bringing your unit back?"

They look at each other.

I pop the locks and toss Skinny the keys—"You drive."

He slides behind the wheel, turns the key, puts it in drive, heads into traffic, signaling Fat with his lights three times. We head over to Belmont, east to the LSD, and south.

I am already figuring that this is the death of my so-called career, even if it all goes perfectly and I end up covered in glory. I am thinking of the four months in the hospital, the six months of home care, the eight months of physical therapy. The hot baths. The ice packs. The four years of disability, every day of which ages me a year. The ceaseless AA meetings, the grinding therapy. Kissing their ass, biting my tongue. The three years of walking a beat and keeping my head down. The bad food and the flat ginger ale. My year in Narcotics, enough said. Now Homicide again, and directly Do-Not-Pass-Go into the middle of a Grade-A Full-Court Press with two dead and one maimed and more to come.

I turn my head toward the window, close my eyes and just like that we're at headquarters and Fat is on my side of the car and opening the door. This is two days in a row I try not to spill out of the car like a load of laundry. Skinny flips me the keys, an underhand toss. I drop them in my coat pocket, stride for the door.

We short-march down the hall and my cell phone rings. It is Amatucci. Fat and Skinny are right there, so I play dumb. Amatucci gets it and hangs up. Ali is sitting at his desk. "Ken," he says, smiling, "you're looking good, how's it going?" He grabs my hand, shakes.

"Actually," I say. "I'm about whipped. I—" He cuts me off.

"Let's go right in and see the captain," he says, and marches me through the inner door.

This time, the man-made light dominates. It is cold, professional, crisp. Not the dark clubby den of my last visit.

The Big Man comes out of his chair, rises up, holds out his

hand. I stick out my hand. He puts the clasp on top with his left, shakes two times. Then releases me into Ali's embrace.

Washington is getting settled, moving papers from five small piles into two large ones, clearing his mind as he clears his desk. He reaches into his desk drawer, pulls out an ashtray and a cigarette. He offers me one. I lean forward, tempted, but wave it off. He lights up, exhales. He leans in, his elbows denting the mahogany.

"I think we can all agree that Saturday night was worthless." He turns to Ali, whose face has become invisible. "He must have spotted us and given it a pass. You were right, Ken, and we should have listened to you."

"Well, Captain, it could have been anything. Who knows . . ."

"Ken," he says, holding up his hand like the traffic cop he once was, "don't argue. It was a perfect setup for him, but we blew it. If it had been only you, maybe one or two back-ups, maybe you would have had a shot . . . But with all our people . . ."

"And all the Indiana people," Ali inserts.

"*And* all the Indiana people," he says. "Shit, what a motherfucking mess."

He is pondering something. He glances at me, making sure I'm still there.

"You know, Ken, it's not like it was back in the day. You know, get the call, get the evidence, get the perp. Now the motherfucking lawyers have taken over. There's almost no room for solid old cops like you and me, Ken, cops who remember . . ."

I do not know where this is going. I let him talk.

"In some ways, it's almost flipped upside down, you know?" he says. "Like, for instance, this situation in Indiana. If we know about something, and don't do anything about it, we're *in the shit*. The city could get sued. Negligence. If we do something, it almost has to be some big mess with dozens of people deployed . . . And what does that do? It scares the perp away, screws it all up. But if, say, for instance, something happened to go down and an officer happened to be on the scene, and he or she happened to take some initiative based on the, uhh, the *exigencies* of the *situation,* so to speak, well, that's different. We're in the clear."

Is he saying what I'm hearing?

"I mean, if we know something in advance, the threat of a civil suit almost forces us to do things that are not in our best interest. If it appears that we just stumbled onto something, that's different. You can use some discretion. You can be a fucking cop, like you're supposed to be."

He takes another drag. My brain is racing.

"Of course, I'm just speaking hypothetically, here."

And there it is: the trigger, the phrase he always uses to give an order when he doesn't want to be on the record. "Just speaking hypothetically."

"Well, I don't have to tell *you* this, Ken. You're an experienced detective. You've put in your time in Narcotics. 'Nuff said."

Narcotics? Where to bust people you pretty much have to set them up?

"Well, just the philosophical ramblings of a tired old man," he says. "Speaking of which, Ken, you look like *shit!*"

He chuckles. I shrug. "Well, I was just telling Lieutenant Ali, I'm not used to these kinds of hours anymore, and the band's been real busy, ever since Saturday."

He nods. Ali nods, too.

"I mean, they had a private party up north yesterday and they have another one up north tonight and another one down south, booked for tomorrow."

"What's the schedule after that, Ken?" Ali asks.

No "*Where* up north?" No "*Where* down south?" questions anyone would ask.

"After tomorrow there's nothing until the weekend," I say. "So I was thinking, in a couple of days, maybe the lieutenant and I should sit down, figure out what our next move is."

"I think you're right, Ken," Washington rumbles. "I think he'll wait."

He takes another drag on the cigarette, looks at me. "You *do* look like *shit,* Ken. Go rest up and come back in on Wednesday, Thursday. You and Ali can game-plan it from there."

"Right, Captain," I say, and move to stand up. My watch says nine-ten.

"Sounds good," Ali says. "Reach out to me after it's over."

"Sure," I say. But this is all wrong. "After it's over?" What the hell?

The captain looks at me, opens his mouth to speak, closes it. He grinds out his cigarette in the ashtray, places the ashtray back in the drawer, turns back to face Ali.

I turn to Ali. We rise. The captain pushes up out of his chair.

"Oh, David, that reminds me," he says. "The car, the car on Saturday night, the Mercedes limo with the out-of-state plates—we ever get anything back on that, from, where was it?"

"Wisconsin. It was Wisconsin," Ali says. "No, their system is down, some techie thing. They won't have that for us until at least tomorrow, the day after."

There it is. A confirmation. We *know* whose car it was, we *know* what she was doing there, but we don't know *officially,* and we don't *want* to know officially.

"Anyway. You're gonna get this guy, Ken, I just know you are."

He sticks out his hand, engulfs mine with the two of his. Gives it two firm pumps and an extra grasp. He leans forward.

"You're doing a great job, Ken. It's great to have you back. You be taking it easy now, you hear? And watch your back. If they come at you, they'll come at you from the back. That's the way they do it."

"Yes, sir, I'll do that," I say. Right, I think. From the back. The way he did it.

Nothing but smoke and mirrors. If it's not the smoke that gets you, it's the mirrors.

CHAPTER 60
Vinnie Amatucci

In the Fat Man's Cab
Monday, January 27

By eight-fifty we had made three stops, one out west, one on the South Side, and one up north. I was letting the Accountant win at license-plate poker and he was in a fine mood. Then, on the way back to the South Side again, I hit a run of undesired luck.

I was looking to get him comfortable, a little bit ahead, but not too noticeable. But he was calling the plates for me, and he pulled out an "AL." Two letters only. I couldn't help myself.

"A Loan, Any Left, All Longer, Amazing Linguist, Ass Licker, Aardvark Love, Artichoke Lover, Alcoholic Liqueur, Absolutely Lovely, Affected Lisp, Astounding Lies, Astonishing Lips, Astronomical Levels, Aeronautical Lessons, Astral Learning—"

"Time," he called. "Well, look who's back in the game after a brief respite. Fifteen quick points, and some interesting pairings along the way."

"Are you referring to 'Astronomical Levels, Aeronautical Lessons, Astral Learning'?" I asked.

"Actually, I was thinking of Amazing Linguist, Ass Licker, Aardvark Love. You *do* have the nastiest mind, Vincent."

"All the better to *beat* you with, my dear," I said.

A car cut in front of us. We both looked up. It was my turn to call, his turn to play.

"FCK." Bad letters, I thought to myself. He was going to get FCK'd, for sure.

"Uh . . . uh . . . Four, uh . . . Four Christian Knights . . . Five Cold Killers, uh . . . Fifteen Classic Kalliopes . . ."

Calliopes starts with a "C," but I let it pass. He was still stuck when the timer beeped.

"Time's up," I said. "Tough letters to work with. That was a three." I paid up.

We stopped at a light. The clock on the dash said nine o'clock. I looked down at the phone on the seat to my right. Nothing yet.

"Time out," I said. "I have to drive for a minute or two here."

"If I didn't know you better, Vincent, I'd wonder if you're trying to give me a break."

I smiled at him in the mirror. "Why, do you need a break?"

He waved me off, chuckled to himself, and looked out the window.

In three minutes we were there, a residential neighborhood, all double-deckers shoulder to shoulder, a few scrawny trees out front. I pulled in at the curb and popped the locks. He slid forward, grabbed his briefcase, said, "I shall return," and hopped out the door.

He took five quick strides toward a doorway, and went in. As soon as the door closed behind him, the phone rang. It was nine-twenty. I picked it up.

"Metro Car Service," I said.

"Can you talk?" Ridlin asked.

"He just went inside. Your timing is perfect."

"Where are you?" he asked.

"Southwest Side," I said. "Vincennes and Eighty-fifth."

"I'm downtown. If he goes anywhere north or west I can get there before you do."

I glanced to my right and saw the Accountant coming out of the doorway.

"Here we go," I said into the phone. "Follow my lead."

Before the door opened I was into my rap.

"But I *did* submit the trip sheets, goddamnit," I said, "I left the fucking things where you told me to leave them, man. Just because you can't find them doesn't mean it's *my* fucking problem. Why don't you ask the other drivers?"

He slid the rest of the way in, and I looked up as if in surprise. I was going "Uh-hunh, Uh-hunh" into the phone, and motioned to my watch and held up one finger.

I listened along, rolling my eyes, shaking my head, for a minute. Ridlin was filling the air with nonsense—"The sky is blue. The temperature is thirty degrees. The humidity is twenty percent. Traffic conditions are normal," like some reporter on the radio.

I jumped in. "Hold on a minute, just hold on," then listened some more. "No, I'm supposed to be making some money for you, and I've got a passenger here who needs to be going somewhere and I can't find out where he wants to go, so hold on a minute, OK?"

I held the phone to my chest, like I was covering the speaker, turned in my seat, and said, "Sorry, my boss can be an asshole sometimes. Where next?"

The Accountant chuckled. "*Your* boss? I could tell you stories . . ."

I waited expectantly, neither encouraging him nor discouraging him.

"454 North Goethe," he said, pronouncing it in the Chicago style, "GO-Thee."

"454 North Goethe it is," I said, the phone an inch away from my lips, my voice plenty loud enough for Ridlin to hear. I put the car in gear and headed back into traffic. I put the phone back up to my ear.

"Listen, I gotta run. Can we talk about this later? Would that be OK?"

"4-5-4 North Goethe," Ridlin said, almost a whisper, and clicked off.

CHAPTER 61
Ken Ridlin

On Goethe Street
Monday, January 27

I park just past the target location on Goethe. I am early. I sit back and wait.

Five minutes pass. I focus on not falling asleep again.

I hear a car coming up behind me and check the side-view mirror. It's Amatucci in that big black cab. I hunker down while they pass. I count to ten, then sit up in the seat and peer out.

The cab stops, and a guy gets out. A little guy, five-three, five-four. Can't weigh more than 140, soaking wet. Dark gray topcoat, black fedora, light gray gabardine slacks. And the shoes, those white ones with the black on the toes and in back.

He goes up to the door at 454, rings the bell. Someone comes right away, lets him in.

I get out of the car, walk to the corner. The wind is coming in from the west.

All it takes is a minute and he is back out the door and

down the steps. Here we go. I reach into my jacket pocket, get my shield, clip it onto my breast pocket, cover it with the lapel of the overcoat. I take out the gun, holding it down against my side.

Amatucci turns his signal on, edges into traffic. I start into the street, like I'm crossing. He brakes. I turn, hold up my hand. He rolls the window down, sticks his head out.

I flip the lapel over, show the badge. "Police business. Open the back door."

He pops the locks. I step to the back door, open it up, get in.

"Drive," I say.

"Yes, sir, officer," he says. "Where to?"

"Take a left, go two blocks south. Then pull over."

He does, and we stop. The Accountant is holding onto his briefcase like it's a defibrillator and he's having a heart attack.

I turn to him.

"Open the bag."

"You have a search warrant?" he asks, his voice a little breathy.

My gun is in my right hand. I show it to him. "This work?"

He rolls his eyes. "Oh, sure," he says.

I reach across with my left hand and punch him in the nose. It is like popping a balloon. Blood spurts onto his white shirt. He teeters forward, holding his face with both hands. I pull his handkerchief out of his breast pocket, hand it to him.

"Steady pressure. Pinch it. Hold it there. Don't take it off."

He nods. Holds the pocket square to his nose. I pat him down while we wait for the bleeding to stop. He's not carrying.

"Open the bag."

He takes the handkerchief away from his nose. Looks at it. It is bright red. Another spurt bounces off his chin and onto his shirt.

"Like I said, don't take the pressure off."

He nods.

"Open the bag."

He fiddles with the clasps. "It'll queer the bust, you know," he says. "Illegal search. You start with that, it doesn't matter if I confess that I'm the fellow on the grassy knoll in Dallas. You won't be able to use anything I say, anything I do, anything that happens at all. 'Fruit of the poisoned tree,' right? You know all this, right?"

"I know it," I say. "I just don't care."

He sighs. He pops the clasps. Plops it down on the middle seat between us. Amatucci has turned around. He's been wondering what's in this bag for a long time. He's curious.

I look inside. It is full of envelopes. Fat ones. I pull one out. It has an address on it, today's date. Handwritten. It's not sealed, the flap is just tucked in. I open it. A lot of cash money. Hundreds, fifties, twenties, nothing smaller, in order from big bills to smaller bills. I count it. Fifty-eight-hundred-fifty in this envelope. Open another one. Twelve-thousand-two-hundred. There must be dozens of these in there.

He is still holding the handkerchief to his nose.

"If this isn't a bust, what is it, a rip-off? Pretty stupid rip-off, Officer Number Twenty-Five-Eighty-Five. Go ahead. You won't live long enough to buy yourself a cup of coffee."

"Not about the money," I say.

"So if this isn't a bust, if this isn't a rip-off, what the hell is it? You are aware that this isn't *my* money, aren't you? And you are aware of whose money it *is*, aren't you? And you're aware that these people do not take kindly to people taking their money, aren't you?"

I turn to him. "A while ago, you had somebody waiting for you, some address on the West Side. Some muscle." I turn to Amatucci. "What was the address again, Amatucci?"

He lowers his head, gulps. He murmurs, "Forty-seven hundred block of South Cicero."

The Accountant looks up, tries to stare a hole in Amatucci through the rearview mirror.

"This guy," I say. "You need to call him out again. It's not you we want, it's him."

"Careful what you wish for, friend," he says.

There is a look of terror there. "Yeah," I say, "but we still need you to call him out."

He turns sideways. "Well, it's not that easy."

"Sure," I say. "What is it—you call a guy who calls a guy who calls him?"

"Well . . ."

"So call the guy who calls the guy who calls him." I reach into my jacket pocket, pull out one of those cheap cell phones you can buy at the corner store, which is where I bought it. It's got twenty dollars of calls in it. Plenty for what we need. And can't be traced.

"What do I say?" he asks.

"Same as last time. Same location, South Cicero. Say the same guy stiffed you. That's what it was last time, right? He stiffed you?"

He nods his head, his left hand moving up and down clamped to his nose. I could tell him he can take the pressure off. But it would take the pressure off of him, a little bit.

"The bleeding's probably stopped," I say. "You can lose the handkerchief."

Carefully, he pulls it away. The blood has dried to a dark maroon. No more bright red.

I lean over, hold out the cell phone. He takes it.

"Don't do anything stupid," I say.

"No," he says. "That seems to be *your* specialty."

He dials the number. And I think: maybe he's right.

CHAPTER 62
Vinnie Amatucci

On South Cicero
Monday, January 27

I dropped Ridlin back at his car and the Accountant and I drove up in the cab. He was hunched over in the corner, where I couldn't quite see him, his chin in his hand. I pulled over on Cicero as soon as I got to it, about twenty blocks north of where we wanted to be.

"I don't think we want to be seen talking when we get there," I said. "It might look like we're plotting."

"When *do* we get around to the plotting part, dear boy?"

"Hold on," I said, and slid out the door. I opened the left rear door, motioned for him to slide over, and hopped in, closing it behind me.

"Here's the plan," I said.

I reached down and untied one of the Accountant's shoes, the left one.

"You see him come up, you get out, you look down, you see your shoe is untied. You motion to the guy and lean down and tie it. That's when Ridlin is supposed to show up."

"And you?" he asked. "What is your role in this caper, Vincent?"

"My role is to get us there, and to get us out of there, and to keep my head down."

He nodded. "Affecting disaffectation, as usual," he said. "How typical."

Gee, thanks for the analysis, as if I don't know how fucked up this is.

I pulled out into traffic and drove until I recognized the building, and when I saw an open parking space, I pulled in.

The space was behind an old Buick, and I left plenty of room in case we had to leave quickly. I put it in park, cracked open the window, and lit a cigarette. I looked in the rearview mirror at the Accountant. He was staring darts at me.

"Listen. It's not about you. It's about the other guy."

"Vincent, I appreciate your thoughtfulness about the possible consequences incurred by this situation to a minor entity such as myself, who, of course, you do not really even *know*," deep breath, "but if it's about 'the other guy,' as you call him, we may have played our last game of license-plate poker."

"I know," I said. "I know."

We waited for five minutes, then ten. It was quiet. There was no sign of Ridlin. I was just lighting a second smoke when the Accountant twisted around in his seat.

"He's here," he said. "Keep your head down. Cover your eyes with your hat, and don't look at him. I mean, don't even *look* like you're looking at him."

"OK," I said, shading my face. I didn't see Ridlin anywhere.

He opened the right rear door, and slid out, closing the door after him.

From under the edge of my cap I could see a pair of legs coming toward the car on the sidewalk from the north, pulling even with the side-view mirror.

I could glimpse the Accountant in the right side-view

mirror; then he dipped down to tie his shoe and I lost him. I caught something out of the corner of my eye, just a blur, and when I swiveled my eyes the trunk of the beige Buick in front of us was opening and Ridlin was rolling out and with two steps he was right on top of the guy, pressing a gun to the back of his head. He reached behind himself, murmuring in the guy's ear, and just like that he cuffed both of the guy's hands behind him. He leaned him against the cab and patted him down, taking away two guns and a knife and a set of brass knuckles. Ridlin loaded it all into his pockets, then walked him into the back of the cab. The Accountant got in the front. I looked at Ridlin.

"Holy shit!" I said. "I don't fucking believe it! It was exactly like you said!"

Ridlin muttered, "Lucky. Just got lucky."

I looked at the guy. He was maybe fifty, fifty-five, five-foot-ten or so and a bit under two hundred pounds. He looked . . . nondescript. Harmless. He also looked like hell. His color was bad and his eyes were bloodshot. His face looked drawn and pale.

I pulled into traffic, and drove to where we had left my car.

My car was parked on the right, and Ridlin's unmarked brown Crown Vic was parked in front of it. There was a space on the left, legal. I grabbed it.

"Let's switch cars," Ridlin said. He turned to me. "Can you leave the cab here?"

"Yeah, the Fat Man will pick it up, if I call him."

I took my keys out, and he reached out and grabbed hold of my wrist. "You take the Accountant. He's going to threaten you, bribe you, con you. Don't listen. Just drive."

I got my stuff out of the cab and tossed it on the front passenger seat of my car. Ridlin uncuffed the Accountant from the cab and cuffed him into the right rear seat of my Jetta, snapping the free end to the grab handle over the door. Then he moved the Cleaner to his car, and cuffed him to a bar on the back of the front seat.

At the edge of my awareness I heard the distinctive ring of the phone in my pocket. So did Ridlin, and we listened to it playing its tinny version of the opening phrase of Beethoven's Fifth.

Maybe it's Paul, I thought, checking on why we're not at the meeting point. Maybe it's the Fat Man, telling me not to do this. I let it ring.

Ridlin looked at me. "You gonna get that?"

"No," I said. "I'm busy."

"Then," he said, "let's get going."

I locked up the cab and hopped into my Jetta, buckling in and starting it up. Within minutes we were on the Stevenson, with Ridlin glued to my bumper all the way.

Finally, the Accountant said, "Where are you taking me, Vincent? What do you want?"

"Like I said, you know, this is not about you," I said. "This is about someone else."

He looked at the floor. "Do you know who I am? Do you know who my 'friend' is?"

I looked down, stared out the window. "I have some idea . . ." I said. "But mostly, you're someone who can get to someone we need to get to."

There was a pause before he spoke again.

"You really do *not* know what a debacle you are about to—"

He pronounced it "DEBB-ickle."

"Oh, I have some idea," I said. "But thanks for your concern,"

"Vincent?" the little guy asked. "Where are we going? And, if you don't mind my impertinence in asking, what is this ridiculous little contretemps all about?"

"We're going north," I said. "And it's all about love."

CHAPTER 63
Ken Ridlin

On Lake Geneva
Monday, January 27

We are gathered at the house on the lake. The isolation feels like it's worth the distance.

The Accountant and the Cleaner, if that's what they call them, are sitting in two chairs back-to-back, handcuffed to each other. Amelia and Landreau are off in her room, the door locked. Laura and Akiko are in another room, that door locked, too. Amatucci is on the deck, checking the perimeter. I am watching our hostages.

The slider opens and Amatucci comes in from the deck. He hands me the phone.

I think: this could work. This could stop all the whispers. This could put me at the top, back where I used to be.

I punch in the eight-hundred number, then the access code. A dial tone comes on.

I walk over to the Accountant. "OK," I say. "Time to call the guy who calls the guy who calls the guy. Tell me the number."

He speaks it out. I punch it in. Hold the phone up to his ear.

The Accountant jumps. "Hello?" he says. "It's me calling in? From the field? From Collections? I'm with our other friend, who joined me at that function we had arranged? Out on South Cicero?" He waits, blinking his eyes.

"No. He's tied up right now," he says. "Listen? I need to speak to Mr. C.?" Another pause. "Mr. C. Senior?"

A long pause.

"Yes, yes, I know it's highly unusual, but trust me, he'll want to speak with me."

Out of the corner of my eye, I see Landreau and Amelia enter the room, with Laura and Akiko behind them. The Accountant is listening carefully. He opens his mouth, jumps in.

"I have met you before, haven't I? Tall guy, greasy hair, one big eyebrow? You're the weight lifter, the one who stands around with his mouth open, aren't you? With the brain the size of a walnut? Your name would be Rocco, isn't that correct? I hate to use names over the phone. It can get one in such trouble with the authorities, whomever might be listening, don't you think? But Rocco? You hold up this call for one more minute, and you're not going to have to worry about anyone listening. If the person I am seeking discovers that you obstructed this call, he is going to cut your puny little heart out of your muscle-bound chest and feed it to you for your last high-protein meal. Oh, and while you're bleeding to death, he's going to cut your tiny little dick off and bring it home so his cat can lick it with its sharp sandpaper tongue. In other words, he would be seriously displeased if you waited one more second. Are you following this, or would you like me to repeat it so you can take notes?"

There is a short pause. Then his eyebrows jerk up.

"Thank you, Rocco, I understand this may take some time. You *can* transfer the call from there, can't you?" His tone changes from menacing to mincing in a heartbeat.

His eyes turn back to the phone. "Sir?" he says. "Yes, that's right, sir, it's me, and I hate to bother you and would not presume to do so, but we—"

I take the phone away from him.

"It's about your daughter," I say. "And her girlfriend."

There is a pause on the other end, then, "Who is this?"

"And it's about your wife, and your courier here, with his bag full of Franklins, and someone he calls the Cleaner."

"Who the fuck *is* this?"

"I'm, uh, I'm with the band. And people are dead and it's time for all of this to stop."

"Who are you to presume to tell me about my business, my *family* business? Who the fuck do you think you are?"

"The girl is a friend of mine. She—"

"Stop," he says. "What do you propose?"

"A deal," I say. "A swap."

"Of course. A swap. What else?" He sounds weary, tired. "Let me talk to my friend. Not the one with the money, the other one."

I pause.

"He can talk to you, but you can't talk to him," I say. I walk over to the Cleaner, hold the phone in front of him.

"Zep," he says. "Do not do this. It's the Riddler, he's—"

I take the phone away. Hold it to my ear.

"All right," he says. "We'll meet. Where? When?"

"There's a club down in Calumet City called the Nickelodeon," I say. "Midnight. Tonight. You can bring one other person, no more."

There is a pause at the other end; then he hangs up.

I turn off the phone, flop down in the big leather chair. I realize that everyone is there.

The Cleaner speaks.

"This is gonna be a repeat. Last time? It did not turn out too good for you."

As if it's the only thing that ever happened in my life. It doesn't follow me around anymore, it has *become* me. I'm 'the cop who . . .'

"No," I say. "Your source is bad."

"My source is me. I was there. Standing right behind you. When you got yourself shot."

Amatucci jumps out of his chair.

"Shot? You got shot?"

"It was a long time ago. And he wasn't there."

There *was* someone standing behind me. Was it him? I was too drunk to know.

He turns to the Accountant. "He's Kenny Ridlin, you remember? 'The Riddler,' the cop who got shot by his own people?"

They talk like they're two old ballplayers remembering a long-ago play-off game. One they had won.

"Lower Wacker Drive, east of Michigan. Late at night. Me and Zep, Ridlin and his boss, some other guys. We're supposed to be negotiating."

"I think I remember hearing about this," the Accountant chimes in.

"And Ridlin here starts to rag Mr. C. Drunk, of course, always drunk, those days. Foam is coming out of his mouth. All of a sudden, he makes a lunge at Mr. C., and there's a shot from behind him. He turns, looks at his lieutenant—what was his name? Jefferson? Washington?—and he drops to the ground."

"Where did the projectile enter?" the Accountant asks.

"In the back, right side, middle. It nicks his spine and takes out half his liver." He cranes his neck my way. "That right, Ridlin?"

"You weren't there. It was somebody else," I say, and the words hit my own ears and I realize I do not know what I'm saying.

"Standing right behind you. See, my job? What I'm there for? You take one more step and I'm the one blows you up. Your boss just gets there first."

He turns the other way, talks to the Accountant, "You know how it works. Evidence gets lost, people lose their memories. The lieutenant? He's a captain now. Our friend here? Long road back, way I hear it. Ridlin sticks it out. Works his way back into the Dicks. Robbery. Narcotics. Then Homicide. Where he starts. And his first case? Getting ready to stare Mr. C. in the face. With me standing behind him. All over again."

"Ken?" Amatucci asks.

"The report said the evidence was contradictory and inconclusive," I say.

The Cleaner clears his throat.

"And I know him, too," he says. "The piano player."

Amatucci stands up. "*I* know *you*. You're the traffic cop who pulled me out of the 1812 Club, and walked me into the arms of the two whack jobs who fucked up my hand."

"I'm talking about the other piano player. Him I know, too."

We turn to Landreau. He is standing next to Amelia. They have joined us while we are talking.

"Isn't that right, piano player?" the Cleaner asks.

Landreau looks up. The toe of his left foot is tapping some weird kind of rhythm. I look over at the Cleaner. His right foot is tapping the same rhythm.

We all look at the floor, as if there is some answer there. The weight of the past becoming present hangs over the room until Amatucci stands up, says, "I need some air," and the rest of them follow him out onto the deck, single file.

It is just the Accountant, the Cleaner, and me.

I sit in the big chair facing them. Slowly, the two of them fall asleep where they sit. My own eyes start to get heavy. The coffee has turned to sludge in my veins. Images start to peck at my brain. I see the carousel at the Nickelodeon, all the mechanical instruments on the walls. I hear the slaps of imaginary gunfire, and each one makes my body twitch. I hear shouting but cannot understand the words. My head is pounding but my limbs are numb. A ragged sleep begins to overtake me. My last image is of the bandstand at the Nickelodeon spinning faster and faster until it throws us all over the side.

CHAPTER 64
Vinnie Amatucci

At the Nickelodeon Club
Monday, January 27

At around five o'clock, we roused ourselves, used the bathrooms, and shrugged into our coats. As Akiko and Laura stepped through the doorway, they were framed by a split sky: the sun was setting in the west over Akiko's shoulder and a thick bank of black clouds was backing in from the east toward Laura.

Ridlin had handcuffed our two captives' inside wrists together, and then handcuffed their outside wrists to the grab handles above the doors of his car. Just like that, they were secure.

As we were loading up, Amelia strode out of the house with Jack half-hidden behind her and turned toward Ridlin. We clustered around and looked up at them.

"I can't see the purpose in us coming, Detective. If Giuseppe is actually going to be there, my presence can only stir him up. And having Franco there . . . We're no good to you, *worse* than no good to you. If you still need me as a bargaining chip, I'm right here," she said.

To me, it was instantly obvious. She was right; they would be a provocation, separately or together. Having them was one thing. Bringing them was another.

I looked at Jack, Franco, whoever. He was looking out across the lake.

Then he turned, dropped Amelia's hand, walked around her and said, "No, I'm going."

Amelia held her hand to her chest.

He looked at her. "I can't hide anymore. It's time to stop running . . ."

She stared straight at him with a look I couldn't read. Then she shivered once, turned around, and walked into the house.

The door closed behind her. There was nothing more to say. We piled into the cars, backed out of the cut, and headed out, with me in the lead.

After a couple of days of warming, the temperature was dropping, and the Hawk was coming in off the lake. I had my coat buttoned up to my neck and the heat jacked up to full blast, but I still felt cold to the point of shivering.

Laura and Akiko were in the backseat, but they weren't talking. Akiko was huddled against the door on the right, watching the sun go down. Laura was sitting straight up on the left, watching the storm roll in. I was looking straight ahead and glancing in the rearview mirror.

By the time we reached the highway, the sky was full of clouds, roiling higher as the warmer air off the lake was sucked into the colder cumulous sky. I switched on my lights and tested the wipers with a flick.

It was going to start snowing again, soon, and snowing hard.

The miles flew past, and we cruised down the Tri-State and bent east on the Kennedy and wove south on the Ryan, and soon we were back in Indiana, winding through the maze of streets toward the club. When we pulled into the parking lot, there was only one car there, an old beat-up Buick the color of diarrhea. Ridlin got out of his car, motioned to us to wait, walked up the steps and knocked on the door. It opened and he went in. Less than a minute later, the owner, the beefy guy with the ZZ Top beard, rambled out and headed to his car, flipping through a roll of bills. I couldn't tell from where I sat if he had it in a Chicago roll or an L.A. roll. He wedged himself into the Buick, then started it up and sliced through the crease in the tall grass. Ridlin came out, walked to his car, uncuffed the Accountant and the Cleaner, and walked them inside. The rest of us got out and followed.

Ridlin walked them onto the bandstand, found two folding chairs, and sat them facing each other around the pole in the center of the carousel. He cuffed their free hands together, so they sat right hand to left hand, left hand to right, like maids around a maypole.

Laura and Akiko sat facing away from each other, on the edge of the bandstand. Jack walked along the wall, inspecting the player instruments, his face close up against them, his hands behind his back. It was only nine o'clock; we had three hours to kill. I looked for a thermostat, found it, and cranked the heat up to seventy-four. I was still shivering.

Ridlin split us up for sentry duty. He put his foot up on a chair, rolled up his left cuff, and unstrapped a small revolver, which he handed to Landreau. "You watch those two," he said. "Don't shoot them unless you have to."

I had assumed that Laura and Akiko and I were all going to be on sentry duty, but Ridlin told Laura to stay inside. I grabbed my hat and coat and headed out the door.

I gave the place a perimeter of about thirty yards and went around clockwise, keeping my eyes open, letting my ears get tuned in. After three laps I veered off my path to go to the trunk of my car, unzip the gym bag, take out the gun, and slide it inside my cast. It wasn't comfortable, but comfort wasn't my priority. Ten minutes into my shift, fat snowflakes began to fall, lazily at first, then harder. By the time my thirty minutes were up, the snow was coming down sideways. There was no sound except the whistling of the wind and it gave the place an eerie stillness.

Akiko came through the door, surprised by the snow, and pulled up her collar. She wasn't wearing a hat; I don't think she even owned one. I went inside and slid behind the bar to put some coffee on. I busied myself finding the grounds and pouring the water, letting my fingers thaw. The Accountant and the Cleaner had moved their chairs closer together so they could rest their hands on their knees. The Cleaner looked pale. Ridlin was checking for back doors.

When the coffee was ready, I offered some all around. Ridlin took his black. Landreau and the Cleaner both passed. The Accountant wanted lots of cream and lots of sugar. As I mixed it for him he kept saying, "Just a touch more, Vincent, if you please." I had mine black, with sugar. It was basic American coffee, but just then it tasted great.

I was finishing my first cup when Ridlin pointed at his watch. It was ten o'clock. I got my hat and coat and headed out the door. As I passed Akiko on the porch, I muttered, "Fresh coffee, behind the bar," and she nodded. She wasn't much of a coffee drinker, but on a night like this she'd pour a cup just for the warmth of it.

At the next changeover, Ridlin called us. "They may be early, so stay alert. They may come in with their lights out, so keep your eyes and ears open." We nodded and went back to it.

The hours passed, with no sign of anyone. When I looked at my watch, it was twenty minutes past midnight. "They're late," I said. "It must be the storm. The roads are probably all fucked up."

He nodded, and returned his gaze to the window. "Either that," he said, "or they're letting us stew, waiting for us to get edgy."

"If that's what they're doing," I said, "it's working."

I poured some more coffee, took a sip, and immediately went off to find the men's room. I stood by the urinal, leaning my cast on the wall in front of me, and pissed for what felt like an eternity. It was the coffee, it was the nerves; I was like a sponge being squeezed in a vise.

At twelve-thirty I grabbed my hat and coat and headed to the door. Akiko saw me right away and hustled inside. The snow had piled up, and was now three or four inches deep, with drifts against the side of the club more than a foot deep. By this point, we had worn a groove around the building, and I just followed it. I kept my eyes on the perimeter, peering into the storm. There was nothing, there was no one, just a stream of white streaks riding the wind.

One o'clock came and Akiko spelled me, then one-thirty, and I was back outside. At one fifty-five I saw a shaft of light through the tall grass, and jogged toward the club sideways as I kept my eyes on it. When I got to the porch Akiko was already there—she must have seen the lights—and she grabbed my arm, the good one, and held me tight. We backed up the stairs and crossed the porch. The lights were closer, and Ridlin was standing behind us in the doorway. We stood there and watched as the lights and the car they were attached to fishtailed into the parking lot and groaned to a stop.

It was black, a Lincoln Town Car. It sat there, revving, the wipers fighting the snow. Ridlin tapped us on the shoulder and said, "Inside. Let's go."

We backed through the door, closing it after us.

Laura was sitting in a booth near the bandstand and Akiko walked over and sat down next to her and took her hand. Maybe it was symbolism of a sort, or maybe it was just comfort.

Ten seconds later the front door opened and two men walked in.

The first was Giuseppe Della Chiesa, the Boss of all Bosses, the Big Guy.

He wasn't actually all that big, maybe five-foot-seven or so. But he was barrel-chested, not fat but wide, and was impeccably dressed, in a dark charcoal two-button suit, black cashmere overcoat, white shirt with a straight collar, burgundy shoes and belt, and a maroon silk tie. He wore a white silk scarf under the topcoat, a thin pair of what looked like black calfskin driving gloves on his hands, and a black fedora pulled down over his steel-gray hair. He could have been a banker or a lawyer or a captain of industry: the suit was conservative, but perfectly tailored. Armani, or Zegna. Bespoke, not off the rack.

His nephew, Johnny Chase, was also well-dressed, but in the more modern style, with gray flat-front slacks, a black three-button blazer, and a black silk mock turtleneck beneath it. He had black half boots on his feet, and what looked like the same black driving gloves as his uncle. No scarf for him, no coat, no hat. His wavy black hair was frosted with snow.

The Don immediately walked over to the Cleaner, put his hand on his shoulder, and leaned down. "Relax, my friend. This is no fault of yours. We will have you out of this shortly." The Cleaner just dipped his head. The Accountant, looking expectant, looked up at the Don, who gave him back a withering glance of contempt, which forced his eyes back to the floor.

The Don looked around, saw Laura and Akiko in the booth, Jack at a rickety table, me on the bandstand, and panned his gaze over to Ridlin.

Ridlin looked him in the eye and said, "Let's talk."

The Don nodded, and pulled up a chair at a table next to the bandstand. He opened his topcoat and carefully placed his hat on the table before him. Ridlin sat down across from him, his hand in his coat pocket.

"Talk is cheap," the Don echoed. His voice was all weary resignation. "Let's take care of business."

"But that's what we wanted to talk about. This has nothing to do with business," Ridlin said. "That's the thing—"

"In the business I'm in," he said, "*everything* has to do with business. People need to know that I keep my word. That's all I have."

Akiko turned to him. "Like, OK, I get the principle, keeping your word and shit. That's, like, a good thing. But what's it got to do with her and me?"

He turned to her, stared at her appraisingly, and nodded in Laura's direction. "She made me a promise, she broke that promise," he said. "There have to be consequences. I told her that, right at the start."

Akiko turned to Laura.

"What?" she asked her. "What promise?"

Laura looked away. Akiko turned to her.

"He asked you to stop seeing me, and you promised you would?" she asked. "And then you kept seeing me, even after you knew he was going to try to kill me?"

Laura looked down. "It wasn't like that, baby. If I had thought anything was really going to happen . . ."

Akiko leaned back.

"Akiko," I started.

"No, Vince. Like, I don't know what to think, you know? I mean, was she so self-centered she didn't even think about me? Or was she so in love with me she couldn't stay away? I don't know whether to feel violated or, like, adored."

Ridlin roused himself. He was staring intently at the Don.

"OK," he said. "Contracts and consequences. Basic rule of civilized society. But, because she's sleeping with your daughter, you have to kill her? Isn't that a little extreme? You know, 'let the punishment fit the crime'?"

Chase cut in. "Hey, mistakes were made. Some of our intelligence may have been inaccurate. There are areas of execution that got a little fucked up and are currently under review, and you can be sure any changes that need to be made will be fucking implemented and—"

Akiko let out a laugh, a single mad cackle, then put her hand over her mouth. It stopped him.

Ridlin leaned over the table, his brow wrinkled. "Listen, I think you might agree with me, this thing maybe requires consequences, but maybe not death—"

The Don looked at him. "Ahh," he sighed. "I see that the

talking is over and the negotiating has begun. What have you got for me?"

Ridlin looked up at him. "You get the Accountant and the money, you leave the ladies alone, and I get the assassin."

The Don looked at him calmly.

"You think this is fair?"

Ridlin nodded.

"You think it's so fair, flip it. You keep the courier and the money, and I'll keep my friend, hmmm?"

Ridlin shook his head.

"Then where's the value for me? It's all on your side."

"He's of no use to you anymore. We've all seen him, there are others who can identify him, at headquarters. You can't use him. He's done."

The Don glared. "Do you think that if he didn't want you to recognize him, that you would? There have been times *I* didn't recognize him, and he's my oldest friend in the world. Besides, say you're right, say he can't work. I *still* want him with me."

Ridlin shook his head.

Della Chiesa stared at him. "What can you do to sweeten the deal?"

"Sweeten the deal . . . ?"

"There's not enough in it for me. Like, maybe you could throw in the piano player."

I looked at Ridlin. He shook his head "No."

Della Chiesa saw this, and said, "No, not *that* piano player. The other one," he said.

"What do you mean?" Ridlin said.

"Give him to me. Maybe there's something I could do with him."

Ridlin shook his head. "I don't think so."

"You see?" the Don said. "We've been negotiating less than two minutes and we've already hit a stalemate. I won't give you my friend, and you won't give me the piano player, and neither one of us really cares about the money. So what the hell kind of a deal is this?"

"But we can talk this thing through," Ridlin said. "Let's just talk about the options—"

"Talk, talk, talk," Chase said. "What a waste of fucking time."

"But you've got nothing to lose by talking. Maybe there's a way to settle this. Maybe—"

"Enough with the fucking bullshit," the Nephew said.

Ridlin stood up, took a step toward the Don. "This is stupid," he said angrily, "the two of them aren't hurting anybody. But three people are dead, the cops are in a full-court press, you've got to be feeling the heat, I mean, what the hell is the point?"

He took another step forward.

A shot rang out, and Ridlin fell to his knees, curled to his right, and crumpled to the floor, all in slow motion. A puff of smoke wafted up from the gun that had appeared in Chase's hand.

We all stood there, frozen. He turned and pointed the gun at me. I put my hands in the air.

He turned to Akiko and sneered. "You see? This is why I gave up that martial-arts shit. You assume the Cobra Posture and people will look at you like you are out of your fucking mind. You pull out a Glock Nine and they will stop what they're doing and put their hands in the air. Much more efficient. Plus you don't have all that fucking practice."

I looked over and saw the Cleaner working a key into his handcuffs, and just like that he had them off, both sets, and was standing up, rubbing his wrists. He leaned over, tucked the key into his sock. Did the Don slip it to him, I asked myself? Did he have it all along?

I started to back toward the piano. It was big, it was solid, it was something I knew.

My eyes flicked to a small metal junction box next to the old upright, with two electrical cables coming out of it and two toggle switches on its side, a handmade thing with a popsicle stick duct-taped across its base. I tried to remember what those switches did, why the popsicle stick was

there. My brain was racing, but it was stuck in neutral:
revving, spinning, frantic.

The Accountant walked over toward the edge of the
stand. He was about to step off. Chase held up his hand,
and stopped him on the edge. "Where's our money?" he
asked.

I reached down and flipped the switch on the left, and
the bandstand started turning with a jolt. The Accountant
stepped back, off balance, and grabbed the railing to stabilize himself. My memory clicked in: I knew what the
switches were for.

"Where's our money?" the Nephew asked. The Accountant opened his mouth to speak.

I flipped the switch on the right, and all the player pianos, mechanical trumpets, violins, saxophones, trombones, and drums along the walls started playing "When
the Saints Go Marching In." The whole thing was horribly
out of tune, and the cacophony was deafening. The bandstand was turning counterclockwise, slowly.

I reached for the switch on the left and tried to jam it
down further. I pried off the popsicle stick that was taped
under it and leaned on the switch, but the switch kept popping back up. I reached into my pocket, took out my tuning
fork, my A-440, and jammed it down onto the switch, the
tines trapping it between them, and the top wedged tight
against the housing. It held. The bandstand started to gain
velocity. In a few seconds it was racing at carousel speed,
and I had to grab hold of the old-fashioned bolted-down
piano stool to keep from spinning off.

The Accountant tried to shout over the din, and Chase
cupped his hand to his ear but couldn't hear him. Chase's
gun exploded, cutting through the cacophony, and a bullet
whanged into the piano next to my shoulder. I scooted
deeper behind the stool. He stood there and waited for the
bandstand to come full circle. When it did, he faced the Accountant and shouted over the din, a few syllables each
revolution, "Where is . . . our fucking . . . money?"

The next time around the Accountant pointed at the floor beneath the table where Ridlin was slumped over, dead. The Nephew followed his finger over. The Don reached over, picked the briefcase up an inch off the ground, testing its heft. He nodded.

The Accountant was holding on to the pole, and each time he came around to the open spot near Chase he would reach a dainty foot out toward the floor, then pull it back. He was smiling and frowning at the same time. As he came around toward where he had started, Chase looked up at him. "Thanks," he yelled, tonelessly. "And by the way," he said, waiting a revolution, "you fucked up," he said, "you're fired," and shot him in the forehead. The Accountant flew off the edge of the bandstand, but his foot caught on the railing post, and the carousel started to drag him around, facedown, leaving a dark red smear behind him. His body was knocking furniture out of the way as he made the circuit, and as he came back around again Chase had to hop back to avoid him.

Laura suddenly stood up in her booth and turned to Chase. "Why are you doing this, Johnny?" Her voice was tight, her eyes were blazing. "What does it have to do with you? You have no idea who these people are, you have no idea at all!"

He looked over at Laura and Akiko, and said, "That's the thing about me. I've got *lots* of ideas. We're barely getting started on all the ideas I have," and he pointed the gun at Akiko.

A shot rang out, and Akiko jumped back. She looked at her chest, but there was no blood there. A red bloom of it was spreading across Chase's abdomen. I looked around. Ridlin was lying on the floor, not moving.

Then I saw Jack Landreau. He was standing with Ridlin's extra gun in his hand. A wisp of smoke drifted up from the barrel. Chase turned and saw him, and chuckled. "Yeah, I deserved that," he said. "It wasn't about her. No, this is the fucking cunt that started this mess, this is the fucking cunt that needs it. Right, cuz?" His leaned back, leveled the pistol, and shot Laura, twice.

The first bullet hit her in the chest, and she fell back, hitting a chair. The second caught her under her chin, and she slithered to the floor. Akiko went down with her, holding on tightly, screaming. She grabbed Laura, held her tight, sobbing. Chase advanced on her.

Another shot crackled, Chase's left leg buckled, and he staggered. Jack was still there, holding the gun. A gun appeared in the Don's hand and he turned and fired at Jack, and caught him in the neck. He went down, falling to his left, dropping the gun, clutching his throat, blood arcing everywhere. Chase turned and loomed over him. He tilted his body back and aimed his gun at Jack's head. Akiko jumped up, screaming, took two steps to her left, then wheeled to her right, swung her left leg up and kicked him in his throat. He went down in a heap, and she leaped behind him, chopped the gun from his hand, and got his head in a leg-lock, his neck bending at a sickening angle.

The bandstand jerked, sparks shot out of the junction box and it ground to a halt. The music wound down, each instrument fading at its own pace.

Akiko looked at the Don and yelled, "Put your gun on the table, now, or I'll break his neck! Put it down!"

The Nephew's face was starting to turn blue. The stain was spreading across his shirt. You couldn't tell it was blood against the black; it looked like he had spilled a drink on it.

The Don turned to the Cleaner. "She's a tarantula, this one, isn't she? Would you take care of her for me?"

The Cleaner took two steps forward, and looked down at him, a frown on his face.

"Put the gun down!" Akiko shouted. "Put the fucking gun down!"

The Cleaner turned to the Don. "Why are we doing this?" he asked. "These people, they're no threat to us. This isn't business."

"Put the gun down!" Akiko screamed. "He's your flesh and blood! Do you want me to kill him?"

The Cleaner crossed in front of me. I reached into the cast with my right arm and pulled out the little twenty-two, held it up against the back of his neck, and cocked it. "Don't move," I said. "It's loaded."

He stood still.

I called out to the Don. "Maybe you don't care about your nephew, but this is your *friend*. Put the gun on the table or I'll pull the trigger!"

"Put the gun down!" Akiko echoed. "Put it down!"

The Don hesitated, a crease forming between his eyebrows. He sighed. His arm started to move.

"No," the Cleaner said. "Don't do it. I'm dead anyway."

"Dead?" the Don asked, incredulous. "You're standing right here. What—"

"Put the fucking gun down!" Akiko yelled, her voice starting to break.

"As good as dead. Got maybe a month, maybe two. It's the cancer."

The Don was frantic. "We can get you help. We can get you doctors. The best doctors. What's in that bag alone is enough to pay for whatever it takes. Whatever it is, we can get it fixed. We can get a transplant, the things they can do—"

"No, they can't," he said. "It's the pancreas. No operations, no chemo. Just pills, for the pain, and they ain't working much anymore. A matter of time is all. Might as well be now."

He and the Don locked eyes.

"Don't go saving me, Zep. Be doing me a favor, tell you the truth."

"No!" the Don yelled. "This is not acceptable! I am not going to let you die . . ." His face was turning red. His eyes were wild; he looked frantic. He rose out of his chair, took a deep breath, and turned toward the two of us.

The Cleaner took one step forward and I clubbed him on the skull with the pistol. He went down to his knees, holding his head. I had hit him hard, but he was just dazed, not out. I bent down over him, the gun still pointed at him.

The Don raised his gun up to shoulder level, aimed it casually at me.

"This is not your thing, is it? Drop the gun, you might walk out of here in one piece."

His gun had lowered while he talked. He raised it up again, aimed it, cocked it.

A shot rang out. And another. I flinched. The Don went all loose and slid to the floor. Behind him, Ridlin was leaning up on one elbow, his gun trying to hold its aim, and failing. He grunted and flopped back down, groaning.

Della Chiesa looked at the blood in his hand with shock in his eyes, then craned his neck up toward the Cleaner.

"Josef," he said.

"Zep."

The Don's mouth opened and blood poured out of it. His eyebrows moved up in surprise and he toppled forward.

My skin felt tighter than Akiko's snare drum. I looked around and all I saw was death.

The Cleaner was still kneeling in front of me. Chase was still caught between Akiko's thighs. She must have relaxed her grip, because he started to croak, "Kill them . . . Fucking kill them . . ."

The Cleaner staggered to his feet and stepped off the bandstand.

"Stop!" I yelled.

He didn't. I hopped off the bandstand and followed him, waving the gun wildly.

He walked over to where Ridlin was lying. Reached for his neck, felt for a pulse. He lifted up his coat, looked at where he had been shot.

He looked over at us and chuckled. "The Riddler strikes again," he said, chuckling. "Looks like he got shot right through the scar. Same place as before. See? He'll live."

He stood up. He looked at Akiko. She had relaxed her grip, but was still in control.

"Go ahead," he said to her. "Finish it."

She squinted up at him.

He nodded slowly to himself. "You don't want to. Not your nature. Not what you would do, you had the choice, right? Doesn't matter. He killed Laura, your lover. He killed her for no reason. You have to finish it."

"What the fuck are you doing?" the Nephew croaked. "Kill her! Kill them all."

"See?" the Cleaner asked. "Go ahead. Finish it. Do it quick or do it slow. You can do that, right? Either way, right? All that dojo stuff?"

She nodded, but her eyes were pleading with him.

"I'll do it, you want me to," he said. "But it should be you. You don't, he's going to kill you. He's going to kill the piano player here. He's going to kill me. You know this, right?"

He stared at her.

"I kill him, it's me doing you a favor. Later on it'll be worse, 'cause you couldn't do it yourself."

She straightened up, looked him in the eyes. She looked like she saw something there. She turned her head, looked at me. There was no pleading in her, no questioning.

I may have nodded. I may have trembled. I may have stood there, frozen.

She leaned back on her elbows. I saw her legs clench, just a twitch.

The Nephew slumped against her, his mouth open, his eyes open, his hands by his sides.

Akiko scrambled to her feet. Her face was flushed; she was breathing hard.

The Cleaner looked at her. "It'll change," he said. "How you feel about it, it'll change."

Akiko looked at him, sideways.

He walked over, stopped, turned toward me.

"One bullet," he said. "In the head. Quick. Simple."

I jumped. "What the *fuck* are you talking about?" I shouted.

"You got to shoot me, got to finish it," he said.

"No fucking way! We're calling nine-one-one and you're going away. Let them handle it. You can rot in jail until you die and feel the pain all the way to the end, for all I care!"

He looked around the room, then looked at me.

"Two things," he said. "One. I start walking, you have to shoot me, right?"

"I could shoot you in the leg," I was saying it but I wasn't believing it.

"So I limp toward my dead friend. Get his gun. Point the gun at Ms. Jones here. What you gonna do? Shoot me, the other leg? You have to kill me. Eventually. That's the thing, see?"

He was right, but I didn't say so.

"Two," he said. "What you gonna tell them, the cops? Got an explanation for all this, this . . . ?" He waved his arm around the room. I couldn't look at all the dead bodies. My eyes blurred them into geometric shapes with slashes of bright color. There was a metallic taste in the air.

"Nobody left to back you up. Just you and the drummer girl," he continued. "Ridlin'll live, but he's out of it. Won't remember a thing. What kind of story you gonna come up with? How long you think you can both stick to it? Want to spend the next two years talking to the cops? Lawyers? CNN? The *Trib*? The *Sun-Times,* for Christ's sake?"

Words were forming in my mind but refused to come out of my mouth. Akiko wasn't doing any better. She kept glancing over to where Laura was laying on the floor.

"Think," he said. "I'm dead already. They can't let me suffer, it's cruel and unusual. Half-decent lawyer? Be in the prison hospital inside a hour. Get better stuff for the pain in there. Morphine drip. Little button to push. Retribution? Justice? Forget about it."

He paused, looked at both of us.

"No one who knows you were here is alive. How many things you touch? The coffeepot? A cup? The door handle? The railing, getting on and off the thing there, the carousel? The back of one of the booths maybe? The handle of the urinal in the can? And you," he said, pointing to Akiko. "Same thing with you. Maybe less. The smooth floor next to the Nephew, there? The booth you were at with Laura? Damp rag. Ten, fifteen minutes max. Leave all the bodies where they are. Don't step in the blood. Wipe it all down. Take the cleaning supplies with you. Dump them, some rest area, the interstate. Take your car. Go anywhere you want, start over. Snow'll cover up every tire-track. You got the money there, you want it," he said, nodding toward the bag, "Buy yourself a good piano, a doctor for the hand. Buy the drummer girl her own dojo. Set yourselves up. Who's to say you don't deserve it, what you been through? Don't have to look over your shoulder. Everybody is dead. It's a new day."

I could see his mind working, each point as sharp as a shark's tooth, all lined up in a row.

"But you," I mumbled. "It would be suicide. Why would you want to—"

"It's way past what I want," he said. "Time is up." His hand was at his abdomen; he was making an intense effort to speak. "Best this way. Best for everybody. And you know it."

He had thought it all out. I was paralyzed by logic.

"Wait," he said. "One more thing. Gotta do this right. Use the Riddler's gun," he said. "You do it with that gun. Make him the goddamn hero. He blasted Joe Zep, he got me. Here, I'll walk closer to make it look right. You do it with that gun, wipe off your gun, put it in my hand. I gotta have a gun, doesn't matter which one. This one registered to you?"

"No," I said. "Someone left it in my cab . . . I just kept it . . ."

"Perfect," he said. "A lost gun, a stolen gun. Perfect, see?"

He stopped. A crease of pain split his face. He took a few deep breaths.

"The hotshot assassin, holding a puny twenty-two, gets shot by an old alky cop. Ridlin? He survives. Don't remember a thing. He's a big hero. Cops'll love it."

I had followed him over to where Ridlin lay on the

ground. I felt Akiko's eyes on me. He pulled a handkerchief from his back pocket, grabbed a corner and flicked it open, reached out, took my gun from me, wiped it with the handkerchief, tucked it under his armpit. He leaned down and picked up the gun in Ridlin's hand with the handkerchief. For a second he was holding both of the guns. I felt a sudden rush of panic, but in the time it took to skip a heartbeat he put Ridlin's gun in my hand, the handkerchief still wrapped around it.

"Wait," he said. "Don't move. Stand still." I froze, my finger tightening on the trigger. He aimed my little gun over my shoulder, fired it twice at the wall. I jumped an inch off the floor. He brought the barrel up to his nose and sniffed it. I flashed to Proust and the madeleine. I thought I saw a sweet nostalgia. I thought I saw a sad disgust. I don't know what I saw.

I looked at Akiko. She was standing still. I don't know what I saw in her face either, because I didn't look for anything there; she was carrying enough already.

I looked at the gun in my hand. I turned it over, seeing one side, and then the other. I waited. I don't know what I was waiting for.

"You know it's the way to go, right?"

I nodded my head. It was all I could manage.

"Problem is, you don't *how* you know it. And you're thinking about that."

I turned to him, startled. "How did you—?"

"You're the one with all the schooling," he said. "You're the one with the big brain. You'll figure it out. Later. Now, you have to step up. Be free of this. Do what's gotta be done."

The gun in my hand rose up in front of my face. My hand was trembling.

"By the way," he said. "You're not a bad piano player, for what it's worth. Just work on that right hand."

CHAPTER 65
Vince Amatucci

Leaving the Nickelodeon
Tuesday, January 28

We held each other for a long long time. And then we did as he said and cleaned what we could, making sure not to leave any sign of ourselves behind. The bar, the booths, the bandstand, the bathrooms—we went over them all with a soft wet rag, every crack and crevice. I washed the coffeepot, the coffee machine, the cups and spoons. I wiped the cream pot and the sugar bowl and the places where they'd been. Akiko did the booths and the bathrooms and the doorknobs and the bar. Then we tackled the bandstand, the piano, the railings, the poles, even the thermostat I had turned up at the start and now turned back down.

There was nothing there but death. A smell lay heavy in the air, metallic, tangy, fecund; we fought our way through it and stayed at it until it was done. At the end she wandered over to where Laura lay on the floor. She knelt down, reached out her rubber-gloved hand, then pulled it back. Her elbows were on her knees, her hands were laced to-

gether, her head was bowed. I turned away and busied myself behind the bar and let her have as much privacy as I
could.

Two minutes later she stood and wiped her eyes. We
rounded up the cleaning supplies, turned out all the lights,
and got ready to close the door. Akiko was holding the
briefcase full of cash, and I had the cleaning bucket full of
rags.

And the phone rang.

I looked at my watch. It was three forty-five. It rang again.
Akiko looked at me, her face all twisted up. I put down the
bucket, grabbed a rag, and walked behind the bar.

"Vince," she said.

I looked at the phone, let it ring one more time, then
picked it up with the rag.

"Hello?" I ventured.

There was a pause.

"Well, I'm glad to be hearing it's you," said the Fat Man.

"What the fuck?" I almost shouted. "You—"

"Yo, yo, don't you be saying *nothin'*," he said. "You got me?"

"Yeah." I got him immediately.

"Good. Good. Now, uhh . . . who's there?"

I looked at Akiko. "My, uh, friend, from the North Side,
she's still here," I said.

"Hunh . . ."

"And I'm still here," I said.

"You sound, I don't know, man, you sound—"

"Blasé? Numb? Totally fucking zombified? Something
like that?" I said.

There was a pause.

"Hunh," he said. "Alright, now. Call me later, whenever . . .
But get outta there, now. You hear me? Go on already. Go."
And the phone clicked off.

I placed it back in its cradle, gave the whole contraption
another wipe, and walked back over to Akiko. She was still
looking at Laura, and I put my hand gently on her shoulder.
Her eyes turned up and questioned me, and I just said,

"The Fat Man, I don't know how, I don't know why . . . Let's just . . ." I bent down, picked up the bucket and walked toward the door. We walked through it, and I set the bucket down to grab the handle with my rag.

I stopped myself, and turned to her.

"Wait," I said. "My tuning fork."

Still holding the rag, I opened the door, walked inside, flipped on the lights, and walked over to the bandstand. I stepped onto the carousel and walked to the metal box on the floor near the piano. I reached down with the rag in my hand and pulled the tuning fork free, stuffing it into my pants pocket. I gave the switches and the box a careful wipe, then walked back to the door.

Jack's funny-looking case was sitting there and it stopped me. Still holding the rag, I opened the zipper of the bottom compartment. There, inside a black velvet drawstring bag, was his cornet. I slid it out of the valise. The mouthpiece wasn't attached. I flipped the case open with my shoe and looked inside, and found it, in a small rubber pouch next to some valve oil. I slipped both into my coat pocket, slid the cornet under my arm, and, holding the rag with some care, re-zippered the bag, turned out the lights, stepped out, closed the door, grabbed the bucket, and walked down the stairs. Akiko waited there, clutching the briefcase, her hair frosted white.

The snow was close to six inches deep, and it was wet and heavy. We picked our way over to my car one step at a time, our knees rising to our waists. I unlocked it, slid the cornet onto the dash, put the bucket behind the front seat, started her up, cranked up the heat, then got back out and brushed off as much snow as I could. I got back in the car, buckled up, and flipped the wipers to MAX and the rear defroster to ON. She had the briefcase in her lap, clutching it to her. I picked the cornet up off the dash and looked for someplace to put it.

She looked at me. "What's that, Vince?" she asked.

"Landreau's horn," I said.

She gave me a puzzled look.

"I don't know," I said, "sentimental value? Or, maybe, if my left hand doesn't heal, I might need something to play that doesn't require all ten fingers. This only needs three."

I gently tucked it back behind the stick shift. I looked over at Akiko.

She nodded, snapped her seat belt on, and set the briefcase on the floor between her feet. She squeezed my hand, and held it. I squeezed back, and we sat there for a moment. Finally, I gently disengaged my hand, engaged the clutch and started to roll forward.

It was virgin snow, and the going was slow. I kept it in second all the way out. "No sudden moves," I thought. "Just keep it moving, nice and steady, straight ahead, like skiing." As we broke free of the back streets, the way was more passable, and it took the roar of the revving engine to remind me to shift up to third.

A half a mile ahead we followed the signs and shushed into the left-turn lane for 94 South. The light turned red. I eased us to a stop, put the blinker on, and looked at her. It was understood that we couldn't go back. I could call the Fat Man later and have him send us our stuff. Of course, I didn't own much stuff, and she had even less.

The light turned green, and we mushed through the heavy snow onto the expressway. There were ruts in two of the three lanes, so I stayed right, eased into the grooves, and locked into the flow. The traffic seemed to be all tractor trailers. They were doing no more than forty, and that was just fine with me.

After twenty quiet minutes we saw the signs for Route 80. I hit the emergency flashers and pulled onto the shoulder, as far from the traffic as I could get. I put the car in neutral and turned toward her. I reached out and traced the line of her jaw with my fingertips. She was looking straight ahead.

"So, what do you think?" I asked.

"I think we're going to make a very interesting couple," she said.

I wasn't sure what to say. Finally, I asked, "So, you understand that I'm a male, right?" I asked. "With all the usual attachments and such."

And she leaned right in and kissed me. It started with a gossamer brush of her lips on mine, then became something softer and sweeter, then turned languid and luscious and tender and moist. And then she reached down and squeezed my cock.

Except it wasn't my cock. It was my tuning fork. She pulled back, frowned.

"See how hard you got me, with just one kiss," I said. "Stainless fucking steel." I pulled the fork from my pocket, reached out, and tapped it on the steering wheel. An A-440 rang out.

She giggled, then turned quiet.

"Here's the thing," she said. "You're a very bright and perceptive man, Vince, I mean, but, like, sometimes you have no fucking clue . . ."

"But I thought—"

"No, wait," she said, holding up a hand. "Don't think."

I paused, looked at her. Her dark eyes were locked onto me tight.

"I don't know, Vince. You've always had this little-sister thing with me, trying to look out for me, you know? Trying to bring me along? But I wasn't looking at you like a big brother. So who knows? After tonight, I'm, I'm not sure what to believe about myself, you know? . . . But I've always believed in you."

I held her hand up, kissed it. "You don't really look like my sister," I said.

I kissed her again, and we held each other, and the boundaries shifted a notch.

Until the sudden blare of a truck horn Dopplering by our window brought us both to a full, upright, and locked position.

We shook ourselves.

"OK," I said. "Which way?"

We sat in silence for a moment. I looked at the signs up ahead—east or west.

"Vince," she said. "I say we go where neither of us has ever been, you know, start new."

"West?" I asked.

She nodded.

"L.A. or San Francisco?" I asked. "Do you have a preference?"

"Do you?" she asked.

"Well, Frisco always looks pretty in the pictures."

"You're not supposed to call it 'Frisco.' San Fran, or the whole name."

"Really? Where'd you hear that?"

She paused, looked away.

"Friend of mine, from out there," she said.

"Really? A friend from out there?" I said.

She looked at me with a glint in her eye. "Lot of bitchin' lesbians out there, in San Francisco," she said. "Hot bi chicks, too, I hear."

I looked over at her. She was grinning.

"Like me, I guess," she said. She was looking half-away from me. Her mouth was a straight line, but her eyes were smiling.

Half an hour ago we're cleaning an abattoir with our bare hands, I thought, and now we're cracking jokes. Jesus.

I put the car back in gear, and checked the traffic coming up behind us. It was all trucks, in herds of three or four. I got rolling and found a gap in the flow, and spun my wheels pulling into the same set of ruts as before. As soon as we were back on 94 South, I flipped the directional to the right, and looped onto the exit for 80 headed west. She had her hand on my right leg as we slopped around the turn and up to the toll booths.

We had a long way to go, and a lot to put behind us. My brain raced back through it all—I thought about why the two of us had been spared and what it all meant. I had no idea, and I had every idea, and no way to tell the merest speculation from the cold hard truth.

We slogged along heading west at thirty miles an hour for what felt like forever. At seven the sky started to lighten behind us but the snow continued to fall. At eight the snow tapered off but the wind bent the trees toward the ground. And at nine we came over a rise and rounded a bend and the sky was blue before us and the road was clear beneath our wheels.

A big green sign loomed ahead and slowly came into focus—DAVENPORT, IOWA, 10 MILES.

How appropriate, I thought.

I turned to Akiko. She nodded. We would stop there, for a day, maybe two. Lick our wounds. Count the money. Make some plans.

My fingers reached down and touched the cornet, briefly. Her hand settled softly on top.

This one's for you, Jack.

Or Franco.

Whoever you were.

"The ultimate cat-and-mouse thriller. Nonstop action."
—*Book Crossing* on *African Ice*

Jeff Buick

As the vice-president of a Washington, D.C., bank, Leona Hewitt knows her new position will have greater responsibilities. She doesn't know they may cost her life. Her boss made it pretty clear that he expects her to approve a particular conversion for one of their largest corporate clients, no matter how questionable it may seem to her.

Both the head of the bank and the head of the corporation have a lot to lose if this doesn't go through…and they're not about to let anything or anyone get in their way. If Leona and her conscience prove to be a problem, they know a very effective way of getting rid of her—permanently. As Leona races to stay one step ahead of the killer on her trail, the only man who can help keep her alive is fighting for his own life halfway around the world.

DELICATE CHAOS

ISBN 13: 978-0-8439-6038-9

TRIPLE IDENTITY

HAGGAI CARMON

Dan Gordon used to work for Mossad, the Israeli intelligence agency. Now he works for the U. S. Department of Justice. All of his intelligence training is coming in very handy in his current mission—tracking a mysterious Romanian who might have fled the U. S. with ninety million dollars stolen from a failed California bank.

Just as he thinks he's getting close, Gordon discovers this is no ordinary mission, and the Romanian is no ordinary money launderer. He'll need all of his training, contacts, resources and cleverness to unravel a Byzantine plot that will lead him across Europe and into the Middle East in a frantic race to stop a rogue nation…before its operatives can stop him.

ISBN 13: 978-0-8439-6040-2

STEVEN TORRES

The big party in the town square should have been one of the happiest moments of Luis Gonzalo's life, celebrating his twenty-five years as sheriff. But in the middle of the ceremony a blaze is spotted on a nearby hill. The Ortiz home is on fire. Inside is what's left of the Ortiz family—bound and shot. This isn't just a murder...it's a message. But who's it for? As the violence continues and Gonzalo digs deeper and deeper, he starts to worry that his twenty-fifth year of service might be his last.

MESSAGE IN THE FLAMES

ISBN 13: 978-0-8439-5998-7

GREGG LOOMIS

The newest secret is about to be uncovered....

A scientist in Amsterdam—murdered. Another scientist in Atlanta—murdered, and his journal stolen. Lang Reilly worked with them both. And when someone took a shot at Lang, it only made him more determined to find the truth. Lang's search will lead him along a twisted trail to Brussels, Cairo, Vienna, Tel Aviv…and deep into the secrets of the past. What's the connection between the murdered scientists and an ancient parchment, recently unearthed? What revelations does it contain, and what powerful group is willing to kill to make sure its secrets remain hidden? With the balance of power in the Middle East at risk, Lang has to stay alive long enough to find the answer to a mystery that has puzzled historians for centuries.

THE SINAI SECRET

Available March 2008 wherever books are sold.

ISBN 13: 978-0-8439-6042-6

W. L. RIPLEY

PRESSING THE BET

What else could Cole Springer do? The cops said an old friend of his had been murdered in Las Vegas. So when the friend's father asked Springer to look into it, the ex-Secret Service agent had no choice but to return there, even though the local mob had warned him never to set foot in the town again. But the mob's only part of his problems. There are also dirty cops and one honest detective, the exotic Tara St. John, who will stop at nothing—even a romance with Springer—to find the killer and advance her career. The more Springer digs into the case, the harder the syndicate pushes him to butt out. But when anybody pushes Springer, he always pushes back.

ISBN 13: 978-0-8439-5994-9

CAILTIN ROTHER

NAKED ADDICTION

A ticket to Homicide.

That was the first thing disgruntled narcotics detective Ken Goode thought when he found the body of a beautiful murdered woman. But his transfer became the last thing on his mind when more victims turned up—all linked to the same beauty school his sister attends. With time running out, a killer on the loose, and the danger hitting too close to home, Goode has to stop this murderer while fighting his own growing obsession with one of the very women he's trying to save.

ISBN 10: 0-8439-5995-9
ISBN 13: 978-0-8439-5995-6
